Praise for
New York Times bestselling author
Brenda Jackson

"The only flaw of this first-rate, satisfying sexy tale is that it ends."
— *Publishers Weekly*, starred review, on *Forged in Desire*

"Leave it to Jackson to take sizzle and honor, wrap it in romance and come up with a first-rate tale."
— *RT Book Reviews* on *Temptation*

"Brenda Jackson is the queen of newly discovered love... If there's
those h

"[Jacks
to craft
steamy, sweaty sex. Here's another winner."
— *RT Book Reviews* on *A Brother's Honor*, 4½ stars, Top Pick

"This deliciously sensual romance ramps up the emotional stakes and the action.... [S]exy and sizzling."
— *Library Journal* on *Intimate Seduction*

"Jackson does not disappoint...first-class page-turner."
— *RT Book Reviews* on *A Silken Thread*, 4½ stars, Top Pick

"Jackson is a master at writing."
— *Publishers Weekly* on *Sensual Confessions*

Also available from
Brenda Jackson

The Protectors

FORGED IN DESIRE
SEIZED BY SEDUCTION
LOCKED IN TEMPTATION

The Grangers

A BROTHER'S HONOR
A MAN'S PROMISE
A LOVER'S VOW

For additional books by
New York Times bestselling author Brenda Jackson,
visit her website, www.brendajackson.net.

BRENDA JACKSON

LOCKED IN TEMPTATION

HQN™

HQN™

ISBN-13: 978-0-373-80214-2

Recycling programs for this product may not exist in your area.

Locked in Temptation

Copyright © 2017 by Brenda Streater Jackson

This edition published by arrangement with Harlequin Books S.A.

For questions and comments about the quality of this book, please contact us at CustomerService@Harlequin.com.

® and TM are trademarks of Harlequin Enterprises Limited or its corporate affiliates. Trademarks indicated with ® are registered in the United States Patent and Trademark Office, the Canadian Intellectual Property Office and in other countries.

www.HQNBooks.com

Printed in U.S.A.

To the man who will always and forever be
the love of my life: Gerald Jackson, Sr. Remembering you
on our 45th Wedding Anniversary, July 8, 2017!

To everyone joining me in Barbados
for the Brenda Jackson Readers Reunion 2017.

Special thanks to Detective Willie "Jay" Collins of
the Carmel Police Department for sharing your expertise
and answering my endless questions.

Special thanks to Dr. Angela Martin, OB/GYN,
for taking the time to provide me with
so much valuable information for this book.

To all my readers who are enjoying The Protectors series.
This book is for you.

To authors Iris Bolling and Adrianne Byrd.
Thanks for the brainstorming sessions.

Let us not become weary in doing good, for at the proper
time we will reap a harvest if we do not give up.
—*Galatians* 6:9

PROLOGUE

I HAVE TO keep moving.

Although her entire body ached with pain and felt as cold as ice, Mandy Clay continued to force one foot ahead of the other. Ignoring the icy wind whipping through the thin dress she wore, she continued to walk in bare feet as fast as she could, making her way someplace…anywhere but back there. That god-awful, evil place.

By now they would have discovered her missing and someone would have sounded the alarm. There was no doubt in her mind they'd be searching for her. She had no idea where she was, wasn't even sure if she was still in the United States. The only thing she knew was that she had to keep moving. It was dark and she was in some wooded area. She didn't want to think about all those sounds she was hearing. Animals? Predators? She was determined to stay alive. Sooner or later she would reach some sort of civilization. Right?

Mandy could tell it had snowed recently because the ground felt cold and squishy beneath her feet. Her toes were numb. She had to find somewhere safe. Hopefully someone would help her and call the police. Then she could tell them about the others. Those poor women… being forced to…

She slowed her pace when she thought she heard a sound. Looking through the trees, she couldn't see anything, but she could swear she heard the sound of a dog barking. Were the dogs being used to look for her? Hunt her down like the animal they'd treated her as? She wrapped her arms around herself, using all her strength to move faster. It had started snowing again. Heavier now. She felt stiff from the cold, and the pain she felt in every part of her body was almost unbearable. But she couldn't think of any of that now.

She had to keep moving. No matter what.

CHAPTER ONE

Five months later

"WHERE ARE WE GOING, Stonewall? This is not the way to my house."

Stonewall Courson brought the car to a stop at a traffic light and glanced at Joy Ingram. They had attended Striker and Margo's wedding together, and she was right. This was not the way back to her home. She was staring at him with those beautiful brown eyes that had the ability to send desire twisting in his gut and give his libido a high five whenever their gazes locked for any length of time. He would never forget the first time he'd looked into them and been totally mesmerized.

A sensual mist seemed to surround them whether they were alone or in a crowd. Those vapors were in full force now and had been from the moment he'd picked up her from her home earlier today. Stonewall had always known sexual chemistry was a powerful thing. He hadn't known just how powerful until he'd met Joy. Now he was tuned to her every breath.

Looking at her lips, he was entranced by the memory of their one and only kiss. He could recall every lip-licking detail. Just the thought sent a needy rush through his veins and made sexual excitement curl in his stomach. That single kiss was all it had taken to deeply embed her in his system. But then, he would admit the scent of her was mind-boggling, as well. In the small confines of the car, he breathed in her sensual aroma. She was wearing the same fragrance she had the night they'd met. It had been hypnotic then and it was hypnotic now.

He couldn't help but smile. It hadn't taken her long to notice he was driving in the opposite direction of where she lived. Joy was a cop, after all—a detective. Being observant and perceptive and paying attention to detail were essential parts of her job.

Today she was off the clock and she was with him. He didn't want her in cop mode. He much preferred having the element of surprise on his side. He'd known when he'd decided on this plan of action that it wouldn't be easy, given the astute person that she was. But he was determined to pull it off anyway.

"No, this is not the way to your house," he finally said. "Where we're going is a surprise." He decided to at least tell her that much.

"A surprise?"

He liked the way her brows shot up whenever she received new information. "Yes, Joy, a surprise."

He liked her name. Something about it, especially whenever he said it, made him think of pleasure, contentment and sexual bliss. They had met six months ago, at a charity function at Charlottesville's Martin Luther King Jr. Performing Arts Center. While standing in a group conversing with friends, he'd glanced around the room and seen her.

Actually, he'd caught her staring, checking him out.

And she'd been pretty damn bold, not stopping when their gazes connected. He'd boldly checked her out in return, and had definitely liked what he'd seen. She was a beautiful woman. And the silky-looking emerald green dress she'd worn that night had complemented her body and clung to her curves. It had showcased a pair of gorgeous long legs in a pair of gold stilettos.

He'd even liked the way she'd worn her dark brown hair that night, chin-length and cut into a trendy and sassy style. But then, he would admit that he liked how she wore it now, as well. It was a lot longer and fluttered against her face while falling in fluffy waves to her shoulders. And speaking of her face… He would admit to having a thing for her high cheekbones, sable-brown complexion, straight nose and rounded chin.

On that night, even from across the room, the sexual chemistry had flared between them, nearly tripping his pulse and definitely stirring his libido in all kinds of ways. His attraction to her was stronger than any he'd ever felt, and he knew there was no way he would leave the charity ball without learning her identity. In less than twenty minutes he'd finagled an introduction. And the strange thing was, he'd always had an intense dislike for cops. At least, he had…until her.

"And since it's a surprise, that means you won't be getting any more information out of me," he added, studying her outfit. He thought the blue lace dress she was wearing today looked good on her. Sexy as hell. Clinging to her curves as if they were a lifeline. Definitely his link to sensual fantasies. He'd told her more than once today just how nice she looked.

This was only his second time seeing her in something other than a pair of dark slacks and a nondescript button-up shirt. He knew that as a police detective, she intentionally downplayed her beauty. But her looks and curves were things that couldn't be hidden no matter what she wore.

"Normally I don't like surprises."

The corners of his mouth twitched in another smile. That's what he'd heard from one reliable source, but he intended to make sure she liked this one. "Just keep an open mind, Joy. I decided it was time for our first official date."

"I thought attending Striker and Margo's wedding together *was* our first official date."

Turning his eyes back to the road when the traffic light turned green, he said, "Attending the wedding with me doesn't constitute a date."

"And why not?"

He quickly stole a look at her in time to see her brows shoot up again. "Because you were invited to the wedding anyway. We just happened to ride in the same car together."

She chuckled, and the feminine sound stirred something deep within him, assaulting his senses in ways he definitely wasn't used to. "I guess that's a different way to look at it, Stonewall." The way she said his name, in that sexy voice, made his insides shiver.

He knew how her mind worked. Already she was trying to figure out where they were going and what he was up to. His goal was to get her to relax and be comfortable with him. He didn't want her to think of work. All he wanted her to think about was him, just like he was thinking only of her.

On four different occasions since meeting six months ago, they'd made plans to go out on a date. However, each and every time those plans got canceled due to their work schedules. His job as a bodyguard for Summers Security Firm took him away from Charlottesville quite a lot. And hers as a police detective kept her busy solving homicides.

Whenever he was in town and their busy schedules allowed, they would meet up at a café on Monroe Street for doughnuts and coffee or grab a beer at Shady Reds Bar and Grill. However, as far as he was concerned, those brief good-to-see-you-again-and-goodbye-until-next-time encounters didn't constitute dates, either. Since meeting Joy, even though he'd never gone out with her, he hadn't been able to muster interest in any other woman. A part of him felt he wouldn't be able to move on until that changed, which was why he was taking her on a real date. A date that was long overdue.

"So, what do you have planned for this date, Stonewall?"

He chuckled. "Like I said, it's a surprise and I'm not answering any more questions, Detective, so let's talk about something else."

She didn't say anything for a minute and then, as if she'd decided to concede—for now—she said, "Margo was such a beautiful bride, wasn't she? And her wedding gown! OMG! It was simply gorgeous, and to think, she designed it herself."

Good. Stonewall figured if he kept her talking, chances were she wouldn't think about where they were going. Hopefully she would let her guard down and relax. Joy had met Margo while working a case that had her racing against time trying to solve a deadly puzzle that had placed Margo's life in danger.

"Yes, Margo looked beautiful and her gown was gorgeous," he agreed. "Striker is a lucky man. Margo's a lucky woman. I'm glad they have each other."

Stonewall truly meant it, although he still found it hard to believe that Striker Jennings, one of his two best friends, had gotten married that day. Like him, Striker had enjoyed his life as a single man too much to think about getting serious with any one woman. Until Striker was assigned as a bodyguard to protect Margo Connelly. The man Stonewall figured would never fall in love had done that very thing.

The same held true for his other best friend, Quasar Patterson, who was engaged to marry a woman by the name of Randi Fuller. After both his friends married, that would leave him as the lone bachelor with all the women. However, Joy was the only woman he thought about. Constantly.

"I thought it was pretty neat how both of Margo's uncles walked her down the aisle."

"I thought so, too," Stonewall agreed. "Margo's quick acceptance of Roland into her life is special."

Roland Summers. CEO of Summers Security Firm and his boss as well as a man he considered a good friend. Years ago, Roland had been a cop for the Charlottesville Police Department when he'd discovered some of his fellow officers on the take. Before he could blow the whistle, he'd been framed for murder and sentenced to prison for fifteen years. Roland's wife, Becca, had refused to accept Roland's fate and worked hard to get him a new trial. In retaliation, the dirty cops had killed not only Becca but also Roland's half brother and sister-in-law—Margo's parents.

"Roland looks good. It's hard to believe that only six months ago he was in the hospital, fighting for his life."

Roland had been shot earlier that year in an attempted carjacking. Just so happened, it was the same night that Stonewall and Joy had met.

"And it was good seeing Randi again," Joy said.

Randi was a psychic investigator. She and Joy had met earlier this year when the two worked together to solve the very case involving Margo. Several people lost their lives before the assassin had been taken down. Stonewall had never believed in psychic powers until meeting Randi. Her help on the case had been instrumental and had made a believer out of him.

"I wouldn't be here today if it wasn't for Randi," Joy continued. "I will never forget the day she saved my life."

Stonewall nodded. From what he'd heard, Joy had been about to drink a cup of coffee tainted with poison. Luckily, thanks to her psychic powers, Randi had detected it and stopped Joy just seconds before it was too late.

"Randi and Quasar look good together," Joy added. "And just the thought that they're engaged is wonderful."

Stonewall smiled in agreement, happy that for the time being, Joy was so caught up in the wedding and the people she'd seen that day that she'd temporarily forgotten she had no idea where they were going.

"And Carson Granger looks simply radiant pregnant," he heard Joy add. "So do Caden Granger's wife,

Shiloh, and Dalton's wife, Jules. I can't believe there are three pregnant women in the same family and all due around the same time. How cool is that? Sheppard Granger will definitely have his hands full becoming a father and grandfather."

Stonewall couldn't help chuckling. Shep's wife, Carson, would be having a baby in a few weeks, around the same time that two of his sons' wives would be having theirs. "Yes, Shep will definitely have his hands full. But if anyone can handle an expanded family with ease, it would be Shep," he said of the man he considered a father figure and mentor.

Dalton, Shep's youngest son, was almost twenty-nine. That meant Shep would be starting all over with the diapers, preschool, high school, college…practically everything. Like Roland, Shep had been locked up for fifteen years for a crime he didn't commit, and if starting over in fatherhood was what he wanted, then Stonewall was happy for him.

When Joy ran out of people to discuss from the wedding, he kept the conversation going by telling her about his recent trips to Dubai, Australia, Thailand and Cape Town. His extensive travels were part of his job assignment to protect wealthy businessman Dakota Navarro, who preferred to be called Dak. Over the past six months, his and Dak's relationship had moved beyond that of client and bodyguard to good friends.

Stonewall brought the car to a stop. "Well, here we are."

He watched as Joy looked out the window before glancing back at him. "A private jet?"

He smiled. "Yes, and no, it's not mine. It's belongs to Dakota Navarro. He loaned it to me."

She lifted a brow. "*Loaned* it to you."

"Yes, he loaned me the plane and the pilot."

"Why?"

Stonewall unsnapped his seat belt and smiled at her. "Because he's aware of how I've been looking forward to finally taking you out on a real date. Dak's also aware that jet-setting around the world protecting him is one of the reasons I couldn't do so. He figured the least he could do was help our romance along."

"Our romance?"

"Yes." There was no need to tell her that romance hadn't been the word Dak used. The international playboy and businessman considered each date with a woman as a conquest of the most sexual kind.

"And just where is this jet supposed to be taking us?"

"Martha's Vineyard. I've made reservations for dinner." Anticipating her next question, he added, "And I promise to have you home before midnight."

CHAPTER TWO

Dinner for two? On Martha's Vineyard? And they would fly there on a private jet owned by Dakota Navarro?

Although Joy had never met the man, she'd heard about him. Who hadn't? And she was well aware Stonewall had been working as Navarro's bodyguard. But still...

She switched her gaze from Stonewall to the sleek jet. On their first official date, he planned to whisk her away on a private jet from Charlottesville to Massachusetts?

She glanced at Stonewall only to find him staring at her with the same intensity he'd looked at her with from across the room the night they'd met. The desire in his eyes was easy to read. It said, *I want you.*

Drawing in a deep breath, she broke eye contact with him to look out the window again, to make sure the jet was really there. When she glanced back at Stonewall, the deep desire that had been in his eyes just moments ago had been replaced with something else. Amusement. However, there was that seriousness she could always detect, even when she figured he was working hard to keep it hidden.

"I don't know what to say," she said against the lump

in her throat. And honestly, she didn't. She had been excited that after six months he'd finally arrived at her house to take her somewhere, even if the destination had been to their mutual friends' wedding.

"You can start off by saying that you'll fly away with me. Quasar was quick to remind me today that kidnapping is a federal offense. Jail time is something I don't want to do again."

Joy swallowed tightly. There it was. Anyone who knew her would find it surprising. That someone who was as straightlaced and by-the-book when it came to upholding the law as she, would even consider dating an ex-con.

But she was a believer in second chances. Stonewall had served his time, and since his release over eight years ago, he'd become a model citizen. She didn't know his story, but she hoped he would eventually trust her enough to tell her.

Joy was convinced that, considering everything about him, there had to be a reason she was so attracted to him. At least a reason other than the obvious. And the obvious was that the man was so drop-dead gorgeous, he could take a woman's breath away, literally. She might be a cop, but around him her hormones boldly reminded her she was also a woman.

And Stonewall Courson had the ability to make her want to be all woman whenever she wasn't busy arresting criminals. That was one of the reasons for this short, sexy, lacy dress she was wearing. She'd seen it in the store months ago and had imagined it on her when she would be with him. That had been months before she'd received an invitation to Striker and Margo's wedding.

"So, do I kidnap you or do you come willingly?" he asked, breaking into her reverie.

She smiled over at him. "I'll come willingly, Mr. Courson."

The smile that curved his lips from corner to corner was sexy as hell, just like the rest of him. In his black tux he looked scrumptiously delicious. It had been hard to keep her eyes off him during the ceremony, and more than once she'd checked out his broad shoulders, commanding biceps, muscled arms and firm thighs.

"Give me a minute so I can check with the pilot, and then we'll be on our way. And like I said, I'll have you home before midnight."

He opened the door and got out, and she watched him walk away. He moved with long strides and a swagger that she doubted he realized he possessed. And because of the way his slacks fit him, she could see the thick muscles in his thighs with every step he took. Like always, whenever she ogled him her wild, needed-to-be-censored imagination would kick in. When he entered the building and closed the door behind him, she drew in a deep breath. *Be still my hormones.*

It had turned out to be a beautiful day in June, the perfect day for a wedding. The sun was shining brightly through the windshield, nearly blinding her. She decided to close her eyes for a moment, and when she did, memories of the night six months ago when she and Stonewall met floated through her mind...

JOY GLANCED AT her watch. Less than five more minutes and she would be free to leave the charity ball. When an informant had gotten word to Police Chief Harkins that an organized pickpocket ring would be working the unsuspecting crowd here tonight, several law enforcement officers were enlisted to work undercover. She was one of them.

Already three individuals had been arrested without incident and without anyone in attendance knowing they'd been targeted. All in a day's work, which for her would be coming to an end in three minutes and two seconds she concluded, glancing at her watch again.

Unlike some of her fellow detectives, she hadn't griped about being chosen to come here tonight. She supported Chief Harkins's belief that every member of the police force should be flexible, regardless of whether they were uniformed officers or detectives sitting behind a cushy desk. When you were needed, you stepped up. Plus, working an undercover gig that actually required wearing something other than her dark slacks and plain button-up shirt? She'd enjoyed getting dressed up for tonight's event. She'd even called her neighbor, Cherish Greenleaf, to help do something with her hair. She hadn't expected Cherish to take the scissors and whack it off, though. But then, Joy had to grudgingly agree that the shorter style looked good on her.

When she had arrived tonight, several of her fellow male officers had blinked more than once to make sure it was her. Even her former partner, Darrin Chadwick, had told her she looked good, and had even gone so far as to ask her out on a date. Seriously, Darrin Chadwick? The man who'd been a thorn in her side since she'd arrived in Charlottesville for work almost two years ago? He'd thrown a hissy fit at having a woman for a partner and more than once had tried making things hard for her. She'd survived all Darrin's BS and felt she was an even better cop because of it. Rumor had it that Chadwick had applied for a lieutenant position in Ohio. Personally, she hoped he got it. She would do the good-riddance dance all over the precinct if he did.

She glanced at her watch again. Less than a minute to go. She might as well grab another one of those delicious treats off the snack table on her way out the door. One thing about doing a gig like this—you definitely wouldn't leave hungry.

Joy chose a couple of chocolate fritters. She couldn't resist anything chocolate. She bit into one and closed her eyes. Delicious.

She opened her eyes and found herself staring across the room at a stunning man while thinking the same thing. Although she couldn't see his face, from his profile he appeared as sinfully delicious as the fritter tasted. He was tall, his hair was cut low on his head and he had broad shoulders with a nice physique. She couldn't help wondering who he was.

She studied the people around him and recognized the Grangers. Sheppard Granger had made news a little over a year ago when, after serving fifteen years for a crime he hadn't committed, he was exonerated as the case was solved. And it had been solved in a big way, with the bust of a computer network fraud scheme that resulted in several CEOs and politicians being indicted. Presently Sheppard Granger was making his rounds on the talk-show circuits, pushing for prison reform.

Included in the group were three men she recognized as Sheppard Granger's sons, along with their wives. Joy knew Jules Bradford Granger, who had married the youngest Granger a year ago. Jules, who used to be a street cop and detective while living in Boston years ago, was now a top-notch private investigator. One of the best the city of Charlottesville had to offer. Joy had gotten to know Jules when they'd collaborated on a cold case that resulted in a murder from five years ago getting solved.

Joy could only assume the remaining people in the group were friends of the Grangers. Her eyes found their way back to the one man who, even from across the room, was sending flutters of heat all through her, seeping into her every pore. How was that possible when he hadn't even looked her way?

She stopped staring at him long enough to check her watch. She was officially off work and could leave. That meant going home to an empty house with hopes of getting a good night's sleep without any interruptions. However, as a homicide detective, it wasn't unusual to be awakened in the middle of the night and summoned to police headquarters because of some murder case she'd been assigned to.

Joy decided to take one more quick look at that man before leaving. Nothing like a good drool before going home.

She released a slow, deep sigh, and as if the sound carried across the room, he suddenly turned his head and looked right at her. She knew she should have looked away, broken eye contact. It wasn't nice to stare. But it was as if their gazes were locked and she couldn't break the hold. She practically forced air into her lungs. He had to be the most gorgeous specimen of a man she'd seen in long time. A very long time. Just looking at him had her heart racing at top speed in her chest. What in the world was wrong with her? She'd never in her life been this affected by a man.

Everyone appeared to fade into oblivion except for the man whose gaze was holding her captive in the most delectable way. Then his gaze began scanning over her, boldly checking her out from head to toe, returning to look into her eyes every so often as if daring her to look away. His silent and bold appraisal filled her with heat of the most intense kind. Suddenly her dress felt too tight. It was obvious her nipples had hardened and were stretching against the material.

She could see more of him now that he'd turned his body. Like the other men present, he was wearing a black tux, and she definitely appreciated the way it fit him, defining all those muscles. He had a very handsome face, and even from where she was standing, she liked the shape of his lips. Even more, she appreciated the neatly trimmed beard that covered the lower part of his face, making him even more handsome. From the distance separating them, she could only speculate about the color of his eyes. Were they black or dark brown? Either one worked in such a gorgeous face.

He suddenly broke eye contact with her when one of the men with him said something and regained his attention. That was her cue to exit. She needed to get home and turn up the air as high as it could get to cool her off while she drank a glass of wine.

She moved toward the exit, which would put her in closer proximity to the hottie, but there was no way of getting around it if she wanted to leave. She felt flutters move inside her once more and knew his gaze was back on her. Although she was tempted to take one last look, she refrained from doing so.

Joy kept walking, determined to make it to the door, when suddenly she heard someone call her name. She stopped, her heart nearly in her throat when she realized the person calling out was Jules Granger.

Jules was all smiles as she walked toward her. "Joy, how are you?"

Joy returned Jules's smile. "I'm fine. What about you?"

"I'm doing great. You're leaving already?"

"Yes." She wasn't at liberty to admit she'd been working undercover.

"It's still early. Come over and join us for a minute. I'd love for you to meet everyone."

Joy knew that meant she would also be meeting the guy who'd caught her staring. Mr. Oh-So-Fine-And-Sexy. It would be easy to tell Jules that she really had to go. But instead, she heard herself say, "Okay."

Jules hooked their arms together as she led her back over to the group. "Everyone, this is Joy Ingram, a homicide detective here in the city." She then introduced her to everyone, including the man who had so intrigued her. "Joy, I'd like you to meet another good friend of the Grangers, Stonewall Courson."

He was even more handsome up close. His dark brown eyes were striking, and she felt a tightening in her midsection when a pair of flawless lips eased into a smile. "Joy, it's nice to meet you."

Joy thought he sounded delicious, as well. His deep, throaty voice sent pleasurable shivers up her spine. "Nice meeting you, too, Stonewall," she said, taking the hand he extended. The touch suffused her with heat. When she was about to pull her hand back, his fingers tightened their grasp, holding her hand captive even as she was introduced to the next two guys.

"And these two are also family friends, Quasar Patterson and Striker Jennings."

She smiled up at the two men. "Quasar. Striker."

"Nice meeting you," both men said. Although he didn't say anything, the one named Quasar showed a hint of a grin when he saw Stonewall still holding her hand.

"YOU'VE FALLEN ASLEEP on me?"

Joy opened her eyes to find Stonewall sitting beside her again in the car. She hadn't heard him return. "Not asleep. Just blocking the sun from my eyes." There was no way she would tell him what she really had been doing. "Is everything okay?" she asked him, feeling excited about their first official date.

A smile crinkled the corners of his lips. "Everything's fine. The pilot is filing our flight plans. Ready to go?"

She couldn't help returning his smile. "Yes, I'm ready."

CHAPTER THREE

STONEWALL HAD FLOWN on this jet many times over the past four months with Dak, but he doubted he'd ever enjoyed it more than he was now with the exceptional woman sitting across from him. He'd seen the way her eyes had lit up the minute he'd escorted her on board. Dak's jet was impressive, to say the least. However, what impressed Stonewall the most was Joy.

He recalled the night they'd met. It was the same night Roland was shot. He and everyone in his group had immediately left the charity event to go straight to the hospital.

To Stonewall's surprise, Joy had followed them to the hospital in her own car, and he was grateful that she had. He'd discovered that night that having a police detective in your corner could cut through a lot of red tape. She'd been able obtain information quickly, about both Roland's condition and the attempted carjacking.

It had been a long night, and although she had never met Roland, Joy had stayed at the hospital with them, throwing her weight around as a detective to get up- dates whenever she could. It had been close to four in the morning before they'd gotten word that Roland had survived surgery and would be okay. Everyone had thanked Joy for her help, and Stonewall had walked her to her car. Even now he remembered that night as if it had been yesterday…

THE NIGHT AIR was cold as they walked beside each other in the hospital's parking garage. The sexual chemistry that had pulled them together most of the night had taken a temporary back seat while they'd awaited word on Roland's condition. Everyone had let out a sigh of relief when the doctor appeared to announce Roland had come out of surgery and was on his way to the ICU, where his condition would be monitored.

"I'm glad your boss will be okay," Joy said, breaking into his thoughts.

He glanced over at her. "Roland is more than just my boss. He's a good friend."

"I gathered as much tonight. It's obvious that he's special to a lot of people." She didn't say anything for a minute and then, "You didn't have to walk me to my car, you know."

In truth, Stonewall didn't know anything. The only thing he was certain about was the fact he wasn't ready for them to part ways. "It's the least I could do for all your help. Getting information from those cops was like pulling teeth. You didn't have to do what you did, and we're grateful for your intervention."

They walked slowly and in silence for a few moments. "So, how long have you been a cop?"

"About five years. I entered the police academy right out of college. I did my time as a beat cop before being promoted to detective."

"I understand you're new to the city."

"Yes. I've been here for almost two years now."

"From where?"

"Baton Rouge."

"Nice city."

"Yes, it is. I loved it there."

If she loved it so much, then why did she leave? He would save that question for another night because he had every intention of seeing her again…but only if she said no to his next question.

"Are you involved in a serious relationship with anyone?"

She looked thoughtfully at him. "No, I'm not involved with anyone. Serious or otherwise. Don't have the time."

Stonewall knew she would discover that excuse wouldn't work with him. He didn't have time for a relationship, either, but for her, he would make time. The fact that she was a cop and he was an ex-con didn't matter.

"Here's my car," she said, coming to a stop beside a dark SUV. "Thanks again for walking me out."

"I'd like to see you again, Joy."

The parking garage lights were dim, but he could see her gnawing on her bottom lip. Was he making her nervous? He released the breath he'd been holding when she said, "I'd like to see you again, too."

He tried keeping the grin from spreading too wide across his face. "Great. What about next Friday night? I'd love to take you to dinner."

"I work next Friday night."

"What about Saturday? And before you try finding an excuse, do I need to remind you that you need to eat sometime?"

She met his gaze, held it for a minute and said, "I'm off Saturday night."

"Okay then, will Saturday night work for you?"

She paused a minute before answering. "Yes, Saturday night will work for me."

"Good." He pulled his cell phone from the pocket in his jacket. "What's your number? I'll call you later in the week to figure out details."

She rattled off a number that he used to call her. When her cell phone rang, he said, "Now you have my number and I have yours."

"Alright."

He put his phone away. Neither said anything for a minute. He inched closer to her. "There's one other thing I need to get from you, Joy."

She lifted a brow. "What?"

"This." He placed his hand at her waist, leaned in, angled his head and took total possession of her mouth. The moment their mouths touched, red-hot passion, the likes of which he'd never encountered before, flared through him, rushed fire through every pore, nerve and pulse.

When he took control of her tongue, he began sucking on it like it was the most delectable thing he'd ever had inside his mouth. He found her taste uniquely satisfying. And when he heard her moan, his erection began to throb.

After she somehow managed to ease her tongue from his hold and began mingling it sensuously with his, he suddenly felt robbed of his senses. He knew at that moment this would be one kiss he wouldn't want to end. One he definitely wouldn't ever forget.

Desire, deliriously intoxicating, joined forces with the passion already consuming him. He wasn't sure how any kiss could absorb him, consume him and enthrall him like this. Feeling greedy, he intensified the kiss, wanting more of her taste, getting addicted to her flavor, while erotic sensations flooded his bloodstream.

The sound of people approaching had her pulling her mouth away from his, and he all but growled in protest. Determined to get one last taste, he leaned in and flicked his tongue across her lips. He knew that might have been their first kiss but it wouldn't be the last.

"WE ARE FLYING at twenty thousand feet. Feel free to unbuckle your seat belts and move around the cabin." The pilot's words snapped Stonewall back to the present.

The pilot had said they were free to move around. However, what he wanted more than anything was to reach out and pull Joy from her seat, into his lap, and take control of her mouth. Then he would proceed to kiss her again, even more deeply than he had the last time.

He had to constantly remind himself that this was their first official date. He was trying really hard to act like a gentleman. The last thing he wanted was to come across as some greedy ass who was interested only in her body. Although he *was* enthralled by her body, he also wanted to get to know her. They'd met occasionally for coffee and beer over the last six months, had talked on the phone a lot, yet to him the communication they'd shared lacked real substance. It had mainly been small talk and not too much more.

"You're frowning, Stonewall."

He blinked, not realizing he had been. "Sorry. I was just thinking."

"Nothing too serious, I hope."

"It was about you," he said, deciding to be honest.

She didn't say anything at first. Instead, she looked at him as if considering his words. As far as he was concerned, she had every right to do that, and it wouldn't have been so bad if she hadn't used her tongue to lick her lips as if it was imperative that she moisten her entire mouth right then. Full lips painted a shiny turn-you-on red. Although he was trying to remain calm, the action had an arousing effect on him. He could feel every nerve in his body starting to hum.

"And what about me would make such a frown?" she asked, releasing her seat belt and slowly easing forward in her seat as if she expected him to share a secret with her and she didn't want to miss a single word.

"It wasn't a frown, actually."

She arched a brow. "Oh? What was it, then?"

"Intense concentration."

"And what about me would cause intense concentration?" she asked in a voice that said she really wanted to know.

He wished he could tell her. Everything. However, doing so would make her assume he had a one-track mind. "We've known each other for about six months now, but this is our first official date. I realized how much I don't know about you and how much I want to know."

She shrugged what he thought were beautiful shoulders as she settled back in her seat. "Then ask away. At twenty thousand feet in the air on a trip that will take at least an hour, I have plenty of time. What do you want to know?"

"Everything." Even as he said it, he really wasn't interested in her work. He knew what she did as a detective, and the last thing he wanted was for her mind to snag on the cases she had yet to solve. Tonight he wanted her focus to be on *them*. "Let's start with parents. I know you're from Louisiana. Is that your birthplace?"

He figured if he kept her talking, he wouldn't be tempted to get out of his seat, cross the aisle, pull her into his arms and assault her mouth. The same one he couldn't stop looking at.

"Yes. I was born in Baton Rouge. My parents are still alive and together, although they did separate for a year when I was younger."

He lifted a brow. "They did?"

"Yes. My father's profession drove them apart."

"And what's his profession?"

"Chief of police in Baton Rouge. When they separated, he was a cop. He'd gotten shot too many times for my mother's peace of mind."

"You father got shot in the line of duty?"

"Yes, three times. I guess you can say the bad guys don't care for him too much. One time nearly cost him his life. The other two were superficial wounds, so he was treated at the hospital and released. Mom gave Dad an ultimatum. Get another job—one that wouldn't place his life in danger—or she would walk. Not sure if he believed her, but when he didn't change professions, she left him, moved to New Orleans and took me and my three siblings with her."

"But they did get back together."

"Yes. Not sure who made the first move, but since Dad didn't give up his job, I figure Mom made some major concessions. Dad would always be his own man, but he loved her and his family. Once they got back together, they never argued about what he did for a living again."

He released his seat belt and got out of his seat. "Want something to drink?"

"No, I'm fine. Thanks for asking."

He nodded as he walked over to the bar to pour a cup of coffee. Columbian blend. He'd acquired a taste for the strong brew since working for Dak. The man loved the stuff. Stonewall figured he would drink coffee now and enjoy a glass of wine at dinner. "So, I take it your mother didn't like your decision to follow your dad into law enforcement."

"No, she didn't, especially since my other siblings have what she considers safe jobs. My oldest brother, Vernon, is five years older than me and an attorney. My brother Orient is four years older and is a dietician at a hospital in Florida. My sister Cheer, who is two years older, is an educator in Atlanta. Everyone is married with kids but me."

"Your name is Joy and your sister's is Cheer?" he asked her, grinning.

"Yes. For some reason Mom thought those names were cute for us. She claims she knew my sister would bring her cheer and I would give her joy." She chuckled. "I'm sure she began having her doubts when I decided to become a cop."

Joy shifted in her seat, and his gaze followed the

movement and saw a flash of thigh. Although he was certain it hadn't been intentional, he couldn't help but appreciate it. "We try to get together around the holidays. I last saw everyone at Mother's Day."

She paused a minute and then asked, "What about you? I know you have a grandmother and sister living here."

"Yes, my grandmother and sister live in Charlottesville," he said, then took a sip of coffee. He intended to tell her about himself, as well. No need to keep anything hidden. He would be the first to admit he'd made bad decisions in his life, decisions he wasn't proud of but had definitely paid for making. He believed at thirty-four he was a better person because of those experiences, and he looked at things a lot differently than he had while in his teens and early twenties, when he thought the world owed him something and he intended to get it.

Returning to his seat, he stretched his legs out in front of him. "I was born in Charlottesville thirty-four years ago. My grandmother lives in the same house I grew up in as a kid. Nothing my sister and I said or did could get her to move. She says they don't build houses like hers these days."

He paused a minute to take another sip of his coffee. "Now, in a way, I'm glad she didn't move. The area she lives in went through a revitalization and resurgence. A lot of the abandoned homes were renovated, and new small businesses opened up shop. Magnolia Oaks is now a sought-after diverse community of young professionals, artists and revelers who enjoy the numerous nightlife hot spots in the area. With roads shaded by magnolia trees, you can get to practically anywhere by either foot or bicycle. Granny Kay's home has quadrupled in value. She loves being one of the eldest neighbors amid 'a sea of young folk,' as she puts it. They spoil her rotten, and she does the same for them."

"Granny Kay?"

He smiled. "Yes. Her real name is Katherine, but to me and my sister, she's always been Granny Kay. Her only child was my father. When my parents were killed, she became our legal guardian."

Joy shifted in her seat again to cross her legs, and he couldn't stop the heated sensations that stirred inside him. There was nothing indecent about the movement and he couldn't fault her for owning such a gorgeous pair. They were legs that looked simply amazing in a pair of heels. "How were your parents killed?" she asked.

"Hurricane Andrew. We were left with Granny Kay while they vacationed with friends in Miami. They weren't able to evacuate in time, and their hotel was demolished, killing everyone."

"I'm sorry."

"Thanks. It was hard on me and my sister. I was nine and she was five. Luckily we had our grandparents." He sighed. "My grandfather never got over losing his only child and died of a heart attack less than a year later. Granny Kay said it was grief that killed him."

He took another sip of his coffee when he realized that in just a short span of time, he'd shared more about himself with her than he had with any other woman.

JOY LIKED THE sound of Stonewall's voice. From the first night they'd met she'd thought it oozed with sexiness, just like the rest of him. If he'd had any idea what see-ing him sitting across from her with his legs stretched out in front of him was doing to her, he would have sat up straight. When had she allowed any man to totally capture not only her attention and interest, but also her desire?

She'd been attracted to him from the first. There was something about Stonewall Courson that kept her in-trigued, mesmerized. She knew that was why she made it a point to show up every morning before the start of her workday for coffee and doughnuts at the Monroe Street Café, hoping she would run into him there. Or at Shady Reds after work, anticipating their paths cross-ing. Their encounters, when he was in town, lasted only five to ten minutes. Enough time to get a feel for his personality and decide he was someone she wanted to know better.

She wasn't interested in anything serious, just a di-version from the complexities of her job. And he had definitely been that. She had enjoyed their brief encoun-ters, the how-are-you-doing text messages she would get whenever he was traveling, and the occasional phone calls that had promised one day they would find the time for more. It was hard to believe that day had fi-nally arrived.

What he'd just shared with her definitely went be-yond small talk. After becoming fascinated with him months ago, she'd done her research, but what she'd found had covered only his later years, his arrest at the age of nineteen and his life after that. She appreciated him filling in the blanks.

"What about your name?"

He quirked a brow at her. "What about it?"

"There has to be a story behind it."

He chuckled. "Really, there's no story, other than Stonewall is my mom's maiden name. She was Vivienne Stonewall. Her mother died of cancer when she was in college, and her father died a year later of the same thing. I never knew either of them, but I knew she adored them both and thought giving me her family's name would be a way to honor their memory."

"She was the only child?"

"Yes. She was her parents' only child.'

Joy didn't say anything for a minute, thinking she really liked being here with him. "How old is your grandmother?" she asked him, trying to stay relaxed and finding it hard to do so.

When they'd boarded the jet, he'd removed his tux jacket and loosened his bow tie. Some men looked okay in a tux and some looked as if the masculine formal attire had been made just for them to wear. Stonewall was one of the latter.

She was a very observant person and was aware each time his gaze roamed up and down every single inch of her body. She was aware of what she did to him with something as inconsequential as shifting in her seat or crossing her legs. She was not intentionally trying to affect him in any way, but the woman in her couldn't help appreciate that she had the ability to do so.

"She will be seventy-two in a few months."

She watched his lips move and wondered how any man could have such a luscious pair. And that beard surrounding his mouth was a total turn-on for her. Deciding to keep him talking, she said, "Tell me about your sister."

He smiled, and from that single expression she detected an extreme fondness. "Amelia, who everyone calls Mellie, is four years younger than I am, and is a doctor at St. Francis Memorial."

"She lives with your grandmother?"

"No, but she lives close enough. Right around the corner. That way both Granny Kay and Mellie can have the independence and privacy they both enjoy since both are dating age."

She blinked. "Your about-to-turn-seventy-two-year-old grandmother dates?"

"Yes."

"Good for her."

He stroked his bearded jaw, and the gesture sent desire throbbing through her veins. "Hmm, now you sound like Mellie. I used to worry about Granny Kay, but then I realized if there's anyone who can handle her business, she can."

He took another sip of his coffee, his gaze never leaving hers, still locking her into all that blatant temptation. It was obvious that she knew he was staring, just like it was obvious she was staring back. One of his brows raised a mere fraction, and a smile touched her lips.

"Are you trying to out-stare me, Joy?"

Sexual tension between them was a constant undercurrent, no matter what they were doing or how serious the conversation they were having. The desire she would see in his eyes held her spellbound. "No, actually I was enjoying the view."

As he placed his coffee cup aside, a sexy smile

spread across his lips. She'd hoped he would get a re-
fill. Any reason that would give her the opportunity to
check out his masculine thighs flexing in those black
trousers would have been appreciated.

To her disappointment, instead of getting up, he
leaned back in his chair as if to get comfortable. "Do
you always say whatever is on your mind?" he asked
her.

She shrugged. "Most of the time. Comes with the
job. It doesn't pay to beat around the bush if you truly
want to know something."

She watched as his dark brown eyes roamed up and
down her body again, the impact hitting her right between the legs. Evidently he liked what he saw. "I've
got a question for you, Stonewall."

"And what is it that you want to know?"

She'd warned him that she had no problem saying
what was on her mind, so here she went. "Are you going
to wait for this plane to land before you kiss me?"

CHAPTER FOUR

OF ALL THE things Stonewall thought Joy might ask, that definitely wasn't one of them. Funny how her thoughts fell in sync with his. Whenever he looked at her mouth, at those full, luscious lips, he thought about kissing her. Those thoughts had sent jolts of desire through him most of the day while in her presence. Even at the wedding, his gaze would seek her out in the crowd. Find her. The one kiss they'd shared had made a lasting impression on him. He had no problem kissing her before the plane landed, when the plane landed, and anytime in between.

"Do you want me to, Joy?"

The smile that touched her lips sent his libido skyrocketing. Beats of arousal drummed through his blood. "It's your call, Stonewall. Either way, regardless of whether you do it now or later, I'll be ready."

She would be ready... Now why did she have to let him know something like that? Her bold declaration made his already fired-up blood that much hotter. He could actually feel his breath catch in his throat. He felt the pressure against his zipper and knew the sexual vibes between them were to blame. The pounding in his crotch was relentless.

He eased out of his seat, at the moment not caring that she was getting a full-frontal view of a deeply aroused man. "I was trying to be a gentleman."

He watched her gaze lower to his crotch before easing back up to his face. "I wasn't aware gentlemen didn't kiss."

Her flippant response made him smile. "Not the kind of kiss I had in mind."

The heat he saw in those gorgeous brown eyes almost did him in. "I'm a big girl. I can handle it."

"We'll see," he said, taking a step toward where she sat and extending his hand to her. "It might be more than you're prepared for, Joy."

"Let me be the judge of that." She placed her hand in his, and the moment she did, he felt a crackle of fiery-hot energy, unmistakably raw, pass between them.

He gently tugged her to her feet, bringing their bodies tight against each other. The moment the lower part of his body touched hers, a spike of intense heat seized him low in the gut.

He stared down into her eyes as he wrapped his arms around her waist. "You sure you want this now?"

"Like I said, now or later. It's your call, Stonewall."

His gaze became fixated on her lips and anticipation jolted him to the bone. "In that case, I choose *now*."

He all but growled the words before lowering his mouth to hers.

JOY FELT HER senses soar the moment his tongue touched hers. She had waited for this moment, and it was just as she remembered it…and more.

She felt every single hormone in her body sizzle and awaken as desire overtook her and began making urgent demands. Like returning the kiss with even more fervor and greed. She tried but could barely keep up with the relentless strokes of his tongue.

The hands that had been around her waist were now skimming up and down her backside. The intimate caress was heightening the beat of her pulse, causing her core to contract, her nipples pressing against his chest to tighten into buds. She thought the same thing now that she had months ago. Nobody could kiss like Stonewall Courson.

The first stroke of his tongue had nearly brought her to her knees that night, and even now she heard herself moaning as she leaned closer to him, felt her tongue trying to out-stroke his and once again discovered it couldn't. He angled his head, directed his mouth to take even more of hers. Leading the kiss deeper and kissing her harder was like a work of art he'd perfected, and he had no problem putting his skills on display.

He'd given her fair warning. Had made it clear this wouldn't be a regular kind of kiss, might be more than she was prepared for. She had to grudgingly admit he'd been right. It wouldn't take much to push him back into the seat he'd vacated earlier, unzip his pants, lift up her dress, straddle him and let nature take its course. Hadn't she decided it would be a great diversion from her crazy and hectic life?

"Please fasten your seat belts. The plane will be landing in fifteen minutes."

The pilot's voice was like water on a burning flame. Stonewall snatched his mouth away and she immediately felt the loss. She watched him through glassy eyes as he drew in deep breaths as if to steady his breathing, get it back under his control. She wondered if that control also included the rock-hard erection that had been pressing against the juncture of her thighs the entire time they'd kissed.

The look in his eyes promised more than just something hot and steamy. It promised rapture of the most illicit kind. She licked her lips, loving the taste of him still there. "I guess we need to take our seats now and buckle up."

His eyes tracked the movement of her tongue. "Yes, I guess we should."

When he continued to stand there, she took a step back and eased into her seat. She reached for her seat belt, but he said, "No, let me."

He leaned down to buckle her in, and the scent of him sent a sensual throb of desire racing through her veins. He leaned in and whispered hotly against her lips, "Do you want to continue this later?"

Did she! "We'll see," she said, deciding not to commit to anything just yet.

A smile spread across his lips as the strong sexual chemistry continued to sizzle between them. "Yes, we'll see."

He snapped her seat belt in place and moved to take his own seat. A part of her knew whatever happened later tonight was meant to be. They had been imprisoned in this deep, mind-blowing attraction even before they'd officially met.

His gaze held hers, and she thought that no man had ever made her skin tingle and the area between her legs throb just by looking at her. Sexual vibes were pouring off him, and at that moment she hoped she would make it through dinner.

SENSATIONS WERE WASHING over Stonewall in a way that he'd never experienced before. He definitely recognized the intense heat and the ragged tug of desire when he'd kissed her, but nothing could have prepared him for the longing that was settling deep in his soul. Had ten months without a woman in his bed brought him to this?

Even now, while sitting across from Joy, he had to fight to tame his breathing and heartbeat. What was it about her that had his vital signs reacting crazily whenever he saw her? And it didn't matter if she was dressed as a police detective or a seductress; the assault on his senses was the same. The last few months had all but proved that.

After watching Joy lick her lips a few times, he decided to lick his own. The taste she'd left there was extraordinary. Not only did her lips have the same luscious, sweet flavor as before, but they'd felt soft beneath his. The shape of them had fit his perfectly, and when he'd applied greedy pressure, she had reciprocated. There was no doubt in his mind if the pilot's voice hadn't intruded over the intercom, they would still be kissing. Or he might have changed his mind about being a gentleman and joined the mile-high club, after all.

He finally broke eye contact with her to stare out the window when the plane began its descent. It was either that or embarrass himself when the pilot saw him with a hard-on as big and solid as the Rock of Gibraltar.

"I'm excited about dinner, Stonewall."

He glanced back over at Joy. "I'm excited about dinner, as well." What he decided not to say was that he was more excited about the prospect of continuing where they'd left off earlier. He knew she was well aware that the next time they kissed, he intended to take things further. Or die trying.

"Have you ever eaten at this restaurant before?" she asked.

He shook his head. "No. This will be my first time." And he would be sharing the experience with her. "But the restaurant came highly recommended. You once mentioned how much you liked seafood, and I understand this place has the best. They catch their own."

The smile that touched her lips right then was priceless, he thought, as his mind tried drowning him in the memory of her taste. "I can't wait to try it," she said.

And I can't wait to try you. He felt the plane touch down on the runway as it landed. He smiled over at her. "We're here."

An hour and a half later, after finishing her meal, Joy decided if being at Martha's Vineyard with Stonewall was only a dream, then it was one she didn't want to end. A private car had picked them up at the airstrip. This was her first time on the island, and since it was still daylight when they'd arrived, she'd been able to see just how beautiful it was.

The pilot had called their attention to a large group of whales in the Atlantic. It was definitely an OMG moment. Something else that had captured her attention from the air was the five lighthouses that signified the island's maritime heritage. When the plane dropped altitude for the landing, she could see several rows of gingerbread-looking houses painted in bright colors as well as a number of small, impressive estates, most likely owned by the rich and famous who made the island their summer home.

During the car ride to the restaurant, she saw not only the island's scenic beaches, but also miles and miles of lush farmlands. Stonewall told her about the six townships that made up the island as well as the fact that the Steven Spielberg movie *Jaws* had been filmed in one of them.

"I hope you enjoyed dinner," Stonewall said, breaking into her thoughts.

She couldn't help smiling at him. "I loved dinner. It was perfect. This restaurant is perfect. I've never had a dining experience quite like this one."

And she truly meant it. Undoubtedly the restaurant had expected their arrival and had escorted them to a private room in the back overlooking the ocean. And once they'd been seated and served drinks, it wasn't long before several platters of delectable seafood had been placed on their table for them to enjoy.

She had started off with a bowl of the best clam chowder she'd ever tasted, followed by grilled shrimp over a bed of vegetable rice. Then there were the steamed lobsters and mouthwatering crab cakes.

"I'm glad you enjoyed everything, and I hope that our first date met with your approval," he said, smiling across the table at her.

"It most certainly did, Stonewall. Thank you for everything. It's been a wonderful evening. You went above and beyond." Not only was the food and atmosphere of the restaurant wonderful, she also enjoyed Stonewall's company. He was a great conversationalist, very adept at keeping the chat between them moving without dominating it.

"I hope you saved room for dessert," he said when the waiter had removed the last of their dishes.

"Dessert? You've got to be kidding. Who can eat dessert after all that?"

"I can. And I refuse to eat it alone. At least share it with me. We're having butterscotch peanut butter cake."

Her eyes lit up. "Butterscotch peanut butter cake?"

"Yes. Will you share a slice with me?"

She shook her head, chuckling. "Okay, I will share a slice, only because I'm curious to see how it tastes."

Within minutes the waiter returned with two smaller plates and forks. Stonewall returned one of the forks to the waiter. "We're sharing."

Desire clawed through her at the thought that not only would they share the cake but the eating utensil, as well. He glanced over at her. "If you prefer your own fork, I can call him back and—"

"No, that's fine. I only want a tiny taste anyway."

When the waiter delivered the slice of cake, she thought it looked delicious. "That's a rather large slice, don't you think?"

He chuckled. "Not really."

Stonewall was definitely a man with a healthy appetite. And if the kisses they'd shared were anything to go by, she had a feeling that appetite wasn't limited just to foods.

She watched him slice into the cake with the fork and extended it toward her, offering her the first bite. She opened her mouth and he slid the cake between her lips.

"Mmm, it's delicious." She couldn't help licking her

tongue around her lips and noticed his gaze followed the movement. There was something so darn sensuous about his rugged good looks, especially the lines of his face that were in perfect symmetry.

"I'm glad you like it. It's one of Granny Kay's favorite recipes," he said, sliding the fork into the cake again.

She lifted a brow. "Your grandmother?"

He chuckled. "Yes. One of the reasons I selected this particular restaurant is that, upon request, they'll make your favorite dessert. All you have to do is provide them the recipe."

He leaned forward as he slid another piece of cake between her lips and whispered, "Although they did a good job duplicating it, I think Granny Kay's is better."

She swallowed the bite he'd fed her. After taking a sip of her wine, she asked, "You're kidding, right?"

"About my grandmother's version being better? No, I'm not kidding."

She shook her head. "No, about providing them with your grandmother's recipe to make this dessert. You were kidding about that?"

"No. Dead serious."

She stared at him. Felt a tightening in her stomach while watching him slide a piece of the cake between his own lips. When a bit of icing clung to the lower part of his mouth, he used his tongue to swipe it away. That same tongue he'd used to mate with hers earlier. The memory had every hormone in her body sizzling. "Why would you go out of your way and do something like that?"

He sliced the fork into the cake again, and when he extended another piece to her, she automatically opened her mouth to him. "Because it was our official first date, and I wanted it to be as special as I think you are."

She didn't know what to say. His compliment had rendered her speechless. And then there was that warm feeling that washed over her she just couldn't ignore. The last thing she wanted to think was that he'd merely given her a line to score, although maybe she should think it. She couldn't let anything Stonewall—or any man—said go to her head. Her career was front and center in her life. She'd worked too hard to get where she was without letting anyone, especially a man with flowery words, deter her focus.

But still, a part of her couldn't help saying, "Thank you for the compliment. But do you honestly think I'm special?"

He chuckled again, and the sound was low and seductive. "Hell yeah. You're a beautiful woman who's smart and intelligent and who can also kick ass when you have to. What man wouldn't think you're special?"

"Plenty of men. You want a list?"

STONEWALL SLOWLY CHEWED another piece of the cake while looking at her. It was not what she said that concerned him but basically what it implied. He recalled that first night when she'd told him she wasn't seriously involved with anyone and cited her lack of time as the cause. Was that the only reason?

"You want to tell me about that list?" he asked, slicing his fork into the cake again.

"Not really. It was their problem, not mine."

"Well, just so you know, kick-ass women turn me on."

He watched as a sensuous smile touched her lips. His groin tightened in response. "Do they?" she asked.

"Yes. Nothing stirs my blood more than a confident woman. A woman who knows how to take care of business and doesn't mind doing so."

She stared at him, as if trying to decipher the truth of his words. There was something ultrasexy about the way her hair tumbled around her face when she tilted her head. "Why?"

"Why what? Why do I admire such a woman? Why would I find such a woman sexy as hell, hot, a total turn-on?"

"Yes."

He shrugged his shoulders. "Not sure why I like strong women. I guess the main reason is that most of the women in my life are strong or have been. Including Mom. She was my father's partner in all things. He was a dentist, and she was his office manager. He would always say she ran his office like clockwork, which allowed him to concentrate on his patients."

He paused before continuing. "Then there's Granny Kay. After my grandfather died she became the one in charge. The one who had to protect her family, namely me and my sister. My grandfather owned several guns, and Granny Kay sold them all and bought one she could handle. She even took classes on how to use it. When decent people began moving out of the neighborhood and thugs began hanging about, word got around that she was an old woman who would shoot first and ask questions later. Just in case they got the mind to test her."

"Did any of them try?"

"I understand a few did. They soon discovered she was as serious as a heart attack." He paused a minute and then added, "I'm glad she was able to protect herself and Mellie since I wasn't around to do so."

"During your stint at Glenworth, right?"

There was no need to ask how she knew about that. She was a cop, after all, and had access to any information she needed to know. "Yes," he said, "it was during that time."

He offered her the last bite of cake, and when she shook her head and said, "No thank you," he slid it into his own mouth.

"Tell me about it," she said softly.

He usually didn't talk about this with women. And yet… "What can I tell you that you probably don't already know? There's no way I'll believe you haven't looked at my file. After all, you're a cop." He knew she must have heard the bitterness in his tone.

"I take it you have something against cops?"

"Depends on the cop. Let's just say I have a reason not to have a favorable impression of the few I've come into contact with."

"Sorry to hear that. I would be a liar to say all cops are good. There are some who give the rest of us a bad name," she said with bitterness in her tone, as well. "But I believe most of us do what we're paid to do and uphold the law while being fair to everyone."

All he had to do was remember how the cops had worked to get that assassin off the street to know what she said was true. And when Striker's and Margo's lives had been threatened, the cops had shown up ready to kick ass.

"And another thing, Stonewall," she said, interrupting his thoughts. "I agreed to go out with you before researching your history. The reason it took us six months to finally have a date wasn't for lack of trying on both our parts, and it had nothing to do with you once being a convict."

"I never said it did, Joy."

She'd spoken matter-of-factly, self-composed, while trying to maintain her cool. There was something sexy about the way her lips curved in a frown and the way she'd tilted her head as if to make sure he fully understood what she'd said, because she had no intention of backing down. The thought that such a gorgeous-looking woman could hold her own made him feel good inside. She reminded him of Mellie, who didn't take foolishness from any man.

"I merely pointed out that I'm aware you know everything you're asking me about," he added.

"But not your side of the story."

He shrugged. "Does my side matter?"

"Yes, it matters to me."

He weighed what she'd said, deciding not to read too much into something about him mattering to her. Leaning back in his chair, he said, "Tonight I wanted to impress you, not depress you."

"You could never depress me. You're too strong a man for that."

He shook his head. "Strong? There was a time I was weak. Acceptance meant everything. I lost my parents, and within the same year I lost my grandfather. My father and grandfather were the two most important and influential male figures in my life. I was angry.

Madder than hell. My life was a mess. Nothing anyone said or did mattered. I rebelled and began hanging with the wrong crowd. I deliberately got into fights, played hooky from school and gave my teachers grief. I was the quintessential pain in the ass."

He paused, remembering that time. "Then one night, less than a month after graduating from high school, two of my friends talked me into driving them to a convenience store for cigarettes and beer. Said they would only be a minute. I didn't know they'd robbed the place until the police pulled us over a short while later. The money they'd stolen was stuffed in their pockets. Stupid me, I'd been clueless that they'd used me as the driver of the getaway car."

He couldn't believe he was telling her all of this. "Granny Kay used the money from my parents' life insurance policy, money that was meant for my and Mellie's college, to hire a lawyer. He was able to get me a lesser sentence since I hadn't participated in the actual robbery. I got five years and they were given ten."

"You ended up doing eight years because you kept getting into trouble while in prison. Three more years were added on to your original sentence," she said.

"Yes, I kept getting into trouble. But all that changed when Sheppard Granger came on the scene."

"Why?"

Like he was certain she'd known his story, he was just as certain she knew Sheppard Granger's. "Shep was a convict who was wrongly accused of killing his wife. He didn't fit. He didn't belong. But even worse, he didn't accept our bullshit. He refused to do so. I tried hating him but ended up admiring him. Especially when he began doing good things for the prisoners, starting educational programs for us and becoming our advocate. He made me realize getting more time added to my sentence was a total waste of my life and my value as a human being. I began believing him and began believing in myself. I got out, went to college, got a good job and have tried to give back to society. I feel good about that."

"And you should. I'd read the news articles about Sheppard Granger and the differences he made in the prison system. Because of him, a lot of changes have been instituted."

"Yes, they have. I owe him a lot." Moments like this, sitting across from a remarkable woman like Joy when he could still be wasting his life getting into trouble, always made him appreciate the day Sheppard Granger came into his life.

Stonewall checked his watch and then glanced at Joy. His pulse kicked up at the thought that their evening wasn't about to end but was truly about to begin. "You're ready to leave?"

She held his gaze and nodded.

He motioned to the waiter for their check. When the man arrived, he also gave them a box containing the rest of the cake. Stonewall slid it over to Joy. "This is yours. Compliments of me."

A smile curved her lips. "Thanks. Whenever I eat a slice, I'll think of you."

He returned her smile. "I'm hoping you will."

CHAPTER FIVE

IT WAS CLOSE to midnight when Stonewall returned Joy to her home, and she couldn't help but reflect on the evening. It was hard to stop smiling, thinking about how much time and attention he'd put into making sure their first official date was special. Everything, from the flight to Martha's Vineyard to the dinner they'd shared at that restaurant, had been carefully thought out and strategically planned in a positive way. And having the restaurant prepare her that special dessert using his grandmother's recipe had shown what a thoughtful person he was.

On the flight back they'd talked about a number of things, while trying to downplay the sexual chemistry floating between them. In addition to being a great conversationalist, he knew a lot about world affairs. It had been interesting listening to his political views, which happened to coincide with hers.

"Beautiful night, isn't it?" she asked as he walked her to the door. The motion lights around her home came on—a security measure she'd installed when she bought the house.

"Yes, it is."

She wasn't sure what cologne he was wearing, but it smelled good on him. Manly and robust. Virile and

sexy. More than once while sitting across from him
on the return flight, she'd been tempted to unbuckle
her seat belt, get up, go curl up in his lap and rub her
nose against his neck to draw the smell of him into her
nostrils.

The one thing she'd tried not to think about was the
kiss they'd shared earlier. The one he'd asked about continuing later. He hadn't brought it back up, nor had she.
However, there was no doubt in her mind he was thinking about it just as much as she was. Would he want to
come inside? Would she ask him to?

She was surprised at how comfortable she felt with
Stonewall. She was a woman who put up a protective
shield where men were concerned, especially after her
disastrous affair with her ex, Omar Elwood. Omar had
taught her an important lesson where men were concerned, one she would never forget. Stonewall thinking she was special, and his reason, touched a secret
place within her, but she knew she must never lower
her guard, at least not completely. Not even for the man
walking beside her. Especially not for him.

She was fully aware of just how attractive she was
to him. Their personalities seemed to mesh, and tonight she had felt relaxed in his presence…at least during those times when she wasn't having fantasies of
tearing off his clothes, or being the one to feed him a
slice of cake.

She would definitely have done things differently,
like licking the icing, the little bit that had clung to his
lips, right off with the tip of her tongue.

"Well, here you are," he said, breaking into her

thoughts when they'd reached her front door. He handed the box containing the leftover cake to her.

Their hands touched and her breath caught on a surge of desire she should have seen coming, but didn't. Drawing in a deep breath, she said, "Thanks, and thanks again for a wonderful evening."

"I'm glad you enjoyed yourself." He suddenly stopped talking and frowned. "I hear conversation inside your home."

She chuckled. "Relax. It's the television. I rarely turn it off."

"Why?"

"A habit I acquired after college when I began living alone. Too much silence drives me mad."

"I see."

She wondered if he truly did. It drove her siblings crazy and whenever they visited, they muted her set. Unlike her, they preferred quiet.

"Would you consider going out with me again, Joy?"

She smiled up at him. "Yes. Hopefully it won't take us another six months."

The sound of his ensuing chuckle sent desire pounding through her veins. She thought what she was experiencing was utterly ridiculous. Since when did the sound of a male chuckle do something to her? Like remind her that she hadn't slept with a guy in almost two years?

"We can hope," he said. "Maybe I should try getting on your schedule now before I leave," he said.

Her smile faded. "Leave? You're off again?"

"Yes. I fly out tomorrow for New York, and from there to London."

"Oh." She tried keeping the disappointment out of

her voice. She didn't have a reason to be disappointed, really. It wasn't like they were a real couple or anything. They'd had their date, although it had taken nearly six months to happen. The important thing was that it had happened. And she was glad it had. "Sounds like an interesting trip. When will you be back?"

"In a couple of weeks."

Had she imagined it or had he just eased a little closer to her? "You will be missed," she heard herself say.

"Will I?"

"Yes. I still drop by that café on Monroe Street most mornings for coffee and at Shady Reds on Fridays for beer," she said. "When you're out of town I miss seeing you around." It was more than that and she knew it. "Would you like to come inside for a drink?"

He inched even closer. "What if I said a drink isn't all I'd want once I'm inside, Joy?"

Wow! Was this the same man who'd been so careful to maintain his role as a gentleman earlier tonight that he'd refrained from kissing her...until she'd egged him on? "And what else would you want?"

"To finish that kiss, for starters."

"For starters?"

"Yes, for starters," he said in a deep, husky tone.

She drew in a long, pulsing breath. At least she knew what to expect, but did Stonewall? If he assumed he would be the captain sailing this ship, then he was vastly mistaken.

Now she was the one to inch forward, and she could tell by the look in his eyes he was a little surprised by the move. Surprised and pleased, just like when she had taken a bold approach earlier.

"Be forewarned, Stonewall Courson. Once you cross over my threshold, you're on my turf."

He held her gaze and she felt the heat. "Meaning?"

"Meaning I'll be calling the shots. What do you have to say about that?"

A smile curved his lips. "I say bring it on."

STONEWALL HAD HOPED when he'd parked his car in Joy's driveway that their time together wouldn't end on her doorstep. Now as he glanced around the huge living room, he felt a sense of relief that it hadn't. Yes, she might be calling the shots, but he was determined to get a few points in nonetheless.

"Nice place."

"Thanks. I'm taking this cake to the kitchen. While I'm there, what can I get you to drink?"

"A beer would be appreciated if you have one."

"I do. Make yourself comfortable. I'll be back in a sec."

Stonewall watched her leave, appreciating the sway of her hips. He drew in a deep breath and felt his body heat from anticipation. Of what? He couldn't be sure, when she was determined to call the shots.

He glanced around the room again. On the drive to her place she'd told him she'd purchased the house a year ago. Upon moving to Charlottesville she had leased an apartment close by and would jog in this neighborhood of historical homes every morning. When this particular house had gone up for sale she had contacted the Realtor immediately and placed a down payment on it. According to Joy, there had been things about the area that she'd liked—the quiet community as well as the treelined streets and a majestic view of the mountains in the distance.

The first thing he'd noticed was just how neat and tidy her home was. Not a single item out of place. Even the pillows on the leather sofa seemed in perfect alignment. What looked like a seventy-inch television hung above a white brick fireplace. She'd mentioned her home's proximity to just about everything: shopping, fast-food places and grocery stores. All those things would be advantageous with her hectic schedule.

"I hope I didn't take too long," she said, returning with two bottles of beer.

He'd noticed at some point she'd removed her shoes, and seeing her out of them was just as sexy as seeing her in them. "No, but I did miss you while you were gone."

"Did you?" she asked, handing him one of the bottles.

"Sure did. And thanks," he said, taking the cold bottle from her and suddenly feeling hot from the brief touch of their fingers. "We're going to have to do something about that sooner or later, you know."

He wondered if she would pretend not to know what he was talking about and was glad that she didn't. "I was just thinking the same thing."

"Were you?" he asked, screwing off the cap to the beer bottle. He took a long, delicious gulp and licked his lips afterward. It was then he noticed she was standing there staring at him. He lifted a brow. "Is anything wrong, Joy?"

"No, THERE'S NOTHING WRONG." Joy knew there was no way a woman could tell a man that the mere sight of him drinking a beer, of his muscles in his throat flexing as he swallowed, was a total turn-on. And it didn't help matters that she knew the shape and fullness of those lips he'd placed on the beer bottle, mainly because they had been on her mouth earlier. The memory of their kiss almost made her groan, and she quickly uncapped her beer and took a swig. She needed the taste of the cold liquid to cool off the rush of desire clawing at her.

"Joy?"

She lifted her eyes to his and wished she hadn't. She saw concern. But more than anything, she saw something hot and steamy in the gaze staring back at her. "I'm fine." She was practically drowning in the man. His mere presence was having a sinfully erotic effect on her.

"I like the way you've got this place fixed up. Maybe you can give me a few decorating ideas."

"I got most of my ideas from the television."

He chuckled and set his beer on a nearby table. "The television you never turn off?"

"Yes. One and the same." She took another sip of beer. "I would give you a tour of the place but you wouldn't be impressed. Nothing spectacular."

"I find that hard to believe when I think you're spectacular. It stands to reason the place you live would be, too."

She chuckled as she tapped the mouth of her beer bottle to the center of her lips a few times. "Why, Mr. Courson, if you continue to lavish me with all these compliments, I'll begin to think you have an ulterior motive for doing so."

A corner of Stonewall's lips curved into a grin. "And what ulterior motive could I possibly have?" he asked, inching closer. He was standing so close that if she wanted to, she could take the tip of her tongue and swipe his lower lip. So close that she could actually feel the heat radiating off him and onto her.

"Do I need to spell it out for you?" she asked him.

He reached out, took the beer bottle from her hand and placed it on the table next to his. As usual, whenever their hands touched, a crackle of sexual energy passed between them. She felt it and, from the darkening of his eyes, knew he'd felt it, as well. "There's no need to spell anything out to me, Joy."

Why did he have to say her name with that sexy huskiness? With the tip of his finger, he traced the curve of her lips. The touch was so light and sensuous she almost moaned. "But like I said earlier, sooner or later we're going to have to do something about all this chemistry between us. Personally, I prefer sooner, since it seems when it comes to the two of us, we can't count on later. Something always comes up."

That was true. Look how long it had taken for their first date, she thought.

"Then there's that kiss we never finished," he added. He leaned his head closer to hers, and she felt his unspoken question like a warm whisper against her lips.

Her mind suddenly conjured up images of how it had felt to wrap her arms around his muscled back while his mouth totally devoured hers. She couldn't give him a yes or a no. At that moment, with his mouth so close to hers, all she could do was give him a "Hmm." And when he leaned even closer and his tongue did a tantalizing sweep across her lips, a rush of sensations bombarded her.

"I'm tempted to do that every time I look at your lips, you know," he said before doing it again.

No, she didn't know. At the moment all she knew was that she was nearly overcome by a degree of want and need she hadn't experienced in a long time, if ever.

But before things went any further they needed to establish some grounds rules. She refused to make the same mistake with him that she'd made with Omar Elwood. "Stonewall?"

He swept his tongue over her lips again, and she couldn't hold back the moan. "Umm?"

"We need to talk."

He reached out, cupped her face with his hands and whispered, "Later," before leaning in and devouring her mouth.

In his lifetime Stonewall had kissed plenty of women, but at that moment he knew none of those kisses had affected him as much as this one did. Joy was pushing him to the limits of his sanity and with every stroke of his tongue to hers, liquid heat was shooting straight toward his groin.

This was their third kiss, and it seemed each and every time their mouths connected things got crazier and crazier. Their needs became all-consuming. Their desire for each other was so perfectly aligned that he could feel every single pore in his body open up to sensations he'd never felt before.

Joy moaned and he released his hold on her face to plunge his hands into her hair, loving the feel of his fingers running through the strands. Angling his head, he deepened the kiss to get a more intimate contact with her mouth.

Pressing his body closer to hers, he wanted her to feel every inch of him, just like he wanted to discover every inch of her. Her dress was sexy as hell and had pushed his libido to the limit. The result was this. Needs and desires overtaking common sense. She moaned again as their tongues continued to mesh and mate with a ferociousness that had a burst of fire hitting him low in the gut. She pressed closer and he could feel the hardened tips of her nipples against his chest. She was driving him insane and he wanted her to be affected by the same madness.

He suddenly broke the kiss and stared down at her, his breathing hard and labored as if he'd run a marathon. Her lips were wet, proof of just how hungry his mouth had been for hers. Her eyes were filled with a need that mirrored his and her breathing was just as irregular. Even now he could feel the deep, hard thud of her heartbeat against his chest.

She'd said she would be calling the shots and he intended to let her. "No pun intended, baby, but the balls are in your court. How do you intend to play them?" he whispered huskily on a breath surging with desire so intense it was almost painful. So intense he felt a spike of desire in those same balls he was alluding to.

"I intend to play in a way that's never been played before, Stonewall. At least, not by me. Are you game?"

Anticipation rushed through his entire body. "Hell yeah, I'm game."

A smile touched her lips and without saying a word, she took hold of his hand and led him toward the back of her house.

CHAPTER SIX

IT WAS STONEWALL'S intent to let her lead; after all, she did have a firm grip on his hand. But after taking no more than two steps, he suddenly resisted. Some primitive force within him demanded that they make love here. Now. At no time had he ever felt this tight with a need to appease a sexual hunger, this filled with intense desire.

"Is something wrong, Stonewall?"

As far as he was concerned, a lot was wrong. Topping the list was this buildup of need and desire he had for her. Six months' worth. "I want you now, Joy. Here."

"But my bedroom is right down the hall."

"Doesn't matter. I doubt I can make it that far." To admit something like that was crazy but at the moment he didn't care. He wanted her now and that's all that mattered. He would call himself all kinds of fool later.

But at present…

He lifted her and pressed her against the wall. She wrapped her legs around his waist the minute he lowered his head and hungrily crushed his mouth to hers, taking her mouth for all it was worth. She returned the kiss, fueling his desire even more. It seemed that they were both unleashing pent-up need and longing with a powerful voraciousness.

Never had he wanted a woman as much as he wanted her tonight. Everything about her sent him over the edge and there was no way to save himself, other than this way. To devour her mouth…at least for starters. This kiss alone was igniting a degree of bone-melting fire that was quickly escalating through his entire body.

Growling deep in his throat, he dragged his mouth away to breathe in a gust of air that included her lush scent. He used the tip of his tongue to lick the side of her face, needing her taste. Drawing in more breath, he met her gaze. "I want you, Joy." He figured there was no way she couldn't know that with his hard erection poking into her.

"And I want you, too, Stonewall."

Sensations ripped through him with her words. Knowing all this desire was being shared made him lower his head and claim her lips again. He enjoyed kissing her, applying his strong, hard lips to her soft ones. A part of him knew the purpose of making love to her mouth this way. He was setting the tone of just how intense he planned to make love to her body. Continuing with that strategy, he kissed her with a relentless hunger that wouldn't let up. Their tongues were mating as if today was all they had and tomorrow was a dream they couldn't bank on. They would take all they could now, and the memories would be savored later during those days when he was off somewhere protecting Dak and she was back here solving her criminal cases. He intended this to be a night they would not only remember, but one that would keep the flame burning until the next time…and he was determined to make sure there was a next time.

WHEN STONEWALL SUDDENLY broke off their kiss, he gathered her into his arms, took the couple of steps toward the sofa and laid her on it. He then began practically tearing off his clothes. First he tossed the tux jacket aside, followed by the bow tie and shirt. Cuff links were placed on the table as he kicked off his shoes.

Joy watched him through desired-glazed eyes. Never had any man kissed her with such intensity and hunger. She had actually felt his need and his desire for her with every stroke of his tongue.

Tonight he'd put to rest the myth that if you'd had one kiss you'd had them all. Mainly because the ones Stonewall had delivered were in a class all by themselves. He could take your mouth and gobble it up with toe-curling greed one minute and ply it with a tenderness that made you feel as if your mouth was a treasure to be cherished the next.

He lowered his pants down in his legs and his briefs quickly followed. She moaned when he stood before her totally naked, giving her a full-frontal view of the most magnificent male body she'd ever seen. His physique was the kind that would make a woman drool ten times over.

Her gaze took him in, moving down his too-handsome face to a pair of wide shoulders, a broad, hairy chest, a tight stomach and perfect abs. He had a tattoo of a bald eagle in flight on his chest. However, it was the area below his waist that had her leaning up to get a better view. Nestled between a pair of taut, masculine thighs and surrounded by a thatch of thick, curly hair, his manhood stood as erect as any she'd ever seen. It was gigantic, and she wondered how he'd kept all his junk encased in a pair of briefs and behind a zipper. She was beginning to feel light-headed at the thought that anything of such monumental size could fit into anything…especially a woman.

"Ready for me to undress you, Joy?"

His words made her snatch her gaze up to his face. *Undress her?* Did he actually think what he was packing could fit inside her? The thought of him even trying should have made her loins ache in pain, instead of the throb of pleasure she was feeling between her legs. For some reason it was anticipation and not panic ruling her mind.

As if he knew her concerns, he said, "I won't hurt you."

She frowned. "You don't know that."

He chuckled. "I haven't sent a woman to the hospital yet."

Was that comment meant to be reassuring? It was on the tip of her tongue to tell him that there was a first time for everything, but instead her gaze lowered to the area between his legs again. Definitely impressive, and she had a feeling he knew it, which was probably why he didn't appear self-conscious. Not all men owned what he had. She forced her gaze lower, past his genitals and legs to a pair of pretty feet.

"You've seen enough of me. Now I'm dying to see all of you."

Joy suddenly imagined two naked bodies. Theirs. Limbs entwined while going at it beneath the sheets. Just the thought, the very idea, sent a gush of wetness flowing between her legs. Suddenly the thought of being able to handle Stonewall Courson stirred a raw need inside her.

He leaned down, brushed a kiss across her lips and whispered, "There will be no pain tonight, Joy. Just pleasure. I promise."

She didn't see how that was possible but decided she would take his word for it. "Alright, if you say so."

"I do." He slid his tongue between her lips and proceeded to ply her mouth with intense strokes of his tongue. Joy knew at that moment she would never tire of being kissed by him.

Getting caught up in the kiss, for a minute she thought she only imagined the feel of his hand beneath her dress. But when his fingers eased behind the waistband of her panties and began stroking her wetness, she tore her mouth from his and moaned deeply against his neck as sharp sensations invaded her womanly core.

"Remember. More pleasure than pain."

She pulled back and looked at him. "Hey, wait a minute. Moments ago you said *no* pain, just pleasure. Why are you backtracking?"

He licked the side of her face. "Because I felt you down there. You're pretty damn tight."

Pretty damn tight? Maybe in his book but not in hers. His statement only raised her anxiety level a notch. He stared deep into her eyes. "Trust me."

Trust him? Didn't he know she was a cop and a cop didn't fully trust anyone? But that throbbing force between her legs all but demanded that she trust him. It had been a long time since any man had given her pleasure, and she wanted it. She needed it. She would even

go so far as to say that after six months and four canceled dates, they both deserved it.

"I can handle it," she said with a lot more confidence
than she actually felt. And it didn't help matters that
his fingers were still planted between her legs, inside
her, stroking her in a way that would make her agree
to just about anything. This was their first date. Were
they moving too fast? From the relentless throbbing at
her womanly core, one would think they weren't moving fast enough. And she was woman enough to admit,
she wanted to have sex with him. She wasn't looking
for anything permanent, exclusive or otherwise. She
needed something to take the edge off, to relieve her
stress. She wanted this.

She wanted him.

She eased up and wrapped her arms around his neck.
"Okay, Mr. Courson. Show me what you can do with
all that you've got."

STONEWALL INTENDED TO do just that. Starting now. He
reached behind her to ease down the zipper of her dress
before pulling the garment over her head and tossing it
in a recliner chair. He looked down at her and couldn't
help the smile that tugged at his lips when he saw her
matching bra and panties. Pink. And not just any shade
of pink. It was a soft pink. Damn, the mere thought
of the tough, kick-ass Detective Joy Ingram wearing
sexy pink lingerie sent his libido into overdrive. And
the sensual scent of her perfume was arousing him to
enormous heights.

"I'm discovering that underneath all of that hard-
hitting and rough detective facade is one hell of a sexy

woman. I think I'm going to start calling you Sexy Joy," he said, using his fingertips to gingerly stroke up and down her bare arms, loving the feel of her soft skin.

"Whatever you like."

Stonewall chuckled, doubting she would be this agreeable often. He unhooked her bra before easing the straps off her arms and then drew in a sharp breath when two gorgeous breasts were freed. His mouth suddenly began tingling and his tongue seemed to thicken. Without any control he reached out and began stroking the turgid nipples, loving how they felt beneath his fingers. But more than anything he wanted to know how they tasted.

Leaning forward, he drew a swollen bud into his mouth and began sucking hard. She grabbed the back of his head and cupped it in her hands, as if determined that he finish what he started. As far as he was concerned, not only would he finish it, but he intended to brand these two delectable twin globes as his. The thought of that gave him pause. When had he ever wanted to mark any woman with his brand? That was just something Stonewall Courson didn't do. He'd never gotten serious enough about someone to even think to do such a thing.

Lowering his hands, he traveled to the panties he'd invaded earlier. Moments later he lifted his mouth from her breast.

"I think we can dispense with these now," he said, pulling the pink panties down her gorgeous legs. A shudder passed through Stonewall when he saw that part of her he craved the most and thought her feminine mound was simply beautiful. And then there was her scent, driving him insane, making his nostrils flare in response.

"Joy."

Her name was a whispered growl on his lips as he began kissing a path down her body, taking little nips in between. When he reached her navel he used his tongue to lave her there. He glanced up, stared into her face. His gaze was fixated on her lips and he was tempted to ease up her body and take possession of her mouth again. But there was another part of her body that he was eager to give equal time.

It was then that he shifted his body to bury his head between her legs. Parting the soft feminine folds of her womanhood, he dived inside and began using his tongue to stir her wetness and massage her clit. She moaned at the intimate infiltration, and he could feel her lifting her hips to give him total and complete access.

That was exactly what he wanted, and he drove his tongue deeper, sucking harder, getting greedier. He loved the taste of her and doubted he would get enough. She was begging him to stop, but then, in the same breath, she was begging him not to stop, get more, take his tongue deeper. She had grabbed the back of his head to press him more intimately to her. He would give her what she wanted and more.

Maneuvering his tongue inside her, he decided to do what he termed the Stonewall Special. He began by twirling his tongue around and around inside her, loving the sounds of the moans she was making. Using his hands, he tilted her hips at an angle to give his tongue even more penetration and depth. And then he bore down on her, as deep as his mouth could go, and began sucking her clit with the intent of making her feel desired, essential and ravished all at the same time. He knew it was working when her moans turned into whimpers. He was sucking her right into a full-blown orgasm of the most delicious kind.

She screamed. His detective actually screamed, and the sound pierced his ears and aroused his erection all at the same time. He refused to pull his mouth back until he was satisfied he'd lapped her up completely. Even then, he used his tongue to put featherlight kisses over her womanhood, trailing over every inch of her folds.

He finally lifted his head to look at her. She was adorable lying on her sofa, naked with her legs spread open and her eyes closed while trying to regain control of her breathing.

As he continued to watch her, she finally opened her eyes and stared at him. She worked her mouth to say something and then, as if she didn't have the strength, no sound came out. She drew in a deep breath and tried again, and a single word emitted from her lips in a low sound. "Amazing."

He couldn't stop the smile that touched his lips. Not too many women had been the recipients of the Stonewall Special, and he'd added an additional move just for her. "I think you're pretty amazing, as well," he said. "I could get intoxicated off your taste."

She closed her eyes again and he knew she was trying to get another wind. He would let her because she would definitely need it for the next round. In the meantime, he pressed his face into the center of her thighs, enjoying her scent and trying to bring his own breathing under control. Oral sex had always been an optional thing with him, depending on the woman. He had a feeling when it came to Joy, going down on her would be something he would definitely look forward to doing. Her intimate scent combined with her taste was enough to drive any man crazy with desire.

He lifted his head and their eyes connected. The renewed desire he saw in the darkness of her pupils made his heart pound and his erection harden. "You're still down there?" she asked, muttering the words in a voice that was low and purring and sent sensuous shivers rippling throughout his body.

"Not for long," he said. Moments later he eased up her body.

CHAPTER SEVEN

JOY STUDIED THE masculine face looming over hers. The aroma of his aftershave was driving her insane, making her heart beat faster and reigniting that relentless throb between her legs. You would think after what Stonewall had just finished doing down there, sensuous pulsation would be the last thing she would feel in that particular spot.

In fact, just having him staring down at her with those gorgeous brown eyes was making the throb that much more intense. His face was so close to hers, all she had to do was to stick out her tongue to lick his lips, if that's what she desired to do. Hell, why not? And before she could change her mind, she used the tip of her tongue to trace his lips from corner to corner, paying special attention to that cute little curve in between. And then, deciding that wasn't enough, she licked his ear and chin. The hairs on his jaw tickled her tongue.

"Joy."

There was just something about the way he said her name while he was under the influence of sex. "Yes? Is there something you want, Stonewall?" she asked in a sultry tone.

The color of his eyes changed to a darker hue and heat began transmitting from his body to hers. "Yes, there's plenty I want. And before I get it, I'm going to make sure you want it just as much."

He leaned in and kissed her deeply, reminding her he'd done the same thing between her legs earlier and making intense frissons of desire consume her all over. How could a man bring a woman to such an aroused state with a kiss?

Stonewall used his tongue in a way that should have been outlawed. It had been obvious to her from the first that when it came to kissing, he had his own unique style. And it was tailored to drive a woman mad. It definitely had her on the brink of insanity right now.

When he finally released her mouth, she was too weak to do anything but lie there with her eyes closed while trying to regain her senses. Her body and mind were experiencing blissful aftershocks.

She knew the moment his body eased off hers, and she could hear him moving around but was still too weak to open her eyes. When she heard the ripping of a package, she knew he was putting on a condom. They came in different sizes, which was good because she couldn't imagine a regular size fitting him. An extra-large? Umm, maybe a colossal.

A short while later he returned, and she could feel him straddling her body once again. "Take a deep breath for me," he whispered close to her ear.

He'd made the husky request for her benefit. At the same time she felt her legs being spread farther apart with his knees and her hips being lifted with his hands. Joy was fully aware of what he was about to do when she felt the engorged head of him pressing against her center.

She opened her eyes to find him staring down at her as he began slowly sliding inside her. She was amazed how her body automatically started stretching to accommodate his size. "Just a few more inches now, baby," he whispered, and the sound of his voice sent vibrations through her.

She felt tightness, not pain. And she felt something else. Sensations that began overtaking her where their bodies were joined. They were so intense she couldn't stop the moans that slipped from her lips. She was driven to do something, like tighten her inner muscles around the massive invader. Clamp down on him. Hold him. She began dispensing her own method of torture by milking him and establishing a sensuous rhythm while doing so.

"Blazes, Joy."

She knew from his tormented groan that what she was doing was getting to him, working him the way she wanted it to. He broke eye contact with her and threw his head back, releasing a deep, guttural growl before thrusting harder, going deeper while gripping her hips.

The sharp intake of his breath propelled her on, and she wasn't sure how long she would be able to keep it up with the way he was thrusting in and out of her with such keen precision. She could feel every incredible inch of him, and there was a lot to feel. It was mind-boggling to think all that was inside her, pounding hard and giving her pleasure, not causing her pain.

"Joy!"

He called out her name the same time his body jerked hard. His thrusts became more rapid and harder, pushing her over the edge, making her scream his name while violent shudders racked her body.

"Stonewall!"

When the tremors and spasms finally passed, he sucked in a deep breath and slowly slid his body off her. Leaning down, he kissed the side of her neck and throat while panting for breath. "I'll be right back, baby," he whispered moments later while shifting his body to sit up at the end of the sofa. "I need to take care of the condom."

"There's a half bath over there," she said, not having the strength to point in which direction.

"I'll find it."

He stood, and she opened one eye to watch his naked body cross her living room. Just seeing it sent a tingling sensation through her. She closed her eyes and hadn't known he'd returned until she was lifted off the sofa into strong arms.

"Now for your bed," he said.

STONEWALL'S EYELIDS FELT HEAVY, but he forced them open anyway. He slowly glanced around the room and saw nothing familiar. Definitely not the deep shade of blue that Mellie had painted his bedroom last year. This room was a soft shade of yellow. It was then that he remembered where he was and with whom.

He shifted his body and found his legs entwined with Joy's. Her scent was all over the room. All over him. He had no problem with that. They'd made love again in here. Several times. He was glad he'd had enough condoms in his wallet.

Sex with her had been off the charts. Definitely

mind-blowing. He would even go so far as to say it was the best he'd ever had. Although he didn't have the womanizing reputation Quasar possessed before he'd hooked up with Randi, Stonewall had held his own with the ladies and had had a pretty good stream of them in and out of his bed. But none had stimulated him the way Joy had last night. She had delivered satisfaction on a silver platter with all kinds of trimmings to go along with it. And the way she'd used her body to try to pull everything out of him still had his erection throbbing.

He regretted that he would be leaving Charlottes-ville later today. As far as he was concerned, he could stay with Joy spooned beside him in bed forever. He frowned at the thought, thinking maybe that was getting a little carried away. Great sex was great sex, but there was no need to think about something as far-reaching as forever. He'd found out years ago that nothing was forever. At least, for him it wasn't. He learned to take life one day at a time.

He drifted back to sleep and wasn't sure for how long. All he knew was that when he woke again, it was to the scents of bacon and coffee. A great combination, in his book. Had he died and gone to heaven? He no-ticed the pictures on the wall, no doubt of various family members. Probably her siblings and parents since each individual favored her.

Stonewall studied the framed photograph of the man he figured to be her father. He was standing on a fishing dock next to a boat and holding up what had evidently been a good catch for that day. The older man was tall, robust-looking and muscular. He looked like a person who wielded authority even when he was in a relaxed mode. There was just something about a cop. You could recognize one even without the uniform.

With the exception of Joy…

The two times he'd seen her all dolled up, he would not have figured her for a cop. There was definitely nothing rough and tough-looking about her in a pair of stilettos. She was pure woman. Hell, she was pure woman even without the stilettos. But with the heels she was sex on the most gorgeous pair of legs he'd ever seen.

And he didn't want to think about her without any clothes. That would only make his body hard, which would tempt him to go drag her out of her kitchen and back to bed. He chuckled. *Drag her out of the kitchen?* He was smart enough not try it or else he might find a Glock to the side of his head. He had a feeling not anyone—man or woman—would be stupid enough to make any attempt to drag Joy Ingram anywhere. You couldn't let her size fool you.

He shifted on his back and stared up at the ceiling. Yellow ceilings? Who did that? Weren't all ceilings supposed to be white? Who painted their ceilings to match their walls?

"Good morning. I see you're awake."

He jerked his head around and found the giver of so much pleasure from last night standing in the doorway. Immediately that verse about enduring something for a night but finding joy in the morning popped into his mind. Well, he'd lucked out and found it. Joy in the morning. She was definitely his joy. He was experiencing such contentment after spending a night in her bed and waking up beside her.

She wore a short, cutesy floral print sundress that

looked sexy on her. His gaze roamed all over her, appreciating everything he saw and a few things he didn't see but knew were there beneath the dress.

"Good morning to you, and yes, I'm awake. I didn't hear you leave the bed," he said, trying not to stare at her legs.

"You were sleeping soundly, and I didn't want to wake you."

He frowned. He never slept soundly. It was part of his profession never to sleep soundly. Even off duty while in his own bed, he never slept so deeply that he wouldn't awaken at the faintest sound. He must have been more exhausted than he'd thought. But when had sex with a woman ever tired him out?

"I'm cooking breakfast if you'd like to join me. I figure you worked up an appetite last night. We both did."

He lifted up in bed, thinking he would definitely agree with that. "And how do you feel this morning?" He was asking for a reason and they both knew why.

She shrugged. "I'm still somewhat sore even after soaking in the Jacuzzi tub for nearly an hour."

Soaking in a tub? For nearly an hour? He'd slept through her doing that, as well? He rubbed a hand down his face. Damn.

"Are you okay, Stonewall?"

Was he? Hell, he wasn't sure. One night in her bed and he was off his A-game. Sleeping like a damn baby. "Yes, but I feel like an inconsiderate bastard."

"Why?"

"I should have run your bathwater for you. That's the least I could have done."

"Why? It's not like I crawled to the tub, Stonewall. I was sore, not disabled."

Still, something about her doing that without his help bothered him. Just like knowing he'd slept through her getting out of bed. "You wouldn't happen to have an extra toothbrush around here, would you?" he asked, swinging his legs off the bed to get up. He glanced around for his clothes and then remembered where he'd left them.

"Yes, I have an extra toothbrush. I placed it along with a washcloth and towel on the vanity. I also hung your shirt and pants up on the back of the bathroom door. I figured the steam from my bathwater would get rid of any wrinkles."

And he'd slept through it all. "Sounds like you've been busy." He wasn't sure how he felt about that. He appreciated a person who was on top of things, but Joy was too much. It sounded like she needed to learn how to slow down and relax some.

She chuckled. "Yes, that's me. Busy beaver Joy. Breakfast will be ready in ten minutes. I'll be in the kitchen finishing up." And then she turned and left.

He rubbed a hand over his face. Hell, regardless of how off-kilter he felt, he still liked seeing Joy in the morning.

JOY KNEW THE moment Stonewall entered her kitchen, but when she turned around, the air was suddenly sucked from her lungs. In the bright morning sunlight that flowed through the kitchen window, he looked as yummy as the eggs, bacon and pancakes she'd been busy cooking. He'd put on his slacks and shirt, and on him they looked freshly pressed. It was as if the creases in his slacks had automatically fallen in place. She always thought she had a pretty nice-sized kitchen, but once he walked in, it seemed rather tiny.

"I didn't properly greet you yet," he said, crossing the room to her and pulling her into his arms. "Good morning, Joy."

He kissed her, reacquainting her tongue with his. Not that it needed to be done. She was certain there was no part of her body that could forget him. He had such a lasting effect. He'd showered, and the manly scent of him delighted her. He deepened the kiss and she knew if she didn't pull back now, they would be making out on her kitchen table.

She broke off the kiss, but he still kept her wrapped in his warm embrace while nibbling on her neck. She in turn took advantage and rubbed her nose against the side of his face, loving the feel of the manly texture of his beard. "I wish I could make love to you again before I leave," he murmured softly.

A part of her wished the same thing. "Any reason you can't?" she asked.

"Yes. You're still sore and you've taken enough of me in one day."

That was definitely being straightforward, she thought. "Shouldn't I be the judge of that?"

"Not this time. I know your body's limitations."

He really thought so? "And how is that possible?"

A smile touched his lips. "I was inside you last night. Remember?"

How could she forget? It felt strange standing in the

middle of her kitchen, holding a conversation about whether or not she could handle him again today.

He leaned closer. "But you can get as much of this as you want," he said, kissing her more deeply this time. She felt her knees weaken and wrapped her arms around his neck at the same time he wrapped his around her waist.

He finally released her mouth but kept his arms around her. "I could get used to this," he murmured softly against her moist lips.

CHAPTER EIGHT

"I THINK OUR first date was simply spectacular, don't you?" Stonewall asked as his lips moved from her neck to nibble her ear.

"Umm, most definitely."

"I could get used to that, as well."

She chuckled and he could feel the vibrations. She pulled away, out of his arms, and gazed up at him. "Considering how long it took to squeeze in our first date due to our hectic schedules, getting used to anything when it comes to us will be next to impossible."

"Yes, but wasn't the wait worth it?"

A huge smile touched her lips. "Yes, it was worth the wait. Thanks again for everything. You sure know how to make a girl feel special."

"You deserve it, and if you recall, I told you at dinner that you were special." He had a feeling that she didn't take compliments well. As far as he was concerned, the best solution to that was to keep on giving them.

"Need any help?" he asked.

"Umm, you can set the table for me. It's such a beautiful day, I thought it would be nice to eat out on the patio. It's screened in, and on nice days it's one of my favorite places to eat and spend time reading or lounging around."

"No problem."

"The dishes are in that cabinet. The eating utensils are there. And the mugs for the coffee are there," she said, pointing the location of everything out to him.

"Thanks."

He opened the cabinets and took out two of everything. But he couldn't stop his gaze from roaming all over her, thinking she definitely looked good in that dress. And she smelled good, too.

"Just so you know, I can cook," he said as he opened the drawer to get out the eating utensils.

She glanced back over at him. "Can you?"

"Yes. I'm no Chef Emeril, but I can hold my own."

"What's your favorite meal you like to prepare?"

"Lasagna."

"I don't know too many men, including my brothers, who like being in the kitchen near a stove. Who taught you?"

"Mostly my grandmother, but my mom taught me the basics." He moved across the room. "Can you get that door for me?"

"Sure."

She moved ahead to open the door that led to the screened-in patio. Honestly, even with his hands full he could have opened it himself, but he enjoyed seeing her legs in motion. "Thanks."

"No problem. Everything should be ready in a few."

"Okay." He watched her leave and thought that was another thing he could get used to. Seeing her gorgeous legs in a dress instead of the slacks she usually wore.

JOY RETURNED TO the kitchen, thinking that she wasn't used to having anyone, especially a man, in her home this early in the morning. This was definitely a first. It was also a first for her to sleep with a guy on their first date, but she'd done so with Stonewall by convincing herself it was long overdue. Had they gone out six months ago as planned, they probably would have shared a bed by now. And it wasn't as if they'd just met and hadn't kept in contact.

She noticed him opening the door to come back inside. "So, how do you think I did?" he asked, walking into the kitchen.

Although she knew he was asking her opinion about the table he'd set, she was thinking about his performance last night. "You did a great job. Now you can help carry everything out."

He looked at the filled platters. "It looks and smells good, but do you expect us to eat all that?"

She chuckled. "Yes."

They sat down to eat and piled the food on their plates. "At least let me pour the coffee," Stonewall offered when she reached out to do so.

"Okay."

Moments later she watched him dig in, take his first mouthful, close his eyes and moan. "These are great-tasting pancakes, Joy."

"Thanks. While in high school I worked at a café where I learned how to flip eggs and make all kinds of breakfast meals. Pancakes were my specialty. I seldom prepare a meal like this for myself—usually I operate on doughnuts and coffee."

"What do you eat for lunch?" he asked her.

"I rarely eat lunch. Most days I work through it."

"What about dinner?"

She took a sip of her coffee and then answered. "Usually I grab a salad from someplace on the way home, but that could be anytime of night. I have no set time to leave work." No need telling him that she'd pulled an all-nighter more than a few times.

He nodded. "How are things going for you at work?" Stonewall asked while spooning more eggs onto his plate. She was glad he seemed to enjoy the breakfast she'd prepared.

"Hectic as usual. Got at least fifteen homicides I'm working."

"That's a lot."

"Tell me about it. Most of them didn't get the attention they deserved when everyone was focused on the Erickson case. One in particular involves a woman who froze to death one night under suspicious circumstances. I guess you can say Murphy Erickson messed things up in Charlottesville in more ways than one."

Murphy Erickson was infamous. The mobster had promised to kill everyone who'd been in the courtroom the day his sentence had been read, including Margo. Ten people had been killed before the assassin Murphy had hired was taken down by Striker while on the job, protecting her.

"Still no new leads on that? The authorities still don't know who killed Erickson?"

"Not that I heard. It's a federal investigation now and the Feds aren't telling us anything."

Her eyes lingered on him. He was finishing off the last of his pancakes. He'd eaten every single one. Knowing it was rude to stare, she picked up her cup and took a sip of her coffee, diverting her attention to the mountains that could be seen over the rooftops of the homes behind hers. On some days she wished she could see more of them but was grateful for the view she had.

"Breakfast was delicious, Joy," Stonewall said, reclaiming her attention.

"Thanks. Glad you enjoyed it," she said, standing to start clearing the table. No need telling him that she'd enjoyed preparing it for him, as well.

"So, what are your plans for the rest of the day?" he asked, standing to help her.

"I don't have any. It will be one of those rare do-nothing days for me. What time will you be leaving town today?"

"Around five. I'll check on Granny Kay and Mellie before taking off."

"You don't have to help me with the dishes if you're pushed for time."

"Who said I'm pushed for time? Besides, it's the least I can do after you cooked such a delicious breakfast. Next time, I'll fix breakfast."

He'd said it like he was certain there would be a next time. That assumption from any other man would have bothered her, but from Stonewall it had the opposite effect. Made her feel good and gave her something to definitely look forward to.

When they reached the kitchen, she told him her dishwasher was broken and gave him the choice to wash or dry. He wanted to wash the dishes and tossed her the towel. "Don't freak out at all the bubbles," he said, squirting more dish detergent than she thought was needed into the sink. "I like bubbles."

She rolled her eyes. "I like bubbles, too, but in my bathwater, Stonewall. Go easy on that stuff."

He chuckled as he began washing the dishes. She watched, fascinated by the strategy he used in separating everything into stacks. He smiled over at her when he saw how she was watching him. "Anything wrong?"

"Why not just throw them all in together?"

"Not on my watch. My plates will never share the same water with my cups or eating utensils."

She rolled her eyes. "First of all, those aren't *your* plates, and I don't care who shares water with who as long as they're all clean in the end."

"Chill. I got this. Let me do this my way. You like keeping your television on 24/7 and I like separating things when I wash dishes."

"Just trying to help you save time," she said, handing him the stack of plates. "You're the one leaving town today."

"And like I said earlier, I'm not pushed for time. Besides, there's a reason I want to hang around a little longer."

She glanced up at him. "Is there?"

"I get to spend more time with you."

A part of her wished he didn't stay stuff like that. Yesterday he'd told her he thought she was special, and now he'd let her know he wanted to spend more time with her.

"You just got quiet on me," he said, handing her a washed plate that she thought he took longer than usual to rinse. Probably because it had been covered with suds.

"I hadn't expected all this for a first date."

"What's *all this*?"

"You know. Flying to dinner in another state. A special dessert made just for me. A night of great sex. Having breakfast together. Sharing kitchen duties. All of that."

"Umm, is something wrong with all of that?"

Why did he have to ask in such a deep, husky, turn-you-on voice? "No, there's nothing wrong with it. I just wasn't expecting it. Makes me wonder..."

"About what?"

"About what you expect," she said, handing him the frying pan.

He didn't say anything for minute as he handed her another plate. "What makes you think I have any expectations?"

"You're a man."

A smile touched his lips. "Yes, and you're a woman. A woman I happen to like."

"That's a start."

"Yes, I think so, Joy. All relationships have to begin somewhere."

He'd just said the one word she detested. *Relationship*. Mainly because she'd been there. Done that. Refused to go that way again.

"You're frowning. Did I say something wrong?"

Joy met his gaze. She could tell him that no, he hadn't said anything wrong and he was imagining things. Or she could tell him the truth. She chose the latter. "It's that one word I try to stay away from, Stonewall."

He lifted a brow. "And what word is that?"

"*Relationship*. The thought of it leaves a bad taste in my mouth."

He didn't say anything as he handed her another item to dry. "I imagine there's a reason it does. Would you like to share it with me?"

She was about to tell him no, but he'd been honest with her, and about some pretty personal stuff. "His name was Omar Elwood, and we became involved my first year of making detective. He knew what I did for a living, but he began resenting all the hours I put in to work cases and felt he was competing for my time. So I tried to do both, to build a productive relationship with him as well as be a model employee at work."

She drew in a deep breath. It was almost draining just thinking about that time. "That was the worst period of my life, trying to juggle both. But Omar still wasn't satisfied. He worked in management for a shipping company with a nine-to-five job and couldn't understand why my workday couldn't end at a normal hour. Things got even worse after we got engaged and moved in together. His expectations of my time became even more demanding. I realized that he wanted me to be the one to do all the giving, make all the concessions. I tried and always felt under pressure, stressed out, overworked and, when it came to Omar, underloved."

She didn't say anything for a moment as she remembered that time and how she'd bent over backward to please Omar, but it had never been enough. "I found myself making mistakes at work because I wasn't getting enough sleep at home. Definitely no support. I was nearly at my breaking point when I took a look at myself in the mirror one day. I had lost weight and was unhappy and it showed. I knew I had to get away for a while. To go somewhere alone to think about what I really wanted in life."

She took the next item he handed her to dry. "I came here for a week. Just so happened a friend of mine from high school had inherited a house from an aunt here in Charlottesville and leased it out as a furnished rental property. She suggested I come here to get away since the house was temporarily vacant. I took her advice and fell in love with the area."

A smile touched her lips. "It was the best week of my life. I found the people to be friendly, the area beautiful and the town much to my liking. Before returning home I applied for a job with the Charlottesville Police Department. I even got an interview before leaving. After returning to Baton Rouge, I ended my engagement to Omar and returned here within two weeks. Luckily we hadn't set a date for our wedding."

He dried his hands on a paper towel. "I'm sure your fiancé wasn't happy with your decision, though."

She shrugged. "No, he wasn't. He thought I was making a mistake to choose a career in law enforcement over him. Inwardly, I disagreed and knew it was the best decision I could ever make. I had to do what made me happy for a change. Although it gets crazy at times, I love my work."

There was no need to tell him that breaking her engagement with Omar was like getting her life back, finding a sense of the freedom she'd given up to Omar, who'd tried being her ruler. And now that she'd gotten used to her independence the past two years, there was no way she would ever give it up again for any man.

She leaned against the counter. "So, there you have

it. I don't want a relationship, steady or otherwise. I'm not ready to let a man back into my space. However, I'm a person with physical needs just like anyone else, and wouldn't mind getting together with someone to take the edge off every now and then. It doesn't always have to be about sex, mind you. I would also enjoy an occasional movie, dinner, walk in the park, mountain climbing…"

He lifted a brow. "Mountain climbing?"

She chuckled. "Yes. I've never done it before, but it seems like something that could give my body a good workout." She would admit that making love to him had given her body a good workout, as well.

"You've engaged in take-the-edge-off kind of affairs before?" he asked her.

Was she imagining things or was his gaze drifting to her mouth more often than not? She could feel her lips tingling from him looking at them. "No. It will be my first time. Once I moved here and began working, my life was even more hectic than it had been in Baton Rouge. I worked the streets for six months to get used to the city. Then, when I became a detective I wanted to do a good job, which meant putting in long hours. No time for a man."

There was no reason to tell him about some of the crap she took, being one of the few female detectives. She had to earn the other detectives' respect, especially when they found out who her father was. She had to prove she hadn't gotten the job due to any favors.

Deciding to continue to be honest, she said, "I never really thought about men, definitely hadn't shown interest in one until that night I met you." She chuckled. "You definitely caught my eye."

"And you caught mine."

And now here they were, standing in her kitchen after a night of hot, blazing sex. "I'm sure with your hectic schedule you aren't interested in a serious relationship, either, right?" she asked him.

He nodded and then said, "Right. I've never dated anyone seriously. In high school I dated but didn't have a steady girlfriend. And then, after I got out the slammer, I figured I needed to work on improving me and not take on the responsibility of anyone else. I preferred things that way. I guess I still do."

She smiled. "Great! We want and don't want the same thing."

"What I really want is to see you again."

"And I want to see you again, too. Let's keep in touch. Hook up again when we can as a diversion."

"As a diversion?"

"Yes, as a diversion and nothing more. So, what do you think?"

He reached out, wrapped his arms around her waist and brought her body to fit snug against his. "I think if a diversion is all you want, then that's what you'll get, Joy."

And then he lowered his mouth to hers.

A SHORT WHILE LATER, as Stonewall drove away from Joy's home, he still felt a trickle of intense pleasure flow down his spine. He felt that way each and every time he kissed her. And that last kiss, the one they'd shared in her kitchen before he'd left, still had his tongue tingling and his erection throbbing.

He'd wanted more. However, like he'd told her, he knew her limitations. Although she'd tried not to make it obvious, he could tell by the way she moved that her body was sore. And he refused to be a greedy ass where she was concerned.

That meant another hookup with her would have to wait. For how long, he wasn't sure. He definitely wouldn't be like the guy she'd been engaged to who'd tried placing demands on her time. It had taken nearly six months for them to get together, but he hoped it wouldn't be another six before there could be a repeat of last night.

Just thinking about the time they'd spent together and all they'd done sent a spike of heat into his gut. Even now his pulse was kicking in response to the memories. And as far as the diversion thing, that didn't bother him. It was just another name for a relationship of convenience. Been there. Done that. Had no problem doing it again.

At that moment his cell phone rang, and he clicked a button on his steering wheel to answer it. "Yes?"

"You didn't get arrested for kidnapping, did you?" Quasar's voice responded through the car's speakers.

Stonewall chuckled. "I told you that I wouldn't and that most women would think what I did was romantic."

"You never know. How did things go?"

"Dinner was great. The entire evening was great." And that was all he intended to tell his friend. "Don't forget I'm flying out today," he said to change the subject.

"What time do you leave?"

"In a few hours. I'm on my way to see Granny Kay and Mellie before I go. And you know the drill."

"Yep, I know it."

Now that he traveled quite a bit, he'd asked Striker and Quasar to check in on his grandmother and sister from time to time while he was away. "Thanks."

They talked for a few minutes longer and then hung up when he pulled into his grandmother's neighborhood. He didn't want to admit it but he was missing Joy already. But how could he not when he'd had the best sex of his life last night?

After parking his car, he walked into his grandmother's home. He wondered how many times he had to tell her to keep her doors locked. There might be a better crew of people living in the area now, but still a thief was a thief.

"Granny Kay?" he called out.

"I'm in the kitchen. Just got in from church."

He glanced at his watch. He knew church service ended at noon, but as usual his grandmother had hung around for the fellowship hour. One of her own making. She would see church members she hadn't seen since Wednesday night prayer meeting. Wow! Four days. But it had always been that way for Katherine Courson. He recalled she would make him and his sister sit inside the church while she made her rounds saying hello to everyone.

He entered the kitchen, crossed the room and placed a kiss on his grandmother's cheek. She was still dressed in her Sunday best. Big hat and all. His grandmother always had dressed well, and he recalled his grandfather would get into the act and wear a shirt the same color as her dress. For years they'd coordinated their outfits that way. Stonewall had always thought it was amusing.

He glanced around. Except for her, the kitchen was empty. "No guests today?" It wasn't uncommon for her to invite others to dine with her.

"They're on their way. A couple who just moved to the area."

He crossed his arms over his chest. His grandmother was so trusting. "What do you know about them?"

His grandmother smiled. "Nothing. That's why I invited them to dinner."

It would be a waste of his time to tell Granny Kay that wasn't exactly how things worked. In his book it was best to get to know people *before* inviting them into your home.

Stonewall checked his watch. He had some time since he was packed already. Maybe he ought to hang around and meet these people himself. He knew his grandmother considered herself Dear Abby, Dr. Phil and T. D. Jakes all rolled into one. Others in the neighborhood saw her as the threesome as well, and always sought her advice on a lot of things.

"So, how was your date, Stonewall?"

He leaned back against the kitchen counter and raised a brow. "Who said I had a date?"

"Mellie. She was at church and asked had I heard from you to see how your date went."

He needed to remind his sister to keep her mouth closed. The only reason he'd told her was that she'd invited him to a concert in town. He'd turned her down and, without thinking, told her he was planning his own date for that night.

"It was nice."

"Any details you want to share?"

"Nope."

Not a single one. He wouldn't even tell her about the extra step he'd taken with the cake and using her recipe to pull it off. He'd asked her for the recipe and she'd given it to him, no questions asked, and he'd been glad for that.

"You're leaving town?"

"Yes. Later today. I think I'll just hang around and watch a game on television."

"Yes, you do that."

He wasn't fooling his grandmother one bit. She knew what was keeping him there. He would check out this couple she had invited to dinner and then leave. As he grabbed the remote off the table and settled down on the sofa, thoughts of Joy again filled his mind. Mainly thoughts of how she'd looked when he'd made love to her. Beautiful.

"Do you want to join us for dinner, Stonewall?" his grandmother called out to ask.

"No, I'm good." He chuckled to himself while thinking that thanks to Joy, he certainly felt good.

At that moment the front door opened, and automatically his hand went to his Glock. He wasn't as trusting as his grandmother. He relaxed when he saw it was Mellie, and couldn't help but smile. This was the younger sister he adored even if she did get on his last nerve at times. She liked being bossy. Some days he could ignore it. Some days he could not.

He knew he had a beautiful sister. All of his friends had made that fact known to him just in case he was too dense to realize. He hadn't been too dense. But you didn't mess with his sister. Amelia Ursula Courson could take care of herself.

At the age of eighteen she began entering a number of beauty pageants for the scholarships. It still bothered him sometimes that his grandmother had been forced to cash in their parents' life insurance policies that should have been used for his and his sister's college education to pay his legal fees.

Mellie had once been Miss Charlottesville and Miss Virginia. She'd even competed in Miss USA and had come in third. All the scholarships she'd earned had helped pay for medical school.

"I thought you left town today," she said, leaning over to give him a peck on the cheek.

"I do leave today. I just dropped by to check on things before heading out."

She dropped on the sofa beside him. "And how was your date?"

There was no need to tell her to mind her own business, because she wouldn't. "It was nice."

"You want to tell me about it?"

"No."

Mellie laughed and he couldn't help but smile. Then he asked her, "What do you know about this couple Granny Kay invited for dinner?"

"Nothing, which is why I decided to drop by."

Stonewall nodded, feeling more at ease. He shouldn't have been surprised that Mellie had this. "When will I get to meet her?" his sister asked.

He glanced over at her. "Who?"

"The woman you waited over six months to date."

He frowned, wondering who'd told her that. Striker? Quasar? Who else had known?

"It was just a date, Mellie. Don't make a big deal out of it."

She smiled. "Okay. I won't, but only if you don't. If you do then I will. I love you, big brother." After placing a wet, sloppy kiss on his cheek and deliberately making that annoying sound that came with it, she got up and went into the kitchen, where he could hear his grandmother moving around.

He wondered about what he'd told his sister—that his date with Joy hadn't been a big deal. Instantly he knew he had lied. It had been a big deal, and he couldn't wait for it to happen again.

CHAPTER NINE

Joy sat at her desk and stared at the documents she'd taken out of the folder, determined to go over everything again. It was a homicide that had happened during the time she'd been working the Erickson case. The detective originally assigned to the case had transferred to another city, and the unfinished investigation had been reassigned to her.

She had enough cases to work not to get hung up on just one, but there was something about this particular case that kept pulling at her. "There has to be something that's been overlooked," she muttered under her breath. Unfortunately, it would be headed to the cold case files if she didn't get a break soon.

According to her boss, Police Chief Hal Harkins, it would be a waste of the taxpayers' money to continue to pursue any case without strong leads, and there didn't seem to be a single one for this particular homicide. All she had was a Jane Doe, white female, approximate age of twenty-three, found five months ago, frozen to death on the outskirts of town in a rural area known as Sofia Valley. It had been one of the coldest nights in Charlottesville, with temperatures dipping to a record low. The woman had been in her bare feet, wearing a thin dress and no undergarments. And according to the medical examiner, she'd given birth three months prior.

Who are you? Where did you come from? And more important, where is your baby?

The investigative team had ruled out the possibility that she'd been murdered elsewhere and then transported to the area. Although there was a chance she'd been alive and deliberately left there to freeze to death. The autopsy report didn't indicate any trauma or sexual assault. However, there had been old bruises on her back. Could they be linked to some sort of domestic violence? Was there a husband or boyfriend somewhere who'd left her in the woods to die?

Due to the condition of the woman's feet, it was apparent she'd been walking for a long period of time. A thorough search of the area indicated several cabins and a number of hunting lodges in the Sofia Valley. The authorities had gone door-to-door. Those with occupants were questioned, and they had checked the perimeters for those that appeared empty. No link could be made between Jane Doe and any of the places. But she had to have come from somewhere. Any tracks that might have been credible had disappeared with the melting snow. And there hadn't been anything unusual about the positioning of the body. It was as if she hadn't been able to take another step and had fallen in her tracks.

The woman had been found near the Coffers' farm by one of the ranch hands when he'd gone to check out a busted water line. So far the victim's description didn't match any missing persons cases worked over the past five years. If they had anything to go on—especially the victim's name—they could move forward and put together the pieces of a puzzle. But they didn't even have that.

Joy hadn't ruled out using the department's sketch artist to come up with a composite drawing of the woman to put in the newspapers in the area. As far as she was concerned, that should have been an option her predecessor thought of. She didn't want to second-guess a former colleague, but why hadn't he? Someone had to have known her.

Joy stood with her coffee cup in hand, walked over to the window near her cubicle and looked out. Somewhere out there was the person responsible for Jane Doe being out in the woods on a freezing-cold night to face imminent death. That bothered her, and they owed it to the victim to find out who was responsible.

She had suggested to Chief Harkins that they contact Randi Fuller for assistance. Randi's skills as an investigative psychic had been invaluable on the Erickson case four months ago. Since Randi was now engaged to Quasar Patterson, who lived locally, more than likely she would be spending a lot of time in Charlottesville. Chief Harkins had immediately shot down the idea, saying the city's budget wouldn't allow such a thing. Especially not after all the expenses from Erickson case.

Thinking about Quasar and Randi made Joy recall seeing them together at Striker and Margo's wedding. A wedding she'd attended with Stonewall.

Stonewall.

She drew in a deep breath as heated memories consumed her, made her remember in full detail what they'd done in her living room and bedroom. The memories stirred feelings inside her, and she couldn't help the satisfied smile that touched her lips, even days later. This was something she'd never experienced with Omar.

There were days when she walked into her house and it seemed the scent of Stonewall was still potent enough to fill her nostrils. It was during those times when she felt immense pleasure take over her being and she was reminded of certain things, certain ways he'd looked at her. He'd been to her home only once, but she found herself missing his presence.

She'd expected to have heard from him by now. In the past, he would either phone or text every so often to see how she was doing. It had been his way to keep the lines of communication open between them. Had it merely been a challenge on his part? And now that they'd had their date and shared a bed, the challenge was gone? He had said he wanted to see her again. What if those had been nothing but words with no true meaning?

She drew in a deep breath, wondering why, at twenty-eight, she was standing here playing mind games with herself over a man. That was a good question. Another one was, why did she think about him so much, even during times she shouldn't? Like now, when her mind should have been on this cold case. She shouldn't be wasting her time wondering why Stonewall hadn't called, especially when she hadn't called or texted him, either. Still, she couldn't help think how he had stirred feelings inside her that Omar never had.

Irritated that she would allow her mind to often compare the two men, and annoyed that she'd allowed thoughts of Stonewall to interfere with her work, she returned to her desk. A woman was dead. A woman whose death had been ruled a homicide. No leads. And instead of reviewing the file again, she was thinking about Stonewall.

Forcing him from her mind, she picked up the file for Jane Doe. If, after going over the case again, she didn't notice anything new, she would have no other choice but to seal the file as *unsolved*. Moments later her office phone rang. She picked it up. "Detective Ingram."

"Detective Ingram, this is Dr. Lennox Roswell from the medical examiner's office."

Joy knew exactly who she was. The new medical examiner who'd taken over when Dr. Miller had died unexpectedly of a heart attack a few weeks back. Dr. Roswell appeared to be in her late twenties and had moved to Charlottesville from Boston when she'd been hired as Dr. Miller's replacement. She was causing quite a stir among the male officers and detectives, who thought she was the epitome of hot...lab coat and all.

"Yes, Dr. Roswell?"

"I'm in the midst of finalizing some of Dr. Miller's reports. One of them is the Jane Doe found frozen in Sofia Valley five months ago."

Which happens to be the same case I'm presently reviewing. "I thought we'd received everything."

"Yes, but I see there was one other thing Dr. Miller failed to include because test results hadn't come back. There was some major delay at the lab."

Joy straightened up in her chair, fully alert. "So, what do you have?"

"It was confirmed by the lab there were traces of Epinnine in her bloodstream, which I figure was the reason Dr. Miller ordered the additional lab test."

Joy wasn't familiar with that drug. "Epinnine?"

"Yes. Some refer to it as the surrogacy drug. It's used to prepare a surrogate mother's body to accept the implanted cells. Without it the body will reject the pregnancy."

Joy put down her coffee cup. "Let me get this straight. Are you saying Jane Doe was in the process of being a surrogate?"

"Yes. And before you ask, the answer is yes. I believe for her other pregnancy that she was a surrogate, as well."

"A professional surrogate?"

"Possibly. I'll drop off my report to you on my way out of the building."

Joy drew in a deep breath. "Okay, and thanks, Dr. Roswell."

After clicking off the phone, Joy leaned back in her chair. Jane Doe had been a professional surrogate? She'd given birth to one baby and was preparing her body for another? If that was true, then she had to have been under the care of a physician who'd prescribed the medication.

When she got Dr. Roswell's report, she would go over it thoroughly. This just might be the lead she'd been hoping for.

"AND THE AUTHORITIES are certain they got the right man?" Stonewall asked, glancing at Dak Navarro.

For the past four months, Stonewall had been a part of the security team protecting the wealthy businessman. When Dak first received threatening letters five months ago, he hadn't taken them seriously. At least, he hadn't until an attempt had been made on his life. And when the perpetrator sent a letter warning he would try again, that's when Navarro made the decision to hire a bodyguard.

Dak rubbed a hand down his face and nodded. "Yes, they're sure."

Stonewall knew the police had been tracking a suspect. "What evidence do they have?"

"According to the police chief, they raided the man's home and found the gun, the paper and pens he used to write those letters as well as the laptop used in the attempted hack of my phones. They're checking out everything but they feel certain it's him. Of course, I intend to keep you on until I know for sure."

Stonewall nodded. "I think that's a smart move." All he had to do was remember what had gone down months ago in Charlottesville with the Erickson case. The authorities assumed they had the right guy but discovered too late they were wrong, after another life had been taken.

"What was his motive?"

Dak shook his head. "I'm not sure. Hopefully the authorities will find that out during their interrogation."

It never ceased to amaze Stonewall just how laidback and unruffled Dak could be at times, even when his life was in danger. "Well, when they find out, do let me know, Dak. Curiosity is biting me in the ass. Sorry if it's not doing the same to you," Stonewall said sarcastically.

Dak shot him a smile. "Don't get me wrong. I am curious, but I don't plan to storm police headquarters and confront the guy. I'm satisfied with letting the authorities do their job. I'm just glad my comings and goings will no longer be restricted."

Stonewall raised a brow. "Restricted? If your activities were restricted, I'd hate to be around when you operate at full-steam."

Dak chuckled. "I have no doubt you would still be able to keep up." He then checked his watch. "Now that we're able to use the phones again, I'll be tied up with my shippers on that conference call for at least a couple of hours. I still plan on attending that Broadway show tonight in New York. I've already informed Sylvester to get the jet ready."

"Fine. I will be ready, as well."

When Dak left the room, Stonewall walked over to the window and looked out. They were on the grounds of Dak's Winding Rivers Estate in Vermont, which encompassed five hundred acres of the most beautiful land Stonewall had ever seen. Sunny hillsides, lush valleys, huge lakes and scenic streams—the estate had it all. Including this monstrosity of a house that sat right smack in the middle of it. A house that served only as a rest stop during Dak's busy schedule.

Knowing someone was out to kill him hadn't slowed Dak down, which meant Stonewall had to keep up. The man, a self-made billionaire, was a walking business genius who probably even made deals in his sleep.

With Dak's life no longer in danger, Stonewall would admit he was looking forward to ending this gig and returning to Charlottesville. Flying around the world with Dak had been nice, but he was now ready for an assignment closer to home and closer to a certain woman.

His thoughts didn't really have to shift to Joy because he'd discovered she was always there in the back of his mind. And no matter how many times he'd tried to keep her there in the back, she managed to wiggle her way to the front. He'd never had this problem with a woman before. It had always been out of sight and out of mind. But with Joy, he went to bed thinking about her and woke up thinking about her.

Sometimes if felt like a crazy force had been working against them. Trying to squeeze a date into their busy schedules had been as difficult as trying to find a needle in a haystack. But Stonewall was determined not to wait another six months for their next date.

Their first date had given him the opportunity to get to know her better. He now understood her drive and her motivation. She'd shared information about her family just like he'd done his. He knew about her broken engagement and how much a career in law enforcement meant to her.

He'd been the same way when he'd gotten out of prison. He'd been fired up and ready to make something of his life. To be of value to his community and the town he loved. That's what had motivated him to enroll in college and get not one but two degrees. And why he'd signed up with the Boy's Club to be a positive mentor to others the way Sheppard Granger had been to him, Striker and Quasar.

As he continued to gaze out the window, he recalled that before his and Joy's official date, he'd felt an anxiousness about when they would get together and what would happen once they did. Now that they had, the memories of their date and all that followed stirred feelings inside him that he wasn't used to.

According to Dak, when a man was that anxious about a woman, all it would take was them sharing a bed to get her out of his system. That might be the easy remedy for some men, but it hadn't worked quite that way for Stonewall. As far as he was concerned, he'd visited paradise and wanted to go there again.

Squinting his eyes against the fading sunlight, he thought of Joy as he'd last seen her that day. Beautiful with lips he'd kissed…several times. Just thinking about all the kisses they'd shared last weekend made his pulse quicken. And at night while in bed, he had replayed their lovemaking over and over in his mind. How her body had adjusted to accept him, and when she'd tried driving him crazy by flexing her inner muscles, milking him. Pulling every single thing out of him. During the last few days he'd become intensely aware of just how much making love to her had meant to him.

Common sense was telling him not to get caught up in the memories because already they'd begun boggling his mind. After all, she'd made it pretty damn clear what any personal connection to her would entail. It would be as casual as it could get. A diversion, she'd called it. At first he hadn't minded. In fact, he'd been in full agreement. However, the more he'd thought about it, the more issues he had with it.

First of all, who would decide when that diversion was needed? What if he needed it and she didn't? How would they compromise? And what if one day he wanted more? Those questions were definitely important to him now that his assignment to Dak would soon be wrapping up and he would be in Charlottesville and traveling less.

As much as he'd wanted to, he hadn't called her. The authorities had asked that neither his nor Dak's phones be used until they could verify nothing was being traced through them. They'd become suspicious when both of them began receiving calls from random numbers.

Stonewall could have gotten a burner phone in the meantime, but the break from her was probably a good thing. He was convinced hearing her voice would make him miss her like hell. In the past he would call her at night right before going to bed. They would talk for a few minutes to find out how each of their days had gone. Or he would text her during the day and she would text back if she wasn't caught up with something at work at the time. Regardless, she would text back eventually. But now, knowing she was interested only in a diversion, he was uncertain about a number of things regarding her time when it came to him, and personally, he didn't like uncertainty.

CHAPTER TEN

"AND WHY ARE you still here, Detective Ingram? Didn't your shift end hours ago?" Police Chief Harkins asked the woman who was determined to be on his heels. He knew what time she was supposed to leave every day, but then, he also knew about the extra hours she worked, just one of the reasons she had such a high solve rate on her cases.

"It did, sir, but I wanted to go back over that Jane Doe case. The woman who froze to death."

How could he forget? It had been a pretty sad situation. "You got a lead or something?" he asked. Evidently she had or she wouldn't be following him around.

She was tenacious and thorough. Both were necessary qualities for a detective and would be even more so for a lieutenant. The mayor had been leaning on him recently to fill a vacant spot. She was young but damn smart. And unlike some of the other detectives, she knew how to deal with people as well as all the bureaucratic bullshit. She was tough when she had to be and compassionate when necessary.

She hadn't worked for the Charlottesville Police Department long. In fact, less than three years. That didn't matter to him but it would to others. Men who thought the promotion was rightly theirs. Men who did half the work of Detective Ingram but felt entitled simply because of their gender. He had no problem backing up a promotion if it came to that. Her work record as a detective before coming to Charlottesville was impressive, as well.

"Yes, sir, I got a lead, and although I know you're in a hurry, I'm hoping you'll spare me a few moments," she said, interrupting his thoughts.

He stopped walking and she almost ran into him. "I'm only sparing you a minute, Detective. What you got?"

"Well, from the medical examiner's updated report, Jane Doe may have been a professional surrogate." She quickly told him what had been in Dr. Roswell's documentation.

Chief Harkins nodded. "And I'm sure you've done your research already."

"Yes. There are five surrogate agencies in the city. But first I want to get one of the sketch artists to do a composite drawing of Jane Doe's likeness, in case someone at one of the agencies recognizes her. And then, I would like to go back and revisit the area where she was found. Check out those cabins and hunting lodges again."

"I thought that was done already and no link could be made."

"Yes, but it wouldn't hurt for me and Sanchez to check again. She had to come from somewhere, and there might be something Sessions missed, now that we know about the pregnancies."

Chief Harkins didn't say anything for a minute. What Joy didn't say but was probably thinking was that after his divorce, Detective Ervin Sessions had begun making mistakes and hadn't done his job as well as he should have. Most people assumed Sessions had transferred to another police department elsewhere. Unbeknownst to any of them, Sessions had resigned to check himself into a facility in another state to combat his drinking and depression.

Chief Harkins studied Joy, who still managed to get that spark of excitement in her eyes whenever she thought she might be onto something, despite some of the horrors she'd seen. Juan Sanchez was her partner, and Harkins thought they made a good team. "Fine, but first things first. Let's work on that sketch and then we'll go from there."

A huge smile touched Joy's face. "Thanks, Chief."

DR. KELLY LANGLEY glanced up when the man walked into her office. She frowned. "What are you doing here, Anderson?"

He waved off her words as he slid into the chair opposite her desk. "Don't worry. Nobody saw me. The office is closed and I used that special key you gave me. Besides, even if I was noticed, nobody would think it odd. A number of physicians in this complex are clients and I often meet with them. But as far as why I'm here now, I think you know. You wouldn't accept my calls so I decided a personal visit was in order. You know how I feel about getting put off."

She didn't say anything, and for the umpteenth time she wondered how she'd allowed herself to become involved with this man.

"We're ready to begin accepting new clients again, Kelly."

She shook her head. "No, I will not send you anyone. That situation with that woman, the one they found frozen to death, was—"

"Unfortunate. She should not have been allowed to escape, and someone paid for the mistake. At least she didn't live."

Kelly swallowed, wondering how anyone could be so callous and unfeeling when talking about a person's life. When she'd agreed to refer clients, she'd had no idea that the women used as surrogates were being held captive and forced to have the babies against their will.

"And what if the police figure out who she was and what she was being used for?"

"They won't. Chill, sweetheart. You're worrying for nothing. It's been almost six months. The police haven't turned up anything, and they won't. And no other woman will escape, trust me." He stood. "Like I said, we're ready for new clients, so start sending them my way."

He headed for the door but stopped midway, turned back around, gave her that smile that could wet her panties and said, "And expect me tonight around nine."

"I've made other plans," she said, knowing it was a lie. She had no other plans. Another mistake she'd made was to engage in an affair with him.

"Change them," he said, giving her a direct order he expected her to obey. "I assume your brother is still out of the country and you're still doing the house-sitting thing."

Her younger brother was an international freelance cameraman and presently on assignment in Turkey. Because they'd decided to keep their affair a secret, instead of meeting at her place or Anderson's, they'd used her brother's home in the mountains to hold their clandestine rendezvous. "Yes, Barron is still out the country."

"Good. Like I said, expect me around nine." He then turned and left her office.

CHAPTER ELEVEN

JOY'S CELL PHONE rang, and immediately she knew it was Stonewall. She had given him his own ringtone. "Hello."

"I hope I'm not calling too late, Joy."

She tried to downplay the surge of pleasure at hearing Stonewall's voice. After setting aside her laptop, she removed her reading glasses and put them on the nightstand. She was sitting cross-legged in the middle of her bed, completely surrounded by reports. She'd spent the last two hours doing research on surrogate agencies in the city and surrounding areas.

"Not at all," she said, wishing his deep voice didn't always do things to her, like make intense heat settle low in her tummy.

He always said her name with a sexy drawl. And as far as Stonewall Courson calling too late, she would accept a call from him anytime. Day or night. Although she was tempted to do so, she wouldn't inquire why he'd waited four days to call. Four days when he'd been constantly on her mind.

"How are things going in London?" she asked him.

"Trip to London was canceled. We'd been at his home in Vermont. But now we're in New York. Dak wanted to attend a Broadway show. We'll be staying overnight and will return to Vermont tomorrow."

She could tell he was moving around the room, and she could hear him opening and closing drawers. "The reason for the change in our plans was that the authorities contacted us, letting us know they'd gotten a lead on the person trying to kill Dak. They have now made an arrest."

"That's great! And I hope it's the right guy."

"Same here. As a precaution, Dak wants me to stay on until the authorities are certain he is and that he acted alone."

"Smart thinking."

"I would have called sooner, but the authorities strongly suggested that Dak and I turn off our phones for the past week. They suspected our phones had been hacked."

Now that she knew why he hadn't called or texted, she was glad she hadn't let those mind games get to her. "Well, I'm sure Mr. Navarro hopes this nightmare is over and he can get on with his life."

"I hope so, too." Then, changing the subject, he asked, "How are things going at work?"

She shifted in bed to a more comfortable position. "I got a lead on one of my cases. The one involving the woman found frozen to death five months ago." She appreciated the fact that he'd asked about her work. Omar never had.

"That's great, Joy. You're good at what you do. I'm sure if that lead goes anywhere, you'll be able to find it."

It still amazed her that Stonewall was a man who

didn't have a problem applauding her abilities. "Thanks for the vote of confidence."

"No problem. Did you finish off the rest of the cake?"

She chuckled. "Yes, and probably gained a good ten pounds in the process."

"I'm sure that's not the case, and if it is, I'll help you work it off when I get back."

"How? Will you go jogging with me?"

"Yes, among other things."

A jolt of sexual energy rocked her to the bone. She could definitely read between those lines. "I'm counting on it, Stonewall."

"And I plan to deliver, Joy."

She could imagine the look on his face about now. Eyes that were heavy-lidded in desire and lips that promised the best kisses ever. She swallowed, feeling an intense need flowing from him all the way through the phone. Joy wondered if he felt the same coming from her.

"Where are you?" he asked her in a low and husky voice.

"In bed."

He was quiet a moment before saying, "I wish I was there with you."

His words were a seductive whisper that caused a restless throb of desire to invade her veins. "I wished you were here, as well."

"Hold that thought until I come back."

"I will." There was no way she could not.

"I'll let you go while I have a mind to do so, Joy."

Thick beats of awareness pounded her heart. What was there about Stonewall that could get her all hot and bothered while talking to him on the phone? "Good night, Stonewall."

"Good night, Joy. Until next time."

Joy hung up the phone thinking the next time couldn't get here fast enough.

"WAKE UP. I'M about to leave."

Kelly opened her eyes in time to watch Anderson's fleeting back before he walked out of the bedroom. She hadn't heard him leave the bed or move around getting dressed. Like he'd told her he would do, he had arrived last night exactly at nine. She'd been here waiting…just like a puppy that needed to be petted.

After easing out of bed, she slid into her robe and left the bedroom, finding him standing at the front door. He was dressed like the businessman that he was and nothing like the man who'd spent the better part of the night making wild and almost nonstop love to her. She drew in a deep breath, knowing for him love had nothing to do with it. It was nothing but sex.

A few minutes later his words confirmed as much when he reached out, wrapped an arm around her waist and whispered, "As always, sex between us was good, Kelly."

And then he kissed her. She tried to be detached, but the minute his tongue entered her mouth, she weakened. She quickly recovered and pulled back. "Goodbye, Anderson."

One dark eyebrow rose. "Is something wrong?"

Yes, there was a lot wrong, but to him she said, "No, everything is fine. Goodbye, Anderson."

He didn't move, and she knew he was eyeing her curiously. "I'll call you later this week."

She wanted to tell him not to bother. Instead she said, "Fine, you do that."

"And remember what I said about sending us clients."

She refused to agree to that. "Goodbye, Anderson," she said for the third time, trying to keep the annoyance out of her voice.

He didn't move to leave, and she wished he would. Instead he stood there and stared at her. "Whatever thoughts are going through that gorgeous head of yours, delete them," he said quietly in a stern tone. "No need to get a conscience now."

She frowned. "I've always had a conscience. I didn't know you were…" She couldn't even say it.

"I was what?" he asked mockingly. "Filling orders? Why does it matter how the orders were being filled and by whom? Your clients want babies and I'm giving them what they want. Just think of all the happy couples you're helping."

But at whose expense? she wanted to scream. *Whose freedom? Whose lives?*

"We're in this together, sweetheart. Remember that," he said in a harsh tone. "Enjoy your weekend."

It was only then that he opened the door and walked out of it. Kelly felt a distinct chill in the air the moment she locked the door behind him. Heaving a disgusted sigh, she walked toward her kitchen, needing a cup of coffee. She hoped the caffeine would give her the energy she needed to face another day.

As she moved around her kitchen, she recalled the first time she'd seen Anderson. It had been at a local medical conference two years ago. He was employed as a genetic counselor at one of the labs in town. He'd been the suave, charismatic and flirty thirty-two-year-old who'd boosted the confidence of a woman nearly ten years his senior. Playing the role of a cougar had had its merits… especially in the bedroom. Her ex-husband had been too driven by ambition to spend any time with her there, but Anderson had shown her a man could merge both sexual enjoyment and ambitions with results that were so mind-blowing she had to fight off erotic shivers whenever she thought about it.

It was only after she'd gotten into the affair too deeply that he'd told her about an agency he also represented. A surrogate agency that specialized in embryo transfers. An agency that he'd manipulated her into being a part of. She hadn't discovered the truth of what the agency was doing until much later, and now she regretted her part in it. A woman was dead, others were being held against their will and she was partly to blame. Anderson was always quick to remind her that if he and the agency went down, she would sink right along with the ship.

Somehow, someway, she had to come up with a plan. If she went to the authorities and told them now, before things unraveled, would she get any kind of clemency? She needed to talk to her brother when he returned. She had to confide in someone and seek advice. Otherwise, she would find herself in a world of trouble because of Anderson's manipulations.

And she refused to let that happen. She refused to be used or influenced by him any longer.

CHAPTER TWELVE

JOY STOOD TO stretch the kinks from her body before stepping away from her cubicle. She glanced outside her window as she drank her coffee. After Stonewall's call last night, she hadn't wanted to do anything but put all her work away, go to sleep and dream about him. And she had.

She was in total awe of just how he could make her feel with a mere phone call. And when he'd promised to go jogging with her, and in the same breath alluded to doing even more, she could only fantasize as to what he'd meant. All sorts of erotic scenarios had filled her head before she'd fallen asleep.

Awakening that morning, she'd felt fresh, relaxed, well rested and ready to face another day. If talking to him on the phone could do that, she wondered what effect waking up beside him each morning would have.

Joy inwardly berated herself for having such thoughts. The last thing she wanted was for any man to have a constant spot in her bed. She had to remind herself that all she needed was a diversion and nothing constant.

She glanced at her watch and saw that it was midday already. When Sanchez had arrived that morning, she'd briefed him on everything. They planned to hit the streets in an hour or so. First they would drive to the crime scene and do their own assessment of the area to determine what homes they needed to revisit.

She'd compiled a list of all the surrogate agencies in Charlottesville. There were more than the five she'd originally assumed. All of them had received stellar reviews from happy couples who might not otherwise be parents without the agencies' services. Could Jane Doe be connected to any of them?

She heard her phone ring and recognized the ringtone. It was her mother calling. She quickly walked back to the desk and clicked on her cell phone. "Hi, Mom."

"Hi, baby. You okay?"

She smiled. Lesley Ingram always reminded Joy she was the baby in the family. "I'm fine. You and Dad okay?"

"We're fine. Orient, Marcia and the kids just left."

Joy was glad her older siblings were all married with kids, so her mother had no reason to try rushing her to the altar or motherhood. Most of her family knew she was married to her career.

"It was nice having everyone home for Mother's Day."

Joy smiled. Yes, it had been. Like she did every year, she had flown to Baton Rouge for the occasion. It had been good seeing her siblings and all her nieces and nephews. There were a total of five, soon to be six with her sister pregnant. "I'm glad I was able to make it home."

"Me, too. You work too much. I bet you're at work now."

Joy chuckled. "Guilty. Cases to solve, Mom." No need to explain that the Erickson case had stripped the city of already tight funds. The budget was tighter than ever, which meant each detective team had more than their fair share of cases to solve. She glanced at her desk, looking at the active cases piled in a high stack.

Joy liked Juan Sanchez and was glad when he'd transferred from the Gang Task Force a few months ago and became her partner. He was alert, cautious, wouldn't put her life on the line to score brownie points with anyone, and he definitely wasn't a hothead. They were the same age but Sanchez was married, and he and his wife, Trina, had a newborn son, Carlos.

"Omar stopped by yesterday."

Her mother's words intruded into her thoughts. Joy frowned. "Omar stopped by? Why?"

"Honestly, Joy, it's not like he's a stranger to us. If you recall, he was the man you were going to marry."

"Yes, he's the man I *was* going to marry. I broke things off a couple of years ago, so why would he come around visiting now?"

"Your dad ran into him on the golf course and invited him to dinner. It was good seeing him."

"Whatever," Joy said, tossing a paper clip on her desk. "It's your home. You and Dad can invite over whomever you want."

"We never could understand why you let him go."

She wondered why her mother was bringing this up when she'd explained it all to her parents before. "I told you, Mom, we didn't want the same things. He wanted a nine-to-five wife and that wasn't me."

"The two of you could have compromised."

No, we couldn't, she wanted to scream. She was saved from saying anything when there was a tap on her cubicle wall. "Look, Mom, I have to go. We'll talk later."

"Okay, but I don't think Omar has gotten over you."

"Sorry to hear that, because I've gotten over him. Goodbye, Mom. Love you. Give Dad my love, as well."

She quickly hung up the phone when the tap sounded again. "I'm available now."

Mike Gunn, the department's sketch artist, appeared. "I thought you'd want these today since I'm out of the office a couple of days next week. My grandson is graduating from high school."

"Congratulations," Joy said, taking the folder from Mike. "College plans?"

"Yep. He's headed to Penn State. Wants to be an engineer."

She nodded. "Penn State has a good engineering program."

"That's what I heard. Well, I'm out of here."

"Thanks for getting this back to me so quickly."

"No problem. Reconstructing her likeness was easy. She was a beautiful young woman. Heartbreaking what happened to her. I hope you find out why she was out in the cold that night of all nights."

Joy drew in a deep breath. "I'm determined to do that."

Only after Mike left did Joy sit down and open the folder. She shook her head sadly. Mike was right. Jane Doe had been a beautiful woman.

"Who are you really, Jane? And where is your baby?" Shivers ran through Joy's body when she thought of how the woman had been out in the cold, going where? But more important, where had she come from?

She closed the folder, knowing she owed it to the dead woman to find out all that and more.

JOY GLANCED AROUND as she approached another cabin.
This was the sixth in one day. To save time and cover
more ground, she and Sanchez had split up. He would
talk to the occupants of the homes to the east and she
would do the same to those on the west. So far they'd
found nothing. Most of the cabins were rentals and
the occupants had been living in them less than five
months. Anyone around five months ago was gone.

She glanced at her watch. It was getting late. The sun
had gone down. She and Sanchez had agreed to call it
a day in another hour or so. This cabin was just like all
the others in the area. Spacious. Luxurious-looking.
Well maintained. She didn't want to guess how much
the rental would be on such a place.

There was a strong mountain breeze and she wished
she'd gotten her jacket out the car and put it on. It didn't
matter if this was June. The higher up in the mountains
you went, the cooler the temperature got. She thought
about going back to get it and decided to keep walking.
Hopefully the questioning wouldn't take long. If the
place was occupied. There was no car so she couldn't
be certain.

She felt her phone vibrate in her pants pocket. It was
probably Sanchez. She would call him back in a second. For now, she wanted to key in on her surroundings.
Imagine the place and the distance of it from the crime
scene where Jane Doe's body was found. It would have
been a good five-mile trek going south.

Her research had shown there'd been a quarter moon
in the sky that night, which meant not a lot of light there.
She couldn't imagine anyone, especially a woman wan-

dering around the area, with barely enough light and in the cold weather.

"May we help you?"

Joy turned and saw a couple had come out to stand on the wraparound porch. They both looked in their late sixties. She flipped open her badge wallet and held it up. "I'm Detective Joy Ingram with the Charlottesville Police. I'd like to ask you a few questions."

"About what?" the man wanted to know. He was eyeing her suspiciously as if, badge or no badge, he didn't trust her.

"About a woman who froze to death one night a few miles from here, five months ago. Were you staying here then?"

"Yes," the woman said, smiling.

Joy immediately picked up on the contrast between the two. One friendly and one not so much. She directed her questions to the friendlier. "And you are?"

Before she could respond, the man she assumed was the woman's husband said, "We're the Dunmores. I'm Henry and this is my wife Edith. Someone has already been here and asked us about that. Not too long after it happened. Why are you back?"

"Because it's an unsolved case," Joy said.

"It's sad what happened to that girl," Mrs. Dunmore piped up to say. "The police officer who came around told us what happened."

"Yes, it was sad," Joy agreed.

"There's nothing else we can tell you," Mr. Dunmore said, as if he was getting annoyed that she was wasting their time.

"I was hoping that you could tell me if you've seen

this woman before," Joy said, holding up the sketch of Jane Doe.

The woman took it and adjusted her glasses to study it. "She's such a pretty girl, but no, I've never seen her before."

Joy nodded. "What about you, Mr. Dunmore?"

The woman passed the picture to her husband, who didn't study it as long as his wife had. "No, I've never seen her before." He then handed the picture back to her.

Joy returned the picture to the packet she was carrying. "Nice place," she said, glancing around. "You're owners or renters?"

"We're owners," Mrs. Dunmore said proudly.

Joy nodded. "Are there a lot of owners who stay-year-round?"

"We wouldn't know," Mr. Dunmore said. "We pretty much keep to ourselves."

At that moment Joy heard the ding on her phone indicating a text message had come through. She'd gotten a call earlier and now a text. Had Sanchez found something and was trying to reach her? She was about to ask the Dunmores to excuse her while she checked her phone when Mrs. Dunmore's next words stopped her.

"I do recall something."

Joy looked over at Mrs. Dunmore. "And what do you recall?"

Mrs. Dunmore glanced over at her husband as if she wasn't sure he would approve of what she was about to say. Then she said, "It's about Stanley."

"Stanley?"

"Yes, our Yorkie. That's how we knew you were here. Stanley doesn't bark. He runs and hides under the bed. Whenever he does that, we know something is going on."

Joy nodded. "And?"

"And Stanley was acting strange that night. He ran under the bed and stayed there."

Joy mulled that over and then asked, "Did either of you venture outside to see if anything was out there?"

It was Mr. Dunmore who answered. "No, it was cold out. I wasn't going out there. I figured it was nothing but some animal trying to find heat from the cold."

Joy nodded. "Did you mention it to the police officer when he came around asking questions?"

"No," Mr. Dunmore said. "He only asked if we saw anything. He didn't ask if we heard anything."

"Oh, I see. Is there anything else?" Joy asked, looking from one to the other.

Mrs. Dunmore shook her head. "No. I just hope you find the person responsible."

"I hope so, too," Joy said. She noted Mr. Dunmore hadn't said anything.

"Well, if either of you remember anything else, please give me a call," Joy said, handing her business card to Mrs. Dunmore.

"Okay, we will."

Mr. Dunmore gave his wife a look that clearly suggested she didn't speak for him.

As soon as Joy got back inside her car, she pulled out her cell phone. The missed call had come from Sanchez. The text, however, had come from Stonewall.

Missing you like crazy.

Those four words caused every hormone within Joy's body to sizzle. These words, combined with the ones he'd spoken last night, had sexual excitement curling in her stomach. They were sensations she was getting used to whenever she thought about Stonewall.

In the past his text messages had been more casual. This was the first one she'd received from him since they'd slept together, and it definitely had a more intimate and personal tone.

She checked her watch. It was close to six. She wondered what he was doing. Had he returned to Vermont? He'd told her about Dak Navarro's home and how beautiful it was.

She nearly jumped when her phone rang. It was Sanchez. For a minute she'd forgotten about his call. "Hey, Sanchez."

"Did you not get my call?"

Now she felt guilty about not calling him right back. Instead she'd been mooning over Stonewall's text. "I was in the middle of an interview with a couple who owns a cabin. I was about to call you back. What's up?"

"Nothing. That's why I'm calling. All of my cabins were vacant. It's late and I'm checking out to go home. I advise you do the same before it starts getting dark."

"I will," she said, appreciating that with Daylight Savings Time, it didn't get dark until almost eight.

"So, how did your interview go?"

She told him about the Dunmores. "I think I'll get Holly to run backgrounds on them, as well as the owners of all the cabins in the area."

"That should have been already been done by Sessions."

"Yes," she agreed. "I'll see you tomorrow."

"Will do."

She clicked off the phone and was tempted to reread Stonewall's text. Instead she quickly placed the phone in her pocket before temptation got the best of her. She wasn't quick enough. She pulled the phone back out and texted him back an emoji happy face. She couldn't help blushing at doing something like that for the first time with a guy.

Joy heard her stomach growl and knew it was time to grab something because she hadn't eaten much since breakfast. A doughnut and a cup of coffee and that candy bar from the snack machine could fill her up for only so long.

After putting her phone away again, she pulled out of the Dunmores' yard. She was headed toward the office, with plans to stop at a fast-food place and grab a hamburger on the way. She needed to make notes on her interview with the Dunmores while it was still fresh on her mind.

Still blushing, she headed back to town.

"You know she won't disappear if you don't check on her every hour, sweetheart?"

Rachel Carrington glanced up at her husband and smiled. She felt so much love for both him and their beautiful three-month-old daughter. Their miracle baby. She and Brett had been trying to have a baby for five solid years. After two miscarriages, she was finally told by her doctor she would never be able to carry a child to term. That had been devastating and had crushed their world.

She had gotten a second opinion and a third, all with

the same prognosis. Then one day she'd received a call from the last doctor they'd seen, Dr. Kelly Langley. She had suggested the surrogate route. Neither Rachel nor Brett was receptive to the idea until Dr. Langley had put them in touch with couples who'd tried it with success. The more she and Brett talked about it, the more the possibility grew on them.

Less than four months later the embryo transfer procedure was a success, and nine months after that they had little Chasta to show for it. And she was definitely theirs, with Brett's lips, forehead, nose and dimples. From Rachel, Chasta inherited her blue eyes and golden-blond hair.

Rachel couldn't help but think about the woman who'd been the surrogate. A young woman who'd preferred not to meet them in person, a position they'd fully agreed with. They had, however, reviewed a detailed portfolio about her. It was important to know about the woman's health and lifestyle. Although they hadn't been present when Chasta was born, she was given to them within forty-eight hours of her birth.

"I can't help it," she said, wrapping her arms around Brett's neck when he pulled her into his arms. "Every time I look at her I think of what we almost didn't have. Now I can't imagine our life without her."

Brett leaned closer and kissed his wife's forehead. "I know, baby. Just think, we'll have the rest of our lives to watch over our daughter and shelter her with our love."

"Yes," Rachel said, smiling brightly. "We'll have the rest of our lives."

CHAPTER THIRTEEN

THE FIRST THING Detective Joy Ingram noticed when she and Sanchez walked into Beautiful Creations was how the reception area was staged to look like the living room of someone's home instead of a professional office. The surrogate agency was complete with what appeared to be a real fireplace and a spiral staircase.

Joy was convinced those were live flowers around the room and not fake ones. If the intention was to make whoever walked through the doors feel comfortable and at home, then the decor worked. "I hope those stairs really do lead to a bedroom upstairs. The first thing I want to do is take a nap," Sanchez mumbled beneath his breath.

She smiled. "The baby keeping you up at night?"

"Afraid so. But then, I wouldn't have it any other way. I'm getting the hang of this fatherhood thing, and I kind of like it."

The professionally dressed sixty-something woman, who didn't appear to have a hair out of place, was sitting at the desk. She smiled brightly at them. "Good morning. May I help you?"

Both Joy and Sanchez flashed their badges. "We hope that you can," Joy said, returning the woman's smile. "I'm Detective Joy Ingram and this is my partner, Detective Juan Sanchez, Charlottesville Police."

The woman's smile immediately turned into a frown. "Whatever my ex-husband is claiming, I didn't do it."

Joy suppressed a smile. "That's not why we're here, Ms...."

"Stone. I'm Cathy Stone. If you're not here because of Nathan's lies, then why are you here?"

"We're investigating a murder."

"A murder?" the woman asked, touching the scarf she wore around her neck as if in shock.

"Yes, a murder," Sanchez answered, glancing around.

"Then you must be at the wrong place. We create lives here, not take them. And just who was murdered?"

"A young woman," Joy said, pulling Jane Doe's picture out the folder she held. "Have you ever seen her before?"

Cathy Stone looked at the sketch, and she held it a long time as if studying the features. She then glanced back up at Sanchez and Ingram. "No, I don't recognize her. How did she die?"

"She froze to death, and according to the autopsy report, she had Epinnine in her system. The medical examination report indicates she had her pregnancy as a surrogate and was preparing for another the same way."

Cathy Stone nodded as if not surprised. "A number of our ladies are regulars who find the ability to assist couples in becoming parents rewarding."

Joy didn't say anything about that. Most women she knew who'd given birth loved the end result but hadn't necessarily liked being pregnant. As one of her friends from college phrased it, what woman wanted to walk around for nine months looking like the Goodyear Blimp? The first person who came to Joy's mind was her mother, who'd done it four times.

"She froze to death with Epinnine in her system, and for that reason you think she was murdered?"

"There's more to it than that, Ms. Stone," Sanchez said.

"I should hope so. She's a very pretty girl. Reminds me of that woman on television—you know who I'm talking about."

Joy shook her head. "No, ma'am, I don't."

"Who do you think she looks like?" Sanchez asked, taking the picture from Cathy to glance at it.

"She's a dead ringer for Sunnie Clay. The woman who stars on *Real Housemates of San Diego*. She could be her twin."

Sanchez nodded. "But you don't recognize her as one of the women you considered as a *regular* here?

Cathy Stone shook her head. "No, and I usually know most of the women because they are regulars. However, my boss would know for certain."

"Then we need to speak with your boss," Sanchez said, sliding the photo back in the folder.

Cathy shook her head. "Sorry, but Mr. Effington is out of town. He left this morning for the Bahamas to attend a conference."

"The Bahamas?" Sanchez asked. "Nice place for a conference."

"I'm sure it is," Cathy said. "I've never been there, thanks to Nathan. You wouldn't believe all the things he's been doing since our divorce."

And we don't have time to listen. Joy handed Ms. Stone her card. "When your boss returns, please have him call me."

Cathy Stone fingered the card while she stared at it. Then she glanced back up at Joy. "Yes, I most certainly will."

When Joy and Sanchez walked out the door, she glanced over at him. "I take it you're a fan of the *Real Housemates*."

Sanchez chuckled. "Used to be before the baby days. Cathy Stone is right. Our Jane Doe is a dead ringer for Sunnie Clay. I didn't notice it before."

Joy nodded. "I'm sure you've heard the saying that everybody's got a twin somewhere."

"Yeah, whatever. But not my Carlos. I'm convinced there's not another baby like him anywhere," Sanchez said proudly.

"Whatever," Joy said, grinning, while pulling her sunglasses from her shirt pocket.

LATER THAT NIGHT Joy was in bed when her phone rang. It was Stonewall. She tried to downplay the surge of excitement that raced through her. As usual it had been late when she'd arrived home with a chicken salad sandwich and soda from the deli on the corner. Now hearing Stonewall's voice gave her renewed energy.

"Stonewall."

"Joy. How are you?"

"I'm okay. What about you?" She leaned back against the headboard, thinking that no man should sound this good so late at night. There was a sexy coarseness in his voice that had her pulse thumping.

"I'm okay," he said. "Got some good news to share."

"Umm, what news is that?"

"Quasar and Randi set a date. They're getting married in September."

She straightened up in bed. "They are? That's wonderful. When I talked to Randi at the wedding last weekend, she thought they would wait and have a June wedding."

"Like Striker and Margo, they decided not to wait. I guess being in love does that to some people," he said.

"Evidently," Joy said, knowing she couldn't claim it did that to her. Neither she nor Omar had been in a hurry to marry. "I'm happy for them."

"So am I. I have what I hope is more good news."

"What?"

"It appears the authorities got the right guy. Everything that was found in his home checked out. And he confessed."

Joy shook her head. "What was his beef with Dak Navarro to the point that he wanted him dead?"

"The dude lost his job during one of Dak's company mergers. The man found himself down on his luck and blamed Dak for it."

"That's unfortunate, but you can't retaliate by trying to kill someone. You apply for another job or get retrained."

A few moments passed and then she asked, "Does that mean you'll be returning to Charlottesville sooner than planned?"

"If things work out, I'll be back this weekend."

It seemed the moment he said it, the area between her legs began throbbing mercilessly. "This weekend?"

"Yes, this weekend. Saturday morning, in fact."

The low rumble in his voice set her stomach to turning a series of slow rolls. "Saturday morning?"

"Yes, Saturday morning. So, tell me, Joy. Will you be in need of a diversion then?"

Breath lodged in Joy's throat with his question. As if her body wanted to respond for her, it throbbed even more, making her wet and ready when he wasn't there to do anything about it. "A diversion?"

"Yes. You wanted to call the shots about our non-relationship, and I accepted your terms. I don't want to keep you from your work or anything you might have planned this weekend. Besides, I have no idea if you need the edge taken off."

She definitely needed to take the edge off, and it had nothing to do with how things were going at work this week. However, she was certain by Saturday she might be ready to pull her hair out.

"Depends on what you have in mind."

He chuckled, and the sound sent a heated ache to the tips of her nipples. She'd worn a gown to bed, but now it felt confining. She felt the need to get naked. "What if I want it to be a surprise, Joy?"

She squeezed her legs together. *Lordy.* "A surprise?"

"Yes."

"Um, you know how I feel about surprises."

"Yes, but you liked my last one, didn't you?"

Joy thought about it in its entirety. From the moment she'd arrived at the airport to board that private jet until the moment he'd walked out her door the next day. He had certainly rocked her world. "Yes, I did," she said honestly, knowing she couldn't be anything other than honest. He had made love to her in a way that still had her panting whenever she thought about it. Thinking of him hadn't interfered with her work, but she'd found herself sighing a lot during the day.

"Stonewall?"

"Yes?"

"Yesterday your text said…"

"That I was missing you like crazy. And I meant it."

She shouldn't let his words stir her in such a way

that even the air in the room seemed to shimmer with need. "Dak Navarro doesn't have enough for you to do to stay busy?" she asked him.

"I have plenty enough. But when it comes to you, I can't help it, baby," he said in a low tone. She was holding her cell phone close to her ear, and if she hadn't known better she would have sworn he was right there in bed with her, holding her close, with his mouth whispering those words against her ear. She squeezed her legs tighter when the throbbing between them intensified.

"I do miss you, Joy."

She swallowed tightly. She felt the same way about him. Why was she not willing to say it? To tell him the feelings were mutual? "It's nice being missed."

"And you know what else?"

She licked her lips, wondering why she suddenly felt so hot. Putting the cell phone on speaker, she placed it on the nightstand to pull her nightgown over her head. She tossed it across the room to land on the chair.

"No, what else?"

"I've replayed moments in my mind of making love to you."

Lordy. "Again, it sounds like you have too much time on your hands."

He chuckled, and the sound sent shivers up and down her body, made her shift again in the bed. Her naked body felt sensitive against the bedcovers. "I love to hear you laugh," she said, truly meaning it.

"You do? Then tell me something amusing so I can laugh again."

"That's easier said than done."

"Hey, did you put me on a speakerphone?"

"Yes. How can you tell?"

He laughed. "I just can. Why did you do that? Put me on speaker?"

She saw no reason not to tell him the truth. "I needed to put the phone down while I took off my gown. I was getting hot."

He was quiet for a moment and then said, "Are you telling me that you are talking to me naked?"

It was her time to chuckle. "Afraid so."

"Now is not the time to be afraid, Joy. Save your courage for Saturday. And by the way, you do have a pair of handcuffs, don't you?"

STONEWALL HEARD JOY'S sharp intake of breath and smiled. Her breathing was becoming labored. He heard that, as well. Like her, he was in bed, but he wasn't naked since he was wearing pajama bottoms. He felt hot as well, but he felt horny even more. Hell, Saturday couldn't get here fast enough to suit him, and he had no problem letting her know that.

"Just so you know, Joy, I can't wait to make love to you, get inside you again. Your taste is still on my tongue. Your scent in my nostrils. I want you again so much I ache."

She didn't say anything at first, but then she asked in a low tone, with surprise in her voice, "Seriously?"

"Yes, seriously. I want you in a bad way."

He heard her swallow. "Do you?"

"Yes. And I want you to want me just as much, Joy."

And he meant that. He wanted to be more than a diversion for her. He wanted to be the man she was glad to see again no matter what. The man she needed.

And right then and there, he decided he was going to make that his next assignment.

CHAPTER FOURTEEN

"HEY, WHAT DID I tell you?" Sanchez said, grinning as he rounded Joy's desk the next day. "You can make it up to me by buying me breakfast tomorrow. I don't know what type of reward Ms. Stone would want, though."

Joy closed the folder on her desk, tired of reviewing the gory details anyway. A man who'd been cheating on his wife was dead. It seemed the wife found out and took matters into her own hands, literally. Pretending she was about to give him a treat, she had handcuffed him to the bed, then blindfolded and gagged him. After giving him his last blow job she removed the blindfold and proceeded to cut off his balls while he watched in hysteria, unable to do a damn thing about it. If that wasn't bad enough, she'd then driven a butcher knife in his heart, killing the man. The woman was now behind bars, and of all things claiming self-defense.

Joy glanced up. "What are you talking about, Sanchez?"

He was still grinning when he sat down in a chair next to her desk. "I'm talking about the picture of our Jane Doe that appeared in this morning's paper, where we asked anyone to come forward who might recognize her. Well, evidently quite a few people did. They, like me and Ms. Stone, thought she bore an uncanny resemblance to Sunnie Clay. It was picked up by the AP, and someone got word to the *Housemates* diva about it. Seems the two are related."

Joy sat up straight in her chair. "Are you saying Jane Doe is really this actress's twin?"

"No, but she's her younger sister by three years. Chief Harkins has received word from the San Diego Police Department that Sunnie Clay is arriving in town tomorrow to identify the body. If she really is Sunnie Clay's sister, then Sunnie intends to claim the body and take it back with her to San Diego."

Joy picked up a paper clip off her desk and toyed with it for a few moments before tossing it back down. "So our Jane Doe now has a name."

Sanchez nodded. "Yes. If she is Sunnie Clay's sister, her name is Samantha, but she went by Mandy."

Joy nodded. She could visualize Jane Doe being a Mandy. She glanced over at Sanchez. "What kind of show is *Real Housemates of San Diego*?"

He chuckled. Evidently she was an oddity by not being a fan. "Similar to the housewives shows, but I doubt you've seen any of those, either. What you have are women involved with their long-time lovers. They've been living with the men for quite some time but haven't managed to get a ring on their fingers to change status from housemate to housewife. It's reality TV, and the women get all catty and shit when one of them gets close to becoming engaged and the others are left as wannabes—still vying to become a wife."

"And people tune in to watch it each week?"

"Yes, it has high ratings. Sunnie is the most popular of the four women on the show because she can be a real bitch. A first-class manipulator and schemer."

"And that makes it interesting?"

"Yes. When Sunnie thought Mia was going to get a ring before her, she sabotaged Mia and Derek's engagement. Derek plays pro football and Andre, Sunnie's man, is a real estate tycoon. This season Sunnie is trying to make waves with Derek behind Mia's back."

Joy held up her hand. "Enough. I get the picture."

"I suggest you check out at least one episode so you can be prepared when we meet with Sunnie Clay tomorrow. I heard she's worse in person than she is on television."

Joy shook her head. That was all she needed. Some diva coming to town thinking she could throw her weight around.

DR. KELLY LANGLEY angrily slapped the newspaper down on her desk. How could this happen? Anderson had all but assured her the matter with Mandy Clay was taken care of and wouldn't come back to haunt them. Now she was staring at Mandy's picture next to the article that not only identified Mandy, but also stated she was the sister of reality TV star Sunnie Clay. Had Anderson known that when his men had snatched Mandy Clay off the streets of New Orleans? And where was Anderson? She'd been trying to reach him all day.

Kelly got up from her desk and began pacing. This was not good. She could lose everything. Her medical practice especially. None of her partners knew what she'd been involved in. And all because Anderson had managed to manipulate her at a weak moment.

Her cell phone ringing interrupted her thoughts and she quickly picked it up, releasing a deep sigh upon seeing Anderson had finally called her back. "Where are you, Anderson? I've been trying to reach you all morning."

"I had to take a business trip to Seattle. I've been in meetings all day and saw you've been blowing up my phone. What's going on?"

If he was in Seattle, chances were he hadn't a clue as to what was going on. "Mandy Clay's picture is in the local newspapers. She's been identified, and of all things, she's the sister of some hotshot reality TV star who is quoted as saying she won't rest until the authorities find out what happened to her sister. What if their investigation leads to us?"

"It won't."

But she could hear the agitation in his voice. "That's the same thing you said about the authorities identifying Mandy. You said it wouldn't happen. I've worked too hard to become a partner at this medical practice. I can't let my association with you ruin everything."

"Calm down, Kelly. Don't you know I won't let that happen? I care about you too much. Damn, I'm going to fix this."

"You'd better." And she hung up on him.

ANDERSON FROWNED AS he clicked off his phone. The bitch had given him a damn order and then hung up on him. Who the hell did she think she was? He rubbed his hand over his face, definitely not liking the news she'd delivered about Mandy Clay. Not only had Mandy been identified, but she was the sister of some damn actress?

Damn! If that was true, it meant Mandy's death would get national attention, and that was the last thing he wanted to happen. Mandy had escaped on his watch, and the people in charge would blame him. Norm Austen was the new man in charge of the territory and he didn't like mistakes. He hadn't liked it when Mandy had managed to escape, and he wouldn't like hearing the body had been identified. Damn. Anderson had to handle matters and quickly.

Ever since Mandy Clay was found dead, Kelly had begun growing a conscience, and now he knew she had become a liability they didn't need. He could tell from the sound of her voice that she was freaking out. He'd picked up on it the night they'd been together before he'd left town. He figured just a reminder of how deep she was in the operation would curtail any ideas about getting out. But now it seemed Kelly was going to have to be dealt with. He couldn't risk her running to the authorities just to redeem her soul or any of that bullshit.

At that moment, he knew what he had to do, although he regretted it. Damn, he enjoyed her in his bed, but all good things had to come to an end.

CHAPTER FIFTEEN

WHEN JOY ARRIVED to work the next morning she was summoned to Chief Harkins's office. She knocked on the door. "Come in."

She entered to see Chief Harkins pop several aspirins in his mouth and then wash them down with water from a bottle. Then, as if he abhorred the bitter taste the pills left behind, he took several sips of coffee before glancing over at her. "Come on in, Detective Ingram. Please take a seat."

She nodded and took the chair in front of his desk. Unlike her cubicle, his office was large with a nice view of the Charlottesville skyline. "You have a headache already this morning, sir?" she inquired.

He chuckled. "I give you till noon and you will, too. Sunnie Clay was here when I arrived this morning, with her film crew and all."

Not believing what she'd heard, Joy leaned out of her seat. "Excuse me?"

"You heard me right, Detective. The woman is a real piece of work, so be prepared. She thought she could capitalize on what happened with her sister and use it in a segment of that television show she stars in. When I shut the attempt down, the lady—and I say that rather loosely—got downright nasty. So, yeah, I got a damn headache."

Joy frowned. "I figured most divas thought they had the right to sleep until noon. Where is she now?"

"Apparently she wanted to get an early start turning this place into a circus, but I wasn't having any of her BS. Needless to say I'm not one of her favorite people. I hope you're not her fan."

Joy shook her head. "No. Never watched the show until last night." She'd wanted to see what she would be up against today. Chief Harkins was right when he said the woman was a piece of work. Joy often wondered how much reality television was real. She figured no matter what you might want to think, people acted different when they knew the cameras were rolling. From all accounts, it seemed that Sunnie Clay was acting as her true self.

"And as far as where she is now," Chief Harkins broke into Joy's thoughts to say, "she left to compose herself after positively identifying Jane Doe as her sister. I honestly think up until then, she believed it was all a mistake. When she saw that it wasn't, she showed the first signs of any real compassion. She was shaken up pretty badly, and her producer rushed her out of here."

"When will she return, sir?" Joy asked.

"In about an hour, so get ready. I don't know how she will behave once she gets herself together. Now that she knows Jane Doe is really her sister, she might be worse than ever, or she may show us her human side."

He took another sip of coffee before adding, "I suggest you and Sanchez use one of the conference rooms for your interview. I refuse to let her sit in your cubicle and put on a show for everyone who wants to listen and watch."

"Yes, sir. I understand," Joy said, standing.

"And no cameras are allowed during your interview with her."

"Yes, sir." Joy hadn't intended for that to happen anyway and was glad she and her boss were in agreement.

"Good luck with her, Detective Ingram. You might very well need it."

"IF I DIDN'T know better, Stonewall, I'd think you were anxious to leave."

Stonewall glanced up and chuckled when he saw Dak standing in the doorway. Although Stonewall wouldn't be leaving until early Saturday morning, he'd started packing already. "I do miss home," he said.

Dak came into the room and dropped down in the wingback chair. "Tell that BS to someone else. There's more to it than that, and you know it. You miss your detective."

Stonewall shook his head. "Now you sound like Striker and Quasar. They like referring to Joy as 'my' detective."

Dak rubbed his chin as he continued to stare at him. "You ever think there's a reason why?"

"Nope."

"Maybe you should."

Stonewall stopped packing and glanced over at the man he'd been assigned to protect. Somewhere along the way a friendship between them had developed, one that had gotten so secure it surprised the both of them. Dak Navarro was not a man who solicited friendship.

In fact, he had a knack for pushing people away, maintaining a wall so high very few men could effectively act as bodyguard to him.

But Stonewall wasn't having any of that. He of all people respected a man's right to privacy; however, he refused to be ignored like he was some piece of furniture. Little by little he'd brought Dak out of his cold and hard shell. Showed him he was a person who could be trusted. But then Dak had to show Stonewall he was someone who could be trusted, as well. Stonewall was reserved, but not to the degree Dak had been.

"Sounds like you think you have all the answers," Stonewall said.

"No, I don't. But you do."

Stonewall didn't say anything because he knew what Dak was getting at. Late one night in Dubai, over a bottle of bourbon that had given Stonewall one hell of a hangover, Dak had shared a lot about himself, and Stonewall had done the same. During their lifetimes, they had both lost people who'd meant a lot to them, people they'd assumed would be around forever. They weren't. To them, forever didn't mean a damn thing because it didn't exist. Not for them anyway. They lived for today and not for tomorrow.

"There's something about your detective that…"

"Sparks my fire and nothing else, Dak," Stonewall interjected.

"Bullshit."

So what if Stonewall knew what he'd said had been a lie? Truth of the matter was that when it came to Joy, there *was* something else. He knew that even if he wouldn't own up to it. In all honesty, Joy more than sparked his fire. She was keeping it ablaze even while she was a thousand miles away.

Stonewall frowned at Dak. "Don't you have something to do? Deals yet to be made. Millions yet to be banked."

Dak slowly stood. "Yes, you're right. That's the story of my life."

Was that regret Stonewall heard? If so, he understood. Even with Dak's revolving door of women, he still lived a lonely life. At least Stonewall had a group of friends in Charlottesville whom he was close to, like Striker, Quasar and Roland. Then, of course, there was Sheppard Granger as well as other members of the Granger family. And now that Striker had married and Quasar was headed there himself, Stonewall was looking forward to getting to know their wives, the women they'd chosen to spend their lives with. Forever.

He shook his head again. There was that word again. He didn't like the word *forever* any more than Joy liked the word *relationship*.

"I came here to tell you something that might make your day," Dak said.

"And what is that?"

"Something has come up, and I need to fly to California. I've instructed the pilot to make a pit stop in Charlottesville to drop you off. That means you'll go home a day or so early."

Stonewall folded his arms over his chest and eyed Dak. "You trying to get rid of me, Navarro?"

Dak chuckled. "No, but you did the job you came here to do, Stonewall. I thank you for keeping me alive. Now that the threat's over, hopefully there won't ever be another. And just so you know, I intend to keep you on my payroll for another thirty days. That means you have a month to do nothing."

A smile curved Dak's lips when he added, "Unless, however, I need you to fly back here so I can whip your ass in cards again."

"Not hardly. Only reason you won that one time was because my mind was elsewhere that night."

"Bull. Just enjoy your time off. You deserve it."

Stonewall smiled, thinking of all he could do in thirty days, and it involved one particular woman. "Thanks. I plan to use the time wisely." He smiled as an idea formed in his mind. Another surprise for Detective Joy Ingram.

JOY AND SANCHEZ entered the conference room where Sunnie Clay was already seated. "She changed her outfit," Sanchez whispered. "Damn, she looks good in anything she wears."

Joy had no idea what Ms. Clay had worn that morning, but she looked like a serene goddess now. Joy didn't think one strand of hair was out of place. The woman's makeup was flawless and her clothing more demure than the outfits she'd worn on television last night. She was dressed in a cream-colored business suit with a strand of pearls around her neck as well as pearl earrings in her ears. It was as if she'd just attended the funeral of the victim rather than identifying a body. And she was using a pretty monogrammed handkerchief to dab tears from her eyes.

"Ms. Clay?"

Sunnie Clay looked up quickly, and a part of Joy

softened. Actress or no actress, Joy knew those tears were real. "Yes?"

"I'm Detective Joy Ingram and this is my partner, Detective Juan Sanchez. We appreciate you coming all the way from California." Joy and Sanchez joined the grieving woman at the table. Sanchez automatically took out his notepad. "We're sorry for your loss," Joy added.

"I'm taking your regret with a grain of salt until you tell me what happened to my sister."

Ouch. So the grieving sister wanted to get bitchy. Joy would try to understand up to a point. "I know Chief Harkins gave you the specifics earlier about how we found your sister. I don't have any more to add to that. Recently we got a lead and—"

"That nonsense about Mandy being someone's surrogate. That is simply not true," Sunnie Clay said defiantly.

"And what makes you so sure of that?" Joy asked.

Sunnie Clay's blue eyes narrowed on hers. "Because Mandy didn't want anything to do with kids."

Joy nodded. "People can change their minds about many things, Ms. Clay."

"Not Mandy. Did you hear what I just said? Mandy *never* wanted a thing to do with kids."

Joy met the woman's angry gaze. "I heard you the first time, Ms. Clay." If Sunnie Clay intended to go on a warpath, she would do it alone. "When was the last time you saw your sister?"

Sunnie Clay dabbed at her eyes again. "Over a year and a half ago. Mandy and I didn't see eye to eye on a lot of things. She wasn't supportive of my career and I wasn't supportive of hers."

"And what was Mandy's career?"

The woman chuckled derisively while shaking her head. "That's just it. Mandy didn't have a real career. I paid for her last two years of college so she wouldn't be strapped with any student loans. She got a bachelor's degree in business. Used it for six months and quit."

"Where did she work?"

"For a life insurance company in the claims department. She said it was pretty damn depressing because any file that came across her desk meant the person had died."

Pretty similar to her job, Joy thought. "What's the name of the company and where is it located?"

"Burnstone Life Insurance Company, and it's located in Austin, Texas."

"Austin? Is that where she lived?"

"After college, yes. Then she moved on, determined to become a tracker, moving from state to state, doing odds-and-ends jobs to keep a roof over her head and food in her stomach."

"A tracker?"

"Yes. That's what she called herself."

"And who or what was she tracking?"

There was a pause, and Sunnie Clay's lips tightened when she said, "Our mother. She was intent on finding our mother."

Joy lifted a brow. "Your mother?"

"Yes, our mother."

Joy waited, hoping she wouldn't have to ask the woman to expound and was glad when Sunnie began talking again. "We were raised in a foster home, detective. The only good thing is that we were kept together for a while so I was able to watch out for Mandy. When I turned sixteen, we were separated and didn't get back together until years later. I'm three years older and was about to finish college when we met up again."

"How many years later was that?" Joy asked.

"Close to five years. I ran into her in New York. I was there with friends during New Year's and she was a waitress at one of the restaurants we dined in one night."

Sunnie paused, dabbed at her eyes again. "I was so glad to see her, and I believe she was glad to see me, although I could tell she had changed a lot. I was in my last year of college and sharing an apartment with three other women and couldn't offer her anything, but I promised that as soon as I finished college and got a job, I would send for her. And I did."

"So she moved with you to San Diego?"

"No. I landed my first job in Miami, working for a major hotel chain in their accounting department. I convinced Mandy to come live with me while she finished up her last two years in college. She did and then took off for Austin."

"Where did she live while in Austin?"

"At some boardinghouse. When she quit that insurance gig and got behind on her rent, I bailed her out a few times. But when she said she didn't intend to get another job but wanted to try tracking down our mother— the woman who never wanted us anyway—I refused to give her any more handouts."

"Earlier you said that she had changed. In what way?"

Sunnie drew in a deep breath. "My sweet baby sister. I tried to get her to talk about what happened during those five years we'd been separated, but she would clam up and refused to do so. All I know is that she said she would never marry and didn't ever want any kids. She was pretty adamant about it and never wavered, which is why I don't believe she'd been pregnant, and certainly not that she was about to do it again."

"But she didn't have the baby for herself, Ms. Clay. She had it for a couple who might not have been able to conceive. Maybe she thought she was doing a good deed. And it was a way to earn money. Surrogates can demand up to six figures from couples. Some might even negotiate for bonuses."

Sunnie shook her head, as if not convinced. "Although she probably could have used the money, I still can't buy what you're saying. I knew my sister. She said childbearing would have left marks on her body. She was rather vain."

After watching Sunnie Clay's show last night, Joy wondered if it ran in the family. "When you saw her last year, did she seem bothered by anything?"

"No. In fact, she seemed happy. Hinted about meeting this guy."

"A guy? Do you have a name?"

"No. She wouldn't give me one, said they were keeping their relationship a secret for a while. But she assured me that he wasn't married or anything like that."

"Then why keep it a secret?"

"Claimed there was a no-fraternizing policy where they worked."

"And where was she working at the time?"

"As a temp in accounting at some pharmaceutical company."

"Where?"

"In New Orleans."

"Is that the last known address you have for her?"

"Yes. I figured I would hear from her again when she was down on her luck and needed money. And if you're about to ask me what she was doing in this area, I have no idea. I'm wondering that myself."

"The last time you heard from her was a year and a half ago, right?"

"Yes."

"The two of you didn't stay in touch?"

"No. She needed her space to deal with some things, and I felt I owed her that much. I would call but she never returned my calls." Sunnie Clay dabbed at her eyes again. "I never thought her life was in danger."

"What is the last known phone number you have for her?"

Sunnie opened her designer purse that Joy figured cost more than Joy's salary for an entire month. When the woman pulled out her phone, Joy and Sanchez exchanged glances. There was no doubt in their minds the phone case was pure gold.

Moments later, Sunnie recited a phone number to them. "Not sure why I haven't deleted it out of my contacts. It hasn't been in use for over a year."

"Still, we'll hopefully be able to get a record of calls."

"Don't be surprised if the phone was a burner."

Joy released a deep breath. That would certainly make things difficult but not impossible. "Let's hope that's not the case."

"I never thought she would end up like this." Fresh tears filled Sunnie's eyes.

Their interview might have started off rocky, but it

had gone smoother than Joy had anticipated. "Detective Sanchez and I appreciate you answering our questions. We know this is a difficult time for you and intend to do all we can to bring the person or persons responsible for your sister's death to justice."

Joy stood, reached in the back pocket of her slacks and pulled a business card from her wallet. "Here's my card, Ms. Clay. Please call me if you remember anything else."

Sunnie took the card. "Thank you, and I hope you do find the person responsible. Mandy didn't deserve to die that way."

Sanchez stood as well when Joy said, "No, she didn't, and we intend to do our best. One last question—did she ever track down your mother?"

Sunnie Clay shook her head. "I would have to say no. I want to believe if she had, she would have told me."

CHAPTER SIXTEEN

JOY SCANNED HER investigative notes. Figuring out what happened with Mandy Clay was a puzzle she intended to solve. Even with all the interviews they'd conducted at the surrogate agencies, they hadn't picked up any new leads. No one could identify Clay as being one of their surrogates. But Mandy Clay had to have worked with someone. Epinnine was an expensive prescription drug. She had to have been under the care of an ob-gyn, reproductive endocrinologist or some other type of fertility specialist.

Surrogacy was something Joy had never dwelled on…until now. Since she'd been assigned the Mandy Clay case, she'd read anything on the subject that she could get her hands on. She could only admire the couples who'd not given up on their dreams to have a child or the surrogates who helped make the couples' dreams come true.

And Mandy had been one of those surrogates. But why didn't any of the agencies know her? That unanswered question only led to another… Were there illegitimate agencies out there? It wouldn't surprise Joy if there were. During her years as a detective, she'd felt like she'd seen it all.

Joy then looked over the list containing the addresses

of all homes or buildings in Sofia Valley. It also listed the owners. She noted that some of the larger homes were owned by corporations instead of individuals. That wasn't unusual as a number of corporations owned places to serve as periodic retreats for their employees. It appeared all those homes had been vacant the night Mandy died.

She noted several homes hadn't been visited by Sessions because they were located too high in the mountains. The logic was that if Mandy Clay had begun her journey that far up the mountain, she would have died before making it off the mountain because the temperature at such a high altitude was even colder. But still, Joy refused to not consider every possibility, no matter how improbable.

She heard her phone's text alert. Her breath wobbled in her throat as she wondered if Stonewall had sent her a message. He'd been doing that a lot, and she always looked forward to them. Usually the message was a countdown of the days before he returned, and other times he would text her something outlandishly sexy that would make her blush.

Pulling her cell phone from her desk, she saw the text had been from him.

Miss u. Want u.

Smiling, she texted back, How bad?
His reply was, Throbbing bad.
Lust stirred in her abdomen when she texted. For me it's aching bad.
He texted back, Tell me what U need.

She quickly responded. A diversion.

She signed off with a smiley face. Joy liked this texting game they were playing. It gave her something to look forward to and it broke the monotony of her day.

She glanced up when she heard the sound of deep male laughter. Joy would recognize it anywhere because it still grated on her nerves. It belonged to Darrin Chadwick, her former partner from hell. He had taken a job promotion to lieutenant in Ohio a few months ago, so why was he here? More than anything, she hoped he wasn't returning to Charlottesville.

He laughed again and the sound was even closer. He was the last person she wanted to see because she wasn't in the mood to pretend to be friendly. But if she left her cubicle now, there was no way he wouldn't see her.

Too late. She glanced up and there he was, standing within a few feet of her cubicle. She thought now what she thought the first time she'd seen him—he was a handsome man. But once he opened his mouth, any thoughts of his good looks would dissolve. He was a male chauvinist bastard who'd given her hell as a partner and belittled her every chance he got. He thought a woman's place was anywhere other than law enforcement.

"Hello, Joy."

"Darrin," she acknowledged. "What brings you back to Charlottesville?"

"I'm in a wedding this weekend and thought I'd stop by and see everyone."

Don't do me any favors. "That was kind of you. How are things going in Cleveland?"

"Fine. I plan to make chief of police one day."

He definitely doesn't lack confidence. "That's a great goal."

"You know what I keep remembering whenever I think of you?"

She wondered if it was all the times he would tell her what she couldn't do and what he could do better as a detective. "No, what?"

"How you looked in that green dress that night we worked undercover at that charity party. You looked sensational."

She would accept a compliment from anyone. *Even him.* "Thanks."

"How about if we get together while I'm in town? I'll be here until Monday morning."

You've got to be kidding. "Thanks, but I'm pretty busy this weekend."

"Oh."

Is that disappointment? Do I care?

"What about if—" he started.

The phone on her desk rang and she couldn't help but smile. *Great timing!* "Excuse me, Darrin. I need to get this," she said, picking up the phone. "Hello?"

"Detective Ingram, this is Margaret."

Margaret was Chief Harkins's personal assistant. "Yes, Margaret?"

"Chief Harkins wants to see you in his office."

"Okay, I'm on my way."

Joy hung up, stood and grabbed a notepad and pen off her desk. "Sorry, Darrin, I have to go."

"I heard. That was Margaret, which means the chief wants to see you. I hope you aren't in trouble about anything."

She frowned at him. "Why would I be in trouble?"

"You never know. I heard you're working that case involving that reality TV star's sister. I hope Harkins's not planning to replace you with someone who will get less emotional."

That was his thing about women detectives. He swore they got too emotional to do their jobs effectively. She moved around her desk, refusing to engage in conversation with him any longer. "Goodbye, Darrin. It was good seeing you again."

And then she left, leaving him standing there.

"THOSE FILES NEED to be destroyed, Kelly," Anderson said through the phone. "I suggest you shred them, but not at your office. Use one of those off-site facilities. I've come up with a plan to protect you if the shit hits the fan."

Kelly drew in a deep breath. She knew why he would want those documents destroyed. Could she have been wrong about him? Could he care for her more than she realized?

"There's one of those shredding facilities not far from here," she said.

"Good. Make sure you do it today. Then return to your office and wait on my call for instructions on the next step."

Kelly lifted a brow. "The next step?"

"Yes. It's all part of my plan to protect you, sweetheart. I care deeply for you, and it was never my intent to get you this involved in the organization, Kelly."

She tried not to feel all gushy inside. "I appreciate that, Anderson."

"Now let me get back to my meeting. And remember to go back to your office. I should be calling around eight."

"That late?"

"Yes. Remember that I'm in a different time zone here. Surely you can find something in your office to do while waiting on my call."

Yes, she could find something to do, but it was a Friday night, and she had certain television shows she liked being home to watch. But she knew what she had to do was important. Otherwise, she would be risking jail time. "Okay, I'll wait on your call."

CHAPTER SEVENTEEN

JOY WALKED DOWN the long hall to Chief Harkins's office. She wanted to laugh at the thought of how she'd left Darrin standing there slack-jawed. Did he really think she would go out with him? He had stood there as if he'd expected something. He was still so full of himself, she wouldn't have been surprised if he'd assumed she would give him a goodbye kiss or something. The thought nearly made her skin crawl.

But then there was another man who'd definitely gotten a goodbye kiss from her the last time she'd seen him. And she'd planted it on him pretty damn good.

One date and the man had already gotten her to the point where she was always eager to get his calls at night or his text messages during the day. But although she thought of him often, even while at work, she still managed to keep her mind focused on her cases.

She entered the small lobby where Margaret sat. It probably would have looked drab and boring with the white walls and all the metal filing cabinets if Margaret hadn't spruced up the area with several potted plants, a huge throw rug and several art pieces on the wall.

"Hi, Margaret."

"Hello, Detective Ingram. He's on the phone, but

you can go right on in since he's expecting you. He'll be ending his call in a minute."

"Thanks." The chief's office door was slightly ajar so she didn't knock. Chief Harkins was leaning back in his chair while he talked on the phone. She couldn't help wondering why he wanted to see her. Was Sunnie Clay making trouble? She thought that she and Sanchez had assured the woman they would do all they could to find the person responsible for her sister's death, and she'd seemed satisfied with that. Had she decided to go back to her diva mode?

"Have a seat, Detective."

She glanced over at Chief Harkins. She hadn't been aware he'd ended the call. "Yes, sir," she said, taking the seat across from his desk.

"First of all, I want to commend you for the way you handled Sunnie Clay. She likes you."

Joy raised a brow. "What gave you that impression?"

"She told me. I talked to her this morning. She called—believe it or not—to apologize for her behavior yesterday…before seeing her sister's body. I think seeing her sister gave her a reality check. Reality TV is not actual reality. Probably seeing her dead sister was."

Joy had to agree with him. The woman seemed shaken during their interview with her yesterday. "If you need an update on how the investigation is going, I can go grab my file and—"

"No, that's not why I wanted to talk to you, Detective. The reason I called you into my office is to let you know that Mayor Greene has decided to bring back the lieutenant position here in the department."

Joy's brow lifted in surprise. She knew the story—

close to twenty-years ago, right before Chief Harkins was hired as chief of police, the last lieutenant had resigned under a scandal of corruption. The man had eventually gone to jail when it was proved that several cops and detectives, including the lieutenant, had not only framed one of their own when he'd been about to blow the whistle on them for a number of illegal activities, but had even gone so far as to kill the man's wife, brother and sister-in-law. That man was Stonewall's boss, Roland Summers. And Roland's half brother and his wife had been Margo's parents. After that scandal, the department had decided not to fill the vacancy of lieutenant.

"Detective Ingram?"

Joy blinked. "Yes? Sorry, sir. I was trying to wrap my mind around what you just said. I understand it's been years since there has been a lieutenant here."

"That's right, and I'm sure you've heard why."

"Yes, sir. It was sad."

"Yes, and a dark time for this department that men given the task to protect could murder so senselessly for greed. I was hired to clean house, so to speak. It's been a long time since this department has had a lieutenant. Over the years, I thought it best to keep the position vacant, but now I agree with the mayor that it should be filled. I never thought anyone would be a good fit for the position…until now. I have the approval of Mayor Greene, and I am ready to move forward."

She knew the usual protocol. Each detective would be called in individually to be told who had been selected for a promotion so there wouldn't be any surprises when the announcement was made. A sudden thought flared in her mind. Darrin said he was in town for a wedding. Was that true? Or had he been called back to town because Chief Harkins had chosen him for lieutenant? Although Darrin was already a lieutenant in Ohio, there was no doubt in her mind that the offer of a higher salary would lure him back. The thought had nerves dancing in her stomach, her skin crawling. Darrin was a male chauvinist pig.

She took a deep breath against the panic she felt. "I assume I'm here so you can tell me who that person is, right?"

He leaned forward in his chair. "Yes, that's right. You, Detective Ingram, are the person I've selected. Congratulations."

"BEAUTIFUL CREATIONS."

"Cathy, this is Oliver. How are things going at the office?"

"Things are wonderful, Mr. Effington. The Martins were at the hospital for the delivery of Baby Jessica yesterday and were able to take her home with them today. I spoke with both the Turners and the Bristols today, and their babies are doing fine."

"That's great!" Oliver Effington prided himself on the fact that his agency stayed in touch with the new parents for the first four months. Most of them returned as clients when decisions were made to increase the size of their families. "Well, I just wanted to check in before I—"

"Oh, and the police were here."

Oliver tightened his hand on his mobile phone. "What did you say?"

"I said the police was here. A Detective Ingram and Detective Sanchez, and they were asking questions."

Oliver swallowed deeply. "About what?"

"About that young woman who froze to death almost five months ago."

Oliver dropped down on his bed, placing his tennis racket aside. "What woman?"

"Her photo was in the paper a few days ago. It seems she was on Epinnine when she died, so they're checking out all the surrogacy agencies in the area. To see if anyone recognized her. They showed me her photo."

Nervous tension swept through Oliver. "And?"

"And of course she's not one of our regulars."

Hairs on the backs of his arms rose. "Why would they consider her a regular?"

"Because it's been determined she had one surrogate pregnancy and her body was being prepared for another. I told them I didn't recognize her but didn't know if you might. They left their business card for you. They want you to contact them when you return to town."

His heart began pounding. "That won't be a problem. Thanks for letting me know."

"You're welcome, Mr. Effington. And guess what else?"

There was more? "What else, Cathy?"

"The dead woman is Sunnie Clay's sister."

"Who?"

"Sunnie Clay. You know—the celebrity."

No, he didn't know. "The dead woman's sister is a celebrity?"

"Yes. A very popular one on *Real Housemates of San Diego*. I noticed the resemblance right away and told those two detectives that. I bet they only decided to dig further after I told them. You would think they would give me credit or something."

"Yes, you would think. Look, Cathy, I need to go. I will talk to you later."

"Alright, Mr. Effington."

As soon as Oliver ended the call, he immediately placed another and nervously tapped his fingers on the nightstand until the person he needed to talk to came on the phone.

"What the hell is going on, Anderson? Cops showed up at Beautiful Creations asking questions. Mandy Clay's sister is some celebrity."

"Don't lose your cool, Oliver. They won't find out anything. I have everything under control. There is only one person who can connect us to Mandy Clay, and I'm taking care of her."

"Who?"

"Dr. Langley."

"Damn, Anderson. I warned you about getting involved with that woman, and to keep things business only."

"Yes, but we needed more couples and she has a strong clientele. And like I said, I'm taking care of her."

"Make sure that you do. And what about the surrogate impostors?"

In cases where the couples wanted to meet the surrogate before making their final decision, they had women on their payroll who played the part. They would charm the couple into thinking they just wanted to help them fulfill their dreams of having a child. If the couple wanted to meet with the surrogate again during the pregnancy to make sure everything was going okay, they would have the pretend surrogate wear a fake pregnancy belly. So far no one had figured out they were being scammed.

"I'm not worried about them. They are being paid good money not to squeal."

"I hope so. The cops want to talk to me when I return to town."

"Let them. Just keep your cool and remember they have nothing on you."

Oliver hoped so, because panic was a new sensation for him. He'd always been a man in control.

CHAPTER EIGHTEEN

IT TOOK A lot of Joy's willpower to keep her jaw from dropping while at the same time feeling all bubbly inside. She stared at Chief Harkins, knowing her eyes were probably wide like saucers. "Me?"

"Yes, you, Detective Ingram. I don't know of any other detective who deserves it more. You've done a great job for this department. From your first day, you rolled up your sleeves and dug in. I selected you to work with me on the Erickson case for a reason. I knew you would be a good fit for the team. You have a sharp mind, and I knew you would be an asset."

Joy sat there, not knowing what to say. But she knew the first words she had to say. "Thank you for your confidence in me, sir."

"It was confidence that was earned. The day I interviewed you for detective I was very impressed with the credentials you were bringing to the table, and none of them had anything to do with Tate Ingram being your father. Although I'm sure you were always being compared to him, being accused of getting ahead because of him or just being a chip off the old block. Whatever the reason, you made a point to excel, this department has benefited from it and will continue to do so with you as lieutenant."

"Thank you." Joy never considered herself to be the emotional person Darrin accused her of being. But at that moment she was fighting back strong emotions of happiness. From the time she'd made the decision to follow in her father's footsteps and go into law enforcement, she'd known being Tate Ingram's daughter would be a handicap. She was proud of all her father's accomplishments but knew others would hold them against her.

She had refused to let that stop her from being a good detective. She'd known that meant she would have to work harder to prove she was her own person even while standing in her father's shadow.

"There's another thing I need to be up front about. There will be some who question my decision, some who will assert that you got the promotion because of your father. Others who will resent you getting it because you're a woman, regardless of your qualifications. There is nothing I can do to change their thought processes. I will advise you not to let their erroneous assumptions bother you. Just continue to do the excellent work you've been doing and you'll do fine."

Joy didn't say anything. She knew he was right on point. She'd left the biggest offender standing at her desk just minutes ago. Although Darrin no longer worked here in the department, he had friends who did. He still had ties and once he heard about it, he would let his opinions be known. There were others who felt the same way he did. Some of them were still pissed that she'd been chosen instead of them for the special task force working with the Feds on the Murphy Erickson case. It had been a high-profile case and it had placed her front and center while representing the department.

"I understand, sir."

He nodded. "I'm sure you do. Just like I'm sure you know it will be up to you to show them how wrong they are. Note I said 'show them' and not 'prove to them.' There's a difference. You don't have to prove a damn thing to them since they need to earn their paycheck just like you do. Showing them means being a role model, letting them see that the right way to do things pays off. Actions and not lip service get the job done."

Chief Harkins paused for a moment, then said, "And another thing, Detective Ingram."

"Yes?"

"Get a life. You hang around here too much and you don't have to do that. Personally, I don't want the people you will supervise to assume they need to do that, either. You have a smart brain. It doesn't take you hanging around here 24/7 for it to work. Besides, it needs down-time every once in a while. I expect you to find it. A good cop is a well-rested cop, not an overworked one."

He picked up a paper clip off his desk and then tossed it back down. "And how is Stonewall Courson doing?"

Joy had been looking down at her hands but jerked her head up. "Stonewall Courson?"

"Yes. I assume the two of you got something going on."

She swallowed. "What would make you think that, and how do you know Stonewall?"

"I know Mr. Courson because he works for Roland."

Joy swallowed. "You know Roland? Personally?"

He nodded his head. "I know him well enough and

over the years have developed a good relationship with him. After I was hired I went to meet him, introduce myself to him and apologize for what the department I'd been hired to lead had done to him. Not only had he been framed but he'd lost a wife who he'd loved very much. And then most recently, it was discovered those same cops were the ones responsible for the fire death of his brother and sister-in-law."

She nodded. "But why would you think something is going on between me and Stonewall Courson?"

"First of all, I saw your reaction that night when he ran into that burning cabin to save his friend Striker Jennings. Fear had gripped all of us, but yours had been different. You tried to hide it, and I'm certain no one else noticed it. I probably would have missed it had I not happened to look over at you to say something at that moment."

Joy didn't respond. She would inwardly admit to still having nightmares of that night. Of arriving at the cabin and finding the assassin that Erickson had hired on the ground dead and watching in horror as both Stonewall and Quasar raced inside a burning cabin to save Striker and Margo. She figured there was no way the four of them would survive. But they had. She hadn't released her breath until all four of them had run out.

She swallowed hard. Why had Chief Harkins brought up Stonewall? Did he suspect she had shared information with him during the Erickson case that she should not have? She would admit she and Stonewall had talked a lot. She had felt comfortable with him. A special connection to him. He had been someone she could talk to and confide in. And because of it she told him stuff on what she thought of as a need-to-know basis. But never had there been a conflict of interest. At least, in her mind there hadn't been. It wasn't like he was a member of the media and she'd divulged departmental classified information. But did the chief see things differently?

"Sir, during the Erickson investigation I didn't share anything with Stonewall Courson that I feel I should not have."

The chief waved off her words. "That's not why I brought him up. And as for you telling him anything, I'm sure you used common sense and discretion. As a fellow cop, Joy, I know there are times you need to talk to others not in our profession, just to get things off your chest or to make sure you're in your right mind. A confidant, so to speak. My wife is that person for me. I won't hold it against you if, at the time, Mr. Courson was that person for you."

At the time. "And now?"

"What you do is your business. Like I said, you need a life."

He was the saying the same thing her father had told her more than once. Although she'd never confided in him about the true nature of her and Omar's relationship and why she'd ended it, a part of her felt he understood. Her mother could not. She saw Omar as a successful man who would be perfect for her daughter.

"I'll take your suggestion to heart, Chief, although I feel I already have a life. The one I want without any drama. Without any controls. No disrespect, sir, but having someone in your life on a constant basis is not always a good thing."

He shrugged massive shoulders. "Depends on the

person." He leaned forward. "Enough about that. It's your life, and as long as you continue to do the job I know you can do, everything will be alright."

"Thank you."

"I plan to wait and make the announcement tomorrow. That way anyone who wants to be an ass about it will have the weekend to sulk, because come Monday I won't put up with any bullshit."

Joy nodded again. "Alright sir."

"That's all, *Lieutenant* Ingram," he said, stretching out his hand to her. "Congratulations."

She placed her hand in his and he shook it. "Thank you, sir."

"WELCOME BACK, WORLD TRAVELER."

Stonewall paused in the open doorway of Summers Security Firm to gaze at the man sitting behind the huge desk. "Thanks, Roland."

Eight years ago, when Stonewall, Quasar and Striker had left Glenworth Penitentiary, Roland had given them their first jobs. Since they hadn't known the first thing about security work, Roland had enrolled them in one of the top tactical training schools in the country. He'd also hooked them up for a full year with former Secret Service Agent Prescoli, a man who had a reputation as being one of the best in the business after serving under three presidents.

Although the three of them had lacked in-depth knowledge in security, what he, Quasar and Striker had possessed was an ingrained ability to survive and a drive to safeguard and defend anyone left in their care.

Roland saw the potential in them, something Stonewall was forever grateful for.

Roland interrupted his thoughts. "I talked to Navarro a little more than an hour ago. He wanted me to know that he was pleased with how you carried out your duties. He also told me you're on his payroll for another thirty days. Lucky you."

Stonewall couldn't help but smile as he slid into the chair across from Roland's desk. He had come here straight from the airport. "Yes, lucky me, and don't think I won't use it."

Roland chuckled. "There was never a doubt in my mind that you would. Got plans?"

"A few." He had plans, alright, and they all centered on one particular woman, especially after reading her recent text messages. Joy had no idea that while they'd been texting, he'd already arrived back in Charlottesville. She didn't expect him to return until Saturday.

"It's not like I was gone long this time around. Just a couple of weeks. What's been happening?"

Roland leaned back in his chair. "Nothing big, unless you're a Sunnie Clay fan. That woman who froze to death that night in Sofia Valley a few months back was her sister. But I figure you know that since you're friends with Detective Ingram, and I understand she's been assigned to the case."

Stonewall didn't say anything for a moment. To say he and Joy were friends was putting it lightly, especially when the people who knew him were aware of just how hot he was on her tail. Although he'd tried downplaying his desire for her over the past six months, the guys had still picked up on it. And no one was surprised they were together at Striker and Margo's wedding.

"I knew about the body, but I hadn't heard it had been identified. I haven't talked to Joy in a couple of days." No need to mention they'd been sexting quite a bit, though. "Joy doesn't know I'm back in town. She wasn't expecting me until this weekend."

"Wasn't expecting you? Sounds like the two of you are—"

"Friends. Just like you said. Nothing more. Nothing less."

"If you say so."

He did say so, Stonewall thought, and decided to change the subject. "I talked to Quasar. He and Randi have set a date for their wedding."

"Yes, and I'm happy for the both of them."

Stonewall heard something in Roland's voice that made him ask, "Roland, do you think you'll ever marry again?"

If the question was a surprise, Roland didn't let on. But he said firmly, "No."

Stonewall waited a beat before asking, "Why?"

"Because I could never love another woman. Knowing that, it wouldn't be fair to a woman to pretend that I can."

Stonewall nodded. "I know what you mean. I don't believe in forever, either."

Roland stared at him intently. "Don't get it twisted, Stonewall. I do believe in forever. Otherwise, I would never have married Becca. She was my forever. I lost forever with her."

Stonewall didn't say anything. He could actually feel

the pain in Roland's words. Deciding to try to shift their conversation from dismal to lighthearted, he asked, "So, how are the pregnant Granger ladies?"

A smile curved Roland's lips. "I understand they're anxious for it to be over. I know Carson is, and I figure Shiloh and Jules feel the same way." Roland had become close friends with Carson Granger when his wife Becca had convinced Carson, who'd worked for the state attorney's office at the time, to reopen Roland's case. Although Becca had gotten killed, the dirty cops had placed a hit on Carson's life as well, but had been unsuccessful in carrying it out.

"What about the fathers-in-waiting?"

Roland chuckled. "They are anxious, too. I talked to Sheppard last night, and the doctor has told him not to be surprised if the baby comes early. Sheppard and Carson are excited about that."

Stonewall glanced at his phone as he stood. "Need to get home," he said. More than that, he needed to get ready to pay Joy a surprise visit tonight. Normally he wouldn't just show up at any woman's home without calling first, but her last text said it all. A diversion.

CHAPTER NINETEEN

Joy took a sip of her wine as she stared at the flames in her fireplace. So what if the flames were the remote-control kind and it was the beginning of summer? None of that mattered. She was in one of her moods. And it was a good one.

Why wouldn't it be when she'd gotten a promotion today? She'd been tempted to pinch herself more than once to make sure it wasn't a dream. It wasn't and she felt so good about it. She'd come home, taken a shower, changed into a lounger and poured herself a glass of wine. Since no one at police headquarters had been told yet, she could not celebrate with any of her coworkers tonight. She wanted to think there would be some who would be happy for her and truly believed her promotion was well deserved. She couldn't worry about those who didn't.

She had called her parents and siblings and told them her good news. They were happy for her. She had talked to her dad for a few minutes longer than the others and, like always, he had given her words of encouragement. Joy knew he was truly proud of her and that meant a lot.

She couldn't wait to share the news with Stonewall. Normally, because of the nature of his business, she refrained from contacting him in case it was at an inopportune time. Instead she was satisfied in letting him contact her. But not tonight. Tonight she decided to take the initiative. She was too happy and excited to wait.

She placed her wineglass down and moved across the room to her phone on the coffee table. It was close to seven. Was it too early to text him? Should she be doing it at all? What if he was in the middle of something?

Joy shrugged off the thoughts and was about to pick up her phone when her doorbell sounded. Who would be visiting her? It was probably her neighbor and friend, Cherish. She crossed the room to the door and glanced out the peephole. Her heart suddenly began pounding at the same time her body tingled with full awareness of the man standing on the other side of her door. It was Stonewall.

Removing the chain, she quickly opened the door. "Stonewall. This is a surprise." She truly meant that. For someone who never liked surprises, she was starting to like his. Joy tried not to notice how good he looked standing there in a pair of jeans and a pullover shirt that stretched across his broad chest. And why did he appear bigger than life tonight? Of its own accord her gaze moved to his crotch and remembered. Then she thought that yes, he definitely was bigger than life, especially certain parts of him.

"I hope it's a pleasant surprise."

If he only knew, she thought, her eyes moving back to his face. She saw the smile that touched his lips and figured he did know…or had a pretty good idea…what she was thinking when her gaze had lowered to his zipper. "Definitely pleasant. Please come in."

She stepped aside and when he passed by her, his aftershave, a woodsy, masculine fragrance, ignited a response inside her body.

Feeling all bubbly at the realization he was really here, she closed the door behind him and when she turned around, he was standing there staring at her. The dark heat in his gaze was blatantly clear, and she met his gaze with a force so powerful it licked through her body.

"I thought you were still in Vermont. When did you return to town? Why are you here?"

He moved toward her and she appreciated his walk. It was like a panther stalking its prey. He came to a stop in front of her. "I returned today, and the reason I'm here is because of your text."

Desire was blossoming in her stomach. "My text?"

"Yes. The one that said you were in need of a diversion. I answered the call, baby. Here I am."

THE MOMENT JOY had opened the door, a need Stonewall hadn't counted on ripped through him. Oh, he'd known he wanted her, which was the reason he'd shown up tonight. To appease his desires as well as her own. But what he hadn't counted on or expected was such gut-wrenching heat blasting off inside him.

He'd just said he was here because of her text when deep down he knew that wasn't completely true. Even if she hadn't sent that text, he would still have been here because Joy Ingram had gotten into his system in a way no other woman had. His jaw tensed at the thought.

"Do you have to frown about it?"

His jaw relaxed. "Sorry, I was just thinking about something."

"What?"

She would have to ask him. Unfortunately, he wouldn't tell her. But he would tell her something that had been on his mind during the drive over here. And it was somewhat connected to the issue at hand. "That I'm here for you tonight, and I shouldn't want you so much."

She smiled and reached up to run a finger across his bearded jaw. "That's okay. I think there will be enough pleasure to share."

Both her words and her touch were doing him in. "Hell, I hope so."

He leaned down close to her ear. Placed a kiss there. "You know what I've been thinking about a lot since the last time I was here?"

"No." He thought her voice sounded breathless.

"You. Me. In your bed again, with you curled up beside be. But only after I've been inside your body for hours."

"Hours?"

"Yes, hours. You got the time?"

He felt her smile against his face. "Only if you've got the stamina."

Did she honestly think he didn't? In that case…

He moved his lips from her ear to the nape of her neck. Her skin was sweet and felt soft. Using the tip of his tongue, he began to lick her in slow, penetrating strokes. He couldn't help but feel pleased when he heard the choppiness of her breathing and felt her shiver.

"Stonewall?"

Why did she have to say his name like that? With such heated passion? "Hmm?"

"Are you going to play games?"

He released a light chuckle. "No, I'm going to prove just how much stamina I've got. I hope you can handle it," he said, brushing her hair aside to press even more kisses to her neck.

He leaned in closer to her, wanting her to feel his erection. Wanting her to know just what she would be dealing with. "I want you so damn much," he murmured, moving his tongue to lick around her chin.

"Not as much as I want you."

"If you think that, baby, then I need to prove you wrong." He swept her off her feet and into his arms. Moving quickly, he headed toward her bedroom.

WHEN HE PLACED her on her feet by the bed, Stonewall gave her a long, hard kiss. Joy couldn't help the moan that started low in her throat before working its way from her mouth. She felt a throbbing between her legs and even felt her panties getting wet. There was no doubt about it. Stonewall had the ability to stoke her fire in a way that left her ablaze.

By the time he released her mouth, she felt like she'd been kissed into oblivion. And when she looked into his dark eyes, she saw something in their depths that was even more erotic than what had been there earlier. Her heart began pounding, and her senses were on overload.

"I am your diversion tonight, Joy. Forget every damn thing except me and how I will make you feel. Things will get wild. They will get raw. Even urgent at times." He gave her a quick, heated kiss. "And another thing."

She licked her tongue around her lips, tasting him there. "What?"

"This bedroom isn't the only place where we'll be doing it. I like different locations even if they're under the same roof."

At that moment, the image of being taken on the

floor in front of her remote-controlled fireplace heated her blood, and another groan escaped from her lips.

She licked her lips again, and he said in an almost fierce growl, "Let me do that, Joy."

The moment his tongue touched the corner of her mouth, she felt her stomach do a quick somersault at the same time her pulse began pounding near the base of her throat. It took all she had to stand there while he licked to one corner of her mouth and back, while the entire length of his body pressed against her, as if he deliberately wanted her to feel the bulge behind his zipper.

She had no other choice but to feel it and remember how it felt inside her while her muscles clamped down on him, milking him and pulling all she could out of him.

The memory made the center of her ache, and desire throbbed through her veins. He had wrapped his arms around her waist, but now his hands had shifted lower to cup her backside. She could feel the heat in his hands through the silk material of her lounger. He continued to ravage her mouth, licking all around her lips while gently rocking his hips against her so she wouldn't miss the feel of his erection. She knew Stonewall was deliberately toying with her. Nearly driven mindless with primal awareness and intense need, she decided two could play his game.

The next time his tongue moved to lick around the center of her mouth, she snared it with hers. Drawing it into her mouth, she began sucking hard on it, the same way she intended to suck hard on him later. She intended to show him that she knew a little about kissing, even if it was pulling out the mental playbook from the last time he'd been here. That night he'd taught her to kiss in ways Omar never had, and she had no problem showing him that she remembered it all.

He removed his hands from her backside to clamp them to her face and hold his mouth to hers. Or hers to his. She wasn't sure. All she knew was that although he deepened the kiss, her tongue was the one in control. Holding tight to his, even though he was trying to make it a full-contact, wet-and-tasty, all-over-your-mouth probing kiss.

She could feel him shudder deeply right before he lifted his head to disengage their mouths. He stared down at her with wet lips, and she figured hers were the same. Suddenly he swept her up into his arms and carried her the couple of feet to the bed.

She pulled him down on the bed with her. There was something about their bodies together on a mattress and the restful feel of her comforter beneath her back. But she knew Stonewall had no intention of letting her rest. At least, not for a while. The next thing she knew, he had whipped her lounger over her head, leaving her bare except for her panties. She felt a surge of need when he pulled the skimpy lace down her legs.

While she lay there, wearing nothing at all, his gaze moved over every bare inch of her. "You are beautiful," he said in a voice that sounded like an aching rasp.

The words curled through her body on vibrations that shivered right to her soul. Intense heat throbbed between her legs. She couldn't help the blush that stained her cheeks when she felt a flow of wetness deluge between them.

"I missed this," he said, stroking his fingers along her feminine folds, deliberately easing a finger inside to stroke her clit. "God, that feels good," he said as he continued to stroke her as if trying to generate even more wetness from her. She held his gaze and then, as if he was the one in control of her body, a stream of juices flowed down her thighs.

Her heart began beating rapidly in her chest when he withdrew his fingers, but then he parted her thighs as if he needed a closer view of what was between them. And then she watched as he lowered his head. Before she could catch her breath, he thrust his tongue inside her.

"Stonewall!"

His mouth was greedier than before. Ravenous. Voracious. Gluttonous. He was making predatory moans as he locked his mouth to her, taking control of her clit. She began gasping, not for air but for more, and he gave it to her. She moaned, whimpered, tossed around on the bed until the firm grip of his hands on her hips held her in place.

When he did that wiggly thing with his tongue, zigzagging and making circuitous motions, her hips nearly shot off the bed. But he continued his firm hold on her as if he was determined to get every last drop of her juices. She wasn't sure how that was possible when, thanks to him and his insatiable tongue, more was being produced.

When she felt a jolt of sexual pleasure consume her, starting at the soles of her feet and traveling with resonant speed toward her center, she cried out, screaming his name. The booming sound seemed to ricochet off the walls before returning to her and making her buck against his mouth again.

Still, he refused to let up. It felt as though his tongue was imprinting itself inside her. When he finally pulled his mouth away, she opened her eyes to stare at him.

It took a while to focus, and when she did she stared deep into his eyes.

"Your taste is spoiling me," he said in a husky tone.

She was too weak to tell him that his tongue was nearly killing her. "Now to take off my clothes," he said, moving away from the bed. Although it was a struggle, she pushed up on her elbows to watch him. Dog-tired or not, there was no way she was not going to watch this.

"Did I tell you how much I love your breasts?"

"Umm." She couldn't remember if he had or not, and right now, seeing him remove his shirt was at the top of her agenda.

Then he removed his shoes and socks. "I guess you intend to lie there and watch."

"Yes." There was no need to lie about it.

By now his hands had gone to the zipper of his jeans and when he slowly pulled it down, she could feel her breath getting lodged in her throat. And then, in what seemed like a deliberately slow movement, he dragged his jeans along with black briefs down a pair of masculine thighs. When his shaft was free, she blinked. *OMG.* Had it gotten even larger?

"No."

Her gaze shifted up to his face for a quick second. "No what?"

"It didn't get any bigger."

She wondered how he'd known what she was thinking. "You sure?"

He chuckled. "Positive. It's just the angle from which you're looking at it now."

"Oh." She figured she'd take his word for it. It was his body. He ought to know.

Joy could feel herself getting wet between the legs again just from staring at him. And as her gaze held tight, she saw his massive shaft expand before her eyes. Like before, it was jutting proudly from a dark thatch of curls. The head of it was enormous and engorged. The veins running along it seemed imposingly solid.

She forced her gaze to take in the rest of him, appreciating the muscled legs, masculine thighs, tight abs and broad, hairy chest. Once again she admired the tattoo of a bald eagle in flight on his chest. She thought the same thing now that she had the last time. He was pure male perfection on legs.

"Got your fill?"

She shifted her gaze to his face. A very handsome face. "For now."

A smile spread across his lips. "Just as long as you know while you were watching me, I was watching you."

"Were you?" She lifted a brow. Had he been able to see how her womanly core had practically begun dripping with wetness? "I can see how wet and slick you are down there."

Joy felt her cheeks tint. She and Omar never had such intimate conversations in the bedroom. They had sex and then went to sleep. They definitely didn't talk about it the way she and Stonewall were doing. Not even during the early days when they were supposedly madly in love.

She watched as Stonewall rolled on a condom. He made it seem like second nature, and she figured he had to have done it a lot for it to be so easy for him.

"Ready?"

She nodded. Holding her gaze, he headed back toward the bed. Back to her, and she got heated with each and every step he took with his huge erection looking massive and firm and expanding even more. *Lordy.*

When he reached the bed, he drew her up, letting her body slide against him. She felt a tingling sensation in her stomach when the tips of her breasts brushed against his hairy chest.

"I want you now, Joy. I missed you so damn much."

His words, spoken in a deep, throaty voice, sent pleasurable shivers through her body. She would admit the truth to him, as well. "I missed you a lot, too. At night before going to sleep I cleared my mind of everything but you. Even without being here, you were my diversion. I woke up every morning well rested and ready to tackle another day. Thanks to you."

She saw the smug look that came onto his face. "Have I given you a big head?" she asked. It would be fitting if she had, since it would match the one between those masculine thighs of his.

"No big head. But I do think you're sweet."

She chuckled. "Sweet? I'm known to kick ass."

"Not tonight, Joy. Not tonight."

And he captured her mouth while at the same time sliding his hands to the center of her thighs. When he began stroking her there again, she clutched his strong arms. He was filling her with sensations all over again. She moaned deep in her throat.

Without breaking contact he began lowering her to the bed. She opened her eyes and looked up at him when her back touched the bedspread. He was straddled over her body, and instinctively she widened her thighs.

"I'm about to give you the ride of your life. By the time it's over, you won't question my stamina again."

His words made her recall she had done that. "Can't you take a joke?"

"Only if you can take this." He'd moved in position between her legs and she felt him. The huge head of his shaft was there against her womanly mound. He began moving, sliding his head against her. And as if he was communicating with her folds, they seem to part for him.

He pressed down and began sliding into her slowly and as before, her body stretched to accommodate his entry. Inch by delicious inch, her body continued to take him in. She breathed in deeply. And when he had gone as far as he possibly could, she clamped her inner muscles down on him at the same time she hooked her ankles to his back.

He glanced down at her and when he did, she deliberately clamped down on him even more. "You trying to kill me?"

"No. I'm trying to pleasure you," she whispered.

"We will pleasure each other," he said, blowing a strand of hair from her face.

His heated breath caressed her face, and for a moment she felt something that she shouldn't have. Mainly the thought that she could get used to this. Him in her bed. Him inside her to the hilt. Him blowing a strand of hair from her face.

He leaned down, and his tongue began stroking around her lips at the same time he began moving, coursing through her juices with deliberate, tempered strokes. When had she gotten this wet with a man? It was as if Stonewall had the ability to bring it on.

She moaned when he escalated his pace. The feel

of his shaft thrusting in and out of her thickened the air in her lungs. She heard him growl when he began moving faster, thrusting harder. The sound of the bed-springs echoed in the room and she moaned deeper as he pressed her further into the bed.

He continued to pump hard into her, flexing his thighs with every thrust to go deeper, hitting a certain spot in her body. He was intent on angling just right, stroking her over and over again. Penetrating hard. Her ankles kept a tight lock on his back as he rode her just like he'd told her he would.

Over and over. In and out. He kept going. It was as if he couldn't get enough of her. She knew the feeling because she couldn't get enough of him, either. Then suddenly, something inside her snapped the same time it did within him.

She gasped as her body spiraled out of control. With the quickness and precision of a jackhammer, he kept pounding into her, and her body braced to absorb each tantalizing stroke.

"Stonewall!"

"Joy!"

Together they were thrown into an abyss that had her gasping even more for breath as his penetration con-tinued hard, fast and deep. The feel of his abs rubbing her stomach was too much and she could feel another orgasm hit right behind the last, making her come even harder than before.

Shudders racked her body, and the last thing she re-membered was him easing his body off hers and pull-ing her into his arms to hold her close.

CHAPTER TWENTY

STONEWALL STARED DOWN at Joy while she slept, thinking just how peaceful and beautiful she looked. After taking a short nap, they'd gone another round of lovemaking. He glanced across the room at the clock. It was close to midnight. Did she want him to leave tonight? She hadn't said.

He felt totally drained, but not as much as the last time. He had no intention of letting her slip past him and get out the bed without him knowing it. She would wake up eventually. In the meantime, he liked lying here holding her, watching her and wondering how she had gotten under his skin in such big way and in such a short period of time.

So, okay. Maybe it hadn't been such a short period of time. It had taken six months for them to finally hook up, and they had kept in constant contact during that time. And now he had shared her bed twice and enjoyed each time immensely. Would there be another?

He was less and less crazy about this being a diversion, especially since now he would have a lot more time on his hands. Thanks to Dak he had thirty days to do nothing. Of course his greedy-ass mind was considering one particular thing he wanted to do. The thought of making love to Joy every day of the week definitely topped the list.

But that was probably wishful thinking on his part. He might have a lot of time on his hands, but she did not. She had bad guys to arrest, cases to solve and even more cases to solve. But that didn't mean he intended to go another six months without this. The feel of her lying beside him. Her warmth penetrating his insides that could get so cold at times. Especially when he thought about how his life had been once.

His grandfather always said even good could come from evil if you let it. Pop had been right. He couldn't help but remember that each and every time he thought about Striker and Quasar. And then there was Sheppard. He owed him so much, he doubted he could ever repay him for helping him get his life back. For making him see he was a lot better than a cell at Glenworth.

And now there was Joy. His Joy in the morning. Over the next thirty days he would not crowd her or get underfoot, but he intended to make sure she was taking care of herself. Getting the proper rest. Eating wholesome meals. The thought that he had thirty days to take care of her…

But what if she didn't want to be taken care of? What if she thought he was getting too serious? He knew she was a woman who liked her space, and thanks to the asshole she'd been engaged to, she probably had no intention of letting another man invade it. Under normal circumstances he wouldn't want to. It wasn't his style to get emotionally attached to any woman.

But now…

He could see himself doing so with this one. He was

already physically attached and that's all she wanted. A diversion. Not a relationship. What if he were to change her mind? Did he really want to? And could he even if he wanted to?

"You're frowning again."

He glanced down at her. "You're awake."

The beginning of a smile touched the corners of her lips. "Yes, but before you get any ideas, I need to go to the bathroom."

Concern furrowed his brow. "You okay? Do I need to run hot bathwater for you to soak for a while?"

She reached up and patted his chin. "Relax, lover. I'm fine. I just have to go potty. I'll be back."

Relief swept through him. "Okay."

He watched her ease out of bed and walk naked into the bathroom. She had a gorgeous body, and just the thought that he'd been inside her, had touched her all over, kissed her all over, tasted her skin both inside and out, made his boner even harder than before.

Moments later she returned and eased back in bed beside him. He pulled her into his arms. "Glad you're back. You were missed."

"I'm glad to be back," she said, smiling at him. "When you arrived tonight I had been just about to text you. I thought you were still in Vermont."

"I wanted to surprise you."

"You did. Like I said, it was a pleasant surprise."

He shifted their bodies in bed so he could lie facing her. He enjoyed looking into her face. "So, why were you texting me? To let me know you were missing me?" He could hope.

She chuckled and cuddled closer into his arms. "I always miss you, Stonewall."

He wondered if she really meant that. "That's good to know. Is anything wrong?"

She gazed up at him with what he thought were the most beautiful brown eyes. Then, of course, there were her lips that he just loved to death. As he stared into her eyes he saw something. Happiness? Excitement? Glee? "Okay, what is it? You got me curious."

She rose up in bed bubbling over with whatever it was. "I got promoted to lieutenant," she said happily.

Her words sank in, and he couldn't help but smile. Share in her happiness and excitement. A huge smile touched his face. He was genuinely happy for her. "That's great, Joy! Congratulations!"

He pulled her down to him and captured her mouth. He had meant for it to be a little kiss, but the moment his tongue slid into her mouth and he tasted her, he couldn't help but take it to the next level. Heat consumed him, and when she arched her body even closer to his, he deepened the kiss. It didn't help matters that she was naked and her skin against his was driving him crazy. But he knew he had to end the kiss for now. It was her moment and not his.

Breaking off the kiss, he fought to focus on the eyes staring back at him. "Hmm, Stonewall. I'd work on getting even more promotions if I got a congratulations kiss like that each and every time."

He held her gaze. "And you will."

She licked her lips and sighed. "Then I guess I'd better get to work on becoming chief of police."

Stonewall threw his head back and laughed. His Joy

in the morning was priceless. She made him smile, laugh and feel good that he was here with her. "Tell me about your promotion," he said, gathering her back into his arms.

"Nothing changes other than I'll have several people reporting to me. I will still keep my caseload, but depending on what paperwork I need to take care of, I can assign some of them out."

"But you won't," he said, thinking how well he'd gotten to know her. "You like working out in the field."

"Yes, I like handling investigations."

"Well, I am happy for you. You're smart, intelligent and a hard worker."

She gave him a huge smile. "That's the same thing Chief Harkins said."

"Then Chief Harkins is a smart man."

She nodded. "He's also very astute. He knows about you, Stonewall."

Stonewall lifted a brow. "What do you mean, he knows about me?"

JOY HESITATED, DEBATING just what she should tell him and how much. But the discussion about him hadn't been a bad one—in fact, it had been rather enlightening.

"The night of that cabin fire, he suspected you and I had something going on. I guess the concern showed in my face when I saw you run into that burning cabin to save Striker and Margo."

She didn't say anything for a minute as she relived that night. The two of them hadn't even gone out yet, but they'd forged a friendship, and seeing him put his life at risk had nearly done her in. Taken years off her life. At least, she'd felt that way at the time.

"He asked about you and made me aware he'd known that I'd talked to you a lot during the Erickson case and probably shared things with you about it."

He nodded slowly. "And did you get in trouble because of it?" he asked her.

She smiled up at him. "No, not at all. In fact, he was glad I had someone I could confide in and knew I wouldn't have told you anything I shouldn't have."

Joy then bit her lip nervously. She must have given something away, because Stonewall asked, "And what else did he say?"

She sighed. "He thinks I spend too much time at the office. That I don't have a life and he doesn't think that's a good example to set for my detectives. He knows there will be some cases that will require a lot of my time, but I get the feeling he wants me to do a better job managing my days."

"That might not be such a bad idea, Joy. You don't want to get overworked, and I might be able to help you with that. At least for the next thirty days."

She frowned, looking up at him. "How?"

"I'm on call with Dak for thirty days, but with the danger over, I doubt he will need me. So, I'll be here if you need me for anything."

She didn't have to ask what he was alluding to. He was volunteering to be her diversion on a more frequent basis if she needed him. But what would that mean? Seeing him more often than not. Did she want that? Could she handle it? After Omar she'd drawn the line. She enjoyed Stonewall's company. She definitely enjoyed him in her bed, but she wasn't ready for anything more permanent.

For that reason, she said, "Thanks for the offer, but I'll be okay." She paused. He deserved to know why she'd said that. "Nothing has changed about how I feel about my space, Stonewall."

There, she'd said it. Reiterated her feelings. She studied him, and she was glad he didn't seem bothered by what she'd said. Why should he? He'd said during the last time they were together that he wasn't looking for anything serious, either.

"Yes, I know how you feel," he said, gently stoking the side of her face. "I was just making an offer."

"I appreciate you doing so."

He smiled and pulled her closer into his arms. "The offer is out there if you ever want to take me up on it."

She returned his smile. "Thanks. That's good to know." Then, taking the initiative, she leaned up, wrapped her arms around his neck and captured his mouth in a kiss.

CHAPTER TWENTY-ONE

Joy stood at the window in her office and took a sip of coffee.

Her office.

She turned and took it all in, finding it hard to believe she had an office. A real office and not the cubicle where she'd sat since she began working as a detective. The office was spacious and hadn't been used since the last lieutenant. Margaret had done a good job in making it look nice. There were several large plants, a map of the city on the wall, and nice furnishings. Her desk was twice the size her last one had been.

Because of budget cuts, she wouldn't have her own personal assistant, but she'd be sharing Margaret with the chief. Joy didn't have a problem with that. She liked Margaret and thought the fifty-something woman was very efficient at her job. She was definitely well organized.

Margaret had called before Joy had left home this morning and advised her to stop at city hall before coming in to work. Mayor Greene wanted to congratulate her. She had just walked Stonewall to the door when she'd gotten the call.

Stonewall.

She couldn't stop the shudder that ran through her body when she thought of him and all they'd done last night and this morning. She didn't want to think about how many rounds of lovemaking they'd engaged in. But she would remember the last one. She had screamed so many times last night it was a wonder she could talk today.

Joy smiled when she'd returned the favor before he'd left. She doubted she could forget the moment she'd pushed him on his back, settled her head between a pair of masculine thighs and taken him into her mouth, locking her lips on him. He hadn't screamed, but he'd moaned, groaned and growled a number of times as she pushed him over the edge and right into erotic bliss.

She brought her thoughts back to the present at the sound of the knock on her door. "Come in."

It was Sanchez, and he was smiling. She returned his smile, appreciating it. By the time she'd arrived to work after her pit stop with Mayor Ivan Greene, it was apparent by the cool reception she'd gotten from some of her peers that the chief had made the announcement of her promotion. It was obvious from the mean-spirited looks and rolling of eyes that the news hadn't gone over well.

Several men and women had congratulated her. Some had not. She decided not to worry about those who hadn't. She intended to do a good job. If she eventually won them over, that was great. If not, it would be their loss.

"Sanchez, come in." She'd known he'd taken some time off this morning to go with his wife for their newborn's first doctor's visit, and she hadn't seen him at all this afternoon.

"Sure, Lieutenant," he said beaming. "I just heard. Congratulations."

Lieutenant. She liked the sound of that. "Thanks."

"And it's more than deserved. You've worked your ass off here. Everybody knows it."

Joy leaned back against her desk. "Maybe they do. But I'm a woman and some are not ready to be led by one."

"Excuse my Spanish, but eff them, Lieutenant. You got this. And if they hadn't promoted you, I bet they would have brought someone else in from another city. None of these guys deserve it. They either don't have the experience or do just enough to get by and nothing more."

She knew Sanchez was right. Some even had the nerve to brag about how little they did. "Well, that's about to change. Everyone will be pulling their own weight around here." Joy knew she couldn't start off bulldozing her way through, but she refused to let anyone run over her. They would eventually become a team.

Changing the subject, she asked, "How was the baby's first doctor's visit?"

"Great. Carlos has gained two pounds. He'll be ready to suit up for the Chicago Cubs in a few years."

"And when he does, I intend to buy a ticket to watch him play," Joy said.

Sanchez gave a proud chuckle, and Joy knew that Juan Sanchez utterly and completely adored being a father. "Where are you headed?" she asked.

It was close to five in the afternoon. She had spent most of the day in her office going over reports, trying to acquaint herself with the men and woman she would be supervising. Yes, she had one woman. Lisa Perkins. Lisa was a divorcée in her early forties who'd been a detective for five years. Joy had worked with Lisa only once before, and she seemed nice enough. And Lisa didn't seem to care that Joy had been promoted as her boss. The six men were another matter. She believed five of them would accept her position, grudgingly or otherwise. But she could imagine Whitman Snow giving her problems. Whit was a tight friend of Darrin's, and the two men shared the same views when it came to women in the workplace.

"I'm about to make a run," Sanchez said. "I stopped by to see if you wanted to go. I understand that now that you're lieutenant, you might have a lot on your plate."

"Where are you headed?"

"Back over to Beautiful Creations Surrogate Agency. I just got a call from Cathy Stone. Her boss, Oliver Effington, arrived back in town today. She told him about our visit, and he'll be more than happy to speak with us."

"Alright then. Let's go."

"WELCOME BACK. HOW was the honeymoon?" Stonewall asked his friend, who slid into the booth across from him and Quasar. Striker had that I-am-a-damn-happy-man look on his face.

"The cruise was great. I'm ready to go on another one."

"What did you like about it?" Quasar asked after popping a french fry in his mouth.

"Everything. The food. Being out on the ocean. The ports we visited in the Caribbean," Striker said, pulling a menu out of the rack. "It was my first cruise, but it won't be my last. We would have stayed longer if Margo didn't have two wedding dresses to finish." His wife, Margo, was a wedding dress designer.

A waitress came and took Striker's order. He only wanted coffee.

"That's it?" Stonewall asked him when the waitress walked off. Everybody knew Striker had a hearty appetite.

"Yes, that's it. Margo and I are going out to dinner later." Striker then looked over at Quasar. "Congrats on picking a date for your wedding."

"Thanks."

"Any idea where the two of you are going on a honeymoon?"

Quasar smiled. "Yes. South Africa. I really enjoyed myself when I went there for Jace and Shana's honeymoon." Everyone remembered that time. Because he'd been Jace Granger's bodyguard he had accompanied Jace and his wife Shana on their honeymoon. Only thing was, Jace and his wife hadn't known Quasar had been hired to protect them.

"This time when I go to South Africa, I intend to really enjoy myself."

Stonewall chuckled. "Considering it will be your honeymoon, I'm sure you will."

"So, catch me up—how did your date go with your detective?" Striker asked, shifting the conversation to Stonewall. "I guess she didn't have you arrested for kidnapping."

"Ha ha. You and Quasar think you're so funny. No, she didn't. In fact, she told me it was the best date she'd been on."

The waitress returned with a plate of miniature biscuits that she put in front of Striker. He grabbed a couple immediately and popped them into his mouth. Moments later he asked Quasar, "So, is your psychic in town?"

Quasar cut Striker a cool glare. "No, but she'll be

arriving later tonight. And my fiancée's name is Randi. Get it?"

Striker chuckled. "Yeah, I get it." He then glanced over at Stonewall. "I guess me saying 'your detective' is out, too, huh?"

Stonewall rolled his eyes. "It was never *in* for you guys. I've just been ignoring your BS for the past six months."

The waitress brought Striker his coffee and gave Stonewall and Quasar refills on lemonade. "So, the best, huh? Just which parts of your date exactly did Detective Ingram enjoy?"

"All of it."

Striker rolled his eyes. "Shit, Stonewall, everybody knows you're a damn freak of nature. Could she handle it?"

Stonewall knew Striker and Quasar were fishing for details, but they were details he wouldn't be providing. Normally he had no problems sharing a few details with his friends. However, his time with Joy was off-limits. "I've said as much as I'm going to," Stonewall answered.

"The oversize stud is not going to tell you anything," Quasar said, grinning. "Makes you wonder."

Frowning, Stonewall glanced over at Quasar. "Wonder what?"

Quasar's grin widened. "Nothing." He chugged down the rest of his lemonade and then glanced at his watch. "I got to run. Randi and I are going to a movie tonight."

Striker checked his watch, as well. "I need to leave, too." He stood and studied Stonewall for a moment.

Stonewall didn't like the scrutiny. "What?"

"You'll be okay?" Striker asked him.

Stonewall frowned. "Why wouldn't I be?"

Striker shrugged. "No reason, I guess. Check you out later."

"Yeah, see you later, Stone," Quasar added, giving him an equally intense look.

"Okay. You guys better go or you'll be late. And don't worry about your bill. Consider it my treat this time," he said, deciding to rush them off. He didn't like being under their damn microscope. Nor did he need them to worry about him, dammit.

"Thanks," they both said before turning to leave.

Stonewall watched them walk away before releasing a deep sigh. He had understood Striker's concern and the reason for it. For the first time since their friendships had begun, they weren't all bachelors. They felt as if they were abandoning him.

Striker was now married, and Quasar would be, too, in a few months. They had women in their lives, and he was the odd man out with no one. To them he was what they probably now perceived as their desolate and lonely buddy. He knew they were happy and only wanted the same thing for him, but it wouldn't be happening. At least, not that kind of happiness anyway.

From the time they'd forged a friendship in the slammer, it had always been the three of them. Sometimes it seemed like the three of them against the world. Their friendship was more than close. It was like a brotherhood. Sheppard had told them to always have each other's backs and they had. They'd worked hard together to put their lives back on track, had taken classes together and even in the beginning had lived together.

Although they kidded each other a lot, most of the time they knew how far to take it. They knew each other's history—the good, the bad and the ugly. Stonewall knew the guilt Striker felt about the past, he knew Quasar's issue with his fucked-up family in California, and they all knew he never wanted to get serious about any woman and fall in love only to lose her the way he'd lost his parents and his grandfather. Three people who'd meant the world to him. Even now he worried about Granny Kay. Although she kept herself in good physical shape and was more active than any woman he knew at her age, he never liked thinking about a time she wouldn't be here. Same with his sister. Mellie had her life and didn't like whenever her big brother got the urge to stick his nose in it…which he tried doing at times.

Stonewall finished off the last of his meal. He enjoyed Shady Reds. The food was always good and he liked this spot by the window, where he could look out and see the mountains. He wondered what Joy was doing. It had been her first day on the job as lieutenant. How had that gone? It was close to six in the evening. Had she called it a day and left for home? He would call her later.

He couldn't help but think about their night together and waking up this morning with her in his arms. It had been fucking wonderful. She was wonderful, and he was enjoying being with her a lot.

Stonewall had fought hard to keep the disappointment from his features last night when she'd reiterated just what their relationship would be. In other words, she had reminded him that they didn't have one. Although the sex between them was good, she liked her space better and had no intention of letting him invade it.

The crazy thing was that most people who really knew him knew he felt the same way. That's the reason he had gotten his own place when he'd returned to Charlottesville instead of moving home to live with his sister and grandmother. He'd been the first to be released from Glenworth. When Striker and Quasar had gotten out months later, he had invited them to move in with him while they got themselves together and decided what they wanted to do. He'd put up with an invasion of his space for them for about four months. Then they'd earned enough money to put down deposits on their own places.

"You shouldn't be sitting alone. Want some company?"

Stonewall glanced up at the pretty woman who was standing by his table. He'd noticed her when he'd first walked in, sitting at the bar. He'd noticed her and that was about all. He hadn't been interested then, and he wasn't interested now. In the past he was not only known to shamelessly flirt with every woman alive but had bedded quite a few. But all that had changed since meeting Joy.

Why?

He was tired of using the excuse he'd been too preoccupied with trying to nail down Joy for a date. It was more than that, but he wasn't ready to figure out what that more meant.

"Hey, dude, I'm waiting on an answer."

He blinked. He'd almost forgotten about the woman

standing there, and from the frown on her face, she wasn't a woman used to being forgotten. He could definitely see why. In addition to being pretty, she had a nice body and didn't mind showing it off in that midriff top and short skirt.

However, there was that irritated smile, the perfume she was wearing that he didn't particularly care for, her too-long fingernails... Bottom line, she wasn't Joy.

"Thanks, but no, I don't want any company," he finally said.

Her irritated smile turned into a full-blown frown. Damn, she had to be kidding. Did men not turn her down ever? "You sure about that?" she asked, licking her lips.

Watching what she was doing to her lips, instead of getting hard, he was getting annoyed. Now, had those been Joy's lips, he had no doubt his erection would have been pressing hard against his zipper about now.

"Yes, I'm sure. Maybe another time," he said, doubting it very seriously.

Instead of saying anything, she glared at him for a long moment before stomping off like a spoiled child. *Oh, well.* He checked his watch. He might as well head on over to the gym. Stonewall put enough money on the table to more than cover his bill and was about to get up to leave when he immediately stiffened upon hearing Joy's name. She was being discussed by two men in the booth behind him, and they were talking loud enough for him to hear.

And he didn't like what they were saying.

CHAPTER TWENTY-TWO

JOY AND SANCHEZ pulled up in front of the huge building and saw a car parked in front. She couldn't help but
appreciate Oliver Effington's willingness to speak with
them. Unfortunately, the executive directors of the other
surrogate agencies hadn't been as eager. A couple had
claimed they didn't have time to answer any questions
and further stated that their agencies were shielded by
strict privacy rights to protect both their clients and the
surrogate mothers.

Joy had found herself breaking things down to them.
A woman was dead, and she was determined to find
out why. They could answer her questions now, or she
could request their presence in the interrogation room at
police headquarters. She'd told them she didn't see the
need of going through all that trouble since she was convinced they had nothing to hide. However, she would if
she had to. Furthermore, she'd made them aware that
she could also very well go to a judge to subpoena all
their agency records.

If they were determined to make things difficult for
her, then two could play their game. It seemed after
hearing her spiel, which was delivered without a hint
of a smile, the other four directors had decided to co-
operate, after all.

Getting out of their unmarked car, she and Sanchez went around to the side door. After pushing the intercom button and identifying themselves, they heard the click and then the door opened. They entered the corridor and headed for the bank of elevators.

As Cathy Stone had instructed in her phone call to Sanchez, they pushed the button to the third floor. Moments later they stepped off the elevator, and Joy glanced around a lobby that was even more stylish than the main lobby. A very attractive woman sitting at the reception desk stood and smiled at them. Joy figured her to be in her late thirties or early forties, and she had that same elegant air about her as Cathy Stone had. Even at this hour, not a strand of hair was out of place on her head, and she looked ready to walk the runway. And if the clothes she wore were any indication of her salary, then this place obviously paid her well.

"Detectives Ingram and Sanchez?" she asked, her smile widening.

"That's us," Sanchez said, glancing around.

"Glad you arrived on time. Mr. Effington had a long day and needs to get home to rest."

"Hey, don't we all," Sanchez said, still smartly. "But then, not everyone can enjoy a week in the Bahamas."

The smile on the woman's face faded somewhat. "Trust me, it wasn't a pleasure trip. He had a lot of meetings to attend and rarely returned to his hotel room before eight in the evening."

Joy eyed the woman. "And you know this how?"

The woman immediately put the friendly smile back in place. "Because I was there with him. I'm his wife, Audrey Effington."

Figures, Joy thought. "We don't want to keep your husband here any longer than necessary. May we speak with him now?"

"Certainly. Please follow me."

They did. With a graceful stride she led them through another plush lobby with several offices, including one that bore her name on a gold plate. It stated she was the office manager. "I bet that's real gold," Sanchez whispered to Joy.

Probably, she thought. Sure as hell looked like it. But then, she couldn't consider herself a gold expert when she thought of the few pieces she had in her possession.

They finally reached the office door with Oliver Effington's name on it and waited as Audrey gave what Joy thought was a delicate and cutesy knock. "Come in."

Audrey opened the door, and there sat a man who they presumed was Oliver Effington. He looked to be in his midsixties and was tall—over six feet. Bald-headed with a little fuzz around the sides and back. Unlike the friendly smile they'd gotten from his wife, his face indicated that although he'd agreed to meet with them, he was doing it grudgingly.

He stood when they walked into the office. "Thanks, Audrey. We should be able to leave in ten minutes." Joy wondered if that was her and Sanchez's hint he intended for their interview to be short.

"I hope so, sweetheart," Audrey said. She then leaned up and kissed him on the cheek. After smiling at them again, Audrey gracefully walked out the door.

"Isn't she beautiful?" he asked, not taking his eyes off the door his wife had just exited through.

"Yes," Joy said when it appeared Sanchez didn't intend to comment.

Oliver Effington then looked at them. "Care to have a seat?"

"No, we'll stand for the next ten minutes," Sanchez said sarcastically, which seemed to go over Effington's head.

"I hope you don't mind if I sit," Effington said. "I just got back from a taxing business trip."

Joy and Sanchez exchanged glances, reading each other's mind. How friggin' taxing could attending anything in the Bahamas be? "No, we don't mind. Please sit down, Mr. Effington."

"Thanks. When Cathy called and told me you were here about that woman, I looked the newspaper article up on internet. If what you guys think happened to her is true, then that's a shame. A doggone shame."

"So you saw her photo?" Joy asked, taking out her notepad and noticing Sanchez doing the same. He would get whatever information she might miss.

"Yes."

"Did you recognize her?"

He shook his head. "No, not at all. I personally interview all our surrogates, and she was not one of them."

"So where do you think she came from since all five agencies we talked with are saying the same thing? They're all claiming she's not one of theirs."

He tossed an ink pen on his desk. "And you're sure Epinnine was in her system? You sure that possibly a mistake wasn't made?"

Joy thought of Dr. Lennox Roswell and how sharp

she'd proved herself to be as a medical examiner. "We're positive. It's no mistake."

"Then like I said, that's a shame."

"How many surrogates are associated with this agency, Mr. Effington?" Joy asked.

"Hard to say," he said, checking his watch, making them feel as if they were infringing on his time. "Probably close to two hundred. Not all active at the same time, of course, and many are only a surrogate once."

"That many? And you think you can remember each and every one of them?" Joy asked. She found that hard to believe.

He glanced up at her. "Yes. Like I said. Each one is interviewed by me personally. Our clients expect the best, and I intend to make sure they get it."

"By giving each surrogate your stamp of approval?"

"Yes."

Joy nodded. "And how does that work?"

He frowned, confused. "How does what work?"

"Your stamp of approval. What do you look for? What could make or break a surrogate…in your eyes?"

Oliver Effington leaned back in his chair. "For one thing, we don't use women who are only doing it for monetary gain."

Since Joy knew payment could be a powerful incentive, considering how much a surrogate could make, she asked, "Then why are most of them doing it? Specifically, the ones who are considered your regulars? Those who act as surrogates more than once?"

He paused, clearly getting ready for a lecture. "Mainly because they want to help others who love children as much as they do, but who are unable to bring them into the world. They want to give couples unable to conceive beautiful creations."

"What else do you look for in a surrogate?" Sanchez asked.

"Her health and lifestyle." He looked at his watch again. "You wanted to know if I recognized the woman whose picture was in the paper. Well, I don't."

"Did you study the photograph? Maybe you need to take a look at our photo in case the one you saw on the internet wasn't as clear." Not waiting for him to say yea or nay, Joy opened the folder in her hand.

Instead of glancing at the folder, he looked at her with an annoyed expression on his face. "There's no need, I saw it already in the newspaper. I didn't miss a single detail."

"You didn't?"

"No. Not the mole on her face or her freckles, or even her golden-blond hair."

Joy didn't say anything as she and Sanchez exchanged a quick look. Effington was too busy rechecking his watch to notice. He looked back at them expectantly. "Is there anything else? It is getting late."

"That's all. We don't want you to keep your wife waiting," Sanchez said, closing his notepad. "We appreciate you taking the time to meet with us tonight."

"No problem."

Joy and Sanchez walked out of his office, saying good-night to Audrey, who was watering a few of the plants. They didn't exchange any conversation on their ride down the elevator. Nor did they speak while walking through the parking garage back to the cruiser.

Only when they got inside the car and closed the doors did Joy say, "So, Juan, what do you think?"

Sanchez smiled as he turned the key in the ignition. "Golden-blond hair? That's an interesting detail to get from a black-and-white police artist sketch we ran in the paper. Sounds like he knew Mandy Clay or had seen her before. What do you think?"

Joy nodded. "I'm thinking the same thing. Definitely worth checking out."

"I agree."

Sanchez turned the corner to head back toward police headquarters. "Do you want to grab something to eat?" he asked her.

"No, I'm fine. When we get back to headquarters, I plan on getting into my car and heading home. I'll pick something up on the way. Glad it's Friday. I am so ready for the weekend."

Joy wasn't sure why when she didn't have anything planned. When Stonewall had left her place this morning, other than kissing her goodbye, he hadn't mentioned when they would be seeing each other again. But then, what did she expect? She'd made it clear she didn't want him to think he could start invading her space.

"I know what you mean," Sanchez said. "I'm ready for the weekend, as well."

"Damn, Whit, I know how you must feel. I can't imagine Joy Ingram, or any woman for that matter, as my boss. I'm glad I took that job in Ohio when I did." Darrin took a sip of his coffee, then added, "But then, I doubt she would have gotten that promotion over me."

"Probably not," Whitman Snow said, shaking his head. "It's a damn shame."

"I bet you her dad had something to do with it. Ever since the last president handpicked him for that special crime task force, she's been moving up. Joy Ingram has been using that to get ahead."

"I'll admit she's been doing a good job since she's been hired, but that's beside the point," Whitman said.

"Damn right. And I don't think she's done such a great job. Nothing any of us couldn't do if given the opportunity. Harkins proved just how biased he was when he picked her to be on the Erickson case. That put her out there, front and center, so the mayor could see her."

"You think so?"

"Hell yeah, I think so. And if I were you guys I wouldn't stand for it. You gotta oust her."

"Oust her? I wouldn't go that far."

"And why not? Just think about it. She doesn't have a life since all she does is hang around headquarters all the time, working homicides and trying to make others look bad. I asked her out a couple of times, and she turned me down. What woman does that? Hell, I even asked her out yesterday when I dropped by to see you guys and she turned me down then, too. Said she had plans. Yeah. Right. No way she has a boyfriend, working the crazy hours she does. What intelligent man would put up with such foolishness? She's gotten brownie points by working her ass off for show. Now she will expect all of you to do the same."

"You think so?"

"Hell yeah, Whit. She doesn't have a life. She doesn't have a man. She has nothing but a promotion that she will use to drive all of you to become workaholics like her. If I were you, I would get with the other guys and put a stop to her."

"Oh, damn, don't look now, Darrin, but Lieutenant Ingram just walked in. I even hate referring to her as a lieutenant."

"She's here? Good. I intend to confront her about her promotion and what she did to get it."

"Hey, wait a minute, Darrin. You've relocated to Ohio. You don't have to work with her. I do. Don't do anything that might get me fired."

"Just sit there and don't say a thing, and then there's nothing she can do to you. There's certainly not a damn thing she can do to me. Just let me handle this."

IT TOOK ALL Stonewall's will to hold his anger in check. He'd heard everything the two men, Whit and Darrin, had said about Joy. Every single word. And it had been uncalled for, unwarranted and asinine. And for this Darrin asshole to suggest that the people who would be reporting to Joy should make things difficult for her was just plain wrong and unethical.

And what did they just say? Joy was here? She'd just walked into Shady Reds? He was sitting at a booth with his back to the entrance so he couldn't see her. Nor would she be able to see him unless he stood up. He wondered what the two assholes planned to do. He intended to sit right there and find out.

JOY RELEASED A frustrated breath when she saw Whitman Snow. And he was sitting with Darrin, of all people. There was no doubt in her mind that Whit had told

Darrin about her promotion. She would have pretended she hadn't seen them if she hadn't looked directly in Darrin's face. She acknowledged both men with a nod but had no intention of engaging in conversation with them. She would place her to-go order and leave. But now Darrin was beckoning her over to where they sat, and it would be rude of her to ignore them now.

Sighing deeply, she walked over to them. "Hi, guys."

"Hi, Lieutenant," Whitman said with what Joy thought was a nervous smile. At least he'd given her respect as his superior.

"I understand congratulations are in order," Darrin said with a smile that didn't quite reach his eyes. Joy wasn't surprised.

"Thanks, Darrin."

"I just hope you begin chilling for a while and not expecting the people you'll be over not to have a life just because you don't."

Joy told herself to take what he'd said with a grain of salt. After all, this was Darrin Chadwick, who had gotten the Asshole of the Year Award many times over. But she was sick and tired of men like Darrin, and even Whit, for that matter, thinking they knew everything about her when they truly didn't know a damn thing.

"Sorry if you think I don't have a life, Darrin, because I do."

"Could have fooled me."

She bit back saying, *Fooling you wouldn't be hard to do since you're such a nitwit.* Instead she said. "Sorry if you, or anyone—" she added for Whit's benefit "—presumes to know everything there is to know about me."

"I know you don't have a man in your life and probably won't ever have one at the rate you're going. I've even asked you out, and you were too busy for me."

Joy fought back a laugh. She could not believe they were having this conversation and in front of Whit. She decided to end it now before she said something she would regret later. Then she thought, what the hell, why not? Darrin had rubbed her the wrong way and unfortunately for him, it was on the wrong day.

"Being busy had nothing to do with me not going out with you, Darrin. Now if you guys will excuse me, I—"

"Too bad. I was the best you'll ever be able to do," Darrin interrupted snidely.

The laugh Joy tried fighting back earlier came out in a derisive chuckle. "I don't think so."

"And I just happen to know so."

Joy jerked around, recognizing that deep and husky voice. Stonewall.

CHAPTER TWENTY-THREE

JOY COULDN'T BELIEVE Stonewall was standing right there beside her. Where had he come from? How much had he heard? For him to have said what he had, he must have heard enough of it.

Before she could ask him anything, he leaned in, placed his hand around her waist, brushed a kiss across her lips and said, "I thought you would never get here, baby. I've been waiting patiently, but the wait was worth it."

And while her mind was reeling from his words, he looked at both Whit and Darrin and proceeded to introduce himself. "I'm Stonewall Courson. The man in Joy's life."

"Uh, nice meeting you," Whit said, extending his hand.

Stonewall didn't bother taking it. Instead he shifted his gaze back to her and said, "While sitting here waiting for you, I was amazed how conversations carry in this place. You'd be surprised what you can hear, and I've heard enough craziness for tonight. Let's get out of here."

Joy couldn't do anything but nod. Stonewall was playacting because of what he'd obviously heard Darrin say, but she was wondering why his last comments had made a remorseful look appear on Whit's face. Darrin was glaring at Stonewall but otherwise remained tight-lipped. She couldn't blame him too much. Stonewall was taller, more muscular and had a look on his face that all but dared Darrin to open his mouth. "Okay, Stonewall, let's go somewhere else."

"Come on, then," Stonewall said, taking her hand.

She turned to Whit and Darrin, smiled brightly and said, "Have a nice weekend, guys."

Stonewall then led her out of the restaurant.

STONEWALL HELD TIGHT to Joy's hand, loving the feel of it encompassed in his. She wasn't saying anything, and neither was he. Was she upset by what he'd done back there in Shady Reds? If she was, then that was too damn bad. He'd heard enough. And then when that Darrin guy, who evidently thought his shit glistened in gold, had the damn audacity to say that his ass was the best Joy could do, Stonewall couldn't help himself. He didn't give a damn that both men were law enforcement. They were jerks. Bastards. Lowlifes. Any man who would plot someone else's downfall, especially a woman's, didn't deserve to be called a man. He certainly didn't deserve a fucking handshake. And that meant neither of them, although the one named Darrin had done all the talking. But since that Whit guy hadn't put a stop to Darrin's BS, he was just as guilty.

He drew in a deep breath as they continued walking through the parking lot and he still held tight to Joy's hand. It had gotten dark. The night smelled of rain, but it was Joy's scent that filled his nostrils. And why did it seem her steps were perfectly in sync with his?

"Where are we going?" she finally asked, breaking into the night's quietness. Their quietness.

"I'm walking you to your car."

She stopped walking and so did he. He looked down at her and saw the small smile that touched her lips. "You don't know my car, Stonewall. I got assigned a different one today. It came with the promotion. And you also don't know where I'm parked."

He released a deep breath. She was right about both things. "Okay, show me where you're parked, then."

She shook her head. "If you think you're going to get rid of me that easily without telling me what happened back there, then—"

"What happened back there was that those two men came close to getting their asses kicked."

She didn't say anything for a moment, and he was glad. He needed to get his anger under control. When he thought of everything they'd said while he'd sat there and eavesdropped, he had a mind to—

"Darrin is an ass," she interrupted his thoughts to say.

"You don't think I've figured that out? Before you arrived they'd been there a good thirty minutes, plotting your downfall. At least, that Darrin guy was giving good ole Whit ideas. Whit didn't agree to anything, but a real man would have told Darrin to shut the fuck up."

She shrugged. "It doesn't matter. Darrin works in Ohio now, and I can handle Whit. He only becomes an ass around Darrin."

Stonewall's nostrils flared. "Well, at least they think you have a man."

Joy chuckled. "Yes, they do."

The sound of her amusement deflated his anger somewhat. Not a lot but some. "I hope you didn't mind my interference. But I couldn't help myself."

She nodded as they began walking. He was still holding her hand, but he was letting her lead the way. "Considering what Darrin was saying at the time, I understand. He thinks a lot of himself," she said.

"Obviously. I don't blame you for never going out with him." But on the other hand, Stonewall could certainly understand the jerk wanting to go out with her.

"He isn't my type."

That made him ask, "Am I your type?"

She released another chuckle. "Trust me. If you hadn't been my type, we would never have gone out on a date." She stopped in front of a Chevy Malibu. "This is my new ride."

It wasn't all that new, but it was a newer model than the one she had the last time he'd walked her to her unmarked police car. Hard to believe it had been six months ago. "So what do you plan to eat tonight?"

She shrugged. "Not sure. All I know is that I didn't want to say inside there any longer."

"I understand." Seeing her, standing in front of her now, made him own up to just how much he'd missed her. How was that possible when he had just seen her this morning? She had awakened in his arms. Shared a shower with him. Walked him to the door and then plastered a kiss on him that still made his toes tingle. When he'd left she'd not given him any idea of when she would see him again. Only that when would be on her terms.

He had thought about her a lot today. But then, it had

been that way since meeting her. And now that he'd slept with her, had been inside her body, had tasted her inside and out, she was becoming an addiction he didn't need. One he didn't want. But it might be too late to do anything about that now.

"Well, thanks for walking me to my car, Stonewall."

"Anytime." And then, because he wasn't ready for her to go yet, he said, "I've got an idea."

She lifted a brow. "About what?"

"Food. Follow me home and I'll fix you something."

She stared up at him as if considering his offer. His heart began beating faster. Joy was an intelligent woman, and there was no doubt in his mind that she knew that he wanted to do more than fix dinner for her.

Even now, just standing here in the parking lot beside her car, there were sparks going off between them that neither could ignore. "And just to be clear, Joy, I won't be invading your space. I'm letting you invade mine."

She drew in a deep breath and nodded. "Okay, I'll let you feed me. What's on the menu?"

"It's a—"

"—surprise. Right." She smiled and looked down at her hand, the one he was still holding. Then she glanced back up at him. "You know how much I dislike surprises. But…"

"But what?" he asked in a low tone.

"So far none of your surprises have disappointed me."

A smile curved his lips as he pulled her closer. "And I intend for it to always be that way."

He then lowered his mouth to hers to share the kiss he'd desperately wanted since seeing her tonight. The

moment his tongue touched hers, a deep throb erupted
in the pit of his stomach while at the same moment, an
intense flare of heat shot straight to his loins. No other
woman could make him want her so quickly. Desire was
clawing inside him, and he was aware of her in every
cell of his body. Tasting her was always something he
looked forward to, but it was becoming more than that.
It was becoming a need. He didn't like the thought of
that. The only thing he needed was his freedom and to
live a life that made him happy on his terms. A life in
which he appreciated each single day and didn't worry
about tomorrow because it wasn't promised.

When he broke off the kiss, he drew in a deep breath.
It took him a while to get his bearings. The woman was
too damn luscious for her own good. "Do you want to
leave your car here and ride with me?"

"No. I'll follow you," she said softly.

"Okay." He couldn't help the way his pulse was
thumping in anticipation. He would make sure this night
was one she'd always remember.

"WHAT DO YOU MEAN, you might have given something
away?"

Oliver Effington drew in a deep frustrated breath.
"Damn, Anderson, you don't have to yell. What I mean
is that I let it slip I knew Mandy Clay had golden-blond
hair. All I could think of while talking about her was
the first time I saw her, that night she'd been brought
to the holding compound. All that beautiful blond hair.
It was only later I remembered the picture in the paper
was a sketch, not a photo."

"Well, you better hope they overlooked what you said."

"I hope so. Audrey is wondering why I'm so upset about the police visit. Of course I made it seem like it was because of what happened to that poor innocent girl, playing on her sympathy. If she knew I had anything to do with—"

"She won't know if you don't tell her. Your wife has such a bleeding heart. She'd probably go straight to the police and turn you in."

Oliver didn't think she would go that far, but Anderson was right. His wife was too softhearted and doted on the surrogates. Considered them family. She would have convulsions if she ever found out there were surrogates she didn't know about. Surrogates being forced to have babies against their will. "What about Dr. Langley?" he decided to ask.

"Like I told you, she's being taken care of."

"I hope nothing is linked back to us. She does recommend clients to my agency."

"As well as all the other surrogate agencies in town. Relax. There won't be any reason for the cops to get suspicious of anything. The person I hired is a pro," Anderson said. "The plan is already in place."

Oliver stood when he heard the sound of Audrey turning off the water in the shower. "I hope so. We don't need any slipups." He didn't want to think that he might have made a major one tonight.

CHAPTER TWENTY-FOUR

"NICE PLACE, STONEWALL." Joy took in the modern furnishings with several pieces of curvature art around the room. The walls were brick and the high ceiling was flanked by several dark oak beams. To her the beams offset the wooden floor below that was done in a golden pecan.

He lived in what used to be a warehouse, one that had been transformed into three separate living quarters. They'd parked on the side of the street, and on the walk to the private elevator, he'd told her that he'd bought the entire warehouse a few years ago. Over time he had renovated it and kept the entire space on the third floor but leased out the first and second floors.

Stonewall told her he rarely saw his tenants, and they rarely saw him. That's the way he wanted it. A single woman lived on the first floor and a married couple on the second. He thought purchasing the warehouse had been a good investment and didn't regret doing so. In fact, he shared that he also had rental property in Magnolia Oaks, the area where his grandmother lived.

"Make yourself at home, and before you ask, the answer is no. None of what you see reflects any decorating ideas of mine. I hired someone to do it for me."

"Well, she did a nice job," Joy said, easing her Glock

from the waistband of her slacks and placing it on a nearby table.

One wall in his home was completely glass and showed downtown Charlottesville. She could see plenty of businesses with their blinking signs. Because of the wide window, she bet during the day the entire room was filled with sunlight. "This place would spoil me," she said.

"How so?" he asked, moving around the room and turning on several lamps.

"It's feels so welcoming and relaxing."

"So is your home. It has a vintage charm about it. We have different tastes in style, but we both managed to make our homes comfortable for ourselves."

"That's true," she said, smiling over at him and thinking just how good he looked tonight in a pair of khakis and T-shirt. "You need help with anything?"

"No. While I'm in the kitchen, I invite you to look around."

"Thanks. Don't mind if I do."

"What about something to drink?" he asked, heading for the kitchen. His house was laid out in an open concept so she could see straight to the kitchen from his living room. There was huge eat-in area in between.

"No, I'm okay." Already she was moving away from the living room area toward the rooms on the other side. The first one she came to was a room where she figured he spent a lot of his time. What looked to be an eighty-inch flat screen hung on one of the walls and a desk with a small laptop faced another. There was a comfy-looking long sofa that was perfect to accommodate the length of his frame. Instead of a coffee table, in front of the sofa was a huge wooden trunk.

She moved into the room to study a huge framed photograph that hung on the wall. It was that of a group of men at a wedding, and the groom in the center was Sheppard Granger.

"I know you said that you didn't want anything to drink, but I wanted you to taste this."

She turned as Stonewall entered the room carrying a glass of something that looked like iced tea. "What is it?"

"Granny Kay's apple cider."

He handed the glass to her, and she took a sip. It was delicious. She took another sip. "This is good, Stonewall. I like it."

A smile tilted his lips. "Most people do. Whenever she makes it, she gives me my own pitcher."

"Aren't you lucky?" she said, taking another sip. She then turned back to the picture she'd been looking at when he'd entered the room. "I take it this is Sheppard Granger's wedding day."

"Yes."

"There are a lot of groomsmen."

Stonewall had come to stand beside her. As usual, heat was emitting from him to her. "No, all of us were his best men. A little over twenty of us, including his sons."

"That's a lot."

"Yes, and all the men whose lives Shep turned around at Glenworth and Delvers. A lot us went back to school to get college degrees, and others have become business owners. We have a couple who have even ventured into politics."

Joy took another sip of her cider. She had learned that Sheppard Granger had been transferred to Delvers, a prison that housed less-serious offenders, after ten years at Glenworth. While at Delvers he'd worked closely with the warden to ensure that the less-serious offenders didn't become serious offenders in the future. "It's amazing how one man could turn so many people's lives around. I saw him on a few of the talk shows he went on after his release. As a member of law enforcement, I agree with what he says about needing to overhaul the criminal justice system."

"So do I. And Shep's an amazing man. He touched a lot of people's lives while confined. He gave us a reason to hope. To believe we were better than where we were."

He checked his watch. "Go ahead and finish your tour of the place while I get the grill started."

"Grill?"

"Yes." Without saying anything else, he walked out, leaving her alone again.

Joy went back into the hallway that connected to two bedrooms with a Jack and Jill bath she figured were for guests. At the end of the hall was a larger bedroom where she figured he slept.

And where she would be sleeping tonight.

There was no doubt in her mind that Stonewall's invite to dinner was also an invite to spend the night. She'd had no qualms about accepting both. The sexual chemistry between them was stronger tonight than ever.

She glanced into his bedroom. It was huge. Nice furnishings that included a king-size bed and decor in colors of black and chocolate brown. From the doorway she could see into his huge master bath, but her gaze wandered back to the bed. It was made up and neat as a pin with a masculine look. There was no doubt she wouldn't be the first woman to spend the night in that bed and she wouldn't be the last. She pushed the thought to the back of her mind. What he did in that bed and with whom were not her concerns and she didn't intend to make them hers.

She liked his home. It wasn't too big and it wasn't too small. It was just the right size and fit for him. A she headed back toward the front, she could imagine him on one of his off days, lounging around the house, shirt-less, in his bare feet and wearing a pair of shorts while sipping a beer. That definitely made for a sexy fantasy.

She followed the scent of grilling meat and for the first time noticed the terrace off the kitchen. She walked through the double French doors to find him manning the grill. "It's nice out here," she said, looking around and drawing in a deep breath of the night air.

"I think so, too," he said, turning a huge steak on the grill. "I had planned to grill tomorrow, so you're in luck that I had the meat marinating."

She chuckled. "Lucky me. Do you need help with anything?"

"No. Potatoes are done, and I've made a salad."

She raised a brow. "Boy, you're fast."

He glanced over at her, and she felt the heat of his gaze as it trailed over her. "Depends on what I'm doing."

And with whom, she thought. Instead of speaking those thoughts aloud, she said, "Mind if I sit over here and watch you?"

"No, not at all. Help yourself. And you can tell me how your first day as lieutenant went."

Joy eased into one of the patio chairs and found it to be very comfortable. From where she sat, she could see many buildings in historic downtown.

"Do you come out here often? To sit?"

"Yes. Practically every night I'm here. No matter the temperature. This terrace was one of the main things that sold me on the idea of buying this place."

"What were the others?"

"Its proximity to the historic district. I love it there with the brick streets and sidewalks, the quaint shops and the old-fashioned light posts. I've got a good view from here."

"I can't help but notice." She took another sip of her cider. "The chief had already made the announcement about my promotion before I arrived, so today was rather interesting. But I'll survive."

"You'll do more than survive. You'll be the best police lieutenant this city has ever had. I'm counting on you, and I know you won't let me down."

She chuckled. It felt good to know someone believed in her abilities. "Thanks. I'll have to become a jack-of-all-trades to handle my cases as well as supervising other detectives."

"How do you feel about doing that?" he asked, then sipped his beer from the bottle.

She shrugged. "It's all part of my job now and I enjoy what I do, so I think things will go great."

"I understand that case you're working—the one involving the woman found frozen—now involves a celebrity's sister."

"It does. Jane Doe has been identified as Mandy Clay. Sister of reality TV star Sunnie Clay. I'm getting bad vibes with this case. Of the five surrogate agencies in the city, none of them claim to have known Mandy Clay."

"There's always a possibility she worked privately for someone."

"Yes, that's a possibility. If it was legal, then why doesn't the doctor who prescribed her the drug Epinnine come forward? Unless something about her surrogacy wasn't on the up and up." She drew in a deep breath, deciding not to overthink anything. Especially not tonight. And definitely not now. She didn't even want to consider what Oliver Effington's blunder tonight could mean.

She blinked when Stonewall came and sat in the chair opposite her. "You were in deep thought," he said.

She smiled. "Just for a minute."

Suddenly the sound of Ray Charles came through the speakers. She glanced around. When she looked back over at Stonewall, he held up a remote and said, "You use yours to start your fireplace, and I use mine to control my music."

"Gadgetry. Whatever works."

"At the moment, you're working for me, Joy, and that's no gadgetry."

"Then what is it?"

He smiled. "The absolute truth."

STONEWALL TOOK ANOTHER sip of his beer as he watched Joy. He wouldn't deny the fact that he'd brought other women here to his home, but he would deny ever having them get next to him on the same level that Joy did. He couldn't recall them getting to him on any level other than the bedroom. Even that couldn't compare to her. The thought of her waking up in his bed sent a hard humming of lust through his veins.

"The meat smells good," she said, breaking into his thoughts.

"Wait until you taste it." He wondered why every word spoken between them made him think of the hot, rolling-in-the-sheets kind of sex. Especially when his head was between her legs. He shifted in his chair when his erection pressed hard against his zipper.

"So why where you at Shady Reds?"

"Quasar and I went there for dinner. Striker joined us. He came back from his honeymoon yesterday."

She nodded. "And then they left you there, or did they overhear Darrin and Whit's conversation, as well?"

He took a sip of his beer and then said, "They'd left. Striker was in a rush to get home to Margo, and Quasar needed to leave since Randi was coming in for the weekend. According to Quasar, Randi plans to stay through Monday to meet with the FBI. Specifically, Special Agent Felton. I think they might want her help after she helped solve the Erickson case."

Joy grunted. "Agent Felton was the man who gave Randi a hard time when she was using her psychic powers to assist law enforcement to find that assassin. He tried belittling her every chance he got. I was there. I know."

"Well, I guess now he sees things differently since she helped solve the Erickson's case...except that one small piece as to who killed him. The Feds still don't have a clue, and they're hoping Randi can help."

"So they won't continue to look incompetent."

"Umm, do I detect no love lost between the two agencies?"

She rolled her eyes. "Let's just say they have a tendency to try stepping on our toes, and we manage to step back."

Stonewall stood. "Well, I hope Randi is able to help. Although some might feel that he did the city a favor by killing Erickson, it should still bother everyone that a killer is still out there."

He walked back over to the grill to check on the meat. He smiled over at her and said, "Looks like it's ready."

DR. KELLY LANGLEY looked up from the papers on her desk when she heard a sound outside her office door. She listened carefully for a minute, but when she didn't hear the noise again, she figured she must have imagined it. That was one of the reasons she hated being at her office late and alone. All the other physicians occupying space in the complex had the good sense to go home at a reasonable hour. Yet she was still here and would remain here until she received Anderson's call.

She got up and went over to the side table to pour another cup of coffee. Instead of shredding those files like Anderson had told her to do, she had taken them to her brother's place. They would be safe there since Barron wasn't due back in the country for another six months or so. She just didn't feel right about destroying them. What if Anderson's plan to protect her didn't work? At least with those files she could prove whatever part she played in all this didn't include murder.

She heard another sound. Since the pharmacy was also located on her floor, she wondered if perhaps Walter Fowler, the pharmacist, was working late.

She opened the door to the lobby area. After unlocking the main door, she opened it. Then, out of nowhere, a figure appeared directly in front of her. It took a second to see the person was dressed in all black and wearing a face mask. She was about to scream when his words stopped her. "Anderson sends his love."

The last thing she felt was pain.

JOY LEANED BACK in her chair and licked her lips. "That steak was prepared just the way I like it, Stonewall. Not too done and not too raw. You grilled it just right."

"Thanks. I'm glad you enjoyed it."

"I did." And she wasn't just giving him lip service. The steak—the entire meal, for that matter—had been delicious. She felt stuffed. Glancing over at him, she saw he was staring at her with dark, sexy eyes. "I noticed you didn't eat a lot." He'd given her the bigger portion of the meat and ate only half a baked potato and a small salad.

"I'd eaten a big meal at Shady Reds. My intent was to make sure you were fed."

"Why?" Not that she had to ask, but she wanted him to tell her anyway. She hadn't missed the way he'd been looking at her, trailing his gaze over her, as if taking in every single detail. Nothing eye-catching about her outfit—a pair of dark brown slacks, a beige cotton blouse and loafers on her feet. As usual, she'd pulled her hair back into a ponytail, so there was nothing that would be a turn-on about that. Although she wasn't wearing much makeup, she simply refused to leave the house without any. Call her vain. She didn't care.

"I want to make sure you have strength for later."

She smiled. "Need help with the dishes?"

"We can do them later."

She chuckled. "Oh, I get it. Now I understand why you said I would need my strength later. It's for the dishes."

"If that's what you think, then you're way off base."

"Am I?"

"Definitely."

He reached across the table and traced the back of her hand with the tip of his finger. The touch had such an arousing effect. "I've missed you," he said in a deep, husky voice that was full of heated desire. So much she was able to feel it.

"You saw me this morning." She added, "You had me this morning."

The smile that touched his lips had her pressing her thighs together. "Didn't get enough."

"Greedy ass."

"Yeah." He chuckled. "That's me. You shouldn't be so irresistible, sweetheart."

"Am I?"

"With every bone in your body."

His finger continued to softly stroke across her hand while his gaze locked on hers. His jaw suddenly flexed, and her nipples hardened in response. "You make it hard for a girl to say no."

"Were you planning to?" he asked in a voice low and raspy.

Planning to say no? Not hardly. "No. I was not going to tell you no," she said honestly. "I came here tonight for more than food, Stonewall."

The movement of his fingers on her hand stopped. As she watched he slowly stood and came around the table to where she sat. He offered her his hand and she took it. And then his phone rang.

He didn't answer it. Instead he pulled her to her feet. The phone stopped ringing and he lowered his mouth to hers. Their mouths meshed easily, deeply, and the minute she parted her lips he slid his tongue between them. She tasted the flavor of him, one she'd thought about most of the day. And when he tightened his hold on her, she held on while he took the kiss to another level.

And then his phone rang again.

Stonewall broke off the kiss, frowning. "There better be a good reason for Roland calling me since I'm on paid leave."

He pulled his phone out his pocket at the same time her own phone began ringing. While he talked to Roland, she moved quickly to where she'd left her purse in the living room. "Detective Ingram."

"It's Lieutenant Ingram now."

She heard the chuckle and recognized the voice. "Duly noted, Detective Acklin. What's up?" James Acklin had joined the department a year after she had, and she'd always liked him. Down-to-earth and outright witty at times, he was a good detective and had been one of the first to congratulate her today on her promotion.

"Seems the natives have been restless tonight, Lieutenant. Two pharmacy break-ins. Unfortunately, a pharmacist at a second location was working late. Apparently he surprised the intruder and they knocked him off before grabbing the drugs. And it seems a doctor whose practice is located in the building was working late, heard the commotion and came to investigate."

"Good. We can interview him and—"

"It's not a he, but a she. And it's not good. The intruders took her out, as well."

"Damn."

"I know. Gunshots. Both of them. Dead. You want me to call in Sanchez?"

Joy remembered Sanchez's plans for the evening. She could substitute him with Whit, but she wouldn't. She needed to have a talk with Whit on Monday before giving him any new assignments. "No, don't call Sanchez."

She glanced over at Stonewall. He was no longer talking on the phone but was leaning against the kitchen counter, looking at her. She had a feeling he knew she would be leaving. She broke eye contact with him and said to Detective Acklin, "Give me your location. Preserve the crime scene. I'm on the way."

Moments later she hung up the phone and returned to where Stonewall stood. "Sorry, but I have to leave."

He nodded. "And that was Roland. He wanted me to know that Sheppard rushed Carson to the hospital. She's in labor."

A smile touched Joy's lips. "That's wonderful."

"Yes, it is."

Joy glanced at her watch. "Thanks again for dinner, but I have to go."

"Okay."

He didn't sound like he regretted her leaving. Totally different from Omar. Whenever she got such a call he would pitch a fit and then sulk for days. "Thanks for your understanding."

"You don't have to thank me. You have a job to do."

She nodded. "Rain check?"

"Whenever you want one, sweetheart. You're the one with the relationship issues."

"Yes, but you know the reason, Stonewall."

He came to stand in front of her. Reached out and caressed the side of her face. "Yes, but I'm not your ex-fiancé, Joy."

"I never said you were. I'm just not ready to get seriously involved with anyone."

"I know. You told me."

Then why was she repeating it? Or feeling the need to? She didn't say anything for a moment, not liking the fact that even with the words he'd just said, he didn't look annoyed and she was the one feeling agitated. Could anyone be that cool? "Look, I'll call you," she said, quickly heading for the door, and then stopping to grab her Glock.

"Wait up. I'm walking you out."

"You don't have to do that."

"Yes, I do," he said upon reaching her.

It was something about the look in his eyes that told her it was part of his makeup to protect, even if she felt she of all people didn't need protecting. Taking her hand in his, he walked her out to her car. There was just something about him walking beside her, holding her hand, emitting his warmth that felt comforting.

When they reached her car, she said, "Thanks for walking me out."

"You don't have to thank me."

Maybe not, but she'd wanted to anyway. They both remained silent, and then he reached out and pushed her hair out of her face. Then he brushed a thumb over her cheek and said, "Stay safe."

She nodded. "I will." She felt a rush of heat flash through her and she tried forcing it away. She had to return to cop mode. No help for it. But when he leaned down and captured her lips, she felt even more heat, and while their mouths mated she went from cop mode to woman mode. Just that easily and just that quickly.

Ending the kiss, he took a step back and shoved his hands into his pockets. She opened the car door, got inside and snapped her seat belt. Without looking back she drove off.

ANDERSON GOT THE call he'd been waiting for. "It's been taken care of," the deep male voice said.

He nodded, feeling relieved. "And you're sure the police won't make connections."

"No way that they can. We hit another pharmacy tonight to make them seem like random robberies. We lucked up when there was some guy working late in the pharmacy. Unfortunately he was in the wrong place at the wrong time. We took him out, as well. No one will ever figure out the intended hit was Dr. Langley."

"For your sake you better hope not."

"Trust me, they won't. I've been doing this a long time."

Anderson drew in a deep breath, feeling assured somewhat. "Did you give her my message?"

"Yes, I gave it to her. Right before I pulled the trigger. You're one heartless bastard."

Anderson snorted. "It takes one to know one." The people in charge didn't like mistakes. He and Oliver were pulling in a lot of money to make sure things continued to run smoothly. Neither of them could take any chances Kelly Langley would mess things up. It was that simple. "I plan to return to Charlottesville on Wednesday."

Just in case it was discovered that he and Kelly were lovers, Anderson figured he might need an alibi. Making sure he was out of town at the time of her death was his.

"Fine," the voice said. "I'll see you around. Call me if you need me again."

He hoped like hell he didn't.

CHAPTER TWENTY-FIVE

Joy PULLED INTO the medical complex, scanning the parking lot before getting out of her vehicle. First thing she looked for was surveillance cameras, and she saw several. If the intruders had been smart, they would have noticed them, as well. Had they been tampered with? It would make law enforcement's job easier if they hadn't been.

In addition to Acklin's unmarked cruiser, several marked patrol cars were already at the scene. The parking lot was pretty well lit and the complex was on a somewhat busy street facing the library. This was Friday, and the library closed early. It looked deserted with only a few lights shining at the entrance.

On one side of the library was a tennis court and on the other there appeared to be a jogging park. It looked deserted, as well, but then, she couldn't imagine anyone out jogging this time of night. It was close to nine.

After getting out of the car, she leaned back against the door and took stock of the location. During daylight hours this was a busy area of town, but at night, not so much. She glanced toward a traffic light. It was too dark from where she stood to be positive, but she bet it was equipped with a camera, as well. Hell, she hoped so.

With her hands buried deep in the pockets of her slacks,

she headed toward the entrance of the medical building and paused at the information on the huge signage.

PARK RIDGE
MEDICAL COMPLEX
Dr. J. P. Jonas, Orthodontist
Dr. L. K. Vanders, Oncology
Dr. K. Langley, Fertility Specialist
Dr. F. Johnson, Cardiologist
Park Ridge Pharmacy

The complex housed four doctors who treated a number of conditions and a pharmacy. Since all four doctors wrote prescriptions, it would be logical and convenient to have a pharmacy on-site.

"Good evening, Lieutenant."

She glanced around at Sam Henson. He was a uniformed officer and had been for close to twenty years. "Hi, Officer Henson."

"Congratulations on your promotion."

"Thanks." She frowned. "I thought you were going to give up smoking."

He pulled the cigarette from his mouth, tossed it to the pavement and crushed it under his foot. "I tried."

"Try harder. Barbara will appreciate you for it and appreciate me for reminding you." Barbara was his wife. When Joy had gotten hired on and requested to go out on the streets as a cop for a few months, Henson had been her partner. He and his wife Barbara had invited her over to their place a few times, and she didn't know of a nicer couple. They had three daughters and their youngest was in her last year of college. Henson claimed he would think of retirement after that.

"I know. Good woman, that Barbara, even when she tries bossing me around." He looked down at the cigarette he'd just crushed and then back at her with regretful eyes. "The ME is on the way. Crime lab already here."

Joy nodded. "Guess I better go on in."

"Surprised you're here and not one of the others now that you're in charge."

She shrugged. "I figured they all had plans. Besides, I was free tonight."

Joy knew that wasn't true. She knew that if she hadn't gotten Acklin's phone call, she would be naked by now in Stonewall's bed with him thrusting in and out of her. The area between her legs tingled at the thought. How could she think of something like that? And do it now? Easily, because it was the truth and she very well knew it.

Opening the huge glass entry door, she went in. There was that smell. Strong disinfectant. Sterile. Antiseptic. She pulled out her electronic notepad and began typing as she walked down the long corridor. In no time she picked up another scent. Death. The cop in her could pick it up each and every time.

When she rounded the corner, she saw the group of officers. She also saw the victim. Female. Acklin looked up and left the group to walk toward her. "Evening, Lieutenant. This is what we have. The male whose body is in the pharmacy has been identified as Walter Fowler. A pharmacist. Cause of death was gunshot at close range. Same for the female MD here. Looks like she came out of her office to investigate. Surprised the intruder and was shot."

"So, what do we know about this victim?"

"Her name is Dr. Kelly Langley, forty-four, divorced, and apparently working late. They shot her for interrupting the robbery."

Joy nodded. "Fingerprints?"

"Being lifted now."

"Surveillance cameras in the parking lot?" she asked.

"Looks like they were tampered with."

Joy drew in a deep breath. "I'm not surprised. Hitting two pharmacies in one night sounds like a well-orchestrated plan. What about a cleaning crew? Were they not here tonight?"

"Yes. I talked to both of them. They're the ones who found the bodies. They had been working on the other side of the building. Good thing they were. Otherwise we'd possibly have four bodies instead of two."

"Did they hear any shots?"

"Said they didn't."

"Two shots fired and nobody heard anything?" Joy frowned. "That's odd. What about security cameras in the building?"

"They are being checked out, as well."

Joy looked around again. The distance from the pharmacy entrance to where the female physician's body lay was a few feet. Had she heard a ruckus as they assumed and come out of her office to investigate? If she'd heard a gunshot, why not call for help first? Perhaps there was a silencer on the gun?

"How much drugs were taken?" Joy asked.

"It seems as much as their hands could carry."

Joy found that odd, as well. You kill two people for drugs and not clean out the place? She would think they would try to confiscate everything they could. "I need an inventory."

"I'll have it done. I called the owner of the complex."

"Who's that?"

"Dr. Vanders. He's in his office, giving a statement. Pretty shaken up. He was able to call in another pharmacist. That person will be able to take inventory for us. His name is Neal Northern. I told Henson to let him in when he gets here."

"How did the intruder get in?"

"Forced entry. Side door. It was torched open. Same as the other pharmacy."

"Where is that pharmacy located?"

"Five miles from here. Stand-alone mom-and-pop drugstore that's been in the community for years. No prior break-ins. Anything else you want to know?"

Joy shook her head. "No, not now. I want to check things out for myself before talking to Dr. Vanders. Next of kin been notified for the victims?"

"Not, not yet."

The sound of heels tapping against the tiled floor got their attention. Both Joy and Acklin glanced up. The ME had arrived. To Joy's surprise it was Lennox Roswell.

"Be still my heart," she heard Acklin say under his breath.

At least Joy figured it was supposed to be under his breath, but whether he realized it or not, he'd all but breathed the words out in a heated rush. Dr. Roswell was walking down the corridor with a stride that would definitely garner male attention. She looked more like a model than a medical examiner. And who would show up at a crime scene wearing stilettos?

Since Acklin was apparently tongue-tied, Joy said, "You're on duty tonight, Dr. Roswell?"

Dr. Roswell smiled as she placed her black bag aside. "Yes. Nothing better to do."

Joy found that hard to believe. Given how Acklin and a lot of men around headquarters lusted after the woman, Joy would think Dr. Roswell had plenty of dates lined up on a Friday night. "Well, I'm glad you're here. Double homicide."

Dr. Roswell nodded as she took clear gloves out of the pocket of her lab jacket. "Guess I'd better get to work, then."

"Hey, I'm Detective James Acklin. I don't think we've met," he said, offering her his hand.

She gave Acklin a quick smile, accepting his hand. "Oh, hello Detective Acklin. I'm Dr. Lennox Roswell. Nice to meet you."

"The pleasure is mine," Acklin said, smiling all over the place like the kid who'd hit a home run at a baseball game.

Joy was convinced Acklin would have held tight to Dr. Roswell's hand if she hadn't pulled it away. The gesture reminded her of the night she'd met Stonewall and how he'd held her hand hostage. "You're ready to check things out, Dr. Roswell?" Joy asked her.

The woman nodded as she slid the gloves onto her hands. "Yes, I'm ready."

STONEWALL SAW THE crowd of people the moment he stepped off the hospital elevator. He shook his head at the thought that so many were here to await the arrival of one baby. But then, this wasn't just any baby. It was Sheppard Granger's baby.

Everyone turned when they heard his footsteps. "We wondered if you were coming," Striker said, grinning. "I figured if you didn't show it that meant you were ahh...unavailable."

"Whatever," Stonewall said. He greeted everyone— Roland; Sheppard's three sons and their wives; Striker and Margo; Quasar and Randi; Ben and Mona, who were Jace and Dalton's in-laws; and last but not least, Hannah. The older woman had been the Grangers' former housekeeper and nanny but was more like family.

It seemed they were given their own private floor, but when your family had donated this particular wing of the hospital, the Ava Granger Wing, then Stonewall figured you could get anything you wanted.

Glancing around, he said, "I take it Shep's with Carson."

"Yes, Dad's back there with her," Sheppard's oldest son, Jace Granger, said. "It's been a few hours now."

"If you want a cup of coffee, I suggest you get it now before Dalton drinks it all," Caden, Sheppard's middle son, said, grinning.

Stonewall chuckled. "Good idea."

He was about to head over to the coffeepot when a smiling Sheppard emerged through a set of double doors. "It's over. Ava Serena Granger has been born."

Cheers went up and congratulations were given to Shep. "Thanks, everyone. Carson and our daughter are fine. And she's beautiful, just like her mother."

"We thought you and Carson had decided on the name Ashley Jade," Roland said, grinning.

"We had...until we arrived here. Then we decided to name our daughter after our mothers."

"Imagine that. Ava Granger was born in the Ava

Granger wing. Kind of nice," Dalton said, pulling his pregnant wife, Jules, to his side.

"So, are you and Carson going to call her Ava?" Stonewall asked.

"Yes," Sheppard said.

"Call her whatever you like, but I'm going to call her Wild Child," Dalton Granger declared proudly.

Stonewall saw Caden frown at Dalton. "Wonder Woman, Wine Lady, Whirl Wind, Wedded Bliss and now Wild Child. Can you please run out of these ridiculous nicknames?"

Dalton chuckled. "No. Besides, Wild Child fits her."

"Why would you think such a name fits my baby sister?" Jace asked.

A huge grin spread across Dalton's entire features. "Because this has been a wild night. What other baby could get this many people out of their homes on a Friday night just to be here for her birth? Like we don't have anything better to do."

"You probably don't," Jace said to his younger brother.

Stonewall couldn't help but smile. Everyone was used to the three brothers' tit for tat. Roland turned to Sheppard, clasped him on the shoulder and asked, "So, when can I see my goddaughter?"

"You can all see her now."

"Is Carson up to it?" Jace's wife, Shana, asked.

"Yes, she's fine. In fact, when I left she was on the phone talking to her best friend, Roddran. Letting her know our good news."

Stonewall smiled as he followed the crowd. Dalton was right. This was one wild night, and deep down a part of him wished Joy was here to share it with him.

CHAPTER TWENTY-SIX

"GOOD NIGHT, LIEUTENANT. Be careful getting home. There's a fog settling in."

"I will. You, too, Henson."

Joy opened her car door and slid onto the seat. Members of the media were still in the parking lot, but most looked as if they were closing shop and breaking down their equipment. Earlier, the place had been swarming to the point where it looked like opening night for the circus. Several networks were doing on-site live reporting. News reporters had asked questions and plenty of them. She'd given a statement. A robbery gone bad. Innocent lives taken. Case still under investigation.

Before starting the car, she scanned the parking lot and surrounding areas. Yellow crime scene tape had been put up, and a number of uniformed officers had canvassed the area. Since this was a business district there were no residents to be interviewed, just grounds to examine to see if the bastards had dropped or discarded something. Like the murder weapon.

She continued to scan the area. It wasn't unusual for those who committed horrendous crimes to come back and be an onlooker. Damn sickos. Anger always filled her when it came to senseless killings, and these two were as senseless as it got. Two people who contributed to society with their medical knowledge had been gunned down for what? Drugs.

There had been more taken than just the handful Acklin had originally assumed, but even the pharmacist who'd shown up had been perplexed. Some of the drugs that could bring in a pretty penny on the streets had been left behind. It was as if the intruders hadn't been aware of the pot of gold at their fingertips. Why? Amateurs, perhaps? Rookies? She found that hard to believe. The robbery had been too well planned. From the dismantling of the surveillance cameras, to the torching of the entry door in a way not to set off the alarms, to the masks worn to conceal their faces from interior security cameras. Who did all of that without taking at least a garbage bag full of narcotics? Anything less didn't make sense to her.

But then the reason could very well be that killing that pharmacist and doctor had spooked them. Scared them shitless to the point that they took what they'd collected already and hauled ass. The possibility made sense. But still, something about this entire homicide didn't add up. She wasn't sure what. It was just one of those gut feelings she got at times.

She started her car and pulled out of the parking lot. The next of kin had been notified. It was always hard when they arrived. Their lives changed forever in a moment. The pharmacist had been a black male, age thirty-four, married, father of two. They'd had to call rescue for his wife. She'd collapsed right then and there. No one was supposed to have been allowed to enter the crime scene. But the cops hadn't been able to hold her back. The little wisp of a woman had broken through the barrier and raced inside, determined to make liars of the people who'd shown up on her doorstep to say her husband had been killed. When she saw it hadn't been a lie, saw him lying on the cold floor, dead in a pool of blood from a gunshot to his chest, she'd lost it. Joy didn't think she'd ever heard anyone scream so loudly and so tormentedly. The look of anguish on the woman's face had made Joy determined to solve these damn homicides and bring the murderers responsible to justice.

They knew there were two intruders. The inside security camera had picked them up. But because they'd worn hats, masks and gloves, they couldn't even tell from the camera the intruders' gender or race. They'd covered their tracks well. And the security cameras at Skinners Pharmacy five miles away showed the same. The only thing the cops knew for certain was that the same two had hit both places. And without leaving a single clue behind. *Or had they?*

Their only hope was the traffic cam in the intersection Joy first noticed when she arrived.

If they had, she was determined to find it.

The second victim had been a female. Dr. Kelly Langley, Fertility Specialist. Dr. Vanders wasn't sure why she was working late since she usually didn't. Her next of kin was a brother who was presently on assignment in Turkey. He had been notified and was on his way to the States.

Dr. Langley had been a very attractive white female with auburn hair and brown eyes. She was about five-eight and weighed no more than a hundred ten pounds, if that. According to Lennox, like Fowler, Dr. Langley had been shot at close range.

Lennox.

The ME had suggested Joy drop the formalities and

just call her Lennox. Joy didn't have a problem with that and extended the same courtesy. She told Lennox she preferred being called Joy instead of just Ingram. They'd shared a chuckle, knowing it was a woman thing. The two of them would meet Monday morning to go over Lennox's report, as well as those of the officers involved in the investigations of both pharmacies and the medical complex.

Joy tried to do everything to not have her male counterparts notice her looks. Lennox was just the opposite. Beneath her lab coat were short skirts or fitted dresses, and those stilettos hadn't hindered the woman's movements one bit.

Joy had made it to the corner when her thoughts shifted to Stonewall. At that moment, she needed a diversion…and a drink. She had seen two lives snuffed out. Their bodies lying on the floor in pools of blood. Loved ones being told. Pain. Anger. Hurt.

It was after midnight. Around three in the morning. She should go straight home, take a shower and get into bed. It wouldn't be a crime if she decided to sleep all weekend. There was no doubt in her mind Monday would be a doozy, and she definitely needed to be up for it. She might even have to call a news conference before Monday. She would watch the news and gauge the community's reaction.

But at that moment, all she could think about was that she needed a diversion the likes of which only Stonewall Courson could provide. Before she could talk herself out of it, she dialed his number through her car's system, and lush sensations came over her the moment his voice answered.

"Hello."

"You don't sound like I just woke you up."

"You didn't. In fact, I'm just returning home. I've been out."

"Oh." He was just coming in? After she'd left, had he found a willing woman, one with more time on her hands to take out on a date? Was that why it hadn't seemed to bother him when she'd left his place earlier?

As if he'd suspected the questions floating around in her head, he said, "I decided to go to the hospital. The entire gang was there for Carson's delivery."

His definition of *entire gang* meant those she'd been introduced to the night of the charity ball. She'd gotten the chance to meet Roland Summers a couple of months later.

"How's Carson?"

"She and her daughter are doing fine. Shep's ecstatic. They named her Ava Serena."

"I like that. It's a pretty name."

"I think so, too." There was a pause and then he asked, "Where are you?"

"I just left a crime scene in the Park Ridge area. Double homicide. One a pharmacist and the other a fertility specialist. Senseless killings for drugs."

She drew in a deep breath. "I don't want to talk about it anymore."

"What do you want, Joy?"

Joy nibbled at her bottom lip as she came to a traffic light. She knew that she was taking casual sex to a whole new level with Stonewall with this diversion thing, but at the moment her needs were overtaking her common sense. "You. I want you, Stonewall. I want to finish what we started earlier. I need a drink. A glass of wine. Then I need you to make love to me until we both collapse in exhaustion."

"That can be arranged without any problems," he said in a deep, husky voice that sent a rush of heat through her veins.

"You sure?"

"I'm positive."

She nibbled on her lips when her car began moving again. "In that case, I'll see you in a few."

"I'm up…literally. And ready for you," he said.

The thought sent a spark of desire pulsating between her legs.

"Okay."

"Drive carefully."

Joy clicked off the phone and hoped Stonewall knew what he'd agreed to, because she wanted him, and in a bad way.

STONEWALL HEARD JOY'S car the minute it drove up, and he was downstairs at the entry door, waiting. He'd opened it and watched her park her car and get out of it. He noticed how slowly she was walking and figured she didn't need sex to exhaust her. She was already tired. Joy had left his house around nine and now it was close to three in the morning.

When she noticed him, she squared her shoulders as if that would give her more energy. Driven by a need to touch her, give her some of his strength, he moved toward her. As they met he leaned down and kissed her lips. "You're beat."

She nodded. "Long night. Sad night. I need that drink. I need you."

Instead of letting her move another inch, he swept her off her feet, into his arms. "Stonewall, put me down. I can walk."

"I know, but I want to carry you," he said, entering the building and heading straight for the elevator. He maneuvered her in his arms while he pressed the button for his floor. Even in the elevator he refused to place her on her feet. When the elevator opened to his floor, the door was right there. He'd left it open and walked inside, using the heel of his foot to close the door behind them.

He stood her on her feet long enough for her to remove her Glock and place it on the table. Then he swooped her back into his arms again. He kept moving through the kitchen and out onto the terrace. He'd already set a bottle of wine and a glass on the table.

Without loosening his hold on her, he slid into a chair, her in his lap. He then reached out and handed her the glass filled with wine. "Here, take a sip."

She raised a brow. "Where's yours?"

He smiled at her as he fumbled with the band holding her ponytail until it was gone, making her hair tumble around her shoulders. "We'll share."

She didn't say anything, just looked at him, held his gaze while she took a sip. When she licked her lips and handed the glass back to him, he felt a tightening in his groin.

He took a drink, deliberately placing his mouth at the same spot on the glass that she had. He preferred beer to wine, but for some reason, tonight the wine tasted good. After taking another drink, he did the same thing she'd done. Licked his lips. He noticed her gaze holding firm and watching every movement of his tongue.

She whispered, "Take me to bed, Stonewall."

He stood with her in his arms and headed toward his bedroom.

CHAPTER TWENTY-SEVEN

JOY FORCED HER eyes open and squinted against the glare of the sunlight. She closed them and slowly opened them again. Her mind felt fuzzy as she glanced around the bedroom. Not hers—that was for sure. Stonewall's. She shifted in bed only to lie back immediately. She'd gotten just what she'd asked Stonewall for. He'd made love to her until she'd become exhausted. And then some.

She'd forgotten about his stamina. His never-ending energy. His ability to persevere. His unwavering resilience. He'd used all of them on her last night, and now, this morning, all she could do was lie there, still feeling the exhaustion she'd begged him for. He had definitely delivered.

They'd tried so many positions last night she couldn't remember them all, but her body could, which was why she felt so achy. Not sore but achy. There was a difference. Each ache had been brought on by pleasure, pleasure and more pleasure. And it made her forget, for a short while, what had happened at Park Ridge Medical Complex. She was a cop but she was also human.

"You ready for lunch?" Stonewall asked from the doorway.

"Lunch?" She checked the clock on his nightstand. It

was afternoon. It was hard to believe she'd slept away the morning. She rarely slept so late and so soundly.

"Yes," he said. "Now you know how I felt that morning I woke up in your bed and hadn't known when you'd left it. Sometimes exhaustion can get the best of you."

Joy wouldn't deny that. She had needed him to love her into oblivion and he hadn't disappointed.

Glad she was under the covers, Joy pulled herself up in bed and pushed her hair away from her face. "You've been out jogging?"

He was wearing jogging shorts. Or they were wearing him. It was quite obvious from the fit of the shorts that he was a man very well endowed. And he had on a shirt that showed every single muscle of his tight abs.

"This is my usual attire for a Saturday morning when I'm just hanging out here."

"Oh, I see." She was glad to hear that. She could imagine the women who wouldn't hesitate to follow him home if he went out on the streets dressed like that. First and foremost they would be seeking verification that what he was packing was real.

"I am kind of hungry," she admitted.

"I figured you would be."

If he expected her to blush at that comment, he would be disappointed. She'd gotten just what she'd asked for last night. In fact, a few times, she'd been begging.

"You don't have to feed me, Stonewall. It's past lunchtime and I've overstayed my welcome anyway."

"No, you haven't. I don't mind you in my space."

She decided not to go there with him. Not today. "Okay, I'll stay for lunch. What you got?" she decided to ask.

"Chicken salad made by Granny Kay. You'll like it."

"I believe it."

He came into the room, went over to the dresser and pulled out a T-shirt. He placed it on the bed. "This will fit you like a dress."

"Umm, we'll see."

"If you prefer you can wear nothing at all," he said, leaning back against the dresser. At that angle she could see the outline of his engorged penis, bulging against his shorts.

"That's okay. I usually don't walk around in the nude."

"Just so you know, it wouldn't bother me if you did. And I put your things in the laundry room."

"Thanks. You're a real nice guy."

He chuckled. "I try to be. Do you need me to run you some bathwater?"

She shook her head. She'd meant what she'd said. He was a real nice guy. Omar had never pampered her this way. "No, a shower will be okay for me."

"I left you everything you need on the vanity. An unused toiletry kit. I have quite a few of them."

She tilted her head and looked at him. "Have a lot of sleepovers, do you?" The moment she asked, she regretted doing so. His houseguests and their number were not her business.

"No. I have a tendency to collect them whenever I stay at a hotel."

"Oh, I see." Was he going to stand there until she got out of bed? Why was she hesitant about him seeing her naked? It made no sense considering all they'd done last night. And she couldn't forget about yesterday morning and the night before at her place. Being shy of her nakedness was the last thing she should have been. Ignoring the fact he was staring, she eased out of bed. If he was intent on looking, she might as well give him an eyeful.

"It wasn't my intent to brand you."

She lifted a brow, then she followed his gaze and looked down at herself. Passion marks were practically everywhere. On her stomach. Thighs. Chest. She walked over to the mirror and saw a number of them on her neck and shoulders. She tried downplaying the sensations oozing through her at the memory of when each and every one was made. His mouth had practically left no part of her body untouched. The night had started out hot and passionate, and he'd taken her hard and harder. Then he'd gone tender on her. It was as if he'd tried pulling out emotions she usually kept locked inside. Emotions deeply buried. He had somehow managed to uncover them. She glanced back at him.

"No sweat. I'm sure we both did." If she remembered correctly, she'd gone down on him twice, loving the feel of him engorged and erect in her mouth while she…

His phone went off, and she watched him pull it out of his pocket. That drew attention to his crotch. Had seeing all those passion marks on her done that to him? She wasn't blind. It was obvious he'd gotten larger. And why was she standing there staring at it?

"That was Roland."

His words grabbed her attention and she shifted her gaze from the area below his waist up to his face. He was smiling. He'd known what she'd been staring at. "Everything's okay?" she asked.

"Yes. News of your promotion made this morning's paper. He wanted me to congratulate you when I saw you."

She nodded. "And what made him think you'd be seeing me?"

"A hunch. We were seen at the wedding together."

"So now everyone thinks…" She didn't finish because she knew she didn't have to.

"Yes, they probably do. My close friends know we'd been trying to get that date and it happened after the wedding."

She wondered how much else they knew about what happened after the wedding. She shrugged off the thought. She was a twenty-eight-year-old woman, and Stonewall was definitely a grown man. Neither of them had to answer to anyone. "When you see Roland again, please tell him thanks."

"I will. He also mentioned that he saw you on television this morning. I guess it was a repeat of last night's interview."

She nodded again. "The media was all over the place."

"When something like that happens, they would be. There hasn't been this much happening in Charlottesville since Erickson hired that assassin, so everyone's interested. I hope you catch the bastards responsible."

"I intend to."

And then she grabbed the T-shirt off the bed and strolled into the bathroom.

NICE ASS, STONEWALL thought as he watched her leave, closing the bathroom door behind her. He wondered how he could get her to stay. Not just through lunch but through the entire weekend. He enjoyed being with her and not just in the bedroom. She might see him as a diversion, but he was beginning to see her as something more. And that was the crux of his problem.

He could pretend nonchalance for only so long with her. In the past, women had been just a means to an end. Mutually so, since he made it a point to date women with a like mind. He should have been jumping for joy at her attitude, but instead, he was discovering that the more time he spent with her, the more time he wanted. She knew how to push all his buttons, even when she had no idea she was doing so. All she had to do was give him one of those luscious smiles, a sexy walk or something as simple as rolling her shoulder in a shrug. All he knew, which had him confused as hell, was that Joy Ingram was getting to him in a big way.

He wasn't sure how long he stood there thinking about it, trying hard to rationalize things, when his cell phone rang. It was Striker. "Yeah, man. What's up?"

"Margo and I are firing up the grill around six and wanted to know if you'll come over and hang out with us. I called Quasar, and he and Randi are coming over, as well."

Pausing a minute, Stonewall said, "I have company." Why was he saying that when he was pretty sure she'd be gone by then?

Striker chuckled. "Bring your detective with you. We saw her on the news last night, by the way. Tragedy about that doctor and pharmacist. And we read about her promotion in today's paper. We're glad for her. I guess now she's your lieutenant."

Stonewall frowned. "What makes you think she's the person who's here?"

"Seriously? Just bring her. The chow-down starts at six."

"I'll have to ask Joy."

"Ask me what?"

Stonewall glanced up to see Joy. She was coming out the bathroom wearing his T-shirt. It looked good on her. Seeing her in it made him realize he'd never given another woman a shirt of his to wear. And even if he had, he doubted anyone of them could have worn it like this. He'd told her it would fit her like a dress. Well, in her case, not so much. Unless he meant a super minidress. A lot of her skin definitely showed. Skin that, from the looks of all the passion marks, he'd tasted a lot of. The hem hit upper midthigh and the top made her perfectly shaped nipples press against the cotton material.

"Ask me what, Stonewall?" she inquired again. She leaned against the headboard of the bed in what he thought was one sexy-as-hell pose. Long, gorgeous legs, shapely body, beautiful bare arms. He could hardly concentrate on anything, but the look on her face said he'd better.

Stonewall then said to Striker, "I'll call you back." He clicked off the phone and put it back into his pocket, not missing the way Joy's eyes traveled to his crotch when he did so.

"That was Striker. He and Margo are setting up the grill around six and invited us over."

She lifted a brow. "Us?"

"Yes, you and me. He also invited Quasar and Randi."

"And how did he know I was here?"

"A hunch."

She nodded slowly as she held his gaze. "The same hunch Roland had?"

Stonewall shrugged.

"Let me think about it. Besides, just look at me."

He *was* looking. "And?"

"I have passion marks all over me, some in places I can't hide. I don't want anyone to think that we're—"

"In a relationship. I get it. But just because you have passion marks doesn't mean they'll think we're in a relationship. They might just think we enjoy sleeping together with no ties. That is the way you want it."

Before she could say anything, he added, "You think about the invite and let me know your decision. I'll go and prepare lunch." He then walked out the room.

THE MOMENT THE woman was handed the baby, she cried. Tears misted her husband's eyes, as well. Audrey reined in her own emotions as she handed the couple tissues. She glanced over at her husband, and he was smiling, as well. She was glad they were in this together. A team. Making couples' dreams come true.

Cherita and Malcolm Bellary had tried for seven years before they'd decided to go the surrogate route, after they learned Cherita couldn't carry a child to term. Beautiful Creations had been their last hope, and Audrey was glad she and her husband could deliver.

At that moment the Bellarys' attorney, Aaron Singleton, said, "With the paperwork signed, my clients are free to leave."

Audrey knew it was a statement and not a question. This was an attorney they hadn't worked with before.

He was thorough, and she liked that. Thoroughness now meant no sloppiness later, and she believed in things being in order.

"That's right," Oliver said, standing. "Someone from my office will call in a few months to—"

"No calls," Singleton said. "When we walk out that office we don't want any connection. My clients prefer it that way."

Audrey looked to Oliver. He seemed bothered by that, and she understood why. He liked keeping in touch with the parents for at least four months, to make sure things were going fine. It was the Beautiful Creations way.

"Alright. If that's what your client wants."

A short while later, after the couple and their attorney had left, Oliver said grudgingly, "I didn't like him. Aaron Singleton."

She looked at her husband. "I could tell. Don't take it personally, Oliver. I'm sure he's just following his clients' wishes. They wouldn't be the first couple who didn't want further contact."

"I know, but..."

She lifted a brow. "But what?"

"But nothing." He glanced at his watch. "I think it will be a beautiful Saturday afternoon. How about if we go grab lunch somewhere and then—"

The phone in Oliver's office rang and Audrey reached and picked it up. "Beautiful Creations. This is Audrey Effington."

"Ms. Effington, this is Cathy. I remembered that you and Mr. Effington had an appointment at the office today and was hoping I would catch you."

Audrey nodded, fingering the pearls around her neck. "Yes, Cathy, you caught us just in time. We were about to leave. What is it?" She placed Cathy on speakerphone so Oliver could listen in.

"Have the two of you been watching television or seen this morning's paper?"

"No, we left home before doing either. Why?'

"There was a robbery and a shooting. A doctor and a pharmacist were killed."

"Oh, how awful," Audrey said, shaking her head. She hated hearing about such tragic news.

"Yes, but the doctor was someone whose name I recognized as having referred patients to us."

Audrey lifted a brow. Oliver had stopped what he was doing and had walked over to the desk. He asked, "Who was it?"

"Dr. Kelly Langley."

Audrey drew in a sharp breath and threw her hand to her chest in shock. "Dr. Langley? But how? When?"

"According to the news reports, two pharmacies were robbed last night within the span of two hours. The last one was in the same medical complex as Dr. Langley's office. She and the pharmacist were working late. I guess the intruders didn't want to leave any witnesses behind, so they killed them both."

Audrey closed her eyes, not believing what she was hearing. She'd met Kelly Langley and had found her to be a pleasant person. She had referred at least several couples, and things had worked out nicely for them.

"I'm sorry to hear that," Oliver said. "That's unfortunate."

Audrey frowned. *Unfortunate?* Was that the only

word her husband could find to say? What had happened to Dr. Langley and that pharmacist was not unfortunate but barbaric. She did not believe in violence of any kind. Her heart went out to Dr. Langley's family.

"Thanks for letting us know, Cathy. Find out when the services will be held and order flowers to be sent to the funeral home," Oliver said.

"Yes, Mr. Effington, I will. You two have a good weekend."

"Thanks, Cathy. We will and you do the same."

Audrey hung up the phone and thought it was sad that she and Oliver planned to have a good weekend and the families of those two victims would not. More than anything, she hoped the authorities apprehended the people responsible.

CHAPTER TWENTY-EIGHT

JOY WALKED INTO the kitchen to find Stonewall standing at the sink. "Sorry I got detained, but I needed to check in at headquarters."

He turned to her. "No problem. Any new developments?"

"No. The next of kin of Dr. Langley, the female doctor who was killed, is to arrive later today. Her brother is a freelance cameraman working in Turkey."

"She wasn't married?"

"No, she'd been divorced for a good ten years."

He nodded. "I figured we could have fries with our sandwiches."

"Sounds good."

"I've got the fries in the oven."

"The oven?"

"Yeah. I can eat fries every day, so it's better for my health if I bake them instead of frying them. Works for me."

"You like them that much?"

"Yes, always have. I'll take a bunch of fries over dessert any day of the week."

She sat down at the table. "Thanks for taking care of my clothes. When you said they were in the laundry room, I didn't know you'd washed them." And he'd done a good job, separating her underthings from her shirt and slacks, and folding everything in a neat stack on a folding table. A part of her wasn't sure how she felt about a man handling her undergarments. When she and Omar had been together, she'd done laundry for the both of them, but he'd never taken the time to wash any of her things. Would have probably thought it was beneath him to do so.

"No problem. I have a sister and when she was down with the flu, I thought I would help her out and do her laundry. I learned my lesson when I tossed everything into the washing machine. I figured I was saving time. And I added bleach thinking that would get the items extra clean. I guess I don't have to tell you how that turned out."

No, he didn't. She couldn't help the smile that touched her lips. "I guess after that she gave you a class in Laundry 101."

He chuckled and pulled open the oven door. "Yes, she did."

The fries he took out the oven looked yummy, and the sandwiches he placed on the plate in front of her looked delicious, as well. She was hungry, understandably so. Last meal she'd eaten was last night, here.

She bit into her sandwich. "Mmm, this is good. Is there anything your grandmother can't do? Bake cakes. Make apple cider. Put together chicken salad for sandwiches."

Stonewall smiled as he took a sip of his iced tea. "Not much. She's an excellent cook. I wished she'd passed some of those skills on to Mellie."

"Your sister can't cook?"

"Let's just say she's the tofu queen. My grandmother cringes every time she talks about it."

Joy didn't say anything as she took another bite of her sandwich. Stonewall didn't, either. After lunch she would tell him of her decision not to go to the cookout with him. She saw no point in doing so. Like she'd told him, people would speculate about their affair, assume it was the beginning of a relationship. That was not the case, and she didn't want to go there with anyone.

Stonewall began talking, telling her more about his grandmother's neighborhood and his desire to buy more rental properties there. She listened and found what he was saying so informative she considered doing the same herself. It was time she considered looking into investment opportunities. In their time together, she'd discovered he was well versed in a number of subjects. She also learned that he worked as a substitute teacher in the school system and as an adjunct professor at the collegiate level. And then there was his community involvement as well as his work at the Sheppard Granger Foundation for Troubled Teens.

Joy inwardly admitted if she had been in the market for a serious relationship, Stonewall would have been her guy. But her work, especially with the promotion to lieutenant, would be even more hectic. The words Chief Harkins had spoken rippled through her mind.

"Get a life. You hang around here too much and you don't have to do that. Personally, I don't want the people you will supervise to assume they need to do that, either."

And then there were the accusations Darren had leveled at her.

"I just hope you begin chilling for a while and not expecting the people you'll be over not to have a life just because you don't."

"Joy?"

Through her hazy and confused mind, she heard her name being called and blinked. Stonewall was staring at her. "You okay?" he asked her.

She nodded, seeing the concern in his eyes. "Yes, I'm okay."

She wasn't sure if that was entirely true. For the first time since her breakup with Omar, she'd decided to open her mind to possibilities she hadn't considered. Had refused to consider.

Could I consider them now?

She met Stonewall's gaze. "May I ask you something?"

"Yes, anything you want."

She knew that to be true. Over the course of the time they'd known each other, she'd asked him far more questions than he'd ever asked her. Being a detective made her an inquisitive person. Nothing personal. That's just the way she was.

Even now he sat there ready to answer any question she threw at him in that deep, husky voice of his. The same one that could make all kinds of sensations thrum through her. "When you look at me, what do you see?"

If he found her question odd, his face didn't show it. Instead he leaned back in his chair and studied her with one of his heated stares. Suddenly his lips curved into a smile, and she couldn't help wondering what he was thinking. He folded his arms across his broad chest as if her question deserved all the deep thought he was giving it. At that moment, she knew whatever his answer might be, it would be something she could go to bed tonight thinking about. It would be something she remembered.

"When I look at you I see beauty, and I am enthralled by it. Beauty that's not fabricated or fake. It's the real deal, and it goes deep and connects with a sense of caring that goes even deeper. That's why you're so good at your job. Why you're so meticulous in carrying it out."

He paused a moment. "I also see a woman who holds herself in, not necessarily because of a past hurt but because of a chance once taken and a regret about that. Where others fall off a bicycle and get back on, you'd rather walk the rest of the way. You don't like getting bruises. For you they become permanent."

What Stonewall said were some awful truths about her. Maybe they were difficult to hear, but they'd been truths. Truths that up till now she could live with because they were a part of her makeup. Now she wasn't so sure. "What's wrong with a person wanting to protect herself against pain? Against bruises?"

She watched the way his brow furrowed. The way his lips worked their way into a sigh before he said, "Over the years I've asked myself the same question. When you've lost three vital members of your family within a six-month period, you think protecting yourself against future hurt and pain is the only way. I admit I still do at times. Forever is something I don't like thinking about because for me it doesn't exist. My acceptance of there being no forever is like your fear of engaging in a relationship. We're held hostage by the protective gear we've put in place."

She heard his words and understood them. He might believe in relationships but he didn't believe in forever. To be quite honest, she didn't believe in it, either. In her book, a man and woman could enjoy each other without the entanglements of a relationship. It could be an association based solely on physical needs. Whereas he believed that even if a relationship existed, you were still in control. You were the one who decided how far, how long and how deep it went.

Now for her next question. "Have you ever been in love?"

A lone dimple appeared in his right cheek and he said, "No, I can't say that I have." Then he asked, "What about you?"

She found his question strange, especially since he'd known of her engagement to Omar. Did he not think she'd loved Omar? She *had* loved him. Hadn't she? That question gave her pause. Would she have left and walked out of Omar's life so easily if she'd truly loved him? And when she'd walked away she hadn't looked back. Even now she rarely thought about him unless her parents brought him up.

"I thought I was," she heard herself say. "Now I'm not so sure." She then said, "It's hard to read you at times, Stonewall."

"When it comes to what?"

"How you really feel about things. How you feel about us and the time we've been spending together," she said.

"The diversions?"

"Yes."

He was quiet a moment, then said, "My grandmother

always tells me that it's a waste of time fighting about the inevitable. It's not worth the effort."

She held his gaze. "You think we'll engage in a relationship eventually?"

"Yes. There's too much chemistry—sexual and otherwise—for us not to. One day you'll realize these diversions just don't cut it."

Had he realized it? "Why not?" she asked.

"Because we'll want more. Not forever, but more. You being here now proves that point."

Did it? she wondered. "What do I get out of a relationship with you?"

"Whatever you want to get out of it based on whatever you put into it. You can't get anything out if you don't put anything in."

And *that*, she thought, was the root of her problem. "I might not have time to put anything into it."

He slowly stood and began collecting the plates off the table. When he'd gathered everything up he said, "At some point, Joy, you have to concede that you deserve a life besides that of a cop."

She didn't ask if he had one outside being a bodyguard. She knew the answer. He had friends he spent time with. He had his community work, his volunteering at Sheppard Granger's foundation. How did he find the time for it all?

As if he read her thoughts he said, "Another thing Granny Kay likes to say is that you find the time for the things you truly want to do." Then, without saying another word, he walked away.

Joy sat there and watched him discard their trash, and it was then that she made up her mind about something. It was time she took some of his grandmother's advice. "Stonewall?"

He glanced over his shoulder at her. "Yes?"

"If that invitation still stands about Striker and Margo's cookout, I'd love to go with you."

He didn't say anything. He just looked at her, and a part of her knew he understood what she was saying. For now there would be no promises made. No risk of promises being broken later. "The invitation still stands," he finally said.

Joy drew in a deep breath. For the first time in years she felt a sense of doing something for herself. She finally felt as if she was taking charge. She wasn't sure how things would turn out or where they would lead. But at least she was willing to risk finding out.

CHAPTER TWENTY-NINE

"WHAT THE HELL were you trying do? Mark her up for life?"

Stonewall had known he'd get some ribbing from Striker, Quasar or both. The outfit Joy was wearing, a pair or capris with a flowing sleeveless tunic, could cover only so much skin. The parts exposed showed passion marks. He knew she'd tried using some makeup, but leave it to Striker to see beyond that.

"Do you have to notice every damn thing?" Stonewall asked, trying to keep his voice low. Quasar was standing only a few feet away, adjusting the volume on the speakers. The last thing he needed was Quasar overhearing and adding his two cents.

"Why not? This is an intimate group, three dudes with their women and—"

"Joy is not my woman."

Striker rolled his eyes. "If I recall, she wasn't your detective, either."

"She wasn't."

Striker smiled. "Whatever. Besides, her not being your woman is a temporary state since I'm sure you're working on changing that."

Stonewall frowned. "And what gives you that idea?"

"Because I know for a fact you haven't dated another

woman, not even as much as scoped out another one, since meeting your detective."

"Her name is Joy."

Striker chuckled. "Yeah, I know. And the psychic's name is Randi, and that woman standing over there, the one in the blue shorts, who can still be nosy as hell at times, is Margo."

"Smart-ass."

"Whatever," Striker said, waving off Stonewall's words with the spatula. "Besides, if you'd notice, all three women could belong to the Passion Mark Club since each has a hickey showing in plain view."

Stonewall glanced over at the women. *Did they?* If they did, he hadn't noticed.

"You need to be more observant, Stonewall. You're a protector, after all."

Stonewall knew Striker hated the term *bodyguard* and refused to be called one. Instead, he referred to the men and women who worked for Roland as *protectors.* "I am observant," Stonewall said. "I just don't make it a habit to check out another man's wife, namely Margo. Or another man's fiancée, namely Randi."

"What about Randi?" Quasar asked, joining them.

"I was just telling Stonewall about that huge hickey on her neck."

Quasar smiled. "What about it? I put it there."

"Hell, I would hope so," Striker said, laughing.

Stonewall didn't say anything as he observed his two friends. Falling in love seemed to have agreed with them. He of all people would never have thought that. Like him, they hadn't had settling down with one woman on their radars. But according to them, it just happened.

It just happened. He took a swig of his beer, wondering how shit like that could just happen. Striker had been right when he'd said that since Stonewall had met Joy, he hadn't gone out with another woman.

He ignored the conversation going on between Striker and Quasar as he looked over at the women again. They were standing together, laughing and conversing like old friends. This was not their first meeting. Margo had met Randi and Joy the night of the cabin fire nearly five months ago. From all accounts, it seemed as if the three had formed a friendship. He shook his head. Funny how that had happened.

"So, Stonewall, are you and your detective a real item now?" Quasar asked, reclaiming Stonewall's attention.

He recalled the decision he and Joy had made in his kitchen after lunch. There was no need to deny anything. "We're working on it."

Striker's gaze sharpened. "But I thought you said earlier that she wasn't your woman."

Leave it to Striker to dissect his every word. "She's not yet. At least, not the way I want her to be." *Fully and without any reservations*, he thought. "Like I told Quasar, we're working on it. Joy has issues regarding relationships."

"So do you," Quasar said.

Stonewall knew it would be a waste of his time to deny what Quasar said because Striker and Quasar knew him better than anyone…except maybe Sheppard. Besides, what Quasar said was true. He did have relationship issues, but as far as he was concerned, they weren't anything like Joy's. He had no problem being in a relationship. Where it would be expected to go was his issue.

"Like I said, we're working on it." Changing the subject, he asked, "Are Carson and the baby still expected to leave the hospital today?"

JOY SMILED AT yet another thing Margo said. She hadn't enjoyed herself at a social gathering like this in months, at least not since she'd gone home for the holidays. Since moving to Charlottesville, she hadn't had time to make a lot of new friends…other than her neighbor, Cherish. And when she'd met Margo and Randi it had been while working a case. Now with that behind them, she knew she truly liked them.

She was tempted to sneak a peek at Stonewall, who sat talking to Striker and Quasar. She'd known each and every time he'd looked over at her. His gaze had been like a heated caress that she'd actually felt. Only once had she given in to temptation and looked back. Their eyes had met, and the sexual chemistry that instant had stirred had spoken volumes.

After their lunch they had sat out on his terrace and talked some more. She'd gotten so caught up in her time with him, she hadn't thought about all the crime being committed out there in the streets or cases she hadn't yet solved.

He had taken her home to change clothes. Of course her television was on since she never turned it off. But he had switched the station to a sports channel to watch a baseball game. When she'd come out of her bedroom after changing, the way his gaze had scanned over her body had heated her insides. It almost made her suggest they skip the cookout altogether and stay in, just the two of them.

Upon arriving at Striker and Margo's place, no one seemed surprised to see her with Stonewall, and everyone had immediately made her feel right at home. They were a friendly group, and from the way Striker was interacting with Margo and Quasar was with Randi, she could tell the two couples were very much in love.

Why hadn't she and Omar interacted that way when they'd been together? Maybe they had in the beginning, before things started to fizzle. He'd faulted her for it, saying she was putting her job before him, and she would admit she had in a way. But even when she'd tried shifting things to accommodate him, it hadn't been enough.

"So, how does it feel being a lieutenant?" Randi asked her, cutting into her thoughts.

When Joy and Stonewall had first arrived, everyone had congratulated her on her promotion. She smiled over at Randi. "The same, honestly. A big responsibility but I can handle it."

"Of course you can."

"Thanks for the vote of confidence."

Randi waved off her words. "No need to thank me. I worked with you, remember? I know what you're capable of, and you're good at what you do."

"Don't look now but our men are headed this way," Margo said, giving her and Randi a wink.

Our men? Margo meant their men. Before she could open her mouth to correct Margo's assumption, Randi touched her arm and said, "One day he will be."

Randi's words gave her pause. Had Randi read her thoughts? The woman was a psychic. Were her words casual or something more? The guys reached them, and Striker said, "I hate to break things up, but dinner is ready and I just got a text from Roland. Caden is on his way to take Shiloh to the hospital. Her water broke."

"Wow, it seems like those Granger babies are arriving fast and furious."

Joy couldn't help but smile.

"OH NO, NOT Dr. Langley," Rachel Carrington said to her husband in shock. "That's awful."

They had left on Friday morning to visit her parents in Williamsburg, only to return this evening to hear the tragic news about the break-in at the Park Ridge Medical Complex. All Rachel could think about was how, thanks to Dr. Langley, they had their baby girl, Chasta.

"You're right, baby, it is awful," Brett Carrington said, pulling his wife into his arms.

Neither said anything for a minute, and then Brett told his wife, "I'm just glad we got a chance to meet her. And I'll always be grateful for her part in recommending us to Beautiful Creations."

Rachel nodded. "So will I."

The phone rang and Rachel recognized the ringtone. "That's my brother. He probably talked to our folks, and they told him about our road trip to see them," Rachel said, pushing out of Brett's arms to grab the phone.

"Hello?"

"And how's my beautiful niece?"

Rachel smiled. Everyone in her family loved Chasta. Even the skeptical ones who weren't sure of the way she and Brett had decided to have a child had come around the moment they'd seen Chasta.

"Your niece is fine. She slept during most of the drive back home. Brett and I have a feeling she might be keeping us up much of the night. You're still out of town?"

"Yes, I'll be here for a few more days. I talked to Mom and Dad, and they were glad to see you guys. Your surprise visit boosted their spirits."

Rachel sighed. "I'm glad, although my spirits are at an all-time low right now."

"Oh? Why?"

"When we got back today, we learned that Dr. Kelly Langley, the doctor who referred us to Beautiful Creations, was murdered during a break-in at the medical complex where she works."

"That's awful. Why would any want to break into a medical complex?"

"For drugs. There's a pharmacy on-site and according to the news that had been the target. A pharmacist was killed. The same people robbed another pharmacy in the Mixon Town area. Thank God that pharmacy had closed up, and everyone had gone home."

"That's terrible. I hope they catch those responsible. I better go. I need to prep for my meeting on Monday."

"Alright. Thanks for calling."

"Love you."

Rachel smiled. "I love you, too, Anderson. Goodbye."

CHAPTER THIRTY

BRIGHT AND EARLY Monday morning, Joy stood in front of her office window and looked out at downtown Charlottesville. It was a beautiful city, one that continued to grow on her since she'd first visited nearly two years ago.

It would be hard to say goodbye when she got ready to move on, and she knew that one day she would. Most career law enforcement officials, the ambitious ones, at least, were always ready to relocate for better opportunities. Unless you were extremely lucky like her father had been. He'd managed to move up the ranks in the Baton Rouge Police Department without relocating once. He ran a tough ship, and he and his department had brought the homicide rate down to low numbers. Because he was a hometown guy, the people loved him, and more than once they'd tried to get him to consider politics. So far he hadn't, but she wouldn't be surprised if one day he did.

She smiled when she thought about how much she'd enjoyed her weekend. Especially the time spent Saturday with Stonewall and his friends. It was enlightening to witness the close relationship Stonewall had with Striker and Quasar. And according to them, they hadn't gotten along in prison. In fact, for years Striker and Stonewall had been bitter enemies. They credited Sheppard Granger for bringing an end to that hostility. And speaking of Sheppard Granger, they'd gotten word while at the cookout that his son Caden's wife, Shiloh, had given birth to a nine-pound son. Mom, baby and dad were all doing great. Caden was a renowned award-winning saxophonist, so it came as no surprise that he and Shiloh named their son Sax.

Joy's smile widened when she thought of the blossoming friendship between her, Margo and Randi. They decided to get together for lunch and a spa day the next time Randi was in town. They even discussed the possibility of a girls' night out. It had been a long time—probably not since college—since she'd hung out with women other than her mother and sister.

When Stonewall had taken her home he had spent the night. No surprise there given the sexual chemistry that continued to burn between them. Even when Margo and Randi had teased her about it, it hadn't bothered her like she'd assumed it would. She had been more than relaxed around his friends. Other than congratulating her about her work and saying how awful it was about that pharmacist and doctor, no one pried about her work. Without knowing they were doing so, they had shown her there was life beyond work and you didn't have to bring work home with you.

Sunday morning she'd awakened to breakfast in bed. The last time she remembered that happening was when she'd come down with the mumps at ten and her mother had kept her in bed but had made her favorite pancakes for her.

While she slept Stonewall had left to grab muffins,

coffee and bacon from a deli on the corner. He'd joined her in bed to nibble on bacon and muffins and drink coffee. After breakfast he had talked her into a walk around her neighborhood, and she was glad. She'd seen things she'd not noticed before. Like the construction of a new library a few blocks away and several new mom-and-pop restaurants. The house just a few doors down that had been vacant for months now had new owners. When had that happened?

Being outside and walking the neighborhood made her realize what she missed when leaving to go to work at sunup and not returning until after dark. The world moved on without her. A part of her tried not to feel guilty about it or dwell on those things she'd missed by convincing herself that she always had to be somewhere keeping the world safe.

Her thoughts shifted to Stonewall and how he'd dominated this weekend. Not that she was complaining. For lunch they had devoured leftovers from Saturday's cookout. After making love to her, he'd left her Sunday evening with a lot to think about. Going to the cookout was one thing, but she still hadn't decided what place he had, if any, in her life. He was becoming more than a diversion, and she wasn't certain how to deal with it.

His grandmother's wise words ran through her mind on a loop, though. It was something she figured he believed—that at some point what they shared would become a relationship, as a matter of course. She couldn't dismiss or deny their chemistry. That was for sure. Considering the pleasure aches in her body after a weekend of intense lovemaking, she didn't want to dismiss or deny it.

She turned at the sound of the knock on her door. Having an office would take some getting used to. "Come in."

Chief Harkins walked in and glanced around before he looked over at her. "Glad to see you've moved in already. I meant to swing by on Friday but had a dentist appointment."

"No problem. Everything is going great so far."

He nodded. "I heard about that double homicide on Friday. Sad situation. Any leads?"

"Not yet. Acklin and I are meeting with Sykes around ten to compare notes. Then I'm meeting with the ME at noon." Tyrel Sykes was a detective in the Felony Department and had investigated the robbery at Skinners Pharmacy Friday night.

Chief Harkins nodded. "Keep me apprised of what's happening with that one. The city expects us to find the persons responsible and bring them to justice. The last thing we want is for pharmacists to begin arming themselves against possible robberies."

"I agree."

"And what about that Clay case? Any updates on that?"

Joy told him about her and Sanchez's visit with Oliver Effington and what he'd let slip about Mandy Clay's hair color. "It might be nothing, but I plan to check out a few things. I have a gut feeling he knows more than he's admitting to."

"Wouldn't surprise me. Get with Taren. She's good at what she does." Taren Corker was the department's technical analyst and could do research on just about anything or anyone.

"I have a meeting with her today, as well."

Harkins chuckled. "Sounds like you're going to be quite busy today. Remember what I said. Learn to balance work and your personal life, Lieutenant Ingram."

She thought about what she'd done over the weekend, specifically the time shared with Stonewall. A part of her could admit at least she was trying.

"HEY, MAN, JUDGING from your droopy eyes I would think you didn't get much rest this weekend."

Stonewall shook his head as he stepped back and let his friend inside his home. "You're a long way from Alexandria, aren't you, Drew?" Like Striker and Quasar, Andrew Logan was someone he'd met at Glenworth Penitentiary. He had gotten out a few of years ahead of them after being exonerated, and now he was a detective for the police department in Alexandria.

"Was passing through and decided to stop and see the little princess."

A smile touched Stonewall's lips. He knew Drew was referring to Shep's daughter. It was hard to believe with three sons of his own and after mentoring so many young men, Shep had a baby daughter. "Did you see her?"

"Yes. Shep's a proud dad and Carson a happy mom. I can't think of two more deserving people."

Stonewall had to agree with him. "I was about to grab breakfast. Want to join me?"

"Sure, why not?" Drew said, removing his jacket and exposing the Glock he wore in a shoulder holster. Stonewall thought it was amazing how far all of them had come from the days they'd been considered hardened criminals. Drew had given the wardens hell. He'd pretty much given Shep hell as well, but Shep had refused to give up on him.

"So what's with the tired eyes, Stonewall?" Drew asked again as he followed him into the kitchen and sat at the table.

"You're imagining things," Stonewall said, going over to the stove.

"And you're stalling."

Stonewall glanced over his shoulder. Leave it to Drew to have that don't-bullshit-me look on his face. Some things never changed, but then some things did. Not only did they change but they were full of surprises. Drew going into law enforcement was one of them. Who would have thought a man who hated cops would become one? But then, Stonewall could say the same about himself. He'd disliked cops as well, although not to the same degree Drew had. Yet here Stonewall was, dating one. At least, he figured they were dating, although he'd taken her out only once. The rest of the times had been spent at her place or his, mainly in their bedrooms. He needed to fix that.

"I'm waiting, Courson."

Stonewall turned and sat, placing two plates on the table. "I would say interrogation isn't your style, but it is."

"And since you know that, just answer the question."

Stonewall had to remember the man was his friend. There was nothing the two wouldn't do for each other. Shep had made damn sure of that. As long as it was legal. Shep made sure of that, as well. "Busy weekend. Striker had a cookout Saturday. You know how it is when the three of us get together. We played cards well into the night."

"Hmm, and their women let them do that?"

"Okay, so it wasn't well into the night, but I had a busy weekend nonetheless."

"Evidently. I understand you and the detective are an item now."

Stonewall didn't have to wonder where Drew had gotten such information. Either Striker or Quasar had talked. "And what of it if we are?"

Drew shrugged massive shoulders before he began digging into his food. "Nothing. I've known Joy a little longer than you. She's a nice person. Dedicated to the job."

Stonewall stared at Drew. "What do you mean you've known Joy longer than me? I wasn't even aware the two of you knew each other."

"Of course we know each other. We're both detectives."

"So you're both detectives. But you're in Alexandria and she's a detective here. Before transferring here she was in—"

"—Baton Rouge. I know. I met her years ago at a law enforcement seminar. First glance I thought she was a looker, but then I saw that engagement ring on her hand. You know I don't impose on another man's territory."

Yes, I know, and I also know the reason. "You met her that long ago?" Stonewall asked, fighting back his annoyance at knowing that Drew had met Joy before he had.

"It's been close to five years. I was equally attracted

to her friend who didn't have a ring on her finger. She's the one I ended up spending most of my time with."

The smirk on Drew's face left no doubt in Stonewall's mind just how most of that time was spent. He met Drew's gaze. "Yes, Joy and I are an item." He didn't want Drew getting any ideas now that Joy no longer had an engagement ring on her finger.

"Thanks for letting me know."

Stonewall chuckled, knowing he and Drew understood each other. "Don't mention it."

JOY FACED LENNOX and Detectives Acklin and Sykes. Sykes had just finished briefing her on his investigation. Both he and Acklin agreed the robberies at both pharmacies were the work of the same men. Although the two had been careful not to leave fingerprints, they had been picked up by security cameras. Only problem was that the masks they'd worn made identification impossible. There was no guarantee the two were even men. The time recorded on the security cameras indicated they had hit Skinners Pharmacy first, left there and headed to Park Ridge.

The detectives had pulled traffic cams near both places to verify the route taken and the time. Everything fit. A black SUV in the parking lots of both places had been identified as the vehicle used in both robberies. It had also been verified from the license plate that the vehicle had been stolen. Currently police officers were on the lookout for the vehicle. The National Association of Medical Professionals was offering a fifty-thousand-dollar reward for any information, anonymous or otherwise, on the two killings.

Joy switched her gaze from Acklin and Sykes to Lennox. "Are you ready to close the ME case on your end?"

Lennox smiled warmly. "Umm, not exactly."

"Why not, exactly, Lennox?"

Lennox tapped on her bottom lip with a manicured nail a few times. "A couple of things seem off. First, I would agree it appears both victims were caught off guard. That's evident from the position of their bodies. Mr. Fowler had looked over his shoulder, probably to see who was coming into his area, when he was shot, which is why he was shot the way he was, in the back with his head slanted toward his shoulder. However, I'm puzzled by a few things concerning how and where Dr. Langley was shot."

"She was shot in the chest, right?" Acklin asked. Joy wondered if he asked because he needed clarification or he just wanted Lennox to address him directly.

Lennox turned to Acklin, smiled and gave him her full attention. "Yes, Detective Acklin. However, the position of the bullet and the way it entered her body, as well as how her body was positioned in the doorway, indicates the person was standing directly in front of her when the shot was fired."

"What's unusual about that?" Sykes asked.

Lennox switched her attention from Acklin to Sykes. "What's unusual about that is, the person had to have been anticipating her opening that door and was waiting for her to do so."

"Yes, but it's plausible they knew she was in the office. Her car was in the parking lot, and more than likely there was a light showing beneath her door. I would think they would have anticipated someone opening that door to investigate the noise they'd made and were intent not to leave a possible witness behind," Acklin said.

At this point Joy had to agree with Acklin. "Chances are they did know someone was still at the office since both victims' cars were parked in the lot. The intruders had probably sized up the situation already and knew what they were dealing with, although not whom."

"True," Lennox agreed. "However, what's been keeping me up at night is the—"

"Something is keeping you up at night, Dr. Roswell?" Acklin asked, and Joy wondered what vision was floating through the man's mind. Lennox up at night, pacing around her bedroom and wearing hardly anything while doing so. Joy shook her head. Thanks to her two older brothers, who'd been real players before settling down, she knew how the male mind worked.

"Yes," Lennox said. "When something about a case bothers me, even the smallest little thing, I tend to think it to death. Well, what's bothering me more than anything is not so much the entry of the bullet as the mark."

"The mark?" Joy asked.

"Yes, it was a direct hit to her heart at close range. When I say close, I mean *close*. The gunpowder samples taken from her clothes show the gun was pressed to her clothing."

Joy frowned. "Are you saying whoever shot Dr. Langley intentionally shot her in her heart?"

"I can't say if it was intentional or not. It might have been a coincidence. But I find it odd the person got that close and took aim without her having a chance to fight back. It's like her body was at a total standstill."

"Probably because she was in shock," Acklin offered.

"She stepped out her office into the complex's corridor to find a gun pointed right at her."

Joy now saw where Lennox was going with this. "But only if the intruder anticipated her coming out of her office. Then what happened to her and how it happened would make sense," Joy said.

She and Lennox made eye contact, and Joy knew they were thinking the same thing. How could the intruder anticipate such a thing?

"I think I'll go back over to the crime scene," Joy said, tossing a pen on her desk.

"I'll go with you," Lennox said.

Not surprisingly, Acklin quickly stood and said, "I'll join you two."

CHAPTER THIRTY-ONE

"I'M GLAD YOU agreed to meet with me, Dr. Fuller. I certainly would have understood if you've decided not to."

Randi Fuller stared across the desk at the man sitting behind it, FBI special agent Tommy Felton. She clearly remembered the first time they'd met a few years ago. From the first he had refused to believe in her psychic abilities. It hadn't mattered that she'd already assisted various police departments around the country in solving close to fifty cases, most of them unsolved murders, rapes and missing persons. Nor had it mattered to him that she'd garnered national attention when she helped federal agents on a number of cases, such as bringing to light a human trafficking ring and aiding in the rescue of a well-known senator just moments before he was to be put on a plane to Libya for his execution by ISIS. It had taken them working together on the case involving mobster Murphy Erickson that had finally made him a believer.

Her approach to solving a crime was different than those of a number of other psychics. She didn't just depend on her psychic abilities but also an in-depth knowledge of the case. That method was more readily accepted by the skeptics, especially those like Agent Felton who believed their way was the only way. She had the ability to work as both a behavioral analyst and a psychic investigator.

"I understand congratulations are in order, Dr. Fuller. On your upcoming marriage."

Randi smiled. "Thanks."

"Now, down to business. We need your assistance solving the Murphy murder. You've reviewed the file?"

Randi had met Murphy Erickson. Had come face-to-face with the sinister gangster. She doubted there was a more evil individual. "Yes. I see you think Erickson was killed by the person intent on taking over his territory."

"Yes. I want to think the person responsible did all of us a favor, but I have a strong feeling the man is worse than Erickson ever was."

Like everyone else, Randi had heard the rumor that someone new was moving in on Erickson's territory. And it was someone with even more sinister plans than Erickson had ever come up with. Rumor was the person was going to make sure Erickson didn't leave prison. And that's exactly what had happened. Erickson had been found dead in his jail cell. The authorities were still clueless as to how Erickson had died. Footage from the security cam had revealed nothing. And so far the medical examiner hadn't been able to pinpoint the cause of death, either.

"We need your help, Dr. Fuller. I refuse to retire before this case is solved."

Randi mulled over what she knew and said, "I'm going to be honest with you. I'm not sure that I can help. In order to find someone's killer, the victim has to reach out to me. I doubt if Erickson will do that. The one time I met with him, I picked up so many negative and evil vibes I could hardly stand being in the same room with him."

Felton nodded and she could see disappointment in his eyes. "You were our last hope. Trust me when I say we covered that cell from corner to corner, every nook and cranny. We checked out every single person who came within ten feet of his cell in the forty-eight hours before and after the murder. I've looked at the footage from the security camera until my eyes got crossed. I honestly don't know how Erickson died."

"Poisoned, perhaps? If you recall, someone tried to poison me and Detective Ingram with coffee at police headquarters."

"Yes, I remember. That's what we figured it was—poison. But nothing showed up in the tox screens."

Randi knew there were poisons that could go undetected, some that didn't show up for years. "What about his cell at that federal prison? Is it still empty?"

"Yes, it's still vacant and nothing has been touched."

Randi drew in a deep breath. "I plan to be in town for the next couple of weeks. I'd like to revisit the cell and look at the security footage. Maybe when I begin doing so Erickson will reach out to me, but don't hold your breath."

She saw relief in the older man's face. "Thank you, Dr. Fuller. Like I said, you're our last hope."

JOY HAD RETURNED to the office after visiting the crime scene again. She would admit that Lennox had raised some serious concerns. To demonstrate, once they arrived at the scene, Lennox had acted out how she thought that night had gone, tracing the steps Dr. Langley had made to her door with Joy and Acklin acting as the murderer on the other side, waiting for her to open the door. First she'd opened the door from her private office that led into the office lobby and then the door from the lobby into the complex's corridor. She'd gotten shot in the complex's corridor.

According to the timeline, the two intruders would have to have been waiting for her when she opened the door to the corridor or soon thereafter. Then what? For one of them to be standing directly in front of her with a gun shoved in her chest close to her heart meant Dr. Langley hadn't been given time to react.

The three of them had reenacted several scenarios and only one gave them the results that made sense. It would mean they'd intended to target Dr. Langley. But why? It was a big leap to make, and Joy worried they were moving too fast with such an assumption. After all, there had been two burglaries that night, definitely by the same intruders. The way Dr. Fowler had been killed and how his body was found made sense with the theory that the robbers weren't expecting him to be there and acted spontaneously. Applying the same theory to Dr. Langley, it didn't make sense considering where she was shot and how close the person had stood to her.

When Joy heard the buzzing of her phone, she pulled it from her pocket to check the text message.

How about dinner tonight?

She couldn't help but smile at the same moment her

heart began pounding in her chest. Why did receiving a message from Stonewall do that to her? Drawing in a deep breath, she texted back. Doubt I'll leave here before eight.

In her mind she could hear him click the keys as he texted back. No problem. Name the place.

A smile curved her lips as she responded. You decide. Too tired to think.

He texted back. Sounds like you need pampering.

She decided against replying that she could definitely use a diversion after today, and instead asked, Will you do it? Pamper me tonight?

A shiver ran through her body as she waited for his response. Pampering will be just the beginning.

Oh my. Her breath caught at those words. Before she could calm herself, he texted, I will call you around eight.

Joy texted, OK, then there was a knock at her door. "Come in." Whitman Snow walked in, and she could immediately tell he was nervous about something.

"Whit."

"Lieutenant Ingram."

When Whit stood there and didn't say anything else, she asked, "Is there a reason for this visit?"

He stared at the floor before looking back up and finally meeting her gaze. "I was expecting to be called to your office today for my termination papers. I'm sure your boyfriend told you what was said."

Joy met Whit's gaze. "No, he didn't, at least not in detail. However, I can only assume from his degree of anger that whatever you and Darrin said was unflattering."

Whit nodded. "Yes, it was. I won't try to place all the blame on Darrin. I should have shut him up."

"Yes, you should have. But then, I know respect has to be earned, Whit. All I'm asking is for you guys to keep an open mind. I want to do my job well just like I'm sure you want to do yours well. And as long as you're doing your job the way I expect, the way Chief Harkins and the mayor expect, the way the taxpayers expect, then there shouldn't be any problems."

He nodded, turned to go, then paused and turned back. "I'm glad to know you got somebody," he said quickly.

When she lifted her brow, he said, "You know. A boyfriend."

Joy just stared at him for a moment. What was with everyone worrying about whether she had a boyfriend? As if he read the question in her eyes, he rushed on, "No matter how you look at it, Lieutenant, people who tend not to have lives expect others not to have them, as well. Same way with people who don't have children. They don't always understand the sacrifices by the people who do. I'm not married but I do have a daughter I try to see whenever I can."

She shrugged. "I understand you and the others have lives, and all of you can rest assured I have one, as well. That doesn't mean I won't be working late some nights, because I will if the assignment calls for it. Whatever it takes to work a case, I will do it and expect all of you to do the same. I think that's only fair."

He nodded. "It is." He paused before asking, "Are you going to write me up?"

She knew he was eyeing a job with the FBI, and an

unfavorable write-up wouldn't look good. "No. It was not a conversation I overheard. But I will give you fair warning. If you deliberately make my job more difficult, you will be out of here in a flash. Do we understand each other?"

She saw the look of relief on his face. "Yes, Lieutenant, we understand each other. Thanks for the advice, and I will do my job."

"And I will do mine."

He nodded and quickly left her office.

"WHY ARE YOU calling me, Oliver?" Anderson snapped. He was getting dressed to go out. He hoped to meet a woman and have a good time.

"Dr. Langley's obituary was in today's paper."

"And?"

"Her funeral is tomorrow."

Anderson slid the belt through the loop of his slacks, getting more annoyed. "So, is there a reason you're telling me that?"

"I guess not if you have to ask. The police still think she and the pharmacist were killed because of the robbery."

"There's no reason they wouldn't. My people knew what they had to do."

"And what if they're able to find your people and—"

"Will you cut it out? Things will be fine. With the two robberies and the other dead person, there's no way anyone will figure out Kelly was the intended target."

"I hope you're right."

Anderson tried to hold his temper. Oliver was getting on his last nerve. Hadn't he taken a cue from what happened to Kelly? When it came to whiners he had no problem getting rid of them. If it wouldn't raise suspicions with the authorities, he would make sure Oliver had a short life span. "Look, I need to go. It might be best if we don't communicate for a while."

"Yes, maybe that's a good idea."

Anderson hung up without saying goodbye.

JOY HAD JUST received a text from Stonewall saying he intended to pamper her at his place, when there was another knock on her office door. "Come in."

She smiled when Taren walked in. As far a technical analysts went, Taren Corker was the best, simply invaluable. "I got your request, and I wanted to let you know I'm on it. Can we meet in the morning?"

"Sure thing. Will nine work for you?"

"Yes. I did want you to know I did a total body analysis of those two killers captured on the medical complex's security cam."

"And?"

"Although race is still unknown, both were definitely male."

"What else?"

"For the taller of the two men," Taren said, "the density of his body weight puts him between the ages of twenty-six and thirty-two. He's six-two and weighs around 153."

Taren provided stats on the second man. "I entered info on both men into the universal criminal database, and so far there hasn't been a match."

"That means no priors for either of them?"

"Either that or any arrests were made before law enforcement became so technologically advanced." Taren checked her watch. "I was just about to leave. You want to join me at Mony's?"

She liked Taren, and more than once they'd left head-quarters about the same time and ended up dining to-gether. Taren was a widow whose husband, a national guardsman, had been killed a few years ago in the line of duty. As far as Joy knew, Taren had not dated since and spent her free time doing volunteer work at the National Guard Armory and other local charities.

"No thanks. I've made other plans."

"I heard about your boyfriend," Taren said, smil-ing broadly.

Joy leaned back against her desk. She almost said that she didn't have a boyfriend, but instead asked, "And just what did you hear?"

"Not much other than he's real possessive. Whit said that you introduced them last week and you and your boyfriend joined him for dinner."

That wasn't how things went down, but if that was Whit's story, Joy would let him stick with it. She looked at her watch. "I need to get out of here."

"It's about time somebody put some fire under you to leave this place on time. Although I haven't met your boyfriend, I like him already. He definitely sounds like a keeper."

A keeper.

Taren's words were still in Joy's thoughts when she parked in front of Stonewall's place. Was he a keeper? She would admit if she was in the market for a serious affair he would definitely top the list. He was a man who en-joyed taking care of a woman in the most indulgent ways.

No man had ever swept her off her feet—literally—and into his arms. But he'd done just that when she had arrived exhausted at his house after a long night working a crime scene. He didn't have a problem being in a kitchen and he'd even laundered her clothes. Yes, he would definitely be a keeper if a keeper was what she'd wanted. But it wasn't. However, he wasn't looking for a keeper, either. Stonewall didn't believe in forever. Of that she was sure.

She unbuckled the seat belt and got out the car. She had called before leaving the office to let him know she was on her way and had offered to stop and pick up anything he needed. He'd said in his ultrasexy voice that the only thing he needed was her. But she knew that no matter what he'd said, when the time came he would pamper her before taking care of any needs he might have. She'd discovered that was the Stonewall Courson way. And it was a way that she was liking a bit too much.

She really wasn't surprised when the main door to the building opened before she'd even reached it. He stood there, leaning in the doorway and watching her. Her stomach did flip-flops. The closer she got the more active her stomach became.

"Sorry I'm late," she said when she came to a stop in front of him. Not only did he look good in his jeans and shirt, but he smelled good, as well.

"You're here now and that's what matters," he said, taking her hand.

At least he hadn't swept her off her feet. She really wasn't into such romantic stunts but would have to admit that when he'd done it before, it had been nice. With Stonewall, chivalry definitely was not dead.

He pressed the button to the elevator and looked at her. "Today's only Monday. Think you can make it to Friday, Lieutenant?"

Had any other man asked her that, she might have taken offense. But this was Stonewall, the man who seemed to accept her and her intensity for her work. "I think so."

He reached out and brushed his hand against her cheek. "I know so. You are a very determined woman who can do anything you set your mind to doing."

Except balancing work and life...or so others thought. She merely considered it a career choice. She was not intentionally trying to show anyone up just because they had lives outside headquarters. "Thanks for the vote of confidence."

"Anytime."

She studied him for a moment, thinking just how different he was from Omar and appreciating that he was. He tightened his hold on her hand as they stepped onto the elevator. The feel of her fingers encompassed in the warmth of his sent tingles up her spine.

Joy sniffed the air. Was she imagining it or could she smell the food he'd cooked even from here? She decided not to ask. Didn't have a chance to do so because he turned her in his arms, leaned down and captured her mouth with his. Using his tongue, he didn't take long to urge her to begin moaning.

A kiss from Stonewall had the ability to erase all tension from her body. Being held in his arms felt so good and right.

He continued to kiss her and didn't stop until the elevator did. When he pulled back, Joy looked up, and now she was the one to reach up to brush a hand against his bearded cheek. "Keep that up, Stonewall, and you're going to make me forget just how tired and hungry I am. And don't look at me that way."

He smiled. "What way?"

"Like you intend to make me forget anyway."

He threw his head back and laughed. The sound echoed off the walls of the elevator as they stepped out. He tightened his hold on her hand. "No, I intend to feed you and pamper you."

While he opened the door, she drew in a deep breath, and once again the smell of food filled her nostrils. "Good. Feed me first."

"Was this one of those days that you skipped lunch?" he asked as they stepped inside.

"Yes, I had to go back to the crime scene. The ME's report made me reconsider a few things," she said, removing her Glock.

He lifted a brow. "Reconsider a few things like what?"

She smiled over at him. "We'll talk about it over dinner."

NORM AUSTEN ENTERED the room where several men were already seated at the table. All eyes were on him, and he didn't mind. These were powerful men who called themselves the Brotherhood. They had a lot to lose if he ever screwed up. His job was to convince them he wouldn't. He understood their uneasiness. Last month, the FBI had busted a huge criminal cartel out West that included some of their counterparts on Capitol Hill in addition to well-known businessmen. Luckily none of their names had surfaced during the investigation, probably because they hid the dirt they were doing well. But he of all people knew how deep their ties to organized crime were.

"Have a seat, Norm. We called this meeting for a reason."

Norm took a chair as he looked at the three men standing. They were bodyguards who served not only as part of a security detail but henchmen, as well. He doubted there was much these men wouldn't do. But then, he also had his team of loyalists. Two were standing outside the door right now.

"Then what's the reason? I'm a busy man." He'd discovered early not to let anyone—not even these men—intimidate him. They might think they were calling the shots, but they were wrong. In time they would realize that.

Senator Patrick Holland was one of the wealthiest and most powerful men on Capitol Hill. He was well liked and highly respected. Few knew of the senator's dark side. He dabbled in human trafficking, the sale of illegal drugs, prostitution and, most recently, his new baby—no pun intended—the surrogate farm.

The other three men, Sherman Weathersby, Elijah Davenport and Roger Charles were all wealthy businessmen. Well respected. Yet tonight they were here with Holland to try to throw their weight around. He had news for them. It wouldn't be happening. For the time being they were letting the senator be the spokesman. That was all well and good.

The senator leaned close to the table. "Do you think

I give a damn how busy you are? Have you forgotten who you work for?"

Norm smiled. The four would realize soon enough he didn't work for anyone but himself. As far as he was concerned, they were equal partners. But for tonight, he wouldn't ruffle their feathers, especially since one of the bodyguards was flashing the gun he wore. Little did the man know that all he had to do was touch the face of his watch to send a silent signal to his men, and they would burst into the room and take everybody out. But the last thing Norm wanted tonight was to get any blood on his new suit.

"I'm not about to debate who I work for, Senator. Like I said, I'm a busy man. The four of you make sure of it. A loss of my time is a loss of money for yourselves. I like staying on top of things and prefer not being called away. So, what's this meeting about?"

Senator Holland eased back in his chair, seeming a little more relaxed, less tense. "It's about the surrogate farm. We've read the papers. That girl who escaped is the sister of a Hollywood celebrity."

"And?"

Holland frowned, giving him a look that would have a lesser man trembling in his shoes. "And we want to know nothing is going to come back and bite us in the ass."

Norm had news for the senator and his three cronies. If it was ever discovered what they did behind closed doors, it wouldn't come and bite them in the ass. It would bury them three hundred feet under the jail with the keys thrown away. "Nothing is going to come back and bite any of you. Trust me. Have I let you guys down yet? If you recall, thanks to me, Murphy Erickson is no longer a noose around your necks. Can you imagine what would have happened if it was discovered the four of you, along with other well-known men, were part of his operation?"

"Alright, alright, you did take care of Erickson, and we appreciate it," the senator said, rubbing the top of his head in agitation.

"And may I also remind you that as of yet no one, not even the Feds, has figured out how I did it," Norm said, smiling. He hadn't shared the details with anyone except his closest men, who'd carried out his orders.

"No, you don't have to remind us of anything," one of the men snapped.

"Good. Then the Brotherhood should feel confident that I'll take care of any issues regarding the surrogate farm. It's a smooth operation, and the people who allowed that girl to escape were dealt with. It won't happen again."

"You make sure that it doesn't. You can go now."

Norm chuckled under his breath at the bastard thinking he could dismiss him. Oh, well. They would discover soon enough that although Erickson was no longer running things, neither were they.

CHAPTER THIRTY-TWO

"So what's this reconsideration?" Stonewall asked as he sat down at the kitchen table with Joy. He didn't suggest they eat on the terrace because she didn't know it yet, but he had a table set up out there where he planned to give her a full body massage.

She glanced across the table at him and smiled. "First, I want to thank you for this. Just look at it."

He did, very much aware he'd prepared a lot of food. But he'd had plenty of time on his hands today and had been at the grocery store when he'd texted her. He'd never prepared her a full-course meal and decided to do so. "I don't expect you'll eat all of it, but it'll make delicious leftovers, too," he said, although he didn't plan on sending her home anytime soon. At least not before tomorrow morning.

"I still have ribs and chicken left from the cookout on Saturday. I ate a portion for dinner yesterday and planned to do the same tonight."

"Now you won't."

"Well, thanks for going to all the trouble."

"No need to thank me, Joy. It was something that I wanted to do." And it had been. All she had to do was say she needed pampering and he figured a home-cooked meal was the way to start. He'd always enjoyed cooking, but after a while it was much easier to grab something to eat on the run. It had been nice rolling his sleeves up and getting back into the kitchen. It had been especially nice today since he wanted to impress her.

Impress her...

When had he ever gone out of his way to impress any woman? Okay, he would admit taking her to Martha's Vineyard had been to impress her, as well. But then, Joy was someone he didn't mind impressing.

They said grace and she quickly began eating, tackling the huge piece of fried chicken breast on her plate. Over dinner she told him about her meeting that day with two of her detectives and the ME.

"Are you saying that you suspect they weren't random killings but were set up to look as such?"

"Right now it's just a theory, though it seems like a possibility. I have a gut feeling we're onto something much bigger, although I have no idea what. Tomorrow I'm telling the chief what I suspect. Going back to the crime scene helped, and it raised even more questions in my mind."

"What kind of questions?"

"Like, why would she have returned to work after leaving for the day? She hadn't mentioned any plans to do so to any of her staff. According to them she rarely works late."

"That would mean if she was the intended target, someone had to know she would be there."

"Yes. But who?"

"What about the pharmacist?"

"Our investigation indicates it wasn't unusual for him to work late. If anyone had been canvassing the pharmacy for any period of time to plan a break-in, they would have known that."

Stonewall shook his head. "Who would want to shoot a woman, directly in her heart? There has to be a motive."

"I agree. We're obtaining the log of her phone records and talking to her brother sometime this week. Tomorrow is the funeral, and I prefer we not interview him before then."

"What a sad thing for anyone to have to go through."

"Yes, it is. So what do you think?"

He appreciated her asking his opinion. "I think you should follow your gut feelings. While locked up I got to know this man who'd been an assassin for hire. A man paid him to kill his wife. To make it look random, he mapped her movements, and one day when she was at the park, he took her out as well as five others."

"How did the cops find out the truth?" Joy asked.

"Someone filmed it on their cell phone. When he was caught he spilled the beans for a lesser sentence and told the cops the husband had hired him. The cops arrested the husband. If the assassin hadn't gotten caught and fingered the husband, the man would have gotten away with his crime."

Joy took a sip of her iced tea before asking, "Why did the man want his wife dead?"

"He wanted to cash in on her life insurance policy. Nobody, his family or hers, or their friends, had suspected him of anything. In fact, I'm told he played the part of the grieving widower very well."

"Some people have sick minds," she said, pushing away from the table to stand. "I can help with the dishes."

He stood, as well. "Later," he said, knowing he had no intention of letting her help him. "Now I want to pamper you. Come with me."

Stonewall took her hand and led her toward the terrace. "I think you're going to like this."

Opening the door, he kept his gaze trained on her face, and from the look that immediately appeared there, he knew she did. He followed her gaze and saw the lit candles all around the terrace and the massage table draped in a white silk sheet. Beside it was a smaller table that held a number of scented lotions and oils. Draped from wall to wall was a swathe of sheer panels that he'd put up himself, and it hadn't been easy. He'd gotten the idea from watching television earlier that day. Funny how much free time he had these days. And he spent most of it thinking about this woman and about things he wanted to do to her and with her, in and out of bed.

"Stonewall, it's simply wonderful. You did this for me?"

He heard the sounds of awe and amazement in her voice. Had her former fiancé never treated her special like this? If he hadn't, what a wuss. "I did this for you. You asked me to pamper you and I will."

He released her hand and cupped her face. "I'm going to make sure you enjoy every second of it."

JOY WONDERED HOW they'd gotten to this point. When had she ever asked a man to pamper her? When did she begin thinking she needed pampering? She was tough, always. The work she did required it. She didn't go to work looking like a fashion model. She dressed appropriately since she never knew when she might have to wrestle a criminal to the ground.

Being around Stonewall made her want to be soft at times. Made her want to have those things she'd missed out on before. Made her want to be pampered, but then, she wanted to pamper him, as well. He was giving her tonight and soon she would give him his night. He was a man any woman would want to be in a serious relationship with. A man who could have his pick of any woman he wanted. Beautiful women. Women who enjoyed looking like fashion models, sexy goddesses, alluring twenty-four hours a day. That kind of woman wasn't her, so why was he allowing himself to be nothing more than her diversion?

"I'll leave you to undress," he said, breaking into her thoughts. "Don't worry about anyone seeing you out here since my terrace is blocked from the view of other buildings."

She glanced around and saw it was. The light from the candles and the way he had the panels draped gave it the effect of a romantic hideaway. She looked back at him. "In that case, you don't have to leave."

Already she was unbuttoning her blouse and knew Stonewall was watching her every move. "Unless, however, you have something better to do," she said, tossing her blouse aside to remove her bra.

She saw the flare of heat in his gaze as he continued to watch her. "No, there's nothing better. I'll just sit right here," he said, pulling out the chair from the table. "I'm beginning to feel weak in the knees."

She chuckled as she watched him slide his tall frame into the chair. Nude from the waist up, she leaned down to remove her shoes and socks. She glanced up when she heard the sound of his heavy breathing. "Is anything wrong?"

He held her gaze as he shook his head. "No, there's nothing wrong."

She nodded as she began sliding her slacks down her legs, followed by a pair of lacy black panties. When she stood there completely naked, she saw how his gaze roamed all over her. "Now what?" she asked, hearing a strain in her own voice.

"Now you can lie facedown on the table so I can give you a body massage."

She nodded. "Have you ever given anyone a massage before?"

"No, but I figured it can't be hard to do. The lady at that store was very helpful in giving me tips."

"What store?"

"Wonderful Lady Spa. The one in the Town Center Mall."

She was familiar with the place and knew the kind of women who worked there. Young. Beautiful. Curvaceous. Most walked around in those hottie shorts and tops that showed way too much skin. "Yes, I bet she was."

Joy ran her gaze over him. He was sitting with his long leg stretched out in front of him with a huge erection pressing hard against his zipper. The erection she definitely couldn't miss. She would admit for a minute she'd gotten jealous, but now, seeing him aroused and knowing that erection was about her and no other woman tempered the jealousy. Besides, she had no right to be jealous. After all, she and Stonewall were not in a relationship no matter how many times they shared a bed.

Deciding she was thinking way too much and too hard, she walked over to the table, more than ready to feel his hands on her. She merely glimpsed at the bottles on the small table before climbing the portable steps to get on the massage table to lie facedown. "I didn't know you owned a massage table," she said, drawing in a deep breath. Even the silken sheet was scented.

She could hear him move, and knew that he was moving toward her. "I didn't before today."

Joy lifted her head to look over her shoulder and he was there, standing beside the table. She could actually feel his heat. "You bought a massage table?"

"Yes. It's a fold-up table. I figured I could use it again for other things if I wanted to."

"Oh." But still, for him to go out of his way and do all of this for her made her feel special. They had spent the weekend together and today was only Monday. Yet she had awakened wanting to see him and regretted it when he had left her home yesterday. Stonewall Courson was growing on her, and the thought didn't bother her as it had before.

"Which do you prefer," he asked her, "lotion or oil?"

She thought about his question and then asked one of her own. "Which do you prefer using?"

"Umm, doesn't matter. Either way I get to put my hands on you."

Desire, hot and sharp, began clawing inside her. "You want that? To put your hands on me?"

"If only you knew how much."

She doubted it was any stronger than her desire to have him put his hands on her. "Then tell me the benefits of each one."

"No problem. Like I said, the woman who sold me this stuff was helpful."

Joy just bet she was. "And what did she say?"

"She said the oil would make you feel slippery and smooth."

"And the lotion?"

"It will penetrate into your skin and hey, I'm all in for penetration of any kind."

She wished his words didn't have the ability to make her body throb with a need she couldn't ignore, but they did. "In that case, I'll take the lotion."

"Good choice. I like the way it smells. Now close your eyes and enjoy."

Joy did as she was told, and the moment he uncapped the bottle of lotion, her nostrils were filled with the scent of jasmine. "That's my favorite scent."

"I know, and before you ask how, I couldn't help but notice it in your bedroom and bathroom."

She smiled. "I can get carried away with it at times."

"Your home is your place to do whatever you want."

Although she couldn't see him, she could visualize him taking his time to squeeze lotion from the bottle into his hands. Those big, strong, knew-how-to-stroke-a-woman hands. Pretty soon those same hands would be...

Before she could finish that thought, she felt his hands on her, touching her shoulders, rubbing the lotion onto her skin. He was slowly and meticulously kneading tension out of her and making her feel stress-free. Relaxed.

He needed to talk or else she would fall into a state of utopia. His hands moving across her shoulders felt so good. "Thanks to Whit, people around the office think you're my boyfriend."

"Do they?"

"Umm." His hands had moved down from her shoulders, lower to her spine.

"And what did you have to say about that?"

"I told them you were. No need to explain anything to anyone, right?"

"Yes, no need."

She felt his hands move lower to her backside as he continued to rub lotion into her skin. She let out a moan and then another when he began stroking the cheeks of her bottom.

"If you keep making that sound, I'll be tempted to…"

"…do what?" she coaxed. She had an idea but wanted him to tell her.

"Let's finish your massage first and then I'll show you."

He continued to knead her skin and she continued to moan. Not to tempt him but because she just couldn't help it. His hands were making her feel so good.

"Your skin always felt soft to my touch, Joy. Now it feels softer. And you have beautiful skin."

"Thank you." And he had a wonderful touch. She had discovered that the first night in her home when they'd made love and he'd touched her all over.

"Now I need you to flip over on your back."

She shifted from her stomach to her back and stared

up into his eyes. He broke eye contact to roam his gaze over her body. He returned his gaze to hers and asked, "Have I told you what a beautiful body you have?"

"Yes."

"Well, I'm telling you again. You have a beautiful body, Joy."

"Thank you." He could say some of the nicest things. She decided then and there not to compare Stonewall to Omar. Stonewall was in a class by himself and didn't deserved any comparison.

"And your breasts..."

She saw how he was looking at them. No doubt he was seeing how the nipples were responding to his close scrutiny. Hardening before his very eyes. "Yes? What about my breasts?"

"They're perfect."

He'd told her that the last few times they were together, and she knew she would never tire of the compliment. Although she thought he was stretching it a bit.

Joy watched as he picked up the lotion bottle and squeezed some into his hands. She thought he would start with her breasts, but he smoothed the lotion on her stomach instead. Frissons of fire raced through her when she felt the intensity of his touch. He glided his hand from one side of her abdomen to the other. Her breathing quickened as if she was about to draw her last breath.

"Your breasts are tempting me, Joy," he whispered, and she heard the urgency in his voice.

"Tempting you in what way?" She knew she shouldn't ask, but she couldn't stop herself from doing so.

"This way." And then he leaned down and sucked a

budded nipple between his lips and immediately began laving it with his tongue.

"Stonewall!"

"Hmm?"

"You're supposed to pamper me, not torture me."

He lifted his mouth and held her gaze. "You want me to stop?"

The answer was easy yet came out in a shaky breath. "No."

He smiled and lowered his head to her pert nipple again.

CHAPTER THIRTY-THREE

STONEWALL WAS CONVINCED that Joy was the most sensuous woman he'd ever laid eyes on. Definitely the most sensuous one he'd ever kissed or tasted. And he couldn't get enough of doing either. Every time he put his mouth on her, tasted the richness of her skin, he was driven to want more. That's why he lowered his head back to her breasts to kiss each one openmouthed before easing a nipple between his lips. He loved the feel of the nipple swelling inside his mouth.

He felt a twitch in his fingers and knew why. They wanted to stroke a part of her, a part he couldn't deny them because he wanted the feel of her on his fingers, as well. Moving his hand from her stomach, he began inching it lower until he reached the area between her legs. Parting the womanly folds of her feminine mound, he inhaled her seductive scent. A combination of jasmine and Joy.

At that moment he couldn't help but recall when he'd first tasted her there. He was convinced that after the first intimate kiss between her legs, his taste buds hadn't been the same. He could remember her taste no matter what he was eating. Whether it was drinking coffee or consuming one of his grandmother's tastiest desserts. Her taste was simply Joy. There was no other way to describe it. The thought of tasting her again made every nerve in his body sizzle. Joy tasted of honeyed richness, and Stonewall was convinced he was addicted to her flavor. That was why at some of the oddest times he would actually yearn for her essence.

Like now.

Pulling his mouth away from her breast, he stared at her face and met her gaze. Her desire-glazed eyes staring back at him made blood pump fast and furious through his veins. He licked his lips, letting her know he was getting them ready for what he thought of as a very tasty meal.

"Stonewall."

His name was whispered in a way that made his erection harden even more. He could feel her getting wetter beneath his fingers. Wanting her to know how much he was anticipating laving the very essence of her, he removed his hand from between her legs to bring the fingers to his mouth and lick her juices off them.

When she whispered his name again, he lowered his mouth to hers. The kiss they shared was mingled with intense desire. When he finally pulled his mouth away, he began trailing kisses down to her stomach. Then, as if his tongue had a mind of its own, it led the way, licking toward the area between her legs.

The moment his tongue touched her feminine mound he felt rejuvenated in a way that made his penis throb against the tightness of his jeans. His tongue was in control and once it slid between her feminine folds, it began circling her clitoris several times before it finally dipped deep inside her.

He tasted her richness and was so entranced by it, he grabbed hold of her thighs and his lips locked on her core. Locked in temptation, he was yielding to a need he couldn't deny he felt. He began sucking and stroking her gently, aware of her every moan and the way her hands had tightened on his forearms. She was squirming beneath his mouth, moving her body, pushing her hips off the table upward to taunt him to apply even more pressure and encouraging him to delve deeper. With the ravenous hunger he felt in his bones, his tongue worked her clitoris to the point that he could feel it budding in his mouth. Her moans urged him to go deeper still.

"Stonewall!"

Her scream seemed to ricochet through the air. His neighbors might not be able to see them but there was no doubt in his mind they had heard that particular scream. But he didn't care. The only thing he was concentrating on was getting ready to taste the orgasm that he knew was coming.

It did.

Her thighs began trembling and her hips started bucking as a climax besieged her. He was tempted to get on the table with her, but wanted her in his bed when he entered her. When he finally lifted his head and looked at her, the satisfied, pleasure-filled gaze she returned made his erection throb that much more. "We will finish this in my bedroom."

And then he swept her off the table and into his arms.

"Look at me, baby."

As Stonewall requested, Joy looked up at him, into a face so handsome it nearly took her breath away. He had brought her to his bedroom and placed her on the massive bed. She had watched him remove all his clothes, appreciating every inch of skin he revealed. The size of him no longer intimidated her like it had that first time. Her body had gotten used to accommodating him with ease. No surprise there given the number of times they'd made love.

What she always enjoyed most, and what was such a turn-on for her, was watching how he would encase himself in a condom. She wanted to ask him to let her do it sometime.

And now he wanted her to look at him and she had no problem doing so. "I'm looking at you, Stonewall."

The smile that touched his lips made her acutely aware of just how male and powerful he was. "Now I want you to feel me."

He said those words the exact moment she felt the head of his manhood stretching her as it eased inside her body. Going deep until he couldn't go any more. It was such a snug fit that she could feel her muscles automatically tighten around him. Then they began clenching him.

He leaned down and licked around her lips before grazing his bearded jaw against her ear. He growled low in this throat when he said, "I love it when you do that. Try to pull everything out of me. One day..."

He stopped short of finishing what he was going to say. *One day, what?* The thought then suddenly flashed through her mind that he was about to say that one day there wouldn't be a condom to hold him back. Was that wishful thinking on her part? She was surprised to realize the thought of him shooting off inside her, coating her body with the very essence of him, not only made her core contract, but made intense desire curl within her stomach.

"And now to finish pampering you."

He said the words as he began moving inside her, and

she reached out to hold his broad shoulders. The feel of his skin beneath her fingers only made her moan as delicious sensations rippled through her. He was establishing a rhythm for them as he began thrusting in and out of her. Soft and leisurely at first, but now more urgent and hard. She began to twist back and forth beneath him as spurts of pleasure tore through her. Even her toes tingled from the feel of his chest hair against her nipples.

Everything he was doing to her seemed to be in perfect sync. Her pulse kicked, her sexual energy was revved, and the sensations made her breathing ragged as he continued to thrust in and out of her. And when she knew she couldn't take any more, thought her body was about to explode, she screamed his name, even louder than she had on the terrace.

Her body detonated in what felt like a million prisms of ecstasy. She was about to scream his name again when she felt another forceful shudder, at the same time she felt his body jerk and buck. Sexual excitement filled her to the rim as he began stroking inside her with a speed and precision that sent a blaze of desire through her bloodstream. His gaze was transfixed on hers, like it was the end of time. That was crazy but at the moment, logic was being replaced by pleasure to such an extreme that at that moment she was a goner, and in more ways than one.

STONEWALL AWOKE EARLY the next morning when he felt Joy stirring in his arms. He knew it hadn't been her intention to spend the night, but one lovemaking session led to another, and another, and then another, and the last thing he remembered was them drifting off to sleep in each other's arms.

He did recall waking during the night and remembering the dishes hadn't gotten done, nor had he taken the time to snuff out the candles. But he hadn't cared. For him the only thing that had mattered was the woman who slept with her cheek resting on his chest, his arms wrapped around her waist and their legs entwined. He had drifted back to sleep thinking he could get used to this.

"I've got to go, Stonewall," Joy whispered, easing out of his arms. "I need to go home and get ready for work. I have several meetings this morning."

He nodded as he released her. "And I have a flight to catch at noon."

She looked at him, surprised. And was that disappointment he also saw in her eyes? The same eyes he'd stared into while making love to her last night? "You're leaving town?"

"Yes. Striker's next assignment was out of town to protect some socialite in Boston name Mondae Reddick. She's been receiving threats from an old boyfriend. I figured since Striker just got back and still considers himself on his honeymoon, I'd do him a favor."

"That was nice of you."

He reached up and stroked the side of her cheek. "Don't you think I'm a nice person?"

"Yes. A socialite?"

"Yes."

"So, how long will you be gone?" she asked, easing off the bed. He watched her look around for her clothes.

"A week. And your clothes are still out on the terrace."

"Oh."

Was that her response to the location of her clothes

or the fact he'd be gone a week? "Are you going to miss me?"

She glanced over at him and held his gaze. "Yes, I'm going to miss you, Stonewall."

There was something about the way she was looking at him as well as the way she'd said those words that got to him, set something off deep inside him that had nothing to do with lust. Made his heart skip a beat. Several. He eased out of bed and went to her, and without saying a word he lowered his mouth to hers. He didn't fully understand why he wanted to kiss her lips right off her mouth, literally. All he knew was this kiss was different from any other they'd shared. Why? He wasn't sure.

He broke off the kiss and whispered against her moist lips, "And I'm going to miss you, as well."

"Umm, what time will you have to miss me? You're be all wrapped up protecting the socialite."

Was that a twinge of jealousy he heard in her voice? He hoped not because there was no reason. She was the only woman he wanted. *The only woman he wanted?* When had that happened? "I will have free time. She has to sleep sometime." He took a step back. "I'll go get your clothes."

He left the room, deciding he needed distance for a minute to rid himself of all those crazy thoughts. He would miss her. She would miss him. But their relationship wasn't really a relationship. He paused and rubbed his hand down his face. Hell, if they weren't in a relationship, then what did you call what had been going on between them for the past three weeks? Maybe they needed the separation to determine what they wanted. Or what they didn't want. After three weeks it was time they decided.

"HELLO, THIS IS ANDERSON."

"Hopkins, this is Jerome Post."

Anderson swallowed hard. Jerome Post was the top man to Norm Austen.

He had never met Norm Austen. Few people had. But Anderson had met Jerome Post a number of times, and there was something about the man that made his skin crawl. Post's job was to make sure things continued to run smoothly and there were no hiccups. That's why, although he'd told Post about Mandy Clay's escape and subsequent death, he'd assured the man he had everything under control. He hadn't provided Post with any details as to how. The man didn't want details, just results.

"Mr. Post, what can I do for you?" Anderson asked, determined to sound as calm as he could, although he wasn't feeling it. He never felt it when talking to this man.

"You can assure me that all is well with our business on the East Coast."

"Of course things are going well. Why wouldn't they be?" Anderson asked, trying to play off the question.

"That woman's death made national news. Her sister is a celebrity. I gather you didn't know that when she was…selected."

No, he hadn't known. But that didn't matter. He couldn't let it matter now. "I told you I had handled everything," he said, refusing to say whether he'd known or not. "Let me reiterate what I told you before. Everything is running smoothly. Everybody's doing what they're supposed to do. I took care of the people responsible for the slipup that allowed the woman to escape. The new people you sent as replacements are working out nicely."

"Good. I assured Mr. Austen that you had everything under control. Don't make a liar out of me, Hopkins."

"I won't."

"And I hope there weren't any loose ends,"

Anderson swallowed again. "No loose ends."

"And you would tell me if there were, right?" Post asked in a threatening tone.

Anderson felt his skin crawl. "Of course."

Post was quiet for a moment, then said, "Seems like a lot of murders in your city lately." Another pause. "We'll talk again later."

Anderson heard the click in his ear. This was the first time he'd heard from Post in months. Had Post figured out things about Kelly? He was aware that Kelly had been one of their suppliers. She had supplied clients, namely couples who wanted a baby and would pay a lot of money for a surrogate so they could have their own biological child. Most of them thought their surrogacy was legal and well within the confines of the law. Little did the couples know that some were. But most weren't.

Like the one Kelly had arranged for his sister.

Rachel had no idea that he'd had a hand in every single detail of the arrangements. Even the attorney she'd hired had been recommended by him and hadn't been on the up and up. But Anderson had refused to see his sister unhappy any longer. She and Brett had wanted a baby, and her happiness had meant a lot to him. It meant everything.

That's why he had no guilty conscience about Kelly. Had she talked, it would have been detrimental not only to the entire organization but to his sister's happiness, as well. Rachel's eggs weren't viable for the embryo transfer. That meant Chasta was Brett's biological child, but not hers. It would destroy Rachel if she ever found out that her eggs had not been used. Mandy Clay had been handpicked by him because Mandy and Rachel shared similar features, including the same hair color and shade of blue eyes.

He had seen Mandy while in New Orleans on a business trip. She and another woman were dining at the same restaurant. Finding out who she was and where she lived had been easy. So had kidnapping her, thanks to a couple of the men in blue from the New Orleans Police Department who were on the Brotherhood's payroll. Unlike the other women who'd been kidnapped, Mandy had come across as street-smart. He should have known she would cause trouble. As far as he was concerned, she had brought her death on herself and he didn't feel bad about it.

Like he'd told Post, everything was going smoothly, and he was determined to make sure things continued that way. He had too much to lose if they didn't. The police had no reason to think Kelly's death was anything more than her being at the wrong place at the wrong time. And if they hadn't discovered anything new about Mandy Clay by now, chances were they wouldn't. Cases went cold all the time.

Kelly's funeral would be held in Charlottesville today. Too bad things had turned out the way they had for her. Too bad.

CHAPTER THIRTY-FOUR

JOY APPROACHED HER office with memories of last night and that morning still running through her mind. She'd questioned Stonewall's stamina only that one time, but she was convinced each time they'd made love he still went out of his way to put that question to rest. The man had more sexual energy than anyone she knew. Not that she was complaining. His night of pampering had been the best she'd ever had.

She recalled waking up in his arms before dawn this morning and watching him the moment he'd opened his eyes. Those heavy-lidded dark brown eyes had held her within their scope, looking irresistibly drowsy. Just gazing at him, especially that sexy bearded chin, not to mention such a naked and warm body, had turned her on all over again.

She didn't have time for one more roll between the sheets since she'd needed to get up and go home, shower and dress for work. But when he'd returned with her clothes and she'd watched him take a bold sniff of her panties before handing them to her, she decided she wanted him to make love to her again regardless of the time. Of course he'd been more than accommodating, and he'd had her screaming out an orgasm in no time.

He would be gone a week, and if his intent was to

leave her with something to think about while he was gone, he'd definitely done that. He had walked her down to her car and kissed the living daylights out of her before she'd left. She had driven all the way home smiling.

Hell, she was still smiling. When she'd passed several detectives in the hall just now they'd looked at her strangely. Let them look. She now had a life and didn't mind anyone knowing it. She stopped short upon reaching her office. *Did she really have a life?*

How could she when she hadn't committed to trying a relationship with Stonewall? It had been her choice not to. In fact, she'd reiterated that to him a number of times. Was she thinking about changing her tune? If she was, how would he feel about it if she did? And why did the thought of them becoming a couple have such a strong appeal to her now?

She continued walking toward her office. She had a week to figure things out. One whole week. But then, as she looked at the files on her desk, she had a lot of detective work to do this week, as well.

JOY WATCHED CHIEF HARKINS. He'd just finished reading her report and was now leaning back in his chair, eyeing her speculatively. He asked, "And you really believe Dr. Kelly Langley was the intended target, and the thieves went to all that trouble to make it seem like a random act?"

"Yes. I admit I didn't at first. It seemed like the motive was clear-cut. Namely the prescription drugs since two different pharmacies had been hit the same night and by the same individuals within a five-mile radius. Now I think things were done that way to throw us off. The new ME, Dr. Lennox Roswell, noted several irregularities. Dr. Roswell is good at what she does, by the way."

Chief Harkins chuckled. "I hire and promote only the best." Any amusement left his face when he said, "If what you assume about Dr. Langley is true, Lieutenant, there has to be a real serious motive for someone to go to all that trouble. Find a motive."

She stood. "I intend to. She was a divorcée so I'll start there."

"And let's make sure the media doesn't get wind of this until we have something concrete. Otherwise they will hound us to death."

"Yes, sir."

Moments later, Joy had returned to her office and was about to sit when her phone rang. It was an inter-office call. "This is Lieutenant Ingram."

"Yes, Lieutenant, this is Acklin. We have the search warrant for Dr. Langley's phone records."

PSYCHIC INVESTIGATOR RANDI FULLER felt a cold, deathly chill as she glanced around Murphy Erickson's prison cell. The same cell where he'd been found murdered about six months ago. The two federal agents, including Special Agent Felton, had brought her here. They were all hoping that Erickson would reach out to her, but so far nothing. No surprise, since the one time she and Erickson had met, it had been more like a face-off, a clash of wills. He had gone to his grave disliking her as much as she disliked him.

Sighing deeply, she turned to Agent Felton. "Sorry,

but I don't feel anything in here. In order for my powers to work, there has to be—"

Suddenly Randi went still as the sound of a male voice came to her. Had she heard right? Had that one single word been a clue from Erickson?

"Dr. Fuller? Are you alright?"

Randi blinked. Two sets of eyes were staring at her. She drew in a deep breath. "Yes. And I think I have something. Video. Erickson just said the word *video*. I think he wants me to watch the video."

No one looked at her like she'd lost her mind. They were well aware of her psychic abilities. "Video from the security cam?" One of the agents asked to clarify. "We just finished watching it."

Randi nodded. "I know, but that's the video I assume he meant. Evidently we missed something. Is it possible for me to watch the security cam again?"

Agent Felton nodded. "Yes, we'll watch it as many times as we need to."

"I want to go to Charlottesville to check on things there."

Norm Austen glanced over at Jerome Post. He knew Jerome was a man he could count on to make sure things ran smoothly. When Norm had been handpicked to replace Erickson, he knew he needed people around him he could trust implicitly. He and Jerome went way back, and he knew if Jerome wanted to go check on their East Coast operation, there had to be a reason.

"Why? Is there something I should be concerned about?"

"Not sure, which is why I want to go check on things.

Hopkins claims he has everything under control but it appears that he's making mistakes. Too many. Pretty soon they will draw attention, if they haven't already. I have a gut feeling things aren't right."

Norm didn't say anything. He'd been in control only a year. Unbeknownst to Murphy Erickson, Norm had officially taken over the moment Erickson had been arrested on those federal charges. There was no way the federal government would have released Erickson from prison, no matter who he'd tried to intimidate and blackmail. And hiring an assassin to kill everyone who'd been in the courtroom that day had been the man's last-ditch effort at freedom. That was when it was decided by the Brotherhood that Erickson would never leave prison alive.

Now Norm had the power, and he intended to keep it. With Jerome's help he knew that he would. "Alright, go to Virginia and take Conyers with you. If you find a problem, fix it."

CHAPTER THIRTY-FIVE

JOY LEFT HER office and caught the elevator to the basement for her meeting with Taren and Sanchez in the tech department, where Taren's team worked their magic. A serious brain when it came to technology, Taren was a MIT graduate whose skills had helped solve numerous crimes for the department. More than once the FBI had tried persuading Taren to come work for them, but so far she'd turned them down.

Walking into Taren's work space was like being in a NASA command center, with huge screens monitoring various areas of Charlottesville and several projects in progress. She saw Sanchez had arrived already.

After greeting everyone, she knew Taren was ready to get down to business. "First off," Taren said, leaning back in her chair, "I ran that background check on Oliver Effington and his wife. So far I've found nothing. They have been married ten years and before that, both were divorcés. No criminal records for either. Not even speeding tickets. Beautiful Creations seems to be one of the top places if you're in the market for a surrogate. It costs more than the other places, but you pay for the results you get. Their satisfaction rate is ninety-eight percent. They vet the women they use as surrogates thoroughly and have a team of lawyers who are good at what they do."

"And Oliver Effington interviews each potential surrogate before bringing them on board like he claims?"

"Yes, from what I can tell. It's all part of his vetting process. Appears that he's more hands-on than any of the others. I can't get a listing of the women without a warrant, though."

Joy understood. "There has to be a reason Effington was certain of Mandy Clay's hair color."

"There is one thing I did notice," Taren said.

"And what's that?" Sanchez asked.

"Effington does more traveling than any of the other CEOs of similar surrogate agencies. Most are for pleasure trips. In checking Beautiful Creations' tax records, I see they are doing extremely well financially, but I'm not sure if that's how he pays for the trips."

Joy nodded. "I'd like to see a list of all his travels over the past twenty-four months and who went with him."

"Okay."

"What about those prescriptions?" Saying the word *prescriptions* made Joy think of the other homicide she was working. Dr. Langley's funeral was today, and she needed to talk to the woman's brother.

"There are a number of doctors who regularly work with the local surrogate agencies. Here is the list." She handed a copy to both Joy and Sanchez.

"And just so you know, the prescription could have been written by a doctor anywhere and not just in this area."

Sanchez shook his head. "That doesn't make our job easier if we wanted to track one of them down, does it?"

"No."

Joy scanned the list, and immediately one physician's name stuck out. Dr. Kelly Langley. "This is interesting," she said aloud.

"What is?" Sanchez asked.

"Dr. Kelly Langley's name is on this list. She was one of the victims in the double homicide Friday night."

"That's right," Sanchez said. "She was at the wrong place at the wrong time."

"Yes, but now we have reason to believe she might have been the intended target." She brought Sanchez and Taren up on what she knew so far. "I can't believe I didn't make the connection before. Dr. Langley was a fertility specialist."

"Think it's a coincidence?" Sanchez asked, rubbing his chin.

Joy drew in a deep breath. "In our line of business there are no coincidences."

"But in this case, it might just be," Taren pointed out. "There are a lot of doctors who work with these agencies. It would have been just part of her job, referring her patients to surrogate agencies."

Joy nodded. "Is there any way we can get more detailed information, like how many of Dr. Langley's patients got referred to Beautiful Creations versus the other agencies?"

"Due to privacy laws, not without a judge order," Taren said.

"Good luck on getting that," Sanchez chimed in to

say. "I can't see a judge giving us that kind of order without just cause."

Joy knew he was right about that. Still, there was something about Dr. Langley being connected to Beautiful Creations that didn't sit well with her. She couldn't wait to review the woman's phone records.

"WOULD YOU LIKE a cup of coffee, Dr. Fuller?"

Randi shook her head. "No, I'm fine." Already they had watched the video footage five times, and she hadn't seen anything. No one had come into Erickson's cell, not a single person.

She was certain Erickson wanted her to see this particular video, but what had he expected her to find? Not having a clue, she was about to watch it for the sixth time. "I want to see it again, Agent Felton."

She was grateful the man didn't say anything but gave the order for it to be replayed. They had sat through the first hour of viewing when she heard a voice say to her, "There. Look closely."

Automatically she said out loud, "Slow the video."

The technician did as she asked and everyone stared at what was happening in the video. Erickson was sitting at a small table and was about to stand when he put his hand to the back of his neck in a move as if he was working out a kink.

"Go back a few frames, magnify and go in slow motion," she said.

She still didn't see anything other than Erickson making the same gestures and movements. "Magnify frame and slow pace even more."

Randi wasn't sure what she was looking for, but she

knew Erickson would not have given her the word that something was there if it wasn't. A part of her was certain if she continued to watch she would see it. She just had to pay close attention to every single thing. Her gaze took in the whole cell, scrutinizing the walls, the floors and every piece of furniture, but she still didn't see anything.

"Go back another two frames and magnify even more," she said in an anxious tone.

"Can I ask what you're looking for?" Agent Felton said, analyzing the huge screen just as closely as she was.

Not taking her eyes off the video, she said, "I'm not sure yet."

Then suddenly she felt it, the physical signs she always experienced when her psychic abilities were kicking in and she was witnessing something crucial. Cold chills passed through her body and there was the fiery feel of blood rushing through her veins. "Magnify the frame five times, please."

The technician once again did as she asked, and she saw it. It surprised her when she did to the point that she drew in a sharp breath that echoed in the room. "What is it, Dr. Fuller?"

Instead of answering the agent, she said to the technician, "Hold the frame right there."

He did, placing it in a pause mode. She then glanced over at the others. "Take a look and tell me what you see."

The agents did as she requested and then turned back to her, appearing confused.

"Look again," she instructed softly.

They did, and a few moments later they reached the same conclusion. They hadn't seen anything. Randi nodded, then told the technician to go back at least three frames. Erickson was shown pacing around in his cell a few times before sitting down at the table.

"Notice that piece of lint in the air," she told the others.

"What piece of lint?" one of the agents asked as he moved closer to the screen.

Getting up out of her chair and using a pointer, Randi showed them what had caught her attention. It appeared as a piece of lint floating in the air and would have been barely visible to the naked eye if she hadn't asked the technician to magnify the frame as many times as she had.

"Okay, we see it now," one of the agents said. "It's nothing more than a piece of lint. I see small particles like them floating around in the air all the time. If I'm not mistaken, I believe the prison's laundry is two floors up."

"Yes, but I don't think it's a regular piece of lint. Watch where it goes the moment it floats into the cell."

They watched and saw that like a magnet, the piece of lint moved toward Erickson and seemed to attach itself to the side of his neck. That's when Erickson rubbed his neck with his hand before standing. They had watched him do that over and over with each viewing of the video but had assumed he'd made the gesture because he'd gotten tired. But it was clear he had rubbed the side of his neck after that piece of lint had attached itself to him.

"Well, I'll be damned," one of the agents said. "That piece of lint contained poison?"

"No, I don't think so," Randi said. "In one of the classes I teach at Quantico, we were presented data about Vertay VCT, which was developed by someone who worked for the Bureau. Unfortunately it got into the wrong hands. It doesn't introduce poison into your bloodstream but works on your nervous system. Erickson felt a twinge in his neck for a mere second, which is probably why his hand went there and he rubbed the area. He was fine until he lay down. Once he went to sleep, the rest of his body shut down, and within two hours, he was dead."

"But how did that piece of lint land directly on Erickson?"

"It's programmed to a person's DNA," she explained. "It will bypass everyone until it connects to the person's DNA it was sent to attach itself to."

Felton shook his head, amazed. "Not that I don't believe you, Dr. Fuller, but we're going to need scientific proof that's what happened."

"Then I suggest you scan the clothing that was taken off Erickson. Hopefully the lint piece is still there."

"But that will be like looking for a needle in a haystack," one agent said, rubbing a hand down his face in frustration.

"It won't be hard with the use of a high-powered scanner. I believe the Bureau has such equipment," Randi said.

Felton frowned as if he was thinking hard. "Using that weaponized technology is damn serious. I don't want to imagine what could happen if someone gets the DNA of a high-ranking official. Like the president."

Randi nodded and said, "Then you guys need to do whatever you can to stop it from happening."

LATER THAT EVENING, Joy got a visit from Detective Acklin.

"What you got?" she asked him when he sat down in the chair in front of her desk.

"Went over Dr. Langley's phone records. Not a lot of texts but a number of calls on Friday. The last one Dr. Langley received was at noon that day."

Joy nodded. "Do we know who the call was from?"

"The phone number is registered to Anderson Hopkins," Acklin said. "In checking, I saw there were a number of calls made either to his number or from his number over the past two years.

"And what do we know about Hopkins? Is he a fellow doctor? Boyfriend? Church member?"

Acklin chuckled. "Not sure about the last or the first, but I believe he might have been a boyfriend. The calls were made frequently enough that we can assume it. As far as his occupation, he's a genetic counselor at Parkmoore Research."

"Genetic counselor? Interesting. Give me a full report on Dr. Langley's phone activities as well as a report on Mr. Hopkins. We'll visit Dr. Langley's brother first thing in the morning to see if he can shed light on anything."

"And what about Anderson Hopkins?" Acklin asked.

"He'll get a visit from us, as well."

JOY HAD JUST walked out her bathroom after taking a shower when the buzzing of her phone let her know a text message had come through. Dropping the towel, she slid into a short baby doll nightgown before picking up the phone. *Thinking about you.*

She couldn't help the sensations that raced through her in knowing that although they were miles apart, she was in Stonewall's thoughts. Sitting cross-legged in the middle of her bed, she texted back. *U in mine 2.*

Too late to call?

She quickly responded, *No.*

No sooner had her finger finished hitting Send than her phone rang. She hurriedly clicked on. "Hi."

"How are you, Joy?"

She just loved it when he said her name in that deep, husky voice. "I'm fine? How are you?"

"Doing okay."

Before she could stop herself, she asked, "And how is your socialite?" Earlier today when she'd had a few free moments, she had looked up the woman. Mondae Reddick was beautiful, polished and elegant. Her family boasted strong ties to W.E.B. Du Bois.

"Mondae is okay."

Umm, so they were on a first-name basis? Was there a reason they wouldn't be? And why did it bother her that they were? "Define *okay.*"

"I think she's a nice person. Easy to get along with."

Joy knew she should let it go. After all, she had no designs on Stonewall and he had no designs on her. And the one thing she couldn't lose sight of was the fact that he had texted her tonight because he'd been thinking of her. And he had called her. He was talking to her when he could very well be doing other things. She forced to the back of her mind what some of those other things could very well be and with whom.

"So how was your day today?" he asked.

Was he intentionally changing the subject? She drew in a deep breath, refusing to go there. She'd never been jealous over a man before him, but this wasn't the first time she'd allowed the green-eyed monster to rear its ugly head. "Today was busy as usual." She found herself telling him about some of the recent developments.

"I knew you would figure things out."

"Thanks for the vote of confidence. Again." More than once he'd not only expressed his faith in her abilities but also given his encouragement and support.

"Don't mention it." He paused a minute and then said, "I thought of you a lot today."

Her heart skipped a beat at his words. She'd thought of him a lot today, as well, even those times when she'd been busy. She'd discovered that being busy did not eliminate him from her thoughts. And him being in them hadn't sidetracked her or distracted her from the cases she was working. They had been pleasant thoughts. She'd purposely saved the more heated ones for later, after she'd gotten home from work.

"You've gone quiet on me."

His words made her smile. "I was just thinking I thought of you a lot today, as well."

"Really?"

She chuckled. "Yes, really."

"And what did you think about?"

Suddenly feeling shy, she said, "You first."

"Okay. I thought about how beautiful you look in the mornings."

She frowned. *Beautiful? In the mornings? No makeup and hair not tied down?* "You're kidding, right?"

"No. You're beautiful when you sleep but even more beautiful when you wake up. Do you know I consider you my Joy in the morning?"

A gush of pleasure rocked her with his words. "No, I didn't know that."

"Now you do."

His Joy in the morning. *Wow.* "That's real sweet, Stonewall."

"You're a sweet person. And I also thought a lot about making love to you. Being inside you. Hearing you scream my name. Damn, I love it when you do that. Scream my name."

Heat curled inside her, and she was convinced every single hormone within her was sizzling. If this was considered phone sex, then she was enjoying it. Probably a little too much.

"Now, what were you thinking when you thought of me?" he asked her.

"Do you really want to know?" She wondered if she could be daring enough to tell him.

"Yes, I really want to know."

She closed her eyes. "I was thinking a lot about your tongue."

He didn't respond at first. Then he asked, "And what about my tongue?"

She released a deep breath as she thought…*everything about your tongue.*

"I think it's perfect. I love the way you use it to kiss me…in my mouth, on my breasts, all over my body and especially between my legs." Saying the words made her body ache in all those places she'd mentioned, especially the last.

It got quiet on his end of the phone. "Stonewall?"

"Hmm?"

"Was that too much?"

"No, I was just thinking that I'd give anything to be back in Charlottesville with you right now. And I'd do everything with my tongue that you think I'm good at."

Lordy. There was no doubt in her mind that he would. They talked for another hour or so, enjoying phone sex, as lusty as it could get. "I didn't know you were such a bad boy."

"Only a good girl would think that," he said in a tone that thickened desire in her bloodstream. The man was walking and talking temptation. "Will you dream about me tonight, Joy?"

Was he kidding? How could she not after all those erotic and explicit words he'd spoken to her? "Yes, I will definitely dream about you, Stonewall Courson. And just for the record, if I had been a good girl before this phone call, I am definitely not one now. However, you do know what they say, right?"

"No, what do they say?"

"Once a bad boy, always a bad boy."

CHAPTER THIRTY-SIX

"Ask me anything you want, Lieutenant, if you think it will help in finding my sister's killers."

Sitting across the table from him, Joy could see the pain in Barron Driscoll's eyes. There was no doubt in her mind he loved his sister and was taking her death hard. She'd read the interview he'd given with Acklin the day Driscoll had arrived back in the country. There was a ten-year difference between him and his older sister. Their parents had died over twenty years ago, and his and his sister's relationship was a close one.

"Thank you," she said, turning on her digital voice recorder. Acklin pulled out his notepad, still preferring to use longhand. "Mr. Driscoll, when was the last time you spoke with your sister?"

He drew in a deep breath. "Three weeks ago. Because of where I was working, she understood I couldn't make frequent phone calls home. When I took the assignment, I knew I'd be gone a while. I was to return home at the end of the year." He paused before continuing. "We talked about a welcome-back party. I would have liked that."

"I understand Dr. Langley was divorced. I need the name of—"

"Wait," Driscoll interrupted to say. "If you're looking for thieves, why would you be interested in Kelly's ex-husband?"

"We're pursuing all possible leads, Mr. Driscoll," Acklin said. "We're not ruling out anything or anyone at this point."

Driscoll nodded. "His name was Herbert Langley. They got a divorce years ago. He moved away and re-married."

"Moved where?"

"Montana. The two met in med school."

"So, he was also a doctor?"

"Yes. A neurologist. He has a successful medical practice in Helena."

"Do you know the name of the man your sister was currently seeing?"

Driscoll frowned. "Kelly wasn't seeing anyone."

Joy lifted a brow. "How can you be so sure of that? You were in Turkey."

"Because she would have told me."

"What about close friends? A BFF?"

"No. Other than her colleagues at work, Kelly was pretty much a loner. She was into soaps. She would tape them during the day and spend her evenings watching them."

He chuckled. "A lot of the times I called when I would knew I'd interrupted her watching her soaps."

"Yes, but still, your sister was a beautiful woman."

"Yes, she was. If she was seeing someone I didn't know about it."

A short while later, leaving Barron Driscoll's home, Acklin turned to Joy as they got into the unmarked car. "I wonder what he's going to think when he finds out his sister was involved with someone and they were using his place most Thursdays for their secret trysts."

Joy didn't say anything as Acklin started the car. The review of the phone records as well as the signals picked up by the towers verified what Acklin had just said. Why did Dr. Langley keep her affair with Anderson Hopkins a secret? There was a twelve-year difference in their ages, but still. Was the age difference the reason or was there something else? She would not have been the first woman to date a younger man.

"What I also find strange is that Hopkins just got back in town, which meant he didn't attend Dr. Langely's funeral. What kind of lover would not at least pay their last respects?" Acklin said.

"I don't know, but I intend to find out," Joy said.

It DIDN'T TAKE the federal agents but a few hours to scan the clothing that had been taken off Erickson and find the microdevice. But that was only after a high-tech scanner had been brought in. Now they were in the FBI crime lab waiting for the device to be analyzed.

"This is amazing," Dr. Woodrow McClendon, one of the Bureau's top crime analysts, said after taking a look at the device under a microscope. "A drone that's barely visible to the naked eye and contains a poison that works on your nervous system. The moment your body goes into sleep mode, it kills without a trace."

"In that case, how can it be proven that the device is what killed Erickson?" Felton asked.

"By breaking down the code. I bet when we do, it will show Erickson's DNA was programmed into it. It will take a while but our team should be able to do it."

"So you've encountered a similar device?" another one of the agents asked.

McClendon nodded. "A similar killing device, the DHX211, was discovered being used last year. However, it was in the form of an insect. I can understand why the perpetrators switched from an insect to a piece of lint."

"Why?" Randi asked, taking a turn to look into the microscope. Under the lens all parts of the lint had been enhanced and its working body was revealed. Dr. McClendon was right. It was simply amazing how such a device had been created and used.

"Mainly because if it was seen, on instinct most people would try to swat an insect away or kill it. However, a piece of lint would be seen as nonthreatening," Dr. McClendon explained.

"Is there any way we can trace where it came from?" Felton asked.

"Yes, but doing so won't be easy. This device only had a twenty-hour life span once it was released into the air to find the person whose DNA it was programmed to kill. This item served its purpose. Once it hit its intended target it became inoperable."

"Who would have the means to make something like this?" an agent asked.

"You'll be surprised to find out what's being sold on the black market. An item like this in the wrong hands would make assassination simple and anonymous."

Felton nodded. "Yes, that's true. If it hadn't been for Dr. Fuller's psychic powers, we might never have realized how Erickson died."

"It wasn't just me," Randi said, moving away from the microscope. "As much as I don't want to give the man credit for anything, I have to say it was Erickson who told me what we needed to know."

Felton frowned. "After all the people he killed, don't expect me to be grateful. I still want him to burn in hell."

"So what's next?" one of the agents asked as he leaned against the lab door. "If we can't trace where the device came from, how can we determine how it got into the jail?"

"That should be easy enough, although time-consuming," Randi said. "You'll need to screen security cam footage of everyone who visited the federal prison that day for any reason. Everyone's a suspect even if they just walked through the door."

She moved away from the lab table to face Felton. "I'll be glad to help out. Who knows? I might get lucky and Erickson will give me a clue again."

Felton released a deep sigh. "Any additional help you can provide will be appreciated, Dr. Fuller."

ANDERSON GLANCED AT the files on his desk. The bad thing about being away from the office was returning to more work. He liked handling his own files. Besides, he wouldn't want anyone nosing around and discovering anything they shouldn't. Parkmoore Research was a reputable company, founded by Dr. Reliford Parkmoore and his wife years ago. The pay was good and the travel opportunities great. But he would admit it was greed that made him jump at the chance Post offered him.

When Post had approached him one day, seemingly out the blue, he'd been intrigued at what the man had offered. It had seemed simple enough. All he had to do was work with several fertility specialists in the area to persuade them to send some of their patients to Beautiful Creations. The kickback had been more than he'd dreamed of. He wasn't supposed to ask any questions, just do as he was told.

That had worked for him for two years before he was approached again for a bigger role in the organization. It was then that he learned what was going on. At first he'd wanted no part of it. After all, he had a younger sister, and he couldn't imagine something like that happening to her. But when Post had laid out the benefits, Anderson had put his conscience aside. Now he had a bigger role and men reported to him. He had a steady stream of clients for Beautiful Creations.

He should not have gotten so deeply involved with Kelly. He'd intentionally put himself in her path at that seminar. Had deliberately wooed her, bedded her and convinced her to do whatever he wanted. Things had been going great. As lovers went she was okay and never demanding. And as long as she kept the clients coming, all was well. Until Mandy Clay had escaped.

Anderson stood and walked over to the window and looked out. He refused to feel guilty about Kelly. Having her disposed of was proof he'd become a man without a conscience. A man who would stop at nothing to make sure everything ran smoothly for the boss man. Someone he had yet to meet.

It didn't matter. He had a nice amount of money in his Swiss bank account. And if anything happened to him, every cent would go to his sister and niece. No one would ever know that Mandy Clay was Chasta's biological mother.

He turned away from the window when the buzzer went off on his office phone. He frowned. Since he'd had a lot of work to catch up on after being gone for over a week, he'd asked the receptionist to hold his calls.

Crossing the room he clicked on the line. "Wilma, I asked not to be disturbed." He'd gotten back in town early that morning. The only reason he'd come into the office this afternoon was to start working the files on his desk.

"I know, Mr. Hopkins, but they insisted upon seeing you."

His frown deepened. "Who?"

"Detectives Ingram and Sanchez from the police department."

Anderson froze.

Moments passed, and Wilma's next words defrosted him. "Mr. Hopkins. Will you see the detectives or not?"

Detectives? He rubbed a hand down his face. He had to get a grip. Stay calm and not give anything away. "Yes, please send them in."

RANDI RUBBED THE back of her neck and adjusted in her chair. Like all the other federal agents in the room, she'd been watching footage for the last three hours. They watched and matched the log of those who'd entered the prison that day with those on the security feed. It didn't matter if the person was an employee, someone making a delivery or a visitor. If they came through the door they got scrutinized.

"Watch guy in blue shirt."

All of a sudden Randi sat up when Erickson's words came out of nowhere. Everyone in the room noted her movement, and she stared at the screen and said what she'd been instructed to do. "Watch the guy in the blue shirt."

"Which one?" one of the agents asked. "There are four of them."

"Then let's concentrate on each one."

They did and followed their every movement. One guy in particular was wearing a baseball cap, a blue shirt and a pair of jeans. He was a Caucasian male, was tall and appeared to be in his early thirties. From his actions he seemed somewhat nervous about something. Every so often he would glance at his watch as if something needed to be perfectly timed.

"Magnify screen times ten," Randi said, keeping an eye on that particular man when she felt a chill pass through her body.

The screen magnified and in a move that would have been missed if you hadn't been looking for it, the man reached into his pocket and took out what appeared to be a pack of breath mints. However, instead of popping one into his mouth, something that appeared to be a piece of lint was released into the air.

"Magnify times five." This time it was Agent Felton who gave the order.

The viewing screen showed the lint floating in the air and then disappearing. It was noted that although there were a number of people in the prison's lobby waiting to pass through the security checkpoint, the piece of lint didn't attach itself to anyone. It continued to float through the air. Everyone in the room now knew it was on a mission to kill its target, namely Murphy Erickson.

Randi's gaze returned to the man in the blue shirt.

Satisfied that his mission was accomplished, without waiting to go through security, he walked back out through the revolving doors. They would find no record of his identity in the logs.

"Get stats on that guy," Felton ordered. "See if his description fits anyone in the criminal activity database."

He then turned to Randi. "If I hadn't been a witness to all of this for the past ten hours I would not have believed it."

At that moment Special Agent Felton's phone rang, and he took the call. Moments after clicking it off, he said, "That was Dr. McClendon. His team of scientists have concluded that piece of lint is what killed Erickson. It was his DNA that was programmed into it like we thought. We need to identify that guy in the blue shirt. The last thing we want is for that killing device to be used again."

CHAPTER THIRTY-SEVEN

AFTER INTRODUCTIONS WERE MADE, Anderson leaned back against his desk. "Detectives, I'm at a lost as to what this meeting is about."

Joy had begun studying the man the moment they'd walked into his office. Anderson Hopkins was tall and extremely handsome. Well, not as handsome as Stonewall, she immediately thought. And he had an air of coolness, like he was prepared to turn this into a game. Little did he know it would be a game that she had no problem playing.

"Mr. Hopkins, did you know Dr. Kelly Langley?"

She noted he hesitated in answering, as if he needed to decide how he would. "*Did* know her, Detective? Any reason you're referring to Kelly in the past tense?"

"Yes. Because Dr. Langley is dead."

Shock appeared on the man's face. "Dead? Kelly is dead?" As if the impact of what he'd just found out disturbed him to the degree he couldn't remain standing, he moved to sit in the chair behind his desk. He rubbed his hand down his face and looked over at them. "But how?"

"She was murdered Friday night while working late," Joy said. "She and a pharmacist. Appears robbery was the motive."

"So you admit to knowing Dr. Langley?" Acklin asked him.

"Yes, although we were keeping our association a secret."

"Is that a fact? Why?" Joy asked.

Anderson drew in a deep breath. "Our ages. I didn't have a problem with it, but she did. She felt uncomfortable about anyone knowing the two of us were seeing each other. Sorry if I seem out of it, but I just got into town early this morning, and what you've told me about Kelly has shocked the hell out of me."

Then, not waiting for them to ask, he added, "I've been in Seattle the past week attending a biochemical seminar."

Joy noted he'd smoothly established his alibi. "And you didn't watch television or have contact with anyone back home who would have told you about Dr. Langley?"

"No. I was tied up in meetings during most of the day, and at night I went straight to bed. And because no one knew of my affair with Kelly, there would not have been a reason for anyone to call and tell me of her death." He shook his head. "It's hard to believe she's gone."

"When was the last time you talked to Dr. Langley?" Acklin asked.

Joy noted he hesitated again before answering. "I talked to her last Friday, around noon, to let her know when I was returning and to see if she wanted to get together when I got back."

"And did she? Want the two of you to hook up when you got back?" Acklin asked.

"Yes. I was to see her tomorrow night at our usual place."

"Which is where?"

"Her brother's home in the mountains. She never

wanted to use our places or a hotel. Since her brother was out of the country and she would occasionally house-sit, it was convenient."

Yes, Joy thought, she just bet it was. "And you didn't try contacting her since returning to town?"

"No. I went home straight from the airport this morning, showered, grabbed breakfast and went to bed to get a few hours of sleep before coming into the office. I didn't even turn on my television. No one here mentioned Dr. Langley's death."

"Would they? Mention Dr. Langley's death? Is she associated with this facility?"

"No, but with something as tragic as a doctor being killed, I would think it would be part of the conversation today."

"The funeral was yesterday," Acklin said. "It's a shame you missed it."

Hopkins heaved massive shoulders. "I probably would not have gone even had I known. Kelly always wanted to keep our relationship a secret, and I would have honored her wishes until the end."

"That's quite noble of you," Joy said.

"Thanks."

Joy wasn't surprised he hadn't picked up on her sarcasm. "What about friends? Although you mentioned her wanting to keep your affair a secret, did you know of any friends she was close to?"

He shook his head. "No, she never mentioned any close friends. But then, whenever we were together, we didn't spend a lot of time talking."

"I see." At least she saw the picture he was painstakingly trying to paint for them.

"According to her associates at the medical complex, Dr. Langley rarely worked late and never on a Friday night. Do you have any idea why she was still at the office?"

He shook his head. "No, I have no idea, and they're right. I've never known her to work late."

"How did you and Dr. Langley meet?" Acklin wanted to know.

"At a local medical symposium two years ago."

"And as far as you know, no one else knew the two of you were seeing each other? No ex-girlfriends on your part or ex-boyfriends on hers that you know of?"

"Not on my end, and I have no reason to believe there were any on hers."

Joy nodded. She clicked off her electronic notepad and Acklin closed his tablet. She handed Hopkins her business card. "If you think of anything else we might need to know, Mr. Hopkins, please give us a call."

"I will, but first I have a question."

"Yes?"

"Kelly worked hard to keep our affair a secret. How did you guys find out about it?"

Joy smiled. "Don't you know there's no such thing as a secret? Anything you do in the dark will eventually come to the light. Goodbye, Mr. Hopkins."

She and Acklin walked out of the office. When they were back in the car, Acklin glanced at her. "So what do you think, Lieutenant?"

"I think he was being careful to be honest with us because he wasn't sure if we'd catch him in a lie."

"Those were my thoughts, as well. But what could be his motive? It's not as if he was flaunting the affair to make an ex-girlfriend jealous," Acklin said.

"First of all, if Dr. Langley was the intended target like we assume, I doubt an ex-girlfriend would have gone to all the trouble to hire two goons to take her out the way it was done. There has to be something we're missing. I'm calling the chief to see if we can get a search warrant for her medical files," Joy said, snapping her seat belt in place.

"Good luck with that. She was a fertility specialist. She probably has sensitive information people like keeping confidential."

Joy shrugged. "It won't hurt to try."

At that moment her cell phone rang. "Lieutenant Ingram."

"Lieutenant Ingram, this is Barron Driscoll. After you left I got up enough courage to go into my guest room, the one Kelly always used when she stayed overnight." He paused a moment and then said, "I found a sealed package on the dresser. I probably wouldn't have thought much of it but it has her name on it, which I'm certain she wrote. There was also a date under her name. It was dated the same day she died. I picked it up, but didn't open it since it's sealed. It feels like a bunch of papers are inside."

Joy glanced over at Acklin as she said, "Thanks for calling us, Mr. Driscoll. We're on our way back to your place to get it."

ANDERSON PACED THE confines of his office while trying to convince himself those detectives' visit meant nothing. It was their job to investigate a homicide. And hadn't that female cop said it appeared robbery was the motive? He hoped they kept thinking that. But then, he hadn't liked that damn smart response she gave about secrets eventually coming to the light. He hadn't liked that one bit. As long as Kelly did what he'd instructed and shredded her medical records, then he was in the clear. *But what if she hadn't?*

He stopped pacing when that thought flashed into his mind. He needed to stop thinking stupid thoughts. Kelly fancied herself in love with him and during that last conversation, he was convinced she believed his BS about wanting to protect her. Yeah, he was certain she believed him. So there was no reason to think he was a suspect in anything. No paper trail.

Satisfied with that thought, he was about to sit down at his desk when his personal phone rang. Few people contacted him using this number. He pulled it out of his pocket and rolled his eyes heavenward when he saw the caller was Jerome Post. As far as he was concerned, things couldn't get any worse.

Anderson started not to answer it but decided it would be in his best interest if he did. "Yeah, Post?"

"We need to meet."

Anderson drew in a deep breath, wondering. He decided to put the man off. "I can't leave town again now. I just got back and—"

"You won't have to leave town. I'm in Charlottesville."

Anderson felt like someone had punched him in the gut. "You're in Charlottesville?"

"Yes, and we *will* meet, Hopkins. Tonight."

JOY ENTERED HER home and glanced at the television. It was still on the station Stonewall had changed it to this past weekend. The sports channel. She smiled as she removed her Glock while remembering how they'd lain sprawled on the sofa together, watching a baseball game. He'd been surprised to discover that she enjoyed baseball as much as he did. Unfortunately they favored opposing teams.

She entered the kitchen and opened the refrigerator, deciding a beer sounded good. She and Acklin had returned to Barron Driscoll's home to get the package. Since the judge hadn't approved a search warrant, they couldn't review the contents inside. Before returning to headquarters they had grabbed sandwiches and drinks from a deli. She had eaten at her desk while going over information Taren had sent her on Beautiful Creations. She had a gut feeling the connection between that agency and Dr. Langley was more than a coincidence, but so far she hadn't found anything. She did notice that over the past year Dr. Langley had made more referrals to Beautiful Creations than the other agencies.

She was about to take a swig of her beer when her phone rang. She hoped it was Acklin letting her know they'd gotten the search warrant to look through Dr. Langley files.

"Yes?"

"Hello, Joy Elyse."

Joy didn't have to wonder who it was. Nobody called her Joy Elyse but her father and one other man. "Omar, this is a surprise."

"I arrived in Charlottesville today and was hoping I could see you."

Joy's eyebrow's rose. "You're in Charlottesville?"

"Yes."

"Why?"

"For a business meeting."

"Oh."

"So can we get together…for old time's sake?"

She had no interest in seeing Omar, but she knew he'd been paying her parents frequent visits. Maybe she should find out what that was about. "Fine. You can tell me where to meet you."

"I can come to your place."

No, he couldn't. The last man who'd been here was Stonewall, and she didn't want Omar's presence to diminish those memories. "I prefer meeting you somewhere. Tell me where."

"Okay. I'm at the Lakeside Hotel downtown. Room 876."

Did he honestly think she would come to his room? "There's a bar and grill across the street from your hotel. Pearlies. I'll meet you there in an hour," she countered.

He didn't say anything for a moment, and then he said, "Alright. See you later."

ANDERSON DIDN'T LIKE where Post suggested they meet but decided not to complain. He could understand the man not wanting them to be seen together, but the abandoned warehouse gave him the creeps. He glanced around and then checked his watch. Post had said they would meet at eight and it was eight. Where was the man?

He was about to call him when he heard footsteps. He turned and it was Post and the man who always followed him around like he was his damn bodyguard. He probably was.

"Why did we need to meet, Post?"

Jerome Post threw down a cigarette. The minute it

hit the concrete, the man beside him crushed it. "Why didn't you tell me you had arranged a hit on the doctor?"

"I didn't know I needed to tell you everything. She was a problem, and I took care of it."

A deep frown settled on Post's face. "You didn't take care of it. You made a bigger mess of things. Do you think the cops won't eventually put two and two together? I know they paid you a visit today so they are already onto something."

Anderson wondered how he'd known. "No, they aren't onto anything. It was a routine visit. There is nothing to link Dr. Langley with the organization."

"You're a fool if you think so. Otherwise the cops would not have come snooping around. You should never have killed anyone—Mandy Clay or Dr. Langley—without consulting me."

"I didn't kill Mandy Clay. She killed herself by escaping. And as far as Dr. Langley, she'd gotten a guilty conscience."

"And you should have let us take care of her," Post snapped.

"She was my problem to handle."

"You don't have the authority to make such decisions on your own. You went too far. Now we have to clean up your mess."

Anderson began feeling uneasy and didn't like the way Post was looking at him. He took a step back. "There is no mess to clean up." Fear suddenly began crawling up his spine.

The man beside Post pulled out a gun and pointed it at Anderson. "I beg to differ."

CHAPTER THIRTY-EIGHT

JOY HAD SHOWERED and was getting dressed to go meet Omar when her phone rang. She checked caller ID. It wasn't Stonewall like she'd hoped but rather Acklin. "Please tell me the judge approved that search warrant we asked for," she said.

"Yes, we just got it. We also got something else."

"What?" Joy asked, sliding into her panties and remembering how much she loved it whenever Stonewall would take them off her.

"Another murder. And you won't guess who, Lieutenant."

Joy sat on the edge of the bed. "Who?"

"Anderson Hopkins."

She sucked in a sharp breath as she stood. "When? Where?" She wouldn't be wearing the dress she'd placed on her bed earlier. And she wouldn't be meeting Omar.

"About an hour ago. His body was found near an empty warehouse in the Hennery area," Acklin said.

"Text me the address. I'm on my way."

While getting dressed she phoned Omar. "Sorry, something came up and I can't meet with you, after all."

"Why doesn't that surprise me?"

Joy rolled her eyes, annoyed and thinking some things never changed. She really didn't need this from him.

"Glad it doesn't surprise you. Goodbye."

"Hey, Joy, wait!" he said before she could click off the phone.

"What, Omar? I have a job to do."

"I'll be here until Sunday. I hope you'll make time for me before I leave."

Make time for you? With this kind of attitude, like hell. "I'll be busy. You know, murders to solve. Have a nice flight back to Baton Rouge. Goodbye."

And good riddance. Again. She quickly finished dressing.

A short while later she was halfway to the crime scene when her phone rang, and the ringtone made her smile. She clicked on her Bluetooth. "Hey."

"You sound out of breath. Rushing to a fire?" Stonewall asked.

She couldn't help but smile. "No fire. Another murder. And it might be connected to the ones that happened Friday."

"Sounds like a bad situation."

"Nothing I can't handle."

"Not for one minute do I think you can't," he said. "Other than another murder that you can handle, are you okay?"

"Yes. No. Maybe." Knowing she'd probably confused the hell out of him, she explained, "Omar is in town on business. He asked me to meet him for old times."

"Oh, I see."

"No, you don't see, Stonewall. I was only meeting with him to tell him that I'm tired of him using his relationship with my parents to try to get me back."

"Is that what he's doing?"

"I think so. Hell, I really don't know. That's why I agreed to meet with him—to find out. Anyway, I didn't meet with him. I got the call about the homicide and I'm on my way there. I canceled, and he didn't like it."

"You have a job to do."

"Yes, I do." She sighed in relief. "Why are you always so understanding?"

"What do you mean?"

"I've been with you before and had to leave to do my job. You didn't give me grief about it."

"No, just like I know you wouldn't give me grief about my job."

No, I wouldn't. "Enough about me. How are you doing?"

"Fine."

"And your client?"

"Mondae is fine. I don't want to hold you up. Be careful."

"I will, and thanks for calling me."

"You don't have to thank me. I think of you all the time."

"I keep saying it, but it sounds like you have a lot of time on your hands," she said, trying to keep her heart beating steadily.

"I'd rather have you in my hands. My arms. Lying beside me."

"That all sounds good to me. Hold those thoughts until I see you again. You'll still be back Tuesday?"

"Yes, if nothing comes up."

And she was hoping it didn't. "Bye, Stonewall."

"Bye, Joy."

"HERE'S WHAT WE know so far," Joy said to the people assembled in her office. It was a little past three in the morning. All of them had been with her at the crime scene that night, including Sanchez. She had called him right after Acklin had contacted her.

"First of all, we know Anderson Hopkins was having an affair with Dr. Langley. We also know he has an alibi and wasn't in Charlottesville at the time of her murder. We know whoever killed him last night definitely wanted him dead." Anderson had been shot four times and according to Lennox, two of those shots had been fired after the man was already dead.

"The judge has approved our search warrant, and we'll be going through the doctor's files today because I have reason to think what happened to Dr. Langley is connected to Mandy Clay."

She saw surprise light some people's eyes. She had discussed her theory with the chief and after hearing her rationale, he had given her the okay to pursue it.

"And how do you think Beautiful Creations plays into all this?" Sanchez asked, sipping on another cup of coffee. It had been a long night for all of them. None of them had gone home since leaving the crime scene at the warehouse. The media had found out and they had to be dealt with. Joy's team also had to notify Hopkins's next of kin.

"From the reports I've reviewed so far, we know that Dr. Langley was referring clients to Beautiful Creations. They were patients who wanted to participate in embryo transfers using surrogates. We know Mandy Clay was a surrogate who worked for some agency, yet none claim her."

She paused to let all that she'd said sink in. "There has to be a motive for what happened Friday night and last night and we need to find it. Go home, get some rest and tomorrow morning be ready to go at this full speed."

Sanchez stood and glanced at his watch. "It's already three in the morning," he said, grinning.

"All of you deserve some sleep. An exhausted person makes mistakes. I can give you at least six hours. If you think you need more, let me know."

An hour or so later, Joy was entering her own home. The voices from her television were always a welcoming sound to her. She removed her Glock and went to the bedroom to undress. A short while later, after taking a shower and slipping into her nightgown, she glanced at the clock on the nightstand. It was four in the morning and she was determined to be back in the office by nine. She had ordered that Oliver Effington be brought in for questioning.

After sliding into bed, she stacked her pillows a few times but still couldn't settle down for the sleep she desperately needed. Grabbing her cell phone off the nightstand, she texted Stonewall. You up?

His response came back immediately. Yeah, I'm up. I'm also hard.

She couldn't help but giggle. Bad boy.

He texted back. What U need?

That answer was easy. 4 U 2 talk dirty 2 me.

Her cell phone rang immediately and she clicked it on. "Hi."

"Hi, yourself. I miss you. And do you know what I'd be doing right now if I was there with you?" he asked her in a voice so sexually charged she felt electrical currents spike her body.

"No, what?" She tightened her legs together in anticipation of what he would say.

"I would..."

As he told her, she closed her eyes and imagined him doing every single erotic and explicit thing he said. She was convinced she could feel him touching her. She moaned when she felt her body become sensitive as sensations began overtaking her.

Joy knew she was being hurled toward a mind-blowing orgasm. She gripped her bedcovers and screamed out his name when her entire body exploded into a trillion molecules of red-hot sensations.

"I love it when you scream my name, baby."

She drew in several deep breaths as she tried to recover. It was hard to believe she'd had a full-blown orgasm from phone sex. When she was finally able to speak, she said in a raspy voice, "I can't wait until you come back home. I've been dreaming a lot about you."

"I can't wait, either. And when I do, I will turn all your dreams into reality."

CHAPTER THIRTY-NINE

Joy walked into interrogation room T5 with Sanchez. Acklin was observing on the other side of the tinted one-way glass. A uniformed officer had picked up Oliver Effington earlier, and the man hadn't liked it.

"Good morning, Mr. Effington," Joy said, sliding into a chair at the table while Sanchez took another. And as far as she was concerned, it was a good morning. After indulging in phone sex with Stonewall and having the best orgasm of her life, she had drifted off to sleep. When the alarm had gone off at eight she'd felt rejuvenated and ready to go.

"It is not a good morning, Detective Ingram. What is the meaning of this?"

"We need answers. What is your association with Anderson Hopkins and Dr. Kelly Langley?"

"Dr. Langley refers clients to us like several other fertility specialists around town, and I'm not sure I know of a Mr. Hopkins. Describe him to me."

"We can do better than that," Sanchez said, tossing a paper clip back and forth on the table. "We can take a trip down to the morgue and let you look at him."

Color drained from the man's face. "Morgue?"

"Yes. Anderson Hopkins was killed last night," Sanchez replied.

Joy was convinced the man would topple over in his chair. "Anderson is dead?" he asked in a shaky voice.

"Yes," she replied. "If the two of you are on a first-name basis, then I'll assume that you not only knew him, but knew him well."

Effington nervously rubbed his hands together. "Not well. We did business together on occasion. When we verified the medical history of our surrogates, his company arranged genetic testing for us."

"And that's it? Is that why the two of you have been talking a lot lately? Most noticeably, within hours of when Sanchez and I paid you a visit that night to discuss Mandy Clay? What did the two of you talk about?"

The man paled. "How do you know we talked?"

The door to the interrogation room suddenly opened. A tall man with an authoritative air and dressed in a business suit that probably cost more than her entire monthly paycheck walked in with a stern look on his face. "I'm Kerry Robinson, Mr. Effington's attorney, and my client won't be answering any more of your questions."

THE PHONE WAS picked up on the first ring. "What do you have to report, Post?" Norm Austen asked.

"It's a mess just like I thought. Anderson Hopkins botched things pretty damn bad by having that doctor killed. But I plan to straighten it out."

"And what about the primary agency we use? Beautiful Creations? Do we need to do something about them, as well?"

"No. Not a good time now. The cops had Effington in for questioning. Tried to make a connection between him and Anderson but couldn't. Robinson showed up and shut things down."

"Good."

"Yes, but according to Robinson, the detective in charge, a Lieutenant Ingram, is dogmatic. She won't give up until she finds something."

"Make sure she doesn't. That surrogacy operation brings in too much money for us to have to shut it down."

"Don't worry. I'll do what I have to do."

IT WAS LATE when Joy got home that night. Effington's attorney had successfully blocked them from talking with him, but they had a court order in before a judge to counter that. She had a gut feeling now more than ever that he was involved in something shady and it had included Anderson Hopkins and Dr. Langley. Was Effington the one to put the hit on the both of them? If so why? Did it have anything to do with Mandy Clay?

They had spoken with Dr. Langley's brother again. He claimed he hadn't known Hopkins and hadn't been aware of her sister's affair with him or that they'd used his home for their romantic rendezvous. Joy was pretty sure Driscoll didn't have anything to do with Hopkins's death, but he would remain on the suspect wall in her office until it was proved otherwise.

She had requested a search warrant for Beautiful Creations and had hoped to have it by now, but didn't. With the search of Dr. Langley's office, she and Acklin had spent most of the day interviewing her colleagues and reviewing files. While doing so she drank so much coffee that now she felt too wired to sleep. But she would, because tomorrow was another full day. One possible new lead was that package Dr. Langley had left at her brother's home. Joy had decided the move had been intentional. But why? After Sanchez and Acklin had left for the day, she had remained behind to go through more files to see if she could make a connection and to review the suspects' photos on her wall.

Joy had stopped by the library to obtain books on fertility and surrogacy. She'd had a lot of reading material to choose from and intended to start tonight.

One positive development was a break in the Erickson case. The chief had shared with her the good news that they had a lead on the murderer and Randi had been the one to find it. More and more people were accepting her psychic abilities as real.

Joy had showered, dressed in her nightgown and crawled into bed with one of the books she'd checked out the library when her phone rang, and she knew it was Stonewall. She couldn't help but smile. His nightly calls were helping her to unwind and release her daily stress.

She quickly clicked on. "Hello, Stonewall. You call me to talk dirty?" she asked, chuckling. A woman could hope.

"I can do better if you open your door."

Joy's heart began racing. "Open my door?"

"Yes."

That meant...

Tossing her phone aside, she quickly got out of bed and rushed through her house. She did take the time to look out the peephole before opening the door, and there he stood under the porch light, looking so un-adulteratedly male that her heart almost missed a beat.

Her nerve endings seemed to go haywire as she un-locked the door. She was so happy to see him that she rushed forward and threw herself into his arms. He seemed ready for the impact and lifted her up, and she wrapped her arms around his neck and her legs around his waist. He kissed her. Or was she kissing him? She didn't care. It didn't matter. The main thing was that they were kissing each other.

And more than anything, she knew at that moment that Stonewall Courson had become more than a diversion for her. A lot more.

DAMN, HE'D MISS HER, Stonewall thought, closing her door with the heel of his shoe and taking the time to lock it. He quickly moved toward her bedroom. The phone sex had been good but what they were about to get into was even better. There hadn't been one day he hadn't thought about her, missed her, wanted her.

The Reddicks had decided to take an extended trip to Dubai for a month. When they invited Mondae to join them, Stonewall's services were no longer needed since the Reddicks would take along their own private security detail.

It hadn't taken him any time to pack, and he'd come straight here from the airport. He hadn't called her be-cause, like before, he wanted to surprise her. And noth-ing would ever erase from his mind the look on her face when she'd seen him. It had made all those hours at the airport on standby well worth it.

"I missed you, Stonewall," she whispered against

his ear while her arms clutched him around his neck and her legs tightened around him. Was he imagining things or was the heat of her pressed against his zipper making him throb even more?

"I missed you, too."

He knew at some point they needed to talk. He thought that two people who missed each other as much as they did were ready for a relationship of the most serious kind. That was his conclusion and he was sticking to it.

When they reached her bedroom, he wasn't sure who was the quickest in removing their clothes. Probably her because she had less to take off. But he was right behind her. His hands were shaking when he slid on the condom, knowing she was in that bed watching him and waiting for him. Finished, he turned and looked at her, the woman he'd been fantasizing about, lusting over and...

For the moment, he didn't want to think about what came after the *and*. It would cause problems if he did. Instead he quickly moved toward the bed and pulled her into his arms. Tonight he planned to make her scream his name just as often as he screamed hers.

CHAPTER FORTY

STONEWALL GAZED DOWN into the sleeping face of his Joy in the morning. And it was morning. Almost six.

As if she felt him watching her, she slowly lifted droopy eyelids. "I wish I could stay here with you all day," she said in a sluggish voice.

He smiled, just imagining how that would turn out. "Sounds good to me."

"It would," she said, yawning. "I don't want to go to work but I have to. So much going on. I'm convinced those two cases I told you about are connected."

He leaned in and kissed her. "And if they are you're going to find out how."

A smile touched the corners of her lips. "You are so good for my ego, Stonewall." She stretched out. "And on that note, I need to get up and get dressed."

He pulled out a book he felt under the covers and held it up. "*The Essence of Fertility.* Your choice reading?"

"Not hardly. I prefer a good mystery novel any day." Then she brought him up-to-date on the cases as well as the FBI's good news about having a solid lead in Murphy Erickson's death.

"A lot's been happening while I've been gone." And he hadn't been gone that long.

"Well, you are back now, and I'm glad you are. When did you get in?"

"Last night. I came here straight from the airport." He'd needed to see her just that badly.

"I'm flattered, Stonewall," she said, easing her naked body out the bed.

And he was in...

No, he refused to go there. "I know you'll be busy most of the day, but you need to start it off right." When she slid her gaze to his lower extremities, he laughed and said, "Not that. I think you got enough last night."

She chuckled. "I got more than enough. So, if not that, then what do you have in mind?"

"Breakfast. Let me take you somewhere and then I'll drop you off at work."

"And how will I get home?"

"I'll come back and pick you up."

She gave his suggestion some thought. "I'm not sure what time I'll be leaving work. And I might need my unmarked car."

"Doesn't matter. Just text me when you want me to pick you up. I'd gladly be at your beck and call. And I'm sure there are other unmarked cars you can use today if you need one."

"That's true." She gazed at him for a long moment before saying, "My beck and call, huh?"

"Yes, baby. Your beck and call."

She smiled as if the thought of that pleased her. "That, Mr. Courson, sounds like an offer I can't refuse."

"I DON'T WANT to go to work, Stonewall."

Joy couldn't believe she was admitting such a thing,

and for the second time that day. When had she ever preferred spending time with a man to being at work, getting criminals off the street? She was allowing the one thing to happen she swore she never would after her breakup with Omar. She was allowing a man to come between her and her job. Her career. Her life.

"That's just all the sex and omelets talking."

She chuckled, giving him an amused glance. "Sex and omelets?"

"Yes, sex and omelets."

She couldn't feign ignorance. Not when he'd gone back out to his car to grab his luggage before joining her in the shower. It had taken her longer to shower than usual when he had shown her just how wonderful it was to make love while water cascaded over their naked bodies. Just thinking about how he'd taken her hard against the shower wall had her feeling aroused all over again.

She'd assumed he was planning to take her to their café for doughnuts and coffee. Instead, he'd taken her to Fargo, a place known for their breakfast entrées. Especially their omelets. She felt satisfied and stuffed. That, she discovered, was a blissful combination.

Now they were in his car and he was driving her to work. Never had any man she'd been involved with driven her to work. It was going to be a beautiful day, and she believed eventually she would solve all her cases, and she and Stonewall would make love all the time and—

Whoa! She suddenly sucked in a deep breath, not believing how crazy her thoughts were getting. Maybe

Stonewall was right. The best sex and the most delicious omelets was a zany combination.

At that moment his phone rang and she almost chuckled at the ringtone. It was the musical theme from the old television show *Dragnet*. "Sorry, I need to get this. It's Sheppard."

He clicked on the Bluetooth in his car. "Good morning, Shep. What's up? You're on speaker with me and Joy."

"Good morning to you both."

"Good morning to you, as well," Joy said.

"I just wanted to announce I'm a grandfather again," Sheppard Granger said, his voice coming in loud and clear over the car's speakers. "Jules delivered."

"And what did she have?" Stonewall asked. "A boy or a girl?"

"Would you believe both?"

Joy was convinced both her and Stonewall's mouths dropped open at the same time. "Jules had twins," Stonewall said in amazement. "Did they know and not tell anyone?"

Sheppard's chuckle was rich. "It seems Jules knew all along but kept it a secret to surprise Dalton."

Joy watched as Stonewall shook his head, laughing heartily. When he was able to contain his laughter he asked, "And how did Dalton take the surprise?"

"I heard he passed out in the delivery room, but I'm sure he'd never admit to it. Watching his wife deliver one baby was bad enough. But watching her deliver two—I can just imagine."

"I can, too."

"He was still in shock when he came out to the waiting room to deliver the news. He said he was going to wring Jules's neck for not telling him. Then Shana told him he couldn't do that. He needed to keep Jules around to take care of those two babies unless he planned on doing it by himself."

"I guess he doesn't plan to wring her neck anymore."

"You guess right. By the time I left the hospital, Dalton was proudly passing out cigars and taunting his brothers that they could only produce one baby, but he'd managed to produce two."

Joy didn't know Dalton Granger that well. But she had heard he was quite a character. It definitely sounded like it. She slid her gaze to look out the window while Stonewall told Sheppard Granger he'd returned to Charlottesville early and why. They were stopped at a traffic light when the occupants in the vehicle next to them caught her attention. She didn't know the two men in the front but she did recognize the one in the back seat. It was Oliver Effington. Where was he going and with whom?

As if he'd felt he was being watched, Effington turned his head and stared at her. Whatever he said made the other two men turn to stare at her, as well. And then the light changed and their car sped off.

"Follow that car, Stonewall," she said before thinking. "That black sedan just ahead of us."

Without asking for an explanation, Stonewall did as she asked. His expertise in dodging in and out of traffic almost surprised her, but he was a highly trained security professional. Already she had unholstered her Glock and was on the phone with headquarters, giving the dispatcher a description of the car and the direction it was headed.

Out of the corner of her eye she saw Stonewall had removed his Glock, as well. She quickly turned to him. "I can handle this, Stonewall."

"I know. Just giving you backup in case you need it. And just so you know, seeing you getting ready to kick ass makes me hard."

Joy couldn't help but laugh. The man was something else. Suddenly he slammed on the brakes. It was either that or risk hitting a bunch of kids who had just gotten off a school bus. The black sedan had sent the kids scampering in all directions when it nearly hit several of them.

Joy was speaking on the phone. "We lost them near Commonwealth and Beaver Streets when we got cut off by a school bus. I want Effington found immediately and brought in for questioning."

CHAPTER FORTY-ONE

"TELL ME YOU'VE located Effington," Joy said to Sanchez when he walked into her office.

"Not yet. His wife claims she hasn't seen him since he left home this morning for a meeting. We have plainclothes cops staking out his house and agency. And we don't have that search warrant for Beautiful Creations yet. That attorney is trying to block it, citing the clients' rights to privacy."

"He would," she said in disgust.

"I just wanted to let you know the Carringtons are here."

Joy nodded. They might not have access to Beautiful Creations' files yet, but they knew who Dr. Langley had referred, thanks to the packet she'd left at her brother's home. Joy was convinced Dr. Langley had done so for a reason. Had she feared her life was in danger? Upon searching through the documents, Joy had pulled all the embryo transfers that matched the timeline for when Mandy Clay gave birth. She was determined not only to find out what happed to Mandy but also to find her baby.

She had seen the names of Brett and Rachel Carrington, but hadn't known that Rachel Carrington was related to Anderson Hopkins until it was discovered her name was listed as his next of kin.

Joy walked into the interrogation room where the couple sat holding hands. "Thank you for coming, Mr. and Mrs. Carrington."

"We want to know what this is about, Lieutenant," Brett Carrington said with agitation in his voice. "My wife is under a lot of stress, which I hope you can understand. She just lost her brother in a brutal attack. What are you doing to find his killer?"

Joy joined the couple at the table. "We're doing all we can, which is why we asked you here. And I am sorry for your loss, Mrs. Carrington."

Rachel Carrington dabbed the tears from puffy eyes. "Thanks, and Brett and I were hoping you asked us here to tell us you've found the person responsible for taking my brother away from me."

"No, that's not why you're here. I need to ask questions I'm hoping will provide leads that will help us solve the case," Joy said, taking out her electronic notepad.

"But I don't know what we can tell you, Lieutenant," Rachel said. More tears fell, and Brett Carrington handed his wife another tissue.

"When was the last time you talked to your brother, Mrs. Carrington?"

"A couple of days ago. He called to let us know he had returned to town. He'd been in Seattle attending a seminar."

"Did he call you during the time he was in Seattle?" Joy asked her.

She nodded. "Yes, he called to check on us and Chasta."

"Chasta?"

"Our daughter."

Joy shifted in her chair. "Do you know any of your brother's friends?"

"Of course," Rachel said as if the question was rather silly. "I know all his friends."

"Could you provide us with their names?"

Rachel frowned. "Why? Surely you don't think any of them are responsible for what happened. Someone tried to rob him and—"

"We have no reason to believe it was robbery, Mrs. Carrington. His wallet with his money and credit cards were still on him."

"Maybe they got scared and left before they could take his wallet," Brett Carrington said, as if that possibility made sense. It didn't, but Joy decided not to say so. Instead she typed into her notepad the names Rachel was giving her.

"What about a woman in his life?"

"No, he hasn't been in a serious relationship for a long while."

"What about Dr. Kelly Langley?"

"What about Dr. Langley?" Rachel asked, looking confused. "I know she was killed in a break-in at her medical complex last week."

"Yes, that's right. And you know Dr. Langley?"

"Yes, she's the one who referred us to Beautiful Creations. I don't understand. Why would you ask me about Dr. Langley? I thought you wanted to know about the people associated with my brother."

"I do. Your brother and Dr. Langley were involved in a romantic relationship."

Rachel frowned. "That's not true. They didn't even know each other. In fact he called the day after Dr. Langley was killed, and I was upset about it. He asked me what was wrong and I told him about it. That was the first time I ever mentioned Dr. Langley to him. I told him how she died and that Dr. Langley was instrumental in helping Brett and me feel comfortable enough to do the embryo transfer procedure."

Joy didn't say anything as she continued to type in her notes. She did recall Anderson Hopkins claimed he hadn't known about Dr. Langley's death until they'd told him. He'd evidently lied to them.

"Why are you making assertions that aren't true?" Brett asked in an aggrieved tone.

Joy looked back and forth between the couple before saying, "I haven't done that. Dr. Langley and Anderson Hopkins were involved in a secret affair and had been for well over a year."

Joy saw anger flare in Rachel Carrington's eyes. "Who told you such a thing?"

Joy leaned back in her chair. "Your brother did. My partner and I paid him a visit two days ago. We had already done our own investigation, and he admitted to the affair. He told us about it and why they kept it a secret."

The Carringtons stared at her in total shock.

JEROME POST GLANCED over at Ike Conyers when he returned to the car. "I assume Effington has been taken care of."

"Yes. He didn't see it coming. Figured we would be putting him in a safe place until everything blew over like you claimed."

"The fool."

"Yeah," Conyers said. "It will be a couple of days before they find his body. So what's next?"

"Next we handle that female detective. She saw us today, and if she makes a connection and links me to Murphy Erickson's death, that won't be good for the boss man."

"When do we make the hit?" Conyers wanted to know.

Post threw down his cigarette and crushed it beneath his shoe. "Tonight."

"SO WHAT DO YOU THINK?" Sanchez asked her. He had been party to her interview of the Carringtons through the one-way glass.

"I honestly don't think they had a clue. And now they are worried," Joy said.

Sanchez raised a brow. "About what?"

"Whether her brother's association with Dr. Langley had anything to do with their daughter."

Sanchez leaned forward in his chair toward Joy's desk. "Are you saying that you think their baby is Mandy Clay's missing child?"

Joy tossed a paper clip on her desk. "I think so. Same age."

After the shock had worn off with the Carringtons, she'd asked if they'd met the woman who'd been their surrogate. They'd said no and then refused to answer any more questions. Evidently they were beginning to wonder what was going on and what part their daughter played, as well.

"I'm going to get a judge to order a DNA test to see if the Carringtons' daughter is somehow connected to Mandy Clay," Joy said.

She checked her watch. "Still no word on the whereabouts of Effington?"

"No. And that judge hasn't approved our request for a search warrant for Beautiful Creations yet. I guess he's trying to tread lightly on this one."

Joy had presented the judge with what she thought was a strong case. Mandy Clay was not registered with any legal surrogate agency, nor were there any records of her having given birth in any of the area hospitals. And yet, from the autopsy, they knew she had been a surrogate and had given birth. Joy now suspected this had been done through back channels, possibly against Mandy's will, given the way she died, as though she were running from something. Or someone.

Mandy Clay's name wasn't in any of Dr. Langley's records. Would her name be in records belonging to Beautiful Creations? More than anything Joy needed to see who the woman listed as the Carringtons' surrogate was.

There was a knock on her office door, and Taren came in smiling. "It's late but I figured you would still be here. Here's that report on the couple you ask me to research. The one living in Sofia Valley."

Joy remembered the couple. The Dunmores. "Thanks."

Sanchez intercepted the file. "You have enough to

read, Lieutenant. Besides, it will give me something to do."

Joy nodded. Sanchez had told her his wife had taken the baby to visit her parents for a couple of days in Alexandria.

"Okay, I wouldn't want you to be bored at home alone," she said, smiling. "And you're right. I have those files from Dr. Langley's office I'm still going through." She was trying to make a connection with those referred couples. Acklin had visited with half of them. All the ones he'd interviewed had met their surrogates beforehand, but the surrogates had not wanted them in the delivery room. The babies had been given to them within hours of the birth. They'd been told a private delivery was the surrogates' preference.

"Still no word on the whereabouts of Oliver Effington?" Taren asked.

"No. Uniformed officers are still out there looking." Joy didn't have to tell them she suspected the worst, the way this case was going. Two dead bodies—Dr. Kelly Langley, Anderson Hopkins—both connected to each other and Beautiful Creations. And now the CEO of Beautiful Creations was missing.

At that moment the phone rang. She immediately picked it up. "This is Lieutenant Ingram."

It was Detective Acklin. "Just thought I'd let you know, we might have a lead on something. Three of the couples we interviewed agreed to provide a description of their surrogates. Sounds like the same woman."

"For all three?"

"Yes. But that couldn't be possible since the couples'

babies were supposedly born within days or weeks of each other," Acklin supplied.

"A fake surrogate?" He was confirming her suspicions.

"Pretty much looks like it," Acklin said. "I will keep you posted."

"Thanks." Joy clicked off the phone and relayed the information.

"A fake surrogate? Taren asked, surprised.

"Seems so. I wonder who the actual surrogates were, and where are they? This makes me even more suspicious of Beautiful Creations since none of the couples interviewed were allowed in the delivery room to see who was actually giving birth to their babies," Joy said, rubbing a hand down her face.

She glanced at her watch. It was close to ten at night. She hadn't realized it was so late and hoped Stonewall had eaten somewhere without her.

Sanchez stood with the file tucked under his arm. "I hope you're about to leave this place for the night like the rest of us," he said to Joy.

"I guess so. I wanted to wait around to see if Acklin's lead produces anything."

"He'll call you if it does. You need to get some rest. Need a lift since you don't have your car?"

She thought about Sanchez's offer. It would save Stonewall from having to come pick her up and drop her off at home. But a part of her wanted to see Stonewall. A part of her needed to see him. "Thanks, but I have a ride."

Sanchez looked at her. "You sure?"

"Yes, I'm sure."

After Sanchez and Taren left her office she called Stonewall. He picked up on the first ring. "You ready, baby?"

Baby. Did he really think of her as his baby or was it just a casual term of endearment? "Yes, but are you sure you want to come? It's late, and I can get another car from the pool and—"

"I'm already here. Been waiting."

Now she really felt bad. "For how long?"

"Doesn't matter. You're worth the wait."

Joy wished he wouldn't say stuff like that. Comments that could make her pulse kick and send an instant flash of lust through her body. It was lust, right? What else could it be? She forced other possibilities from her mind. "Thanks. Give me five minutes to lock up my office, and I'll be right on out."

CHAPTER FORTY-TWO

STONEWALL GOT OUT of the car, straightened his body and stretched. He'd passed the time sitting in the car by talking with Striker and Quasar. Both had Dalton stories. Everyone had something amusing to say about how Dalton was handling being the father of twins. Now that the shock had worn off, he was in normal Dalton mode. Names for the twins hadn't yet been released. Everybody figured Dalton would be making a big production of that.

Stonewall checked his watch. Joy said five minutes, but he thought he'd head over to meet her and walk with her. He'd tried staying busy most of the day and had even paid a visit to his grandmother and his sister, who were getting ready for the Fourth of July cookout in a few days. Yet Joy had never been too far from his thoughts.

He enjoyed being with her and loved everything about her. Her scent. The way she would roll her eyes when she thought he was handing her a bunch of bull about something. The way she would tilt her head whenever she was paying close attention to what he said.

Stonewall could have gone on and on, but really didn't need to. He recalled dropping her off at work after their morning chase. She had been in her element, pursuing those guys with her Glock firmly held in her hands. What he'd told her was the truth. It had been a total turn-on to watch her.

If he could have done the forever thing, she would have been the one who headed the list. Hell, she would have been the only one on the list. He could never forget when his grandparents had sat him and Mellie down to explain their parents were never coming back. He'd hated hurricanes for years after that and would cringe whenever the weather channel announced there was one stirring in the Atlantic, the Gulf or the Pacific.

Shoving painful memories to the back of his mind, he crossed the street and began walking down the sidewalk. It was a beautiful night. Great weather. Full moon. Bright stars. Several uniformed officers were coming in and out of police headquarters.

He figured Joy hadn't eaten and would be hungry. There was this restaurant that served pretty good food that didn't close until one.

His training as a security expert made him check across the street. He stopped walking and studied the car parked there. There was nothing eye-catching about it, just a light-colored sedan. But it was running. He wouldn't have found that odd had it been winter and cold outside. Why was the driver wasting gas that way?

He shrugged his shoulders, thinking, to each his own. He switched his gaze back toward the entrance and saw Joy the minute she walked out. A feeling in the pit of his stomach had him turning his attention away from her to that car again.

That's when he saw it. The driver had rolled the window down, and Stonewall could see what looked like the barrel of a gun aimed out of it. Aimed right at Joy.

She had seen him coming toward her and was smiling. As loud as his voice could carry, he screamed, "Get down, Joy," the exact moment a shot was fired from the car.

He hadn't realized how quickly he could pull his own gun. He fired several shots at the person who'd had the fucking nerve to shoot at Joy. The car sped away, but he was certain he'd made a hit.

With his heart pounding in his chest, he raced to where Joy was. A crowd had gathered around her, and he couldn't tell if she'd been hit. Had his warning been in time? Suddenly several cops surrounded him with their guns drawn and ordered him to drop his weapon and put his hands up. He complied, while trying to explain what happened.

He wanted to go to Joy, but the cops ordered him not to move.

Then he heard Joy's loud, angry voice. "Put your guns down now!" she ordered the uniformed officers. "He saved my life."

The cops lowered their guns as ordered. He put his hands down but no one returned his gun to him. He would deal with that later. Right now he had to get to Joy. He rushed over to her and, not caring that they had an audience, he pulled her into his arms and held her tight while ignoring the questions being thrown out at them by the police officers.

"I'm okay, Stonewall," she said, pulling herself out of his arms. "Thank you for the warning. You probably saved my life." Then, without catching her breath, she asked him, "Did you get a make of the vehicle?"

It took a second for it to sink in what she was asking him. His woman had nearly gotten herself killed, and she was back to business. Back to her professional mode. Like nothing had happened. Like she hadn't come close to losing her life. Why? Just so she wouldn't appear weak in front of her men? "Well, did you, Stonewall?"

Her words cut into his muddled mind. "No. Yes." Then drawing in an irritated breath, he said, "Yes. It was a light-colored sedan."

"Did you get a look at the occupants?"

He stared at Joy a minute. "No. And are you sure you're alright?" he asked her.

"I'm fine."

"Well, dammit, I'm not. Let's go inside now."

She nodded. "Okay, let's go inside. We'll need to give statements."

"ARE YOU SURE you're okay, Conyers?"

Post was certain Conyers had taken a hit. He just didn't know where and how serious it was. Conyers was still driving, but Post noticed him shivering and having a hard time staying in his lane. He couldn't take a chance the man would end up killing them both. "Pull over and let me drive."

They were on the outskirts of town and luckily there was not another car on this stretch of road. Conyers had to be bad off because he didn't argue the point. When Post got out and went around to the driver's side of the car, he saw Conyers had taken a hit and it didn't look good.

Conyers struggled to slide over and somehow managed to do so. Post got in and started driving. There would be a doctor where they were going, and he hoped like hell he got there in time. Once he had Conyers taken care of, he would go back after the woman if she was still alive.

CHAPTER FORTY-THREE

"AND YOU'RE SURE you're okay, Lieutenant?"

"Yes, Chief. I'm fine." Joy remembered another time the chief had asked her something similar. It was a few months ago when she'd almost been poisoned. Now, fast-forward. Another day. Another case. Like before, a part of her hated that she was the center of so much attention. However, at the same time she was grateful to be alive. Mainly because of the man quietly sitting in the corner with his long legs stretched out in front of him, staring at her.

It was hard to stay focused and not stare back. Evidently it didn't matter to him that she was in a building full of cops and, at the moment, safe. Obviously he felt the need to keep his eyes on her, as well. She wished she could tell everyone else to go away and cross the room and curl up in his lap for him to hold her for a minute. She drew in a deep breath, wondering when she had gotten so needy. So dependent on a man to feel secure.

"Well, I want you to go home and stay there. There's a lot we need to sort out here. Namely, why someone would take a shot at you. You're evidently onto something."

"And that's why I need to continue to work. I'll bet it has something to do with Mandy Clay, Anderson Hopkins and Dr. Langley. I'm convinced more than ever the three homicides are connected."

"You're probably right, but now my main concern is keeping you alive, Lieutenant Ingram."

He turned his attention to Stonewall. "Take her home and watch her like a hawk, since it seems you're doing that anyway. I'm assigning additional cops to patrol the area where she lives."

Stonewall stood. "Alright."

Joy glared at both men. "Excuse me. Don't I have any say about this?"

"About taking a couple of days off? No. My orders." He looked over at Stonewall before looking back at her. "However, it is your choice whether you want *him* as your bodyguard."

Joy frowned. "I don't need a bodyguard."

Chief Harkins shrugged. "That's for you to decide, and I'll let the two of you hash things out."

Joy stood, giving Stonewall a there's-nothing-to-hash-out look before glancing at a picture on the chief's desk. She froze.

"What's wrong, Joy?" Stonewall asked, coming to stand beside her.

She picked up the sketch and then stared at Chief Harkins. "Who is this?"

The chief looked at the photo. "That's the sketch the FBI is circulating of the person responsible for Murphy Erickson's death. The man has been identified as Jerome Post. He is believed to be Norm Austen's main man."

"Norm Austen?"

"Yes, the guy believed to have taken over Erickson's territory. Why do you ask?"

Joy met the chief's stare. "Because this Jerome Post is one of the two men I saw today in the car with Eff-ington."

"Are you sure?"

She nodded. "I'm positive."

Chief Harkins picked up his phone and said, "I need to speak with Special Agent Felton at FBI Headquar-ters immediately."

IT WAS THREE hours later when Joy walked into Stone-wall's home. Adhering to the advice of the chief and Special Agent Felton, she hadn't returned to her house. It would have been easy for Jerome Post to break into her home and leave anything behind that could harm her or install some sort of listening device.

"Let's get something straight, Stonewall. I don't need a bodyguard."

Instead of responding, Stonewall locked the door behind them. He then set the alarm. Turning to her, he said, "You know where everything is, Joy."

"I don't have any clothes with me."

"You and my sister are about the same size. She left a few things in the dresser drawers in the guest bedroom."

She evidently was in the mood to be confrontational, but he refused to argue with her. At the moment all he could remember was seeing her walking down the steps of police headquarters and then spotting that gun aimed right at her. What if he hadn't called out to her in time, or been quick enough to return shots at the assailant? He thought he'd experienced stark fear while in jail but nothing could have prepared him for what he'd expe-rienced tonight.

"Stonewall, we need to talk."

He kept walking toward his kitchen, ignoring the fact she was right on his heels. "There is nothing to talk about," he threw out over his shoulder.

"I think there is."

He turned quickly and had to reach out and catch her when she nearly collided with him. He should not have done that. Touching her, feeling how alive she was, flesh and blood, and knowing things could have been different, that she could be a body lying in the morgue, sent shivers through him. How could he think that he'd almost lost her when he'd truly never had her?

Dropping his hands from her waist, he took a step back. Seeing no end in sight, he heaved a deep sigh and said, "Fine. Talk."

He saw that stubborn look in her eyes and knew she was itching for a fight. He'd taken enough psychology classes to know this was how some people reacted when they'd come close to death. The sudden realization, the unexpected apprehension that there was a limit on their life and that it could be snuffed out at a moment's notice was enough to terrify anybody. Hell, he'd been terrified for her. He still was.

"First of all, I want to thank you for—"

"You did that already and like I told you before, you don't have to thank me."

"But I do. I don't want to think about what could have happened had you not been there at that precise moment."

He didn't want to think about it, either. In all honesty, he preferred not have this conversation. "Okay, you've thanked me twice. Now can we drop it?"

"I don't want to drop it."

He rubbed a hand down his face. "Then what do you want?"

She stared up at him and he looked back at her. This time instead of seeing defiance in her eyes, he saw what she'd hidden before. Vulnerability.

"I want to be held, Stonewall. By you."

Without wasting any time he pulled her into his arms and held her tight. He'd held her tight earlier tonight outside headquarters on the sidewalk, but she'd pulled out of his arms because of their audience, when he hadn't given a damn. But now, here, with just the two of them, she wanted to be held. And dammit to hell and back, he wanted to hold her.

His kick-ass, tough-as-nails detective, whose career choices meant putting her life in danger every day, had discovered when faced with death she was just as human as anyone else.

Stonewall wasn't sure how long they stood there in the middle of his kitchen, and he didn't care. She felt good in his arms, with her body plastered to his. She was going through her own private hell and he was going through his, because he knew at that moment Joy had come to mean more to him than any woman ever had.

She pulled back and looked up at him with those gorgeous eyes that could melt his soul. It was then that he leaned in and lowered his mouth to hers.

WITH THE TASTE of his tongue Joy knew this is what she needed. To be devoured by him. And he was kissing her with an intensity she felt all the way to her toes.

She didn't want to think how close she'd come to dying tonight. How close she'd come to never experiencing this again. This mind-blowing kiss that only he could deliver. The feel of him holding her. Making love to her. Had it taken her almost losing her life to realize how much life she was yet to discover with Stonewall?

At the moment it was hard for her to think. He was dominating her mouth in a way that had her senses riding the edge of being not enough and almost too much. Stonewall had the ability to make you forget your name. Hers was Joy, right? At that moment she wasn't sure and would answer to practically anything.

He deepened the kiss, and not to be outdone, she began devouring him like he was devouring her. She wasn't sure at what point they began tearing off their clothes. It really didn't matter. All that mattered was that they both felt the need to be skin to skin. She refused to consider their actions or how out of control they both were. The only thing that mattered to her right now was that she was alive because of him, and more than anything she was grateful for another chance to be with him.

She felt him lift her in his arms and place her on his kitchen table. Her thighs automatically parted when she felt the hard surface touch her back. "I can't make it to the bedroom, baby," he whispered close to her lips.

Neither could she, but she didn't have the mind to tell him that. Right now her mind was filled with him, so much of him, and all the things she knew he was about to do to her. Things she wanted him to do. Needed him to do.

Joy couldn't hold back moaning his name when she felt his fingers ease into her, at the center of her very existence. He began stroking her, sending all kinds of sensations skyrocketing through her body. When his fingers delved deeper, massaging her clit, a restless throb of desire tore through her. And then it happed, the explosion of all explosions, and before she could recover, she felt him above her on the table, as well.

Before she could ask whether the table could hold both of their weight, he'd eased inside her and begun thrusting hard, pounding, and filling her with sensations she felt only when he was inside of her. He was breathing hard and heavy, his hands clutching her hips. His entire body was filled was sexual energy that he was transmitting to her.

Suddenly, he slowed his pace, nearly came to a stop and she knew why. He'd realized he wasn't wearing a condom. She tightened her legs around him and whispered, "It's okay. I'm on the pill."

He leaned in and kissed her, and immediately her senses were being overtaken by his feel, scent and taste. Slipping her arms around his muscled back, she held on tight as he began riding her hard again.

Suddenly he snatched his mouth away and let out a loud yell of her name when he exploded inside of her. Feeling the essence of him flooding her insides triggered something deep within her, and she felt herself dissipate in tiny sensual pieces. She cried out his name, and when another orgasm hit her hard, she screamed it at the top of her lungs.

He whispered fiercely in her ear, "I don't want to be just your diversion any longer, Joy."

A RINGING SOUND jarred Joy awake. She opened her eyes to find herself stretched out on top of Stonewall.

"That's your phone, Joy," Stonewall's husky voice said. He reached over and handed it to her. She glanced at caller ID and didn't recognize the number.

"Hello."

"Detective Ingram?"

Joy moved to lie beside Stonewall. She pushed a mass of hair from her face. "Yes, this is Detective Ingram."

"I'm sorry to be calling you so late. Henry would be upset if he knew."

Joy glanced over at the clock as she rubbed a hand down her face. It was three in the morning. "Who is this?"

"Edith Dunmore. You told me to call if I saw something suspicious."

"And have you?"

"I'm not sure. Stanley needed a late potty break, and Henry told me it was my time to take him out so I did. I was scared out there by myself. I didn't want to run into any animals. Did you know there are bears in these parts? I remember seeing a coyote one day. That's why I always walk Stanley on a leash."

Joy rubbed her hand down her face again, hoping the woman would hurry up and get to the point. "What did you see that was suspicious?"

"A car."

"A car?"

"Yes, a car, and it was parked in one of the coves. I watched it, wondering why someone would be out here so late at night. Then the men got out and went to the trunk."

"Did they take anything out of the trunk?"

"A shovel."

"And what did they do with the shovel, Mrs. Dunmore?"

"I didn't stick around to find out. I hurried back home and told Henry about it, and again he thought I was seeing things. He says I do it all the time."

"Do you?" Joy asked the woman.

"Not *all* the time. The doctor accused me of having early stages of dementia."

Joy could somewhat believe that. "But you're sure of what you saw?"

"I think so. Do you want me to call the police and have them come out and take a look? Henry is going to be mad if I do. But I don't think he minds me calling you. He likes you."

Joy found that hard to believe. "Where is Henry now?"

"He went back to sleep. Umm, maybe I should call the police. They'll come with their blue lights flashing and make a lot of noise. Can I request that?"

Joy shook her head. "Why would you want to?"

"It will give the neighbors something to talk about. We need excitement around here."

Lordy. Joy was convinced the woman was loony. "Look, Edith, would it make you feel better if I came out?"

There was hesitation on the other end. "I guess so. But I don't want you to get out of bed just to come out here. Those men might be gone by then."

Joy thought there was no need to make the point that they might be gone when the police with flashing blue lights got there, as well. "It's no problem. I should be there in half an hour."

Joy hung up the phone to find Stonewall staring at her. She told him about the Dunmores. "Do you think she actually saw something?" he asked her.

"Not sure. But Oliver Effington is still missing."

"In that case, shouldn't you call the police?"

She chuckled as she eased out of bed. "I am the police."

"I mean on-duty officers to go check things out. Your boss gave you time off."

"I know, but technically the Mandy Clay case is mine. I shouldn't be gone long. Keep the bed warm till I come back."

Stonewall eased out of bed, as well. "If you think I'm letting you drive all the way out there by yourself, then you're crazy."

She wrapped her arms around his neck. "Being a die-hard protector, are you?"

"Whatever." He leaned down and brushed a kiss across her lips. Then another. "We never did have a talk," he whispered against her moist lips.

"We will. I know you don't want to be my diversion any longer. Just so you know, you're not."

"Then what am I?"

If she told him now, exactly how she felt and what she wanted, chances were they would delay leaving by getting back in that bed. So she said, "I'll tell you when we get back and have more time."

He stared down at her, as if weighing her words.

Then he nodded. "Okay. Our clothes are in the kitchen. I'll get them."

Joy was about to head for the bathroom when she thought it would be best to at least let Sanchez know what was going on. She didn't have to worry about waking up the baby since his wife and their son were gone for the weekend.

"Hola."

"Juan, this is Joy."

"How are you doing? I heard about tonight. I thought of calling you, but it was late."

"I'm doing fine, just shaken up some."

"Understandably so. That boyfriend of yours is a keeper. Do I need to repeat that?"

"No, I heard you. The reason I was calling is to let you know I just got a call from Edith Dunmore." She told him about the conversation she'd had with the woman.

"She sounds like a nutcase. Do you want me to go and check things out? You've been through a lot tonight."

"No, I'm awake now and I'm closer to Sofia Valley than you are."

"Since when? Your place is on the other side of town."

"Yeah, but I'm not at my place. The Feds didn't want me to return home until they check over the place."

"Makes sense. But are you sure you don't want me to meet you out there? I don't like you going alone."

"I won't be alone. Stonewall is driving me."

"Okay, but if you need me, call me."

"I will."

CHAPTER FORTY-FOUR

"THIS AREA LOOKS sort of eerie at night," Stonewall said, bringing the car to a stop and glancing around.

"Not used to places with no streetlights, are you?"

He heard the teasing tone in Joy's voice. "Whatever. What I'm really not used to are neighbors who are not within hollering distance."

"That's why people move out here. They want their space and to get back to nature."

He glanced at the house that looked completely dark. He was hoping this Edith person had taken a stiff drink and was knocked out in a sound sleep. That way he and Joy could leave Sofia Valley and return to his place and have that talk.

"Wait here. I'll be back in a minute. This shouldn't take long."

"Maybe I should come with you. It looks pretty dark in there."

She shook her head. "No, I'm on official police duty and you're a civilian. Just stay put. I'll be back."

"Just so you know, if you don't come back after what I consider a reasonable amount of time I'm coming after you, police business or not."

JOY KNOCKED ON the door and thought that while Edith might be glad to see her, she figured Ole Henry wouldn't. Especially this time of night. He would be mad at both her and Edith for waking him up for nonsense.

The door opened at the same time a porch light came on. "Detective Ingram?" Edith whispered.

Following her lead, Joy whispered back, "Yes, it's me."

"No flashing blue lights?"

Joy shook her head, hearing the disappointment in Edith's voice. "Sorry, no flashing blue lights. I came alone." That wasn't totally true but there was no need to mention Stonewall sitting in the car.

"Oh. Come in. Henry is asleep, and I can take you out the back door to where I saw the car."

Joy entered the house, and the moment she stepped across the threshold, she felt a hard hit to her head.

JUAN SANCHEZ TOOK another sip of coffee while reading the documents he'd gotten from Joy. Boring shit. But that was all part of being a cop. He hadn't been able to get back to sleep after Joy's call. He missed his wife and son, true enough, but he'd gotten a funny feeling in his gut that just wouldn't go away. So he'd stayed awake and decided to finish reading the stack of files he'd brought home from the office.

Reading the information on the Dunmores was about to put him back to sleep when suddenly something had him lifting his brow. Both of the Dunmores at one time had been medical professionals? Didn't sound anything like the two strange-acting people Joy had told him about. Interesting.

A short while later the hairs on the back of his neck

stood up. In the report they'd received on the Dunmores, a layout of the house they owned was included. It had been built in the early sixties by a man who believed the next war would destroy the world, and he had built a bunker underground. It was a huge bunker with tunnels that led to heaven knew where.

Picking up the phone, he immediately called Joy, his mind racing at what she might be walking into.

JOY SLOWLY CAME TO, ignoring the pain in her head. She stared at the faces surrounding her. All three she recognized. Edith and Henry Dunmore and one of the men she'd seen in the car with Effington. He was holding a gun on her. He was the same man the FBI had fingered as Murphy Erickson's killer. Jerome Post. "What is this about?" she heard herself asking them.

Edith laughed. "I played the part of a crazy woman and got you out here."

"You were stupid to fall for that," Henry added, grinning.

The man who towered over them said nothing, but Joy could see hatred in his eyes. "Because of you my partner died tonight and you're going to pay for it."

Joy knew she had to keep them talking and buy some time. "Give yourselves up. My police department knows I'm out here and will be sending backup if I don't report to them that I'm okay," she said, wishing that was true.

Post laughed. "Doesn't matter. I've timed this place to blow up in thirty minutes. By then, we'll be gone and you and the others will get blown to smithereens."

Joy frowned. "The others?"

Edith put her hands on her hips. "Mandy Clay might have escaped, but there are others."

Joy had figured there might be, especially when it was discovered a woman was a fake surrogate to so many couples. For now she would play dumb to stall for time. "Other women?"

"Yes. Women who were handpicked and kidnapped to impregnate. You see, Detective Ingram, we have quite a bustling business going on here, a real surrogate farm."

"You've got to be kidding me," Joy said. "Let me guess. Anderson Hopkins ran things."

"Sort of," Henry said. "I liked him. Real businessman."

"So why was he killed?" Joy hoped by now Stonewall was wondering what was going on and why she hadn't returned to the car.

"Because he began making too many costly mistakes," Post said in an annoyed tone. "Having an affair with Dr. Langley was the first. Having her killed was the second. He didn't get permission to do that."

"And the reason she was killed?"

"Because she wanted out. He'd talked her into becoming involved, then she got a guilty conscience."

Joy nodded. "And the Effingtons?"

"Only the old man. The stupid wife knows nothing."

Joy drew in a deep breath. She didn't want to think of the women who'd been kidnapped and impregnated against their will. Women being held somewhere in this place.

At that moment her phone rang and Post said, "That's

probably your fellow officers wanting to know if you need backup. Too bad you won't be answering that."

Joy tried to keep her gaze on the three when something moved behind them, and she knew at that moment it was Stonewall. Her hands were tied behind her back, and they'd taken her gun away. It would be Stonewall against these three and one had a gun. She had to keep them talking.

"Are you the ringleader?" she asked the tall man. She figured the only reason they were telling her anything was because they thought she would be dead soon.

He chuckled. "No. I'm second in command. We have quite a little organization. The Brotherhood. They pay me well to get rid of troublemakers."

"So who's the big guy in charge?"

All of a sudden there was a loud noise of something hard hitting the wall.

SANCHEZ PACED HIS KITCHEN. It wasn't like Joy not to answer her phone. Making a decision, he dialed another number and cringed when a sleepy voice answered. "Hello."

"Chief Harkins, this is Detective Sanchez."

"What is it, Sanchez? What's wrong?"

"I think Lieutenant Ingram might be in trouble, sir."

THE THREE PEOPLE TURNED, giving Stonewall the time he needed. He opened fire. Joy reared back in her chair to knock into the tall man, who was taking aim at Stonewall.

Stonewall swiftly grabbed him by the collar to knock him down to his knees. Before Joy's eyes, Stonewall became a fighting machine. Joy hated feeling useless and tried working her hands from the tight bindings. Using the technique she'd been taught at the police academy, she was able to work her hands free. Right on time. Edith tried coming at Stonewall from behind. Henry had taken one of Stonewall's hits, and Joy wasn't sure if he was alive or dead.

Joy tackled Edith, who didn't put up much of a fight, while Stonewall quickly disarmed the man with the gun and knocked him out. Rushing to Stonewall, Joy grabbed his hands. "He said explosives are set to blow in less than thirty minutes. We need to get everybody out. I'm calling for backup and the bomb squad."

After moving quickly to find something to bind everyone's hands, Stonewall began tying everyone up and dragging them outside.

Stonewall reached out and touched the bruise on the side of her head. "You okay?"

"Yes. I'm fine. While you finish here, I'll look for the others," Joy said frantically.

"What others?"

She told Stonewall what the three had said. "Women are being held somewhere in here?"

"Yes, and I need to find them."

"Help me with this and we can both look."

Henry was alive but had taken a bullet to his shoulder. They made doubly sure the three were securely bound by tying them to trees.

"You can't leave us like this. There are wild animals out here," Edith wailed.

Joy glared at the woman. "I know, and I'm staring into the eyes of three of the wildest, cruelest and most inhuman right now." She and Stonewall then raced back inside the house.

They searched from room to room before Stonewall noticed that the panels on one wall looked out of line with the others. When he checked he discovered it was a movable wall that led to a hallway with a set of stairs going down to a basement. "Come on," he said, taking her hand. They rushed down the stairs and entered a place that looked like a surgical room in a hospital. Or, more precisely, a delivery room. Then they went through another door that opened to several sleeping quarters. Joy kicked open the doors. Women were in each one and, to Joy's horror, most of them were pregnant.

"Jesus," she heard Stonewall mutter under his breath. The women wanted to talk all at once, and Joy tried calming them down. "We're here to get you out. You need to follow me quickly. Is everyone capable of doing that?" Joy felt she had to ask since a couple of the women looked as if they were about to deliver their babies any minute. They all assured her they were, and she and Stonewall led them to the stairway.

"Wait!" one of the pregnant women said. "Dorcas is missing. She delivered her baby a few hours ago."

"Where is she?" Joy asked, desperately glancing around.

"Probably still in recovery. It's located that way," one woman said, pointing. "I'm not sure if they took her baby away from her yet."

Stonewall turned to Joy. "Lead them upstairs and out of here. I'll look for the other woman."

"This place is set to blow up, Stonewall," she said,

not able to keep the fear out of her voice. They were racing against time and didn't know exactly how much they had. At that moment Stonewall wasn't just her protector. He was the protector of all the women present.

"I'll be quick." A smile touched his lips and he tenderly caressed the side of her face near her bruise. "Remember we still need to talk, after you get medical attention." Then, in a voice that brooked no argument, he said, "Get them out of here, Joy. Now!"

He raced toward the area the woman had pointed to and was gone. Joy drew in a deep breath before turning her attention to the women. She'd counted twenty of them. "Ladies, please follow me. We need to get out of here as quickly as we can."

STONEWALL RACED FROM room to room, not believing the setup down here. No wonder they'd managed to go undetected. It was like a medical facility and a dormitory all rolled into one. He remembered one of the victims saying the woman he was looking for was named Dorcas. He began calling out to her. Realizing she might not answer because she wouldn't know he was one of the good guys, he said, "Dorcas, I'm Stonewall Courson, and I'm helping to get you out of here. The cops are outside." Okay, so he lied. There was only one cop outside, but in his book Joy was worth a dozen cops.

"Dorcas?"

He heard a faint sound and then a voice that said, "We're in here."

He moved toward the voice and opened a door to discover a woman sitting in a small room, cradling a baby in her arms. She looked at him with defiance in her eyes. "He's mine, and you can't have him."

He nodded. "I just want to get you and your baby out of here, alright?"

She stared at him, trying to decide if she could trust him, and then she nodded. "Alright."

Stonewall moved quickly. The baby wasn't even covered in a blanket. Pulling the shirt over his head he gave it to the woman to wrap up the baby. He then scooped both mother and baby into his arms.

Joy HAD MANAGED to get the pregnant women out safely, far away from the cabin. She then had to keep them from attacking Edith and Henry when they saw them tied to the trees. That had been difficult.

"You don't understand," one of the pregnant young women said with tears streaming down her face. "They took my two babies from me. They took my babies!"

The women all began talking at once. They had been kidnapped from all over the country, from college campuses, while out jogging or shopping. All were between the ages of eighteen and twenty-two and forced into surrogacy.

"Mandy got away, and then they wanted to let us know what happened to her. That woman told us what would happen to us if we ever tried getting away like Mandy did. It was awful."

After calming the women down, Joy checked her watch. The man had said the explosion was set for thirty minutes. They had less than five minutes left. She looked toward the cabin. Where was Stonewall?

Suddenly she heard police sirens and saw the flashing blue lights of several police cars and several un-marked ones, as well as ambulances. Sanchez, Chief Harkins and Special Agent Felton emerged from their vehicles and raced toward her. Their eyes took in the pregnant women. She'd filled in Chief Harkins when she'd phoned for backup. Uninformed officers and fed-eral agents were untying the three criminals she and Stonewall had bound to the trees. A paramedic was checking Henry's wound and Edith and Post were being handcuffed. A number of other paramedics were tend-ing the pregnant women.

"The bomb squad is here," Agent Felton said. "Is everybody out?"

"No!" Joy said in a loud voice, her body filled with more fear than she'd ever felt before. "Stonewall is in-side searching for a missing woman and her baby."

"Damn!" Chief Harkins said, shaking his head.

An officer dressed in bomb squad gear ran over to them. "The guy who set the explosives won't tell us anything other than it will blow any minute. Not sure if the dogs will have time to sniff out the location of—"

Before the man could finish what he was saying, an explosion shook the ground beneath their feet.

"Stonewall!" Joy cried out and moved to race for-ward. Chief Harkins held her back. "No, no, let me go," she screamed. "I've got to go. He can't die. He can't."

"Sorry, Lieutenant," Chief Harkins said sadly. "I don't see how anyone could have survived that. I am truly sorry."

Suddenly there was the sound of a baby crying.

"Damn, would you look at that?" Agent Felton said amazed.

Joy turned and saw what Felton did.

Walking away from the rubble and flames of the now decimated cabin and heading toward them was a shirtless Stonewall. And he was carrying a woman who was clutching a baby in her arms. Chief Harkins released his hold on Joy and, like the others, she raced toward them.

As soon as Stonewall turned over the woman and her child to the paramedics, he pulled Joy into his arms and held her for the longest time. She finally pulled back and looked up at him. "But how did you escape that?" she asked him. Others were standing around as well, wanting to hear what he had to say.

"I knew I couldn't make it out the front door in time so I took them out the back way. We had gotten far away from the cabin before the explosion hit." He embraced her again. "We still need to talk," he said for her ears only.

She smiled up at him and, not caring that they had an audience, she leaned up and kissed him on the lips. "And we will. Most definitely."

CHAPTER FORTY-FIVE

"WHAT A LEGAL MESS," Joy said, taking the television remote out of Stonewall's hand.

A day had passed since they'd rescued those women. Most had been reunited with their families. Jerome Post hadn't talked but Edith and Henry had. Norm Austen had been arrested and was working out a deal with the Feds. He'd provided the FBI with the name of every man associated with the Brotherhood. Everyone had been shocked to find that the admired Senator Patrick Holland headed the list. Oliver Effington's body had been found and so had the man who'd tried to shoot Joy. He had died from the wound he'd suffered from Stonewall's gun.

Joy had been taken to the emergency room with the twenty-one women and baby. She was released after being check. One of the women had gone into labor before Joy walked out the hospital doors.

The legal mess Joy referred to was the kidnapped women demanding rights to their babies. Babies that were with their parents. Attorneys were fighting to keep records sealed, but a judge ordered all records opened. Beautiful Creations hadn't been the only surrogate agency involved in shady dealings, and a number of CEOs and their attorneys had been arrested, as well.

And that included the man who'd represented Effington, Attorney Robinson. Several women who'd worked as fake surrogates to gain the couples' trust had been rounded up and were now behind bars.

Courts were trying to determine who had legal rights to the babies. DNA tests had been ordered for Chasta Carrington. She was the biological child of Mandy Clay and Brett Carrington. Rachel Carrington's egg had not been used. Joy couldn't imagine how the woman was taking the news. In trying to help his sister, Anderson Hopkins had caused her great pain. It was reported that Sunnie Clay had flown into town, making a legal claim to her sister's child.

"You've become a celebrity," Stonewall whispered to her. She had been credited with breaking the case. She had had to return to Stonewall's house since the media practically surrounded hers. Chief Harkins told her to take an additional week off because she deserved it.

"And you're a hero," she said, smiling. The photo of Stonewall with a burning cabin in the background, carrying a mother and her child, had made the front page of *USA TODAY, The New York Times, The Washington Post* and the *Los Angeles Times*, compliments of a female paramedic who'd snapped the picture. Shirtless, he had looked big, strong and sexy, while carrying all that weight like it had been nothing. The headlines had simply read, The Hero.

"And that woman you rescued is naming her newborn son after you. Just think. Another Stonewall."

Joy was aware that he'd gotten calls from all his friends to make sure he was okay and to congratulate him for his heroism. Dak Navarro had even called.

Stonewall's grandmother and sister had dropped by, and Joy had the chance to meet them. Granny Kay had invited her to Sunday dinner, which Joy had accepted. She had gotten calls from her family, as well. Her father had told her how proud he was, and that made her feel good.

Stonewall pulled her into his arms. "Ready to talk now?"

She cuddled close to him on his sofa. "Yes, I'm ready." It wasn't that they had avoided talking. There just hadn't been any time. When they left the hospital they'd gone to FBI Headquarters and then police headquarters to give statements. As more details came from the twenty-one women rescued, Joy and Stonewall became overnight sensations. Both as celebrities and heroes.

Mandy Clay was also being held up as a hero, and for that Joy was glad. She had been the one bold enough to escape. The men responsible for Dr. Langley's and Walter Fowler's deaths had also been apprehended.

Stonewall lifted her up and placed her in his lap to face him. "So, what am I to you, Joy?"

Joy wrapped her arms around his neck. "You are my everything, Stonewall. I love you. I hadn't realized it until I thought you had died in that explosion. It hit me just what you meant to me and that I could have lost you."

She forced back tears from her eyes and asked him, "I know you don't believe in forever, but—"

"I do believe in forever, with you, Joy. Just like it took me almost dying for you to realize how you felt, the same was true with me. That night you almost got shot was a game changer for me. I knew then how much

I loved you, and that I wouldn't be your diversion any longer. That you would have to accept me as the man who loved you."

"Oh, Stonewall," she said, laying her head on his shoulder. "I love you so much."

"And I love you, too."

She lifted her head and smiled down at him. "We make a great team, don't we?"

"Yes, the best. So you know what this means, right?" he asked her.

"No, what does it mean?"

"It means I want to marry you, Joy. I want you to always be my Joy in the morning, at night, during the daytime. For always. Will you? Will you marry me, Joy?"

More tears flowed from her eyes as she nodded her head. "Yes, yes, Stonewall, I will marry you."

He brought his lips down to meet hers, and she knew this was the beginning of their lives together. The beginning of forever.

EPILOGUE

"This place is stunning," Joy whispered to Margo. They were on Glendale Shores, an island off the South Carolina coast that was owned by Randi and her family. It was a beautiful September day. A gorgeous one for an outdoor wedding. Joy thought Stonewall, Striker Jennings, Roland Summers and Sheppard Granger all looked handsome standing beside Quasar Patterson as his best men. Joy had thought it sad that no member of Quasar's family had been invited. But after Stonewall had explained why she then understood.

Randi had told them that the wedding would be held in the same spot where her parents, her brother, and her sister had exchanged their wedding vows years ago. Randi had looked simply beautiful walking toward Quasar on the arm of her father, Randolph Fuller. A man who Joy thought looked pretty darn handsome, as well.

Now Quasar and Randi stood facing each other, reciting their wedding vows. Joy had to wipe tears from her eyes. They looked so much in love. Joy and Stonewall had decided on a June wedding, and her parents were happy they'd decided not to rush things. That would give her mother time to plan the wedding she and Stonewall both wanted. Or the wedding her mother thought they should have.

The wedding reception was held at the main house on the island. It was beautiful as well, and Joy thought Randi was blessed to have an island in the family. She had been talking to the Grangers earlier. This was the first time they'd left town without their babies, but they knew the woman watching over their little ones, with Hannah's help, would do fine.

Jules and Dalton had named the twins Hannah and Harrison. Jace and Caden had teased Dalton mercilessly about how many diapers he had to change compared to them.

"Miss me?"

Joy turned when Stonewall wrapped his arms around her waist. "Yes, I missed you." It had been two months since the rescue of the women, and Stonewall was still getting offers for television and radio appearances. He'd even gotten a call from a movie director in Hollywood. Sunnie Clay and the Carringtons, among others, were still in court battling out legal rights. Every baby born to the women had been located, and neither side wanted to give up their babies. So the legal feud continued.

"Are the newlyweds ready to leave for their honeymoon?" she asked.

"In a few. They still have to cut the cake."

She had taken Stonewall to Louisiana to meet her parents and siblings, and they'd loved him. Her father had thanked him profusely for protecting her. She glanced over at Roland Summers. The man she had to thank for not only giving Stonewall a job when he'd gotten released from prison but for being a mentor and good friend to him, as well. He was standing alone, looking out over the Atlantic Ocean. To Joy he looked sad. From what Stonewall had told her, Roland never intended to marry again. But she hoped that a special woman would one day come into his life.

Joy and Stonewall would leave here to spend a couple of days in Martha's Vineyard. The place where they had their first date. "Have I told you lately how much I love you?" he whispered for her ears only.

She glanced down at the beautiful engagement ring on her finger before smiling up at him. "Yes, and I always love hearing you say it."

"I love you, my Joy in the morning."

"And I love you, too, sweetheart. My hero and protector."

* * * * *

Don't miss a single story in
THE PROTECTORS *series*
by New York Times *bestselling author*
Brenda Jackson:
FORGED IN DESIRE
SEIZED BY SEDUCTION
LOCKED IN TEMPTATION

*If you like sexy and steamy stories with
strong heroines and irresistible heroes, you'll love
LITTLE SECRETS: HIS UNEXPECTED HEIR
by USA TODAY bestselling author Maureen Child.*

*After a fling with a sexy marine leaves Rita
pregnant, her attempts to reach the billionaire
are met with silence...until now! Brooding,
reclusive Jack offers to marry Rita—in name only.
Will his new family give him the heart to
embrace life—and love—again?*

*Turn the page for a sneak peek at
LITTLE SECRETS: HIS UNEXPECTED HEIR!*

Jack Buchanan listened to his interior decorator talk about swatches and color and found his mind drifting… to *anything* else.

Four months ago, he'd been in a desert, making life and death decisions. Today, he was in an upholstery shop in Long Beach, California, deciding between leather or fabric for the bar seats on the Buchanan Shipping's latest cruise ship. He didn't know whether to be depressed or amused. So he went with impatient.

Why the hell was Jack even here? He was the CEO of Buchanan Shipping. Didn't he have minions he could have sent to take care of this?

But even as he thought it, he reminded himself that being here today, in person, had all been his idea. To immerse himself in every aspect of the business. He'd been away for the last *ten* years, so he had a lot of catching up to do.

Jack, his brother Sam and their sister, Cass, had all interned at Buchanan growing up. They'd put in their time from the ground up, starting in janitorial, since their father had firmly believed that kids raised with all the money in the world grew up to be asses. He'd made sure that *his* children knew what it was to really work.

Now, looking back, Jack could see it had been the right thing to do. At the time, he hadn't loved it of course. But today, he could step into the CEO's shoes with a lot less trepidation because of his father's rules. He had the basics on running the company. But it was this stuff— the day-to-day, small, but necessary decisions—that he had to get used to.

Buchanan Shipping had interests all over the world. From cruise liners to cargo ships to the fishing fleet Jack's brother, Sam, ran out of San Diego. The company had grown well beyond his great-grandfather's dreams when he'd started the business with one commercial fishing boat.

The Buchanans had been on the California coast since before the gold rush. While other men bought land and fought with the dirt to scratch out a fortune, the Buchanans had turned to the sea. They had a reputation for excellence that nothing had ever marred and Jack wanted to keep it that way.

Their latest cruise ship was top-of-the-line, state-of-the-art throughout and would, he told himself, more than live up to her name, the *Sea Queen*.

"Mr. Buchanan," the decorator said, forcing Jack out of his thoughts and back to reality.

"Yeah. What is it?"

"There are still choices to be made on height of stools, width of booths…"

Okay, details were one thing, minutia another.

Jack stopped her with one hand held up for silence. "You can handle that, Ms. Price." To take any sting out of his words, he added, "I trust your judgment," and watched pleasure flash in her eyes.

"Of course, of course," she said. "I'll fax you a complete record of all decisions made this afternoon."

"That's fine. Thanks." He waved a hand at the men in the back of the shop and left. Stepping outside, he was immediately slapped by a strong, cool breeze that carried the scent of the sea. The sky was a clear, bold blue and this small corner of the city hummed with an energy that pulsed inside Jack.

He wasn't ready to go back to the company. To sit in that palatial office, fielding phone calls and going over reports. Being outside, even being here, dealing with fabrics of all things, was better than being stuck behind his desk. With that thought firmly in mind, he walked to his car, got in and fired it up. Steering away from work, responsibility and the restless, itchy feeling scratching at his soul, Jack drove toward peace.

Okay, maybe *peace* was the wrong word, he told himself twenty minutes later. The crowd on Main Street in Seal Beach was thick, the noise deafening and the mingled scents from restaurants, pubs and bakeries swamped him.

Jack Buchanan fought his way through the summer crowds blocking the sidewalk. He'd been home from his last tour of duty for four months and he still wasn't used to being surrounded by so many people. Made him feel on edge, as if every nerve in his body was strung tight enough to snap.

Summer in Southern California was always going to be packed with the tourists who flocked in from all over the world. And ordinarily Jack avoided the worst of the crowds by keeping close to his office building and the penthouse apartment he lived in. But at least once a month, Jack forced himself to go out into the throngs of people—just to prove to himself that he could.

Being surrounded by people brought out every defensive instinct he possessed. He felt on guard, watching the passing people through suspicious, wary eyes and hated himself for it. But four months home from a battlefield wasn't long enough to ease the instincts that had kept him alive in the desert. And still, he worked at forcing himself to relax those instincts because he refused to be defined by what he'd gone through. What he'd seen. Frowning at his own thoughts, he concentrated again on the crowd and realized it had been a couple months since he'd been in Seal Beach.

A small beach community, it lay alongside Long Beach where he lived and worked, but Jack didn't make a habit of coming here. Memories were thick and he tended to avoid them, because remembering wouldn't get him a damn thing. But against his will, images filled his mind.

Last February, he'd been on R and R. He'd had two weeks to return to his life, see his family and decompress. He'd spent the first few days visiting his father, brother and sister, then he'd drawn back, pulling into himself. He'd come to the beach then, walking the sand at night, letting the sea whisper to him. Until the night he'd met *her*.

A beautiful woman, alone on the beach, the moonlight caressing her skin, shining in her hair until he'd almost convinced himself she wasn't real. Until she turned her head and gave him a cautious smile.

She should have been cautious. A woman alone on a dark beach. Rita Marchetti had been smart enough to be careful and strong enough to be friendly. They'd talked, he remembered, there in the moonlight and then met again the following day and the day after that. The remainder of his leave, he'd spent with her and every damn moment of that time was etched into his brain in living, vibrant color. He could hear the sound of her voice. The music of her laughter. He saw the shine in her eyes and felt the silk of her touch.

"And you've been working for months to forget it," he reminded himself in a mutter. "No point in dredging it up now."

What they'd found together all those months ago was over now. There was no going back. He'd made a promise to himself. One he intended to keep. Never again would he put himself in the position of loss and pain and he wouldn't ever be close enough to someone else that *his* loss would bring pain.

It was a hard lesson to learn, but he had learned it in the hot, dry sands of a distant country. And that lesson haunted him to this day. Enough that just walking through this crowd made him edgy. There was an itch at the back of his neck and it took everything he had not to give in to the urge to get out. Get away.

But Jack Buchanan didn't surrender to the dregs of fear, so he kept walking, made himself notice the everyday world pulsing around him. Along the street, a pair of musicians were playing for the crowd and the dollar bills tossed into an open guitar case. Shop owners had tables set up outside their storefronts to entice customers and farther down the street, a line snaked from a bakery's doors all along the sidewalk.

He hadn't been downtown in months, so he'd never

seen the bakery before. Apparently though, it had quite the loyal customer base. Dozens of people waited patiently to get through the open bakery door. As he got closer, amazing scents wafted through the air and he understood the crowds gathering. Idly, Jack glanced through the wide, shining front window at the throng within, then stopped dead as an all too familiar laugh drifted to him.

Everything inside Jack went cold and still. He hadn't heard that laughter in months, but he'd have known it anywhere. Throaty, rich, it made him think of long hot nights, silk sheets and big brown eyes staring up into his in the darkness.

He'd tried to forget her. Had, he'd thought, buried the memories; yet now, they came roaring back, swamping him until Jack had to fight for breath.

Even as he told himself it couldn't be her, Jack was bypassing the line and stalking into the bakery. He followed the sound of that laugh as if it were a trail of bread crumbs. He had to know. Had to see.

"Hey, dude," a surfer with long dark hair told him, "end of the line's back a ways."

"I'm not buying anything," he growled out and sent the younger man a look icy enough to freeze blood. Must have worked because the guy went quiet and gave a half shrug.

But Jack had already moved on. Conversations rose and fell all around him. The cheerful jingle of the old-fashioned cash register sounded out every purchase as if celebrating. But Jack wasn't paying attention. His sharp gaze swept across the people in the shop, looking for the woman he'd never thought to see again.

Then that laugh came again and he spun around like a wolf finding the scent of its mate. Gaze narrowed, heartbeat thundering in his ears, he spotted her—and everything else in the room dropped away.

Rita Marchetti. He took a breath and simply stared at her for what felt like forever. Her smile was wide and bright, her gaze focused on customers who laughed with her. What the hell was she doing in a bakery in Seal Beach, California, when she lived in Ogden, Utah? And why did she have to look so damn good?

He watched her, smiling and laughing with a customer as she boxed what looked like a couple dozen cookies, then deftly tied a white ribbon around the tall red box. Her hands were small and efficient. Her eyes were big and brown and shone with warmth. Her shoulder-length curly brown hair was pulled into a ponytail at the base of her neck and swung like a pendulum with her every movement.

Her skin was golden—all over, as he had reason to know—her mouth was wide and full and though she was short, her figure was lush. His memories were clear enough that every drop of blood in his body dropped to his groin, leaving him light-headed—briefly. In an instant though, all of that changed and a surge of differing emotions raced through him. Pleasure at seeing her again, anger at being faced with a past he'd already let go of, and desire that was so hot, so thick, it grabbed him by the throat and choked off his air.

The heat of his gaze must have alerted her. She looked up and across the crowd, locking her gaze with his. Her eyes went wide, her amazing mouth dropped open and she lifted one hand to the base of her throat as if she, too, was having trouble breathing. Gaze still locked with his, she walked away from the counter, came around the display case and though Jack braced himself for facing her again—nothing could have prepared him for what he saw next.

She was pregnant.

Very pregnant.

Jack's heartbeat galloped in his chest as he lifted his eyes to meet hers. He had a million questions and didn't have time to nail down a single one before, in spite of the crowd watching them, Rita threw herself into his arms.

"Jack!" She hugged him hard, then seemed to notice he wasn't returning her hug, so she let him go and stepped back. Confusion filled her eyes even as her smile faded into a flat, thin line. "How can you be here? I thought you must be dead. I never heard from you and—"

He flinched and gave a quick glance around. Their little reunion was garnering way too much attention. No way was he going to have this chat with an audience listening to every word. And, he told himself, gaze dropping to that belly again, they had a *lot* to talk about.

"Not here," he ground out, giving himself points for keeping a tight rein on the emotions rushing through him. "Let's take a walk."

"I'm working," she pointed out, waving her hand at the counter and customers behind her.

"Take a break." Jack felt everyone watching them and an itch at the back of his neck urged him to get moving. But he was going nowhere without Rita. He needed some answers and he wasn't going to be denied. She was *here*. She was *pregnant*. Judging by the size of her belly, he was guessing about six months pregnant. That meant they had to talk. Now.

She frowned a little and even the downturn of her mouth was sexy. Which told Jack he was walking into some serious trouble. But there was no way to avoid any of it.

While he stared at her, he could practically see the wheels turning in her brain. She didn't like him telling her what to do, but she was so surprised to see him that she clearly wanted answers as badly as he did. She was smart, opinionated and had a temper, he recalled. Just a few of the reasons that he'd once been crazy about her.

Coming to a decision, Rita called out, "Casey," and a cute redhead behind the counter looked up. "I'm taking a break. Back in fifteen."

"Right, boss," the woman said and went right back to ringing up the latest customer.

"Might take more than fifteen," he warned her even as she started past him toward the door.

"No, it won't," she said over her shoulder.

Whatever her original response to seeing him had been, she was cool and calm now, having no doubt figured out that he deliberately hadn't contacted her when he got home. They'd talk about that, too. But not here.

He caught up with Rita in two steps, took hold of her upper arm and steered her past the crowd and out the door. Once they were clear of the shop, though, Rita pulled free of his grip. "I can walk on my own, Jack."

Without another word, she proved it, heading down the block toward the Seal Beach pier. The treelined street offered patches of shade and she moved from sunlight to shadow, her strides short, but sure.

He watched her for a couple of minutes, just to

enjoy the view. She'd always had a world class butt and damned if it wasn't good to see it again. He'd forgotten how little she was. Not delicate, he told himself. Not by a long shot. The woman was fierce, which he liked. But right now, it was his own temper he had to deal with. Why was she here? Why was she *pregnant*? And why the hell hadn't he known about it?

His long legs covered the distance between them quickly, then he matched his stride to hers until they were stopped at a red light at Ocean Avenue. Across the street lay the beach, the ocean and the pier.

While they waited for the light to change, he looked down at her, and inevitably, his gaze was drawn to the mound of her belly. His own insides jumped then fisted. Shoving one hand through his hair, he told himself he should have written to her as he'd said he would. Should have contacted her when he came home for good. But he'd been in a place where he hadn't wanted to see anyone. Talk to anyone. Hell, even his family hadn't been able to reach him.

"How long have you been home?" she asked, her voice nearly lost beneath the hum of traffic.

"Four months."

She looked up at him and he read anger and sorrow, mingled into a dark mess that dimmed the golden light in those dark brown eyes. "Good to know."

Before he could speak again the light changed and she stepped off the curb. Once again he took her arm and when she would have shaken him off, he firmly held on.

Once they crossed the street, she pulled away and he let her go, following after her as she stalked toward a small green park at the edge of a parking lot.

The wind whipped her ponytail and tugged at the edges of his suit jacket. She turned to look up at him and when she spoke, he heard both pain and temper in her voice.

"I thought you were dead."

"Rita—"

"No." She shook her head and held up one hand to keep him silent. "You *let* me think it," she accused. "You told me you'd write to me. You didn't. You've been home four months and never looked for me."

Jack blew out a breath. "No, I didn't."

She rocked back on her heels as if he'd struck her. "Wow. You're not even sorry, are you?"

His gaze fixed on hers. "No, I'm not. There are reasons for what I did."

She folded her arms across her chest, unconsciously drawing his attention to her belly again. "Can't wait to hear them."

Find out what happens when Rita finds out
why Jack has stayed away so long
LITTLE SECRETS: HIS UNEXPECTED HEIR
by USA TODAY *bestselling author Maureen Child.*

Available now from Maureen Child
and Harlequin Desire.

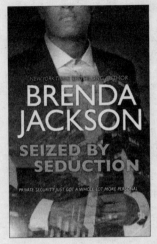

HARLEQUIN® Desire

Family sagas…scandalous secrets…burning desires.

Save **$1.00**

on the purchase of ANY Harlequin® Desire book.

Available wherever books are sold, including most bookstores, supermarkets, drugstores and discount stores.

Save **$1.00**

on the purchase of any Harlequin Desire book.

Coupon valid until September 30, 2017.
Redeemable at participating outlets in the U.S. and Canada only.
Not redeemable at Barnes & Noble stores. Limit one coupon per customer.

52615001

5 65373 00076 2 (8100)0 12297

Get 2 Free Books,
Plus 2 Free Gifts -
just for trying the Reader Service!

STRS17R